He listened to the howling wind outside, knowing that it was bringing with it many inches of snow that would be covering the entrance to the shelter. But it was a warm shelter, so much better than the hastily erected lean-tos down the hillside in the clearing. A good place from which to do work.

Yes.

A good place to become something more. He looked around at the tools hanging from lumber nail hooks; sharp tools, unused for many decades. On the floor beneath them nestled an ancient-looking flintlock weapon, from another time, perhaps even a previous century – no good to anyone now. The tools, however, he could use.

You are strong.

The voice inside him made him shiver with delight.

I hope so.

He looked down at the canvas sack of bones; daring to pull open the threaded mouth of the bag, he glimpsed the small cluster of dark-coloured, almost black bones inside.

You came to me.

Yes. I chose you.

Preston.

You are a good man.

I try so hard to be.

Alex Scarrow lives a nomadic existence with his wife Frances and his son Jacob, their current home being Norwich. He spent the first ten years out of college in the music business chasing record deals and the next twelve years in the computer games industry. Visit his website at www.scarrow.co.uk.

By Alex Scarrow

October Skies
Last Light
A Thousand Suns

October Skies

Alex Scarrow

An Orion paperback

First published in Great Britain in 2008
by Orion
This paperback edition published in 2009
by Orion Books Ltd,
Orion House, 5 Upper St Martin's Lane,
London WC2H 9EA

An Hachette UK company

1 3 5 7 9 10 8 6 4 2

A CIP catalogue record for this book is available
from the British Library.

ISBN 978-0-7528-8429-5

Typeset at The Spartan Press Ltd,
Lymington, Hants

Printed and bound in Great Britain by CPI Mackays,
Chatham, Kent

The Orion Publishing Group's policy is to use papers
that are natural, renewable and recyclable products and
made from wood grown in sustainable forests. The logging
and manufacturing processes are expected to conform to
the environmental regulations of the country of origin.

www.orionbooks.co.uk

Mum and Dad, a small offering of thanks for everything. Most of all . . . thanks for the writer genes – they've come in very handy. This one is for you.

Acknowledgements

As with my previous two books, there's the matter of a thank you to a small group of beta readers who have helped me turn a first draft into a novel. I think a pretty decent one this time.

A big hug of thanks to Robin and Jane Carter and John Prigent for giving both drafts an extensive walkthrough; to Mike Poole for some very well-targeted comments, and my oldest brother Scott, for pinpointing some pretty key issues in a concise way. This was a bloody hard book to pitch right, the hardest for me yet, if I'm honest.

My thanks also to Dad for his encouragement. That came when I needed it most.

And of course, the biggest helping of gratitude goes to Frances, who with every book I write carefully moves those commas to where they *should* actually sit. (Truth be told . . . I punctuate as if I'm doing a *William Shatner*, pausing dramatically, and putting a, comma often where, it shouldn't, really, go.)

I also need to thank my new little laptop for doing such a good job, not crashing and trashing some important files like the previous little bugger did. Also to thank Starbucks in Borders for many coffees and chocolate chunk cookies — without those two ingredients, this book would not have been written.

Finally, thanks to my agent, Rowan Lawton and my editor, Jon Wood, for direction and guidance.

Prologue

The two little girls, playing in the meadow by the stream, were the ones who saw it first: a pale form moving along the edge of the wood, just inside the tree line. They saw it at a distance, moving slowly; appearing, disappearing, reappearing amongst the foliage, a chalk-white stick-man with no face and two dark holes where his eyes should be.

It turned to gaze at them for a moment, swaying slightly as it studied them intensely across the stream surging with recent snow-melt from the peaks above and the tail end of a hard winter.

This was more than enough for the two girls. They turned and ran. As they stumbled up the incline of the meadow towards the edge of town, they thought they heard the thing scream after them — a sound both frightening and pitiful.

They ran across the small town, down the closest thing to a main street, busy with the mid-morning, mid-week trade, to their home, whimpering in broken, garbled sentences, each talking over the other, that they had seen a skeleton walking in the woods.

The skeleton was next seen by Jeffrey Pohenz a short while later. Jeffrey, a willowy teen, was outside by the back door of the trader's store, enjoying a crafty ten-minute reprise from hefting bags of cornmeal, leaning against the wall and savouring the unseasonably early warmth of sunshine on his face.

His mind was elsewhere . . . on a particular promise made to him by a certain young lady last night. Anticipation of *that* was making the day at work drag interminably; his concentration was shot to hell.

Of course, when he saw the skeleton suddenly emerge from a cluster of trees and thick tufts of untamed briar just across the yard, littered with broken and being-mended chassis and wheel spindles, the thought of this evening's exciting promise was instantly dismissed. Like some creature from Hieronymus Bosch's visions of hell, it shambled towards him with a lurching clumsiness, bony arms and hands glistening brightly in the sunlight, reaching out to him.

Jeff decided not to dive through the back door into the store and run the risk of getting entangled with the clutter of goods within. Instead he ran around the back of the low wooden building towards the busier thoroughfare at the front, stumbling out into the dusty open space and tripping over hard-baked wheel ruts that only a few days ago had been mud, churned into grooves and ridges by large steel-rimmed wheels.

'Jesus, help me!' he screamed as he scrambled to his feet again. 'There's a . . . there's a . . . there's a skeleton man round the back!'

The nearest people to Jeffrey were bemused at the sight of the mop-haired, lanky teenager stumbling over his own clumsy feet and bellowing with fear.

Jeff turned to look back at the side of the wooden fencing around which he'd just sprinted, expecting to see that shuffling bone-white creature emerge.

'Oh, Jesus, it's . . . it's . . .'

Gordon Palmer, a loader who worked out the front, shook his head at Jeff's delinquent craziness. The boy was prone to goosing around at work – a practical joker rather than a real grafter.

'What've you seen, lad?'

Jeff looked up at him. 'A skeleton! It just charged out of the woods at me!'

Gordon straightened up, sensing that maybe *this* time the boy might not be playing the fool. It could be some goddamned *Nez Perce*. He'd heard that tribe sometimes wore chalk-white body paint on raiding parties.

'What exactly did you see?'

2

Jeff pointed to the wooden wall leading round to the rear of the compound. His finger wobbled uncertainly. 'Just there . . . I swear I saw someth—'

And then Gordon saw it for himself.

The skeleton staggered forward, one bony hand held out and running along the wooden slats of the wall for support, for guidance. Gordon's first impression was identical to Jeff's, identical to the two little girls'.

But then his eyes picked out other details on the shambling form: the tattered scraps of clothing, fluttering like ragged pennants on a washing line, boots tattered and torn and held together by strips of vine or leather.

'What the hell . . . ?' he muttered, his terror replaced with horror of a different sort.

Jeff, standing beside him, now began to pick out those same details and realised his error.

'Oh shit. It's a man.'

Other heads in the thoroughfare had, by now, turned and witnessed the thing as it took several tentative steps forward, finally stumbling, as Jeff had done, on one of the deep wheel ruts. It fell forward, landing heavily on the hard, ridged ground and then curled up into a pitiful foetal position.

'Somebody get this poor sonofabitch some help!' Gordon shouted as he rushed forward and knelt down beside the thing. Closer now, he could see this quivering pale creature in rags had once been human but could barely be described as that now. Looking at the gaunt, starved-to-within-an-inch-of-death face, the deeply recessed and shadowed eyes, he saw an emptiness that would haunt him for the rest of his life and flavour the way he would tell this story to his children, and their children.

Those were the eyes of someone who had glimpsed the Angel of Death himself.

He leaned closer to the man. 'We'll get you some help. Some food and water,' he whispered, suspecting it was already long past doing the poor wretch any good. Those empty eyes met his

3

and Gordon swore for a moment that he saw the flickering flames of hell in those wide, dilated pupils.

My God, he may die right here.

Gordon reached out and gently held one of this poor man's bony claws. The loose folds of skin on his hands reminded him of the turkey-wattle skin of an old man.

No man should die without a name.

'Can you tell me your name, sir?'

The man's thin, leathery lips parted, revealing impossibly long teeth, gums withdrawn by malnutrition. He struggled to say something – little more than a mucous-clogged rattle.

'Tell me again,' whispered Gordon, his face just inches away now. He could feel tiny, rapid puffs of fetid air against his cheek.

The man tried again, panting with effort, managing just the faintest whisper that sounded like rustling wings.

'My name is . . . Ben . . .'

The Present

CHAPTER I

cave iram Dei

M	T	W	T	F	S	S
				1	2	3
4	5	6	7	8	9	10
11	12	13	14	15	16	17
18	19	20	21	22	23	24
25	26	27	28	29	30	

Thursday
Sierra Nevada Mountains, California

Julian Cooke squatted down amidst the knee-high ferns, looking up at the thick canopy of pine needles and the stout straight trunks of the Douglas firs around them, before turning to look at the camera.

'Ready?'

'Yeah, I'm running,' Rose replied.

Self-consciously he patted down his coarse dark hair and adjusted the round steel-rimmed glasses on the bridge of his nose.

'There's a rich tradition of fire-side tales that come from this part of America, the wilderness of the Sierra Nevada mountain range,' he started, looking squarely at the lens of the digital camera that Rose was holding. 'They come in all shapes and sizes out here: ghost stories, stories of alien abductions, sightings of Bigfoot . . . sightings of Elvis.' Julian arched his thick, dark eyebrows and shrugged.

A trademark gesture. The shrug, the flickering expression of mild disbelief . . . an understated gesture of gently mocking cynicism.

He sighed. 'Some of the people I've spoken to here will tell you of a giant Indian spirit, as tall as a house yet invisible, moving through the woods leaving broken trees in its path. Then, of course, you'll get those who talk of a hooded monk, and others . . . a witch, seen moving in the half-light of dusk. I've spoken to several people who confidently assure me that *a friend* has even captured the hooded figure on camera, something that might just happen tonight . . . if we get lucky.'

His thick *Groucho* eyebrows arched again behind the glasses and the hint of a tongue-in-cheek smile played across his lips. He held the expression for a couple of seconds, then relaxed.

'How was that?' he asked, rubbing his cold hands together.

Rose Whitely nodded. 'Yup, it was good. A bit on the cheesy side maybe.'

'Bugger. It felt cheesy doing it. I hate these talk-to-camera pieces.'

She disconnected the camera and collapsed the tripod with a practised efficiency. 'Well, we need a set-up piece, Jules. At the moment we've got more than enough footage of you interviewing the yokels——' She shot a glance towards the park ranger sitting patiently on a log nearby and sipping her coffee from a Thermos. 'I'm sorry, Grace, I didn't mean it to sound like that.'

Grace shook her head. 'No offence taken,' she replied with a gruff, twenty-a-day voice.

Rose turned back to Julian. 'Anyway, it looked good. You looked like David Attenborough crouching there amidst the foliage.'

Julian smiled. 'Did I?' He liked that.

'Well, no, not really.' Rose looked up at the sky. Through the canopy of leaves and branches, the languid white sky was beginning to dim. 'I think we're losing the last of our daylight for shooting.'

Julian nodded. 'Yup, I think we're done.'

Grace tipped the dregs of her coffee away, screwed the cap on her Thermos and stood up. 'All right,' she said, 'we've got an hour of light. Need to find a decent-size clearing to pitch the tents.'

She bent down and scooped up her backpack, slung her rifle

over one shoulder and pushed through the undergrowth. 'Let's move out.'

Julian watched her for a moment, groaning as he wearily picked up his pack and pulled the straps over his shoulders. Rose brushed past him, carrying about twice the load – camping pack, camera and equipment – and grinned.

'She *is* something of a character, isn't she?'

Rose filmed them using the night-vision filter. Julian sat next to Grace, both of them leaning against a moss-covered hump in the ground, looking out across the large clearing at the tree line around them. It was pitch black, save for the faint light intermittently cast by the moon as heavy clouds scudded across the sky.

They spoke in hushed voices, barely more than a whisper, as Julian interviewed her. And out there, amidst the trees, her microphone picked up the wonderfully atmospheric creakings, rustlings and nocturnal cries of the wilderness at night.

'You ever seen anything out here, Grace? You know . . . whilst you're out patrolling the woods?' whispered Julian, the pupils of his wide eyes entirely dilated as he stared edgily out into the darkness around them. The emerald-green grainy composition of night vision lent the scene an eeriness that Rose knew was going to look good – anticipation of something about to happen.

Grace shook her head. 'Nope, can't say I have. Get to hear a lotta things, though. The woods are as alive in the night as they are in the day . . . mebbe more so,' she replied, her breath puffed out into the cool night air.

Rose had headphones on. She could hear only what the directional mic was getting. To her it sounded delightfully creepy. A light breeze was teasing the firs and spruces around them. The swaying branches produced a chorus of conspiring whispers in the background.

'Why do you think there are so many weird sightings and urban myths around these woods and mountains?' Julian asked, cutting into the silence.

Grace measured her quiet reply. 'We got *a lot* of history here in Blue Valley. I guess when you got a bunch of history, you get a bunch of boogieman stories.' She smiled. 'We ain't so used to having a lot of history around us, not like you Brits are.'

Julian nodded and smiled.

A branch snapped out in the darkness and Julian jerked nervously, spilling coffee from the mug he was cradling in his hands.

'Uh . . . Grace, what the hell was that?' He swallowed anxiously, his prominent Adam's apple bobbing like a fisherman's float. Rose smiled at the grainy-green display in front of her.

Jules plays the fool so naturally.

'Nothing,' replied Grace calmly, 'just dead wood falling. It happens. Relax.'

'God, I hate woods,' he gasped with a cloud of vapour. 'Anyway, you were saying?'

Grace nodded. 'History. We got a lot of it here; Indian history, followed by settler history. You know Emigrant Pass isn't that far away from us.'

'Emigrant Pass?'

'It's the one and *only* way through the Sierra Nevadas. At least, it was back in the 1850s when something like half a million people were migratin' west,' she continued. Rose listened intently to her dry throaty voice; a mesmerising monotone of Midwest vowels, back-woods charm and a lifetime of Marlboros.

A perfect voice for storytelling.

'They called the route a number of things back then; the South Pass trail, the Emigrant Trail, the Freedom Trail . . . I guess you'd know it best as the Oregon Trail. It was the route settlers were taking across the wilderness to Oregon. There wasn't one fixed trail though. It was a bunch of different east-west routes that mostly followed the Platte River towards the Rockies. Those trails criss-crossed each other, each one promising some kinda shortcut that beat the others. But no matter how

10

much they all twisted and turned, they all came together in the end. They converged at one critical point.'

Grace pulled out a cigarette and lit up. The flame of her lighter flared brightly across Rose's view screen, and then it flickered out a moment later.

'Emigrant Pass. Half a million stories came through that gap in the mountains.' She pulled on her cigarette, her lips pursed and lined like a puckered tobacco pouch. 'And they was superstitious people back then. Many strongly religious types, devout types, you know? Like the Mormons, for example.'

Julian nodded.

'You ever hear the saying "seeing the elephant"?'

'Nope.'

'It was a myth that grew up along the trail. All the hazards of that journey, the terrain, the weather, disease, crooks, Indians . . . it somehow all got rolled up into one frightening mythological beast – the elephant; the size of a mountaintop, or a storm front, or the size of a broken cart wheel. If you caught a glimpse of the elephant ahead of you in the distance it was meant to be an omen, an omen to turn back right away, and go no further. And you sure as hell did that and thanked God you saw the elephant from afar, and not up close.'

Julian looked out into the darkness. Rose instinctively panned the camera away from him in the direction he was looking – towards the tree line across the clearing. 'Do you think we'll see anything tonight?' he asked.

Grace laughed – a loose rattling sound like a leather flap caught in a wind tunnel. 'Maybe we'll see that elephant, eh?'

Julian turned round to look at the park ranger, then turned to look directly at the camera, his mouth a rounded 'O', those brows quizzically arched and his eyes wide like a nervous child's.

Rose giggled silently. Jules had the kind of comedian's face the camera loved.

11

CHAPTER 2

cave iram Dei

M	T	W	T	F	S	S
				1	2	3
4	5	6	7	8	9	10
11	12	13	14	15	16	17
18	19	20	21	22	23	24
25	26	27	28	29	30	

Friday
Sierra Nevada Mountains, California

Julian was woken by his aching groin.

Oh great, I need a piss.

He realised that he was going to have to step outside the tent.

'Bollocks,' he whispered to himself. 'Shit and bloody bollocks.'

The campfire would be no more than glowing embers now and both Grace, with her reassuringly large hunting rifle, and Rosie were fast asleep, tucked away in their own tents. He really wasn't that keen on the idea of wandering over to the tree line for a necessary piss. But Grace had warned them to pee well away from the tents, as the smell of urine could confuse a bear — could be construed as territorial marking.

'Oh, come on, you wimp,' he chided himself.

He wrestled his way out of the bag, fumbled for the torch and then, having found it and snapped it on, fumbled for his glasses.

'Two minutes and you'll be back in bed, snug as a bloody bug.'

He squeezed out of his tiny tent and panned the torch around the clearing, Grace's parting words for the night still playing around with his over-active mind.

*Did you know grizzlies can run as fast as a horse? Oh . . .
and the smaller ones can climb trees?*

Julian grimaced. 'Yeah, thanks for that, Grace,' he hissed,
watching the plume of his breath quickly dissipate in the crisp
night air.

He stepped lightly across the clearing, navigating his way
over the lumps and bumps of long-dead and fallen trees. The
beam of his torch flickered like a light sabre through the wispy
night mist, picking out the uneven floor of the clearing, carpeted
in a thick, spongy layer of moss. He was surprised at how much
it undulated and guessed that perhaps some time in the past
someone had been logging here, but never got round to finishing
the job, leaving an assault course of rotting trunks and branches
for him to awkwardly clamber over.

He made his way to the far side of the clearing and came to
a halt on the edge, staring uneasily at a tangle of brambles and
undergrowth leading up towards a wall of dense foliage – the
start of the wood.

He turned to look back at the tents.

Sixty feet . . . is that far enough away?

He decided it would have to do. There was no way on earth
he was actually going to step through the dense web of undergrowth ahead of him and *into* the woods. No way.

This is good enough.

He unzipped, feeling a sudden gotta-go rush that he couldn't
contain any longer, and, with a long groan of satisfaction, he let
rip. His torch picked out the steaming silver arc and he watched
with detached interest as the jet of piss stripped away – like a
pressure hose cleaning a graffiti-covered wall – the delicate
blanket of moss on a rounded log in front of him.

It wasn't until he'd shaken off and tucked away, and then
played his torch more thoroughly across the small arc of exposed dark wood, that his curiosity was piqued enough to take a
step forward.

The exposed wood was curiously smooth, not natural. He
reached out with his fingers and ran them along the surface. It

13

was old and evenly curved. He rubbed a little further along the exposed arc, moss rolling off effortlessly into little doughy balls under his fingers. By the torchlight he could see the remains of a rusted metal band, dislodged dark brown flakes tumbling from it. He ran his torch down and noticed several unnaturally straight ridges in the mossy surface, converging on a bumpy hub. He rubbed the moss off one of the ridges to find the smooth, weathered form of what quite clearly was wood once turned on a lathe.

A spoke?

He straightened up. 'That's a wheel. That's a wagon wheel.'

CHAPTER 3

---

cave iram Dei

M	T	W	T	F	S	S
				1	2	3
4	5	6	7	8	9	10
11	12	13	14	15	16	17
18	19	20	21	22	23	24
25	26	27	28	29	30	

Friday
Sierra Nevada Mountains, California

'See?' he said, waving at the clearing.

Grace and Rose looked around. Through the morning mist they could see it was about a hundred yards in diameter, and roughly elliptical in shape. The floor of the clearing seemed to be one large, rumpled, emerald-green quilt draped delicately over the messy floor of a child's bedroom.

'Whoa . . . the whole clearing's . . . ?'

'One big camp.'

Rose panned her camera round in a slow, steady loop.

Julian stepped towards a rounded hump, knelt down beside it, and rubbed away the covering moss, exposing the spokes of another wheel. 'Another wagon,' he said, and surveyed the clearing. 'There must be several dozen wagons buried here.'

Grace's eyes narrowed. She pulled off her ranger's cap and tucked a loose tress of silver hair behind one ear. 'My God,' she said, blowing cigarette smoke out of her nostrils. 'A whole wagon train, up here in our mountains. Sheeesh . . . been walking these woods for years' – she turned to Julian – 'never knew this was here.'

Rose looked at Grace. 'This *is* quite a find, isn't it?'

Grace nodded silently. 'Hell, could be another Donner Party.'

'Donner Party?'

'Party of emigrants that went missing on the way to Oregon in the 1850s. They were too slow making for the pass and got snowed into the mountains. Not too far from here — about a hundred miles further south.'

'I've heard of that,' said Julian.

She nodded. 'Helluva grim story. They went missing over the winter, but were found come spring. What was left of them.'

'I don't like the sound of that,' said Rose.

'Yeah.' Grace nodded. 'They resorted to cannibalism. The papers at the time were full of made-up variations of that tale. People scared their kids with the story for generations after.'

They studied the clearing in silence, their eyes making sense of — telling stories with — the contours hidden beneath a century and a half of growth and organic detritus.

'What we got here,' uttered Grace, 'is a *heritage* site. That means I've got to call this in to the National Parks Service.'

Julian bit his lip in thought. 'Grace, will you excuse me and Rose for a moment?'

'Change of plan,' he said quietly to her. 'Okay, we came out here to basically poke fun at a whole load of gullible straw-chewing rednecks and their stories of abductions and Big Foot sightings and Glowy Things In The Sky.'

Rose nodded. 'Yeah. I'm guessing we aren't doing that now?'

Julian grinned. 'Christ, no. That's the sort of bottom-shelf schedule-filler I'd love us to leave behind. This' — he gestured at the clearing around them — 'is like finding the bloody *Titanic*.'

'But we won't have it to ourselves for long if she's calling it in, Jules.'

'I know. Grace is a good ol' girl and wants to do the right thing. After all, in US terms, this is ancient history. To them it'll be like finding Stonehenge.'

'That's my point, though. This site will be crawling with archaeology students and American history lecturers.'

Julian nodded. 'But *we* found it, so surely *we* deserve the scoop, do we not?'

Rose nodded. 'That would be nice.'

'There'll be a human-interest story here, Rose. A powerfully strong one. And if we can find out *who* they were and *how* they ended up here, and if they survived . . . ?' He looked around at the uneven floor of the clearing. 'There'll be all sorts of personal artefacts buried here to give us names. There's bound to be family these people left behind, descendants today who'll have a curious family story of their great-great-uncle Bill who travelled west to the promised land and was never heard from again.' Julian turned to her. 'I say we drop the stupid bloody project we *were* doing and instead let's dig up what we can on this.'

'Errrm.' Rose tapped her chin with her finger. 'Didn't someone commission this *stupid bloody project*. You know . . . money? A paying customer?'

'Stuff that. RealityUK are a truly shit reality channel paying us a piss-poor commission for this. Not to put too fine a point on it – screw them.'

Rose looked sceptical. 'But it's money.'

'Look, I know money's tight right now, but I'll find some other small independents who'll front some cash for us to work on this. Or better still, I'll talk to my old contacts at the BBC. I'm still on chatting terms with Sean, and the guys on *Panorama*. Everyone's going to want a piece of this.'

He looked across at Grace, who was squatting down and cautiously examining the wheel spokes he'd exposed.

'We just need a little time,' he said.

Rose swung the strap of her kit bag off her shoulder and started to unpack her camera. 'I should grab as much of this on film as I can, you know . . . whilst it's still pristine.'

Julian nodded. 'You're right. I'll talk to Grace. See if I can't convince her to delay a little before calling it in to her boss.'

*

Grace sucked in cool air through her teeth with a whistling sound. 'See, I'm gonna have to call this in to the park's manager. Seeing as this is a heritage site now.'

Julian nodded. 'Yeah.'

'Mind you,' she sighed, 'Lord knows what they'll do with it. Stick a gift shop in the middle of it, I guess; flag it up as a place of interest to hike to,' she muttered, exhaling a cloud of smoke and vapour and shaking her head. 'Gotta call it in though.'

The park ranger shook her head. 'Sorry, I got to inform someone about this. The proper authorities, you understand? Otherwise, when it gets made public, there'll be all sorts of souvenir hunters out here pickin' this place to pieces.'

'I know,' said Julian, 'you're right, I suppose it has to be done. But give us a little time? Just a week or so? Give Rose a chance to film this site properly, as it is now, pristine. Because . . . even before the Parks Service get a chance to stick up a gift shop and barbecue pits nearby, there'll be heritage buffs pulling this place apart, marker poles pegged out across it. It'll look like a bloody building site, with archaeology undergrads and TV news teams tramping carelessly everywhere.'

Grace regarded him silently with her steel-grey eyes.

'You know how this'll go, don't you?' asked Julian. 'Everyone'll want a piece of this; the Parks Service, state authorities, local press, national press.'

Grace shrugged. The Parks Service had gravelled over a century-old logging camp to build the Blue Valley camp site. They'd even dammed the Tahoe river to produce a scenic lake alongside it. She knew exactly what they'd want to do with this place.

'Grace, give me a chance to find out who these people *were*, to find out their stories.'

Her wind-worn face creased with suspicion. 'You want the scoop?'

Julian offered her a guilty smile. 'Well, yes.'

She said nothing.

'Please. We'll be so very, very careful. I promise you.'

She could already see the gift shop in the very centre, several 'how-it-must-have-looked' dioramas dotted around, and to one side, a children's play area floored with that safety rubber tarmac . . . and for guest convenience electricity outlets embedded in the trunks of the surrounding trees . . .

She pursed her lips.

. . . And discarded Snickers wrappers for miles around this place.

'I'm a researcher, Grace. I used to work for the BBC. It's what I do best. I can give faces and voices to the people who lie here, before this place gets trampled.'

'I'm not sure.'

'Look,' he said, taking a deep breath, 'what do you think a FOX news team would do with this? If there's even a *hint* that these people ended up like the Donner Party, that's *all* they'll focus on. And the likes of the *National Enquirer*? It'll just be a sensational story about cannibalism, that's it. Give me a week, maybe two, and I'll find out who they were, their dreams, what drove them west, how they ended up trapped here.'

'Two weeks?'

'No more. It's sat here for what? A hundred and fifty years? Is two more weeks' rest going to do any harm?'

She pulled a face he couldn't read as she reached for her crumpled packet of cigarettes and eased out another.

'We'll not be up here all that time, either. Just today, and maybe come back for another day in a week or two. We'll let Rose get all the footage she wants, and I'll try and see if I can unearth any personal effects—'

Grace looked at him sharply.

'Gently, ever so carefully,' he said, throwing his hands up in surrender.

'I don't want you pulling this place apart,' she said sternly.

Julian put on his best pleading, beseeching face — a family dog begging beside a laden dinner table.

'All right,' she said gruffly as she lit up. 'You got two weeks.'

CHAPTER 4

cave iram Dei

M	T	W	T	F	S	S
				1	2	3
4	5	6	7	8	9	10
11	12	13	14	15	16	17
18	19	20	21	22	23	24
25	26	27	28	29	30	

Friday
Sierra Nevada Mountains, California

During the morning Rose diligently filmed the site from all angles. She had Julian doing a variety of walk-through shots. She set up the camera in the clearing, filming him and Grace emerging from the tree line and pretending to act surprised at their discovery.

Julian was impressed by how dutifully compliant Grace was. A stern-faced schoolmarmish lady who didn't seem the type to suffer this kind of foolishness gladly, she generously played along. By mid-morning Rose felt she had enough in the can and started taking high-resolution close-up shots of some of the exposed remains.

As they explored the site, delicately wiping away the veil of moss and peat, it was becoming clear that there was a lot hidden beneath; timbers that had once upon a time made up wagons had not fared well; now rotten, black and jagged like decayed teeth. However, nestling amongst these fragile skeletons of wood, they were beginning to discover a multitude of personal effects that had been preserved surprisingly well.

In the last hour Julian had unearthed a stash of ceramic items – crockery, much of it still in one piece, stored as it was in barrels of cornmeal. They found the rusted metal remains of a long-barrelled musket, which Grace called a Kentucky rifle, and the remnants of several wooden tool boxes, one complete with a suite of carpentry tools, their metal blades dull with corrosion.

Nestling at the bottom of a shallow ditch, surrounded by jagged ribs of wood that protruded from the ground like the long gnarled fingers of a clawing hand, Julian found something he'd hoped he'd find.

He squatted in the ditch, teasing the wet peat-like soil aside. His fingers traced around the edge of his find: a small tin chest, black and pitted with rust and decay, but incredibly, still firmly sealed. He found a latch at the front; no longer functioning, of course. Time, moisture and the elements had turned it into one solid nugget of flaking, oxidised metal. He pulled out a penknife and probed the latch with the tip of the blade. It began to crumble.

'What have you got there?' said Grace, standing over him.

Julian lurched. 'Jesus . . . I didn't see you there.' He pointed at the chest. 'The whole thing's still sealed. It's incredible.'

She stepped down into the ditch beside him and looked around at the ribs of wood protruding from the ground around them. 'Seems they built some kinda shelter out of each of the wagons.'

'They knew they were going nowhere.'

Grace nodded. 'And that's when they turned on their wagons and pulled them to pieces. They must've been stuck here for a long, long while.'

A thought occurred to him. 'No bodies so far, Grace. Why do you think that is?'

'The animals will have had them. Anybody died here would have been bear or cougar food before long.'

'Surely there'd be bones lying around, though?'

Grace shook her head. 'Not here. Maybe go looking around hard enough, you'll find them all together stacked neatly into a hillside nook, like hotdogs in a jar. A bear larder. Could be one just a few hundred yards from here, could be a mile away.'

She smiled coolly at Julian, 'I reckon dumping a body up

22

here in the mountains is just about the best way to get rid of it. Nature's a great recycler.'

She looked down at the chest Julian was still holding. 'You goin' to open that up?'

Julian nodded. 'I need to find some names. If we can identify just one or two of the people who ended up here, that'll be enough to get me started on the research.'

Grace looked unhappily at the chest for a moment. 'You gonna be careful with it?'

Julian offered her a reassuring smile. 'I'll be very gentle, Grace.'

She locked her eyebrows suspiciously, studying him for a moment before curiosity finally won her over. 'Okay. You go ahead and do it then.'

'All right.' Julian smiled and then let out a deep breath. 'Nice and gently, trust me.'

With a twist of the penknife's blade the latch crumbled into a shower of flakes and fell away. He tried to lift the lid but it was stuck firmly to the chest. He ran the blade of his knife lightly around the edge of the lid, dislodging more flakes and small clods of earth. With another gentle twist it cracked open and, in the stillness of the moment, they heard the slightest whisper of air rushing in.

'My God, it was actually airtight,' whispered Julian. He looked up at her. 'That's very good news.' He slowly eased the lid open, muttering to himself, 'So, what have we got in here, then?'

It was a small chest, with very little in it, and to his immense relief, bone dry inside. He noticed a leather purse in the corner. Poking it gently, he guessed there were coins inside. He spotted a shaving brush with what he guessed were probably badger-hair bristles, a milk-glass water cup and a mirror with an ornate silver frame. Julian picked up the mirror and turned it over in his hands. There was an engraving on the back.

'B.E. Lambert,' read Julian in a hushed voice.

He spotted a photo frame. Turning it over, there was a fading

23

sepia photographic portrait of a distinguished middle-aged woman, seated. Standing behind her and to one side was a young man in his early twenties, fair hair parted tidily to one side and sporting light-coloured sideburns and a modest moustache. By the likeness of their facial features, Julian guessed them to be mother and son.

Neither were smiling, both looking intently at the camera. It was a formal portrait. He noticed the young man's hand resting gently on the woman's shoulder; a small gesture that communicated a lot.

They were close. Or perhaps this was a farewell portrait?

Julian gently placed the frame back in the box and noticed, beneath the other things, a dark burgundy leather-bound notebook. He reached in and pulled it carefully out. Then, with a quick glance up at Grace, who nodded for him to go ahead, he opened the front cover. There was an inscription on the inside, the gently looping swirls of a woman's hand:

Benjamin,

For all your adventures in the New World. Fill these pages with your exciting stories, and then come home safely to me.

Your loving Mother.

He grinned and looked up at Grace. 'This is exactly the sort of thing I was hoping to find.'

He gently flipped the first page over; fragile, yellowed by time. Overleaf a dated first entry in tidy copperplate, little more than a few hastily jotted sentences, a sketch of a quayside and, as far as he was concerned the most useful scrap of information, a bill of passage from Liverpool to New York on a ship called the *Cathara*.

'Excellent.' He laughed and looked up from the notebook. 'That's more than enough to find out who this bloke was, Grace. More than enough.'

He lightly turned over a few more pages, the entries growing longer and longer, dense with meticulous handwriting and a few pencil sketches. He spotted amidst the spidery pen strokes names used over and over: *Preston . . . Keats . . . Sam . . .*

Emily . . . then the writing became too erratic, too dense and tangled and the ink towards the end too faint to easily decipher.

Watered-down ink. This guy was doing his best to stretch out an emptying inkpot.

There was a lot in this leather book, he sensed: perhaps the complete story of what had happened here. But he'd need to scan the pages and digitally clean them up to make them easily legible, particularly the latter ones.

'Grace, with your permission, I'm going to take just this book with me, okay? Nothing else.'

She looked unhappy with that. 'Ain't yours to take.'

'We're going to need to photograph each page. Get a digital record of this immediately. The paper's fragile, and there's very faint ink here, towards the back.' Julian turned a few pages. 'Very faint. The writing's almost like a watermark. This should come out of the ground right now, and be kept somewhere dark and dry.'

She considered that for a moment.

He closed the notebook gently. 'If I leave it out here, it'll deteriorate. It needs to be taken out and digitised, Grace. As soon as possible.'

The woman considered that for a moment, and then nodded. 'Okay.'

'Thank you,' he said, 'you know . . . for trusting us.' Julian looked up at the cold grey sky. 'You think it'll snow today?'

Grace shrugged. 'Snow's due, I guess. Usually as regular as clockwork.' She looked up at the pale featureless clouds. 'I reckon, though, we'll need to head back soon. We got us about six hours of daylight for hiking back to the camp site this afternoon.'

Julian stood up. 'Where's Rose? I'll get her to pack up her stuff.' He climbed out of the ditch and called out for her. He could see the bright red flash of her anorak amongst the trees on the far side of the clearing; she was stepping slowly through the tangled briar and roots with the camera braced firmly on her shoulder.

Getting some mood footage.

Grace, meanwhile, knelt down and ran her fingers over the rough, pitted surface of the metal storage chest.

'Mr Lambert. Mr Benjamin Lambert from England,' she muttered quietly through a plume of evaporating breath. 'So, you gonna tell us all about what happened here then, are you?'

CHAPTER 5

18 July, 1856

Benjamin Lambert stretched in his saddle and felt the worn leather flex beneath him. His rump was sore and he could feel that his left thigh, rubbed raw by a roughly stitched saddle seam, was beginning to blister beneath the frayed linen of his trousers. It stung insistently with each rub, as the pony he sat astride swayed rhythmically like a heavily laden schooner on a choppy sea.

But the minor aches and pains were rendered meaningless as he looked up from the sweating, rippling shoulders of his pony to the sun-bleached open prairie; thousands, millions of acres of land untamed and not portioned out by mankind. No patchwork of fields, manicured lawns, landscaped rockeries or garden follies, no cluttered rows of terraced houses or smoke-belching mills spewing out grimy workers onto narrow cobbled streets.

And there were no gravel paths or smartly paved roads dividing up this expansive wilderness. Instead just the faintest, almost indiscernible track worn into the summer-baked orange soil by earlier trains of heavily laden conestogas; those that had passed this way earlier in the season.

Ben savoured this infinite horizon, defined so sharply between the swaying ochre of prairie grass and the fierce blue of a cloudless sky, not a single, solitary tree to punctuate it.

My God, this is exactly what I came for.

This was an alien landscape for Ben, a city-dwelling English-man, used to every precious acre, yard, walkway and rat-run belonging by deed to somebody. Until he'd sailed over to the new world and embarked on this exciting journey across an unmapped continent, he realised, every step he'd taken thus far in his twenty-five years had been on ground owned by someone.

Right now he was on land owned by absolutely no one.

He reined in his pony, relieved to have that swaying motion cease for just a moment and give his back, his rump and his thighs a little respite. He took in the horizon, low and undulating gently with a smooth curvature of modest hillocks and spurs. To the west the hills grew more pronounced and shimmering in the heat; the white peaks of the Rockies danced.

Not quite so far away now.

'Oh God, this is wonderful,' he muttered to himself. This — *THIS* — was why he came; to see it all before swarms of humankind descended upon it and broke it up into a million homogenous parcels of fenced in farmland.

Beside him the wagons rolled past, each pulled slowly but assuredly by a six-team of oxen. He twisted in his saddle, looking down the length of the train; in all he had counted forty-five of them. Some open carts, many smaller rigs, and a couple of dozen ten-footer conestogas with flared sides and sturdily contructed traps.

This particular caravan of overlanders was a blend of two parties that had happened to find themselves setting off into the wilderness from Fort Kearny at round about the same time and had merged to form a loose, if somewhat uncomfortable alliance.

The smaller contingent was one he had joined at the very last moment: five wagons that had coalesced outside the military outpost, looking for others to share the arduous and hazardous trip. Fort Kearny was considered by most overlanders readying themselves for the journey as the stepping-off point, the very edge of the United States of America. Beyond that point it was God's own wilderness.

Many families delayed at this outpost longer than they should, gathering their wits, their willpower, supplies, and mustering their wavering courage to commit to the crossing ahead of them. Ben had made his way here and chanced upon these five wagons in his carefree, meandering way. They were amongst the last wagons lingering around the fort, preparing to leave. Over a shared evening meal with them, and too much drink, Ben had casually announced that he intended to journey to Oregon on his own, trading on his skills as a doctor along the way — and to write a book of his adventures and experiences. They very quickly disabused him of that foolish notion, assuring him that to travel alone, with no plan, more to the point, with no *guide*, would see him dead out there on the trail within days.

Ben smiled at his own reckless bravado.

They had successfully managed to scare the shit out of him and he promptly decided to throw in his lot with them and even contributed a substantial portion to the pool of money that purchased the services of 'Wild' Bill Keats, a prairie guide who dressed more like an Indian than a white man. Keats confidently assured them he had led dozens of parties safely across to the far side of both the Rockies and the more challenging Sierra Nevada mountain range beyond.

With Keats came an Indian partner, Broken Wing — a Shoshone, Keats assured his clients, one of the friendlier tribes.

The other contingent, about forty Mormon families led by their First Elder and spiritual leader, William Preston, had travelled down from Council Bluffs, Iowa, and had arrived with great haste just as Keats and the others were setting off. With both groups intending to head west at the same time, both equally keen to beat the season and cross the Rockies, the salt deserts, and the Nevada range beyond before the snows arrived, it was Keats's idea that both groups should combine, there being safety in such numbers.

They set out from Fort Kearny on a fine morning, the last day in May, with the rumpled and leathery old trail guide announcing solemnly that they were the last party who were going to be able to make it across the mountains this year. They left the fort behind with Keats and his party leading the way, and the Mormon wagons behind, led by Preston.

'Hey, Mr Lambert!'

Ben turned away from the distant peaks. Passing beside him was the Dreytons' conestoga. The large wagon was perhaps more than this small family needed. Mrs Dreyton was a widow – Ben guessed – in her early thirties. She dressed, like all the other Mormon women, very modestly, covered from neck to toe in a drab-coloured dress of hard-wearing material, every last wisp of her hair tucked away inside a bonnet for modesty. She shared the wagon with her two children; Emily, a pretty girl of nine or ten who made no secret of the fact that she adored Ben, and her older brother Samuel, a tall, broad-shouldered and muscular young lad of seventeen, with a sun-bronzed and freckled face, topped with sandy hair.

The young man held the reins in one hand and waved with the other. 'Morning!'

'Good morning!' Ben shouted cheerfully across to them. He reined his pony in, and steered it and a second, tethered behind and bearing all his worldly possessions, towards them. He fell into step beside their wagon, which was clattering noisily with pots and pans dangling from hooks along the outside, and the jingling of the oxen harnesses ahead of them.

Samuel and Emily's smiles were as wide as they were warm, a marked contrast to most of the sour-faced and stern-lipped members of Preston's people.

'How's the riding today?' asked Sam.

Ben shuffled in his saddle and winced. 'My blisters have blisters, I think.'

'You can always tie up your pony on the back and sit up here with me,' offered Sam. 'We got room.'

Emily's face, poking through a canvas flap over her brother's shoulder, lit up. 'Oh we got room, Mr Lambert, haven't we, Momma?'

Mrs Dreyton shot a cool glance back at her children, and then at Ben. 'I don't think it would be appropriate,' she said flatly. 'And, Emily, put your sun bonnet on, this instant!'

'Mom,' Emily chimed unhappily, 'it makes my head hot.'

She turned round to her. 'Do you want a face as brown as a savage?'

Emily shook her head.

'Then you best put it back on.'

She then turned to stare at Ben with an expression that quite clearly indicated there wasn't room on the jockey board.

Ben quickly responded. 'That's all right, Mrs Dreyton. I'm just fine where I am.'

Sam shrugged apologetically. Emily wilted.

He liked the two children. The rest of their group had kept very much to themselves under the stern and watchful eyes of Preston and his cadre of loyal elders. They were all a little too sombre and cheerless to make easy travelling companions – 'too churchy' Keats had grumbled after only a couple of days on the trail with them. But these two youngsters were as bright and as welcoming a sight as a couple of shined pennies.

He turned his pony away, wary that tongues amongst the neighbouring Mormon wagons might start wagging if he loitered too close and for too long beside the Dreytons.

'I'll bid you good morning.' Ben doffed his broad-brimmed felt hat.

Sam called out to him. 'Will you take a mug of coffee with us, Mr Lambert? When we stop at noon?'

The young man's mother looked sharply at her son with steel-grey eyes.

Ben nodded. 'That's kind of you, Sam, but maybe not today.'

He turned round and, with a jab of his knees, urged his pony to break into a lethargic trot, taking him up to the front of the column where the small contingent of wagons under Keats rolled on, through the dust.

CHAPTER 6

```
cave iram Dei
M   T   W   T   F   S   S
                    1   2   3
4   5   6   7   8   9   10
11  12  13  14  15  16  17
18  19  20  21  22  23  24
25  26  27  28  29  30
```

Saturday
Blue Valley National Parks Camp Site, California

They emerged from the woods and onto the gravel parking area just as the pallid autumnal sun dipped down behind the brow of tree tops. There were only two vehicles parked up here — Grace's Cherokee, marked with the National Parks Service logo, and the Toyota Prius Julian had rented from Hertz.

They exchanged goodbyes, and Grace gave them her home and mobile numbers to call when they were ready to trek out there again. She firmly reminded them both that she was going to do the right thing and call in the find to the park's manager in a fortnight's time . . . and no later.

Julian and Rose thanked her, watching her dump her pack in the boot and carefully put away the Parks Service issued hunting rifle in a case on the back seat. She climbed in, offered them a wave, started up the Cherokee and swung out of the parking area, kicking up a rooster tail of stones and grit, onto a single lane of road that wound its way down the mountainside to the nearest town, Blue Valley — a half-hour's drive through some of the most beautiful scenery Julian had ever seen.

'You think she'll keep her word?' asked Julian.

'Not tell her boss?' Rose nodded. 'Yeah, I think so. I think we won her round.'

Julian unlocked the car and dropped his pack on the back seat. 'Well, Rose . . . what do you think?'

She carefully placed her camera bag on the back seat, setting the folded-up tripod down beside it. 'I think we might've hit the jackpot,' she muttered, trying to keep an excited smile off her lips. 'So we're going to drop the other project then?'

'Yup,' he replied, pulling open the driver-side door and sitting down. 'It's a no-brainer,' he added, squeezing long gangly legs into the space beneath the steering wheel.

'No discussion about it?'

'Nope.'

Rose sighed as she sat down heavily beside him, pulled the seat belt down and clicked it home. 'Yeah, I really like the way this partnership thing works. You decide stuff, and I get to nod dumbly.'

Julian winced guiltily inside. Rose was a one-woman production studio; deft with a camera, a solid sound technician, a shrewd editor – he'd be buggered without her. She was the talent behind the films they had put together over the last few years; Julian was merely the vaguely recognisable TV face fronting their small company, Soup Kitchen Studios.

Business was ticking over, but it wasn't great. They had a window of time to make their production company work. That window was his rapidly fading C-list celebrity status. The general TV-viewing public still recognised his face; some might even still remember his name . . .

The Cooke bloke . . .

Julian had reached what now seemed to have been his showbiz peak five years ago as a regular host on a late-slot, anarchical, current affairs quiz show. The panellists were the usual mixed bag of stand-up comedians, red-top columnists and publicity-hungry MPs. Julian Cooke had, arguably, been a household name for at least a couple of seasons. Prior to that, he had spent about fifteen years working in the BBC as a production assistant, then as a senior researcher. He couldn't remember exactly how the transition from research-monkey to front-of-camera personality had occurred, but it had happened surprisingly quickly after he'd put together a tongue-in-cheek show reel in his spare time.

The quiz show never really took off, but it led to some work as a presenter on various off-the-wall documentaries. Round about the same time he'd stumbled across Rose – a media graduate knocking out amazingly satirical, biting, short pieces and uploading them onto YouTube. When he first saw her work she was already an established name in the Tube community, routinely getting hundred-thousand-plus views for each of her five-minute films.

For Julian, Soup Kitchen Studios was the right next step; an agile little studio with plenty of technical know-how and a recognisable figurehead and presenter, capable of knocking out TV content quickly and cheaply.

In rapid succession they made half a dozen fly-on-the-walls following around a succession of characters: a British National Party parliamentary candidate; a Muslim cleric recently returned from Guantanamo; a veteran soldier from Iraq attempting to rebuild his life (and his face); an ex-soap starlet trying to launch her pop career; the 'ASBO King', an objectionable hooded thug who enjoyed boasting and blustering about his criminal record; Dennis the Dentist, a charming old man who was serving an indefinite sentence for the serial murders of a dozen of his patients; and Tone, a guitar band from Reading on the cusp of success, but never quite managing to make it.

It was a great series: *Uncommon People*.

Since then he and Rose had failed to capitalise on the success, picking up shitty stocking-filler commissions like this one; a seedy poke at American trailer-trash and the weird crap they reckon they've seen. Rose already had a dozen digital tapes full of interviews they'd had with an auto mechanic, a waitress, several bored college kids and a couple of old guys in the woods who made slow-burn charcoal – swearing blind they'd picnicked with Sasquatch, made love to Jim Morrison, or seen the ghost of Elvis wandering the hills and woods around Blue Valley.

Julian sighed. It would be nice to make some serious TV again.

'Yeah, we're dropping that bloody project,' he said, starting up the Prius.

'Fair enough,' Rose agreed.

CHAPTER 7

20 July, 1856

I should have written more in this dairy than I have. I look in here and find my last entry is more than four days old.

I shall make immediate amends.

So, we have travelled in this loose association for a while now, out of Fort Kearny. We are an interesting mix of people at this end of the train. Our guide, Keats, insists our contingent refer to itself as the 'Keats Party' since he has been employed as our trail captain. Rather than antagonise a man I fancy could skin and fillet me with one flick of his large 'Bowie' knife, I'm more than happy to go along with that.

Amongst our group I've found the most fascinating diversity of people you could ever hope to travel with. Our contribution to the long train of carts is just five wagons long, with myself, Keats and his Indian partner Broken Wing as the only members travelling without the encumbrance of one.

We have the McIntyres, a family of four whose journey west, so they tell me, started in New York, and before that, Cork in Ireland. Their tales of squalor, the overcrowded tenement buildings in New York, the desperate gang fights amongst groups of immigrants, sound quite grim.

Then we have another family, the Bowens, who hail from my

home city; more specifically, from the East End. Just as grim a place as any I've seen in the Five Points.

The other two wagons are occupied by a dark-skinned family. I have spoken with the only one of them who knows enough English to manage a conversation: Mr Hussein, the head of the family. His oldest son, Omar, pilots the second wagon and also speaks a little English.

Finally, there's Mr Weyland from Virginia, who has only a two-wheeled cart, few possessions, and a Negro woman with him. I don't know if she is his property. I would prefer to think not. It is an uncomfortable feeling to witness one soul owned, like a shoe or a brush, by another. But, I have seen him be both respectful and tender with her. Perhaps, she is not his property.

Perhaps I'll ask . . .

Ben sat back, resting his aching spine against the soothing cool oak lid of his medicine chest. He leaned all the way back and looked up at the star-spotted sky. Night-time in this wilderness was the sort of absolute darkness that he was still finding quite novel. The streets and terraced houses of London maintained an ever-present amber twilight of flickering gas and oil-fed lamps.

The wagons of their parties were drawn close together in a circular cluster, the oxen corralled securely in the centre. The Preston party wagons were drawn together in their own cluster thirty or forty yards away; not a huge distance, but far enough to clearly make the point that they wished not to interact any more than was absolutely necessary.

Keats was holding court around their campfire. Ben could feel the heat from where he sat, warming one side of him while the other side gathered goose bumps from the fresh night air.

'. . . seen all kinds right across from Independence to Oregon,' Keats replied in answer to a question from Mrs Bowen. 'The trick of it, ma'am, is to *know* your tribes, and know 'em well. You got some that are so goddamned friendly you wonder how they managed to survive so long. The other tribes? Well . . .' Keats's voice trailed off and he shook his head.

After a moment of silence, Mrs Bowen leaned forward. 'Mr Keats?'

Intrigued, Ben carefully packed away his journal, pen and inkpot into his chest and joined the huddle of people around the glowing, warming flames.

'Mr Keats, you can't just say that and then leave us 'angin' about,' Mrs Bowen persisted and looked at the others gathered nearby, 'can 'e now?'

He shrugged. 'If it weren't for it being mixed company, ma'am . . .'

Ben cleared his throat. 'I think I'd like to know what we stand to face along the way, Mr Keats. Will it be friendly Indians or not?'

Keats's hand cupped his bristly chin. 'Well now, see that's why you got me showin' you the way through to the other side. Ain't it? We'll be passin' through lands of maybe a dozen different tribes; Pawnee, Lakota, Cheyenne, Arapaho, Ute, Shoshone, Paiute, to name just a few.' Keats looked at Ben. 'Six, seven years ago, *most* Indians was friendly, back when the rush began. But they kinda learned a whole lot since then. They know it ain't so smart riding in to greet wagon trains like ours. Too many bored settlers carryin' guns and lookin' for something to shoot at,' he said, settling back against his saddle. 'Ain't that right?' he asked Broken Wing.

The Indian nodded silently, puffing on his clay pipe and gazing distractedly at the flames dancing in front of him.

'I remember, heard a story from a few years back,' Keats continued, pulling out his own pipe and tobacco pouch. 'There was this family . . . mother and father with more kids 'n they could be bothered to count. They stopped and made camp one evenin'. And then, like we do, they was up early the next morning whilst it's still dark an' off they set again. Only, it weren't until they gone some miles before they realised they was *down one child.*'

Both Mrs Bowen and Mrs McIntyre gasped.

'A group of men from the party was organised and they

39

doubled back to try and find it. Led by the father, they headed back to where they was camped and then searched some trees nearby.' Keats paused as he packed his pipe and then produced a match.

'Now see, they found that little child,' he said, then struck the match, held it to the bowl of his pipe and sucked. He took his time puffing, until the tobacco was well alight.

'Well?' asked Mrs McIntyre. 'You were saying . . . the child?'

'They found the child all right,' Keats continued, 'safe and well, being fed and played with by a group of young Pawnee warriors, would ya believe? Some say they was a raidin' party looking to steal horses from the neighbouring Lakota. All tough young warriors these . . . but playin' with the child. Them Indians had made camp right there where they found the child.'

Mrs Bowen smiled. 'Them Indians don't sound so bad after all, then.'

Keats puffed on his pipe and blew a cloud of smoke. 'Camped right there over night, just so's they could *mind* the child until the parents came back to get her. Well, that's what some people say. But we'll never really know.'

'Why's that, Mr Keats?' asked Mrs McIntyre.

'The father fired upon them. The others joined in. Killed most of them right there.'

There was a wary silence around the fire that popped and crackled, feeding hungrily on the buffalo chips.

'I told you the story so's you get the idea what them Indians have seen of us. An' none of it is good,' he said, shaking his head. 'Thing is, they had about enough of us folk comin' through, shootin' their buffalo and lettin' 'em rot, tossing aside our shit and spoils, burning *their* firewood, spoilin' *their* creeks and pools . . . shootin' at them for no other reason than they were within range.' He shook his head. 'They was real slow on the uptake at first. But they got the measure of us folk now.'

'It sounds like you're on *their* side, Mr Keats,' said Mrs McIntyre, shooting a glance at Broken Wing, 'not ours.'

'Don't get me wrong, m'dear,' he replied, 'I'll shoot a Indian if I have to. Or a white man, for that matter.' He turned to the others around the fire. 'I'm just tellin' you what you oughta know. These last few years, Indians started turnin'. Which is why you gotta be lookin' at wagon trains of twenty and over now, if you want to make it across alive. Which is why you need the likes of me and Broken Wing to lead you folks safely across the way.'

'So,' ventured Ben, 'the question still stands: what type of Indians *are* we likely to come across? Friendly ones? Or—'

Broken Wing snorted a muted laugh.

Keats chuckled. 'Well, there ain't no friendly Indians no longer, Lambert. Just real cautious ones, or real pissed ones. And you want to hope to God, young man, that we only run into the first kind.'

Mr Bowen, a broad-shouldered man who habitually shaved his head down to the wood and looked every bit the East End brawler, put an arm around his wife's narrow shoulders.

'Don' worry, Molly, luv,' he said, nodding politely at Keats, 'I reckon we'll be just fine with Mr Keats 'ere lookin' out for us, won't we?'

Keats nodded. 'S'right, Bowen. I aim to lead you folks up a route I took last year. Takes us north of most other well-worn trails, more into Shoshone country than Ute as we cross.'

'But will that take us longer?' asked Ben.

Keats fixed his dark eyes on Ben and nodded. 'Good question, young man. We're late in the season. The only fools who set off now from Independence, or even Fort Kearny, would be damn *stupid* fools. *My* route's a little longer, but a whole lot safer. We want to make it to the far side of the Rockies this side of September, an' across them Sierra Nevada mountains before October hits us.'

'But if we don't . . . ?' Mrs Bowen started to ask.

Keats's salt and pepper eyebrows arched. 'If we don't make it across in time?'

She nodded, her eyes wide and anxious.

'We *will*, Mrs Bowen, we will. Just as long as we push hard, and mind that you take good care of your oxen an' grease your axles daily.'

Ben heard the scuff of several pairs of boots approaching through the darkness, and those already seated around the dwindling flames were joined by Mr McIntyre, Mr Hussein and his son, and Mr Weyland.

Keats nodded with satisfaction. 'Seems like we got at least one person from each of our wagons here . . . good. I guess now's as good a time as any other. One rule you folks should know up front. We ain't gonna stop for nobody.' Keats looked at each of them in turn. 'Whatever happens — oxen die in their harness, wagon tongue snaps, sickness hits a family, any accidents . . . the rest of us gotta keep rollin' whatever.'

'What about those others?' asked Mr McIntyre, gesturing towards the Mormon camp.

Keats looked across at the wagons of the Preston party. 'Hell, it's up to them. They got their own trail captain, that Preston fella. He can take my advice or leave it, up to him. But you folks hired me as your trail captain, so you follow my rules, understand?'

'You're serious?' asked Ben. 'You'd ask us to leave someone behind? But they might die.'

'Oh yeah.' The old man nodded. 'Anyone left behind *will* die, Lambert. And you people are gonna start seein' the graves by the trailside pretty soon — the *left-behinds*. Those're the real stupid folk who had horses pullin' their wagons 'stead of oxen. The stupid folk who ignored a creaky axle a day too long. The stupid folk who got their head blasted off 'cos some dumb ass was ridin' by with his rifle loaded and restin' cross-saddle.'

There was a sombre silence punctuated only by the crackle of the fire.

'The elephant can kill in many diff'rent ways, folks. Sweep you off the trail with one blow of his trunk. You be mindful of him. You see him . . .' Keats took a long pull on his pipe and blew out a cloud of acrid smoke. 'You see him, near or far, that's the time to turn round.'

'Keats, you're scaring my missus,' said Bowen.

'Good. Cause we got plenty to be scared 'bout, not least of all is the weather.'

'The weather's been fine, Mr Keats,' said Ben. 'Lovely, in fact.'

Keats laughed. 'Fine right now, Lambert, but we still yet to beat it.' The old guide nodded westwards. 'That's the thing we all gotta be mindful of though, folks. We don't beat the snow in those Sierras, then we're in big trouble.'

CHAPTER 8

Saturday
MKNBC NEWS studio, Utah

'I like to think I speak for the hard-working man on the shop floor, those regular Joes who pay taxes year in, year out, don't ask for favours, don't run around breaking the law . . . to quote Andrew Jackson, the very sinews of this nation of ours,' he said, offering his host a polite but sincere nod.

'I think in recent years we've lost sight of the quiet guy. The guy that just gets on with it, doesn't complain about the cards he's been handed, doesn't try and find someone to sue if everything isn't going quite right for him.'

Patricia Donnell offered him a calculating smile. 'Which sounds to me, and I'm sure to our viewers, Mr Shepherd, a very noble sentiment. But what I'm trying to understand, what I'm trying to get my head around, is where you really sit in the political spectrum. You see, there will be those who look at your background; an influential family, old money in property and banking, your strong Christian views, and ask themselves whether they're looking at another Republican candidate by a different name.'

'Two things, Patricia. Two things you got wrong right there,' he said, working carefully to keep his voice measured and calm and his pace deliberate and even.

44

'My faith, as you well know, is Church of Latter Day Saints. I am not a Baptist, nor an Evangelical, nor Seventh Day Adventist. I am a Mormon. There's a big difference there, Patricia. Secondly, yes . . . I come from a privileged background, but we've all worked for that. Myself, my father, my grandfather – through generations of putting our backs into it, we've rightly amassed our wealth. And what's wrong with that? This is America. But, because of that,' he said, raising a finger to stop her cutting in, 'because I understand what work is, I truly understand the work ethic, that a man's toil deserves to be rewarded, from the guy operating the factory-floor machine, to the guy sorting letters in the post room, to the shift supervisor. I'm *not* a Republican candidate.'

Patricia shrugged. 'You're making the right noises for the average Republican voter.'

He sighed and shook his head. 'I'm offering something new, something different. A new realism – common sense politics. This nation has been strangled by the shared monopoly of Democrats and Republicans. The man I'm talking directly to . . .' His eyes flickered to the camera in front of them. '. . . is fed up with looking at Washington and seeing this tug of war once every four years between two groups of people who, in fact, differ very little. I mean, these guys are in the pockets of the same lobby groups; they only seem to care about prolonging their terms in office. Meanwhile, out there in the real world, there's problems need fixing.'

Patricia nodded. 'There are those who are saying, Mr Shepherd, that you will end up just like other independent candidates from previous elections. Like Ross Perot, like Ralph Nader, spending millions and millions of your own money and getting lost in the void between the two main parties.'

William Shepherd smiled and held out three fingers in front of him, which he proceeded to count off. 'First, there is no void between the two big parties. They sit right on top of each other, snug as two peas in a pod, aping each other's policies. There's no void at all there, Miss Donnell. Second, I know this country is

45

fed up with the both of them and begging for some new alternative. You can feel it in the air, like the static before a thunderstorm. Third,' he said, tucking down the last finger, 'I have the best campaign manager in the world on my side. He's never put a foot wrong, not yet.'

She smiled quizzically. 'And who . . . ?'

'Well now, it's God, of course.'

CHAPTER 9

3 August, 1856

'If it ain't a wheel, then it's a goddamned axle,' Keats muttered irritably to Ben and Broken Wing as their ponies trotted side by side towards the growing crowd of people gathering around a wagon that had slewed to one side. He stretched up in his saddle and craned his neck to see over the milling circle of broad-brimmed hats and bonnets.

'Someone's goddamned wheel's buckled, I betcha,' he added with a hint of disgust. 'One of them Mormon wagons. If it's the one I'm thinkin' of, I heard the wheel creakin' yesterday. An' I damned well warned them about it too.'

There were several dozen men, women and children around the wagon, which was canted over at an awkward angle, house-hold goods spilled out across the hard-scrabble ground. The team of oxen had been released from their yokes and now grazed, oblivious to events, on tufts of dry prairie grass some yards away.

Keats dismounted and pushed his way irritably through to the front. He watched as Preston, his sleeves rolled up, helped several other men lift the wagon's axle onto a block to level the wagon. He waited until the heaving and puffing was done, and the axle firmly secured, before saying his piece.

'Preston!' he called out and then nodded towards the discarded broken wheel. 'No way you gonna fix that.'

Ben dismounted and politely pushed his way through the gathered crowd to join Keats, whilst Broken Wing remained where he was, a respectful distance back. Standing beside Keats, Ben studied the wheel. Five of the spokes had split and the metal rim had buckled and twisted as the wheel frame had collapsed in on itself. Even to his untrained eye, there was nothing at all to salvage from it.

Preston looked up at Keats, taking his wide-brimmed black felt hat off and wiping the sweat from his face on a shirt sleeve. 'I believe you're right, Mr Keats. The wheel is, I'm sure, quite beyond repair.'

The trail guide pursed his leathery old lips and shrugged. 'Well, we can't sit around here all day talkin' about it. We got eight more miles to make today before we set down to camp.'

Preston nodded. 'I understand. But these people, the Zimmermans, need a new wheel making. We have those skills amongst our party.' Preston pointed to one of the men standing next to him, wearing, like his First Elder and every other man, a white linen shirt, a dark waistcoat and a black felt hat. 'Mr Larkin is a smith and Mr—'

'The job's at least two days,' cut in Keats. 'We don't have the time to spend it so carelessly. The whole train should be moving on.'

Preston's bushy blond eyebrows knotted above his dark sunken eyes. He gestured towards the family, a couple with a little girl. 'And leave these people to fend for themselves? Would two days be worth their lives?' Preston looked at the family. Ben followed his gaze and studied them; both the parents were short and stocky, their child a girl perhaps a year or so younger than Emily Dreyton.

'Because they will die alone out here, Keats . . . these good people . . . this precious child.'

It was the first time Ben had been up close to Preston and

48

heard him speak. There was a powerful resonance to his voice, and a magnetic charm in his long, gaunt face.

'These people trust me to lead them. I will not abandon them. Not over one broken wheel, which can be replaced with a new one.'

Against his initial judgement from afar, Ben found himself warming to the Mormon leader.

Keats snorted with derision. 'Then you *shouldn't* be a god-damned trail captain.' He pointed out across the grassy plain, towards a small cairn of rocks.

'You see those graves by the side of the trail? Those are left-behinds; unlucky folks who saw the beast and didn't turn. Maybe their wheel broke too, or their oxen died, or they drank foul water an' got too sick to travel. Whatever . . . they got left behind 'cause they was slowin' down their party.'

Keats addressed Mr Zimmerman. 'You should head back to Fort Kearny. Leave the wagon, load yer supplies on the oxen and turn back.'

Mr Zimmerman turned to Preston. 'William, perhaps he's right?'

Preston shook his head firmly. 'I'll not leave you behind. No one will be left behind, and that is my final word on this.'

Keats shook his head with irritation. 'Then my people ain't wastin' a moment longer. We're too goddamned late in the season to be losin' time like this.' He turned away from Preston and pushed his way back through the crowd towards his pony.

One of the Mormon men standing beside the wagon's blocked-up axle turned to Preston.

'William, we have an ornate table in our wagon. We could use the table-top, cut to size, to replace the wheel. It would be far quicker, no more than an hour or two.'

Keats heard that and turned round. 'Anythin' but a proper crafted wheel will put a strain on that axle. The damn thing will snap the first rock it hits.'

'Then we will proceed with a greater degree of caution,' Preston replied firmly.

'This wagon will slow us all down, Preston.'

'Then we can start out a little earlier each morning.'

Keats shrugged casually. 'Shit. Do what the hell you want; my party's movin' on.' He swung himself up onto his pony. 'But I'm tellin' you, this wagon will slow you down. And you and your people will get caught in those mountains when the snow comes.'

'God will decide our fate, Mr Keats. Not some little man who chooses to dress like an Indian to impress his clients. If it is His wish that we make it across to the other side, then the snow will come a little later, rest assured.'

'Pfft.' Keats spat on the ground and nodded for Ben and Broken Wing to follow him. 'C'mon,' he grunted.

Ben pulled himself up, and together they headed away from the crowd towards their wagons, taking their turn at the rear of the column.

'Bunch of goddamned fuckin' zealots,' Keats muttered to himself, 'goin' t' get 'emselves in real trouble.'

Ben looked across at him. 'So what are we going to do?'

'What're we goin' do?' he looked at Ben incredulously. 'Hell, we're goin' to leave 'em fools in our dust.'

The group stirred uneasily at the suggestion.

'Leave them?'

Keats turned to Giles Weyland. 'Yes, Mr Weyland, we leave 'em right here and we press on.'

Weyland sported long, almost feminine, auburn wavy hair and a beard carefully trimmed down to little more than a golden tuft on his chin. 'But, sir, did we not unite with them out of concerns for our safety?' he replied in the mellifluous and languid tones of a Virginian. 'The Indians that lie ahead of us, sir?'

It was that particular issue, Ben noted, that seemed to be on their minds – the safety in numbers. Only yesterday they had passed a roadside message, the 'bone express', as Keats referred to it. Carved onto the weathered boards of an abandoned conestoga, surrounded by the withering carcasses of half a dozen horses, they found a warning left by a group of overlanders that had passed this way earlier in the season.

Indians up ahead. Party attacked. Some killed. Be vigilant.

'We got us a choice here,' said Keats. 'We got two different things to busy ourselves worryin' about, folks; the weather and them Indians,' he snorted and spat. 'Now them Indians? May be a problem, may not. But the weather? That's as regular as a goddamned clock. That snow *will* come in October, mark my words' — he looked across at Ben — 'whatever the hell that Preston says about God willing it or not.'

Keats's profanity sent an uncomfortable ripple amongst his party. The dark-skinned man, Mr Hussein, stepped forward.

'My faith is different one to this Preston,' said Mr Hussein, his accent thick and his English laboured. 'The name we are use for pray to him is *Ullah*. But is *same* God. I am agree with Preston, not leaving one behind. It is *haram*.'

Keats shook his head. 'Horse crap,' he muttered.

'Look 'ere, Keats,' said Bowen, 'I ain't too sure I want us splitting up from that Preston lot, not with us 'aving them savages up ahead to worry about.'

Keats looked across to Ben and McIntyre. 'I agree with Mr Bowen,' said the Irishman. He met his wife's eyes and she nodded. 'See, Mr Keats, I think I speak for most of us,' said McIntyre, looking at the others before he continued. 'I think we're *more* worried about the Indians than we are about snow.'

Ben found himself in agreement. 'Is that not why we hooked up with the others in the first place?'

There was a silence amongst them. They watched their trail captain weighing things up. He narrowed his eyes, scratched his chin and cast a glance towards the peaks on the horizon, then turned to Broken Wing.

The Indian shrugged casually.

Keats sighed. 'You folks *all* of the same, stupid, get-yourself-killed opinion?'

Heads nodded silently.

'What if we were to start a half an hour earlier each morning, as Preston suggested, and take a little less resting time at noon – can we not make up for the slower pace?' offered Ben.

Keats stroked his bristled chin as he considered the suggestion.

To Ben's surprise the old man finally nodded.

'Fine,' he said, looking back at them. 'But when – and mark my words, folks – *when* that stupid make-do wheel or the axle holdin' it breaks, we won't be discussin' it like some goddamned town council meeting. We leave them behind. Understand?'

They nodded in unison.

CHAPTER 10

5 September, 1856

It has been hard work in recent days. I have not written a word in here for a while!

We left the plains in the last few days of July and entered the Rockies. The trail through those spectacular mountains was not as hard as I had anticipated. Our trail captain, Keats, put the fear of God in us, ensuring we hasten on at every moment despite being slowed down by the crippled Mormon wagon.

We crossed South Pass on the last day of July, gently descending from the mountains on to land so bare and arid that I can barely imagine anyone could survive here. But Keats assures us they do; Ute, Shoshone, Bannock . . . they all manage after a fashion.

We have started to see graves more frequently by the trailside. Sometimes in ones or twos, sometimes, it seems, whole parties. There are those that have died because their horses have failed them and those that have died from sickness. Some of the graves were opened and the bodies unearthed. Keats said Ute most likely did this, scavenging for items, clothes. Indians, he says, do not bury their dead; once the spirit is gone, they consider what's left as mere carrion.

He said the same fate awaits the Zimmermans when their wheel finally collapses, or their stressed axle breaks. Out here in

this salty plain, he says, they will die quickly and be scavenged
first by Indians, then by vultures . . .

'Mr Lambert?'

Ben stirred.

'Mr Lambert . . . Benjamin?' a voice whispered out of the darkness. He put down his pen and screwed the lid tightly on his precious inkpot.

He recognised the voice coming out of the night nearby. The lad had sneaked out under cover of dark several times before.

'Samuel?'

Into the small pool of flickering light from his writing lamp, the lad emerged, hand in hand with Emily, a grin of mischievous excitement stretched across her small bonnet-framed face.

'Emily too?' He looked at Sam. 'Will she not be in trouble, being out this late?'

'Momma's at an Elders' meeting with Preston.'

'Momma won't find out,' said Emily. 'They pray and talk late.'

Ben smiled. 'All right then. But I'd hate for you two to get in trouble.'

Both of them shrugged.

'Come on the pair of you,' said Ben. He nodded towards the campfire, around which the children from the Bowen, McIntyre and Hussein families sat and played together. 'Why don't we join the others?'

He led them over to the communal fire. There was a moment of awkwardness as the children sized each other up, aware that Emily and Sam were from the other camp. Five minutes later, names had been politely exchanged and Emily was chatting with one of the McIntyre children, Anne-Marie, a girl a year older than Emily, who was eagerly showing and sharing her small collection of dolls.

Sam stayed close by Ben's side, fascinated by the dark skins of Mr Hussein and his family and Weyland's Negro girl, and the quiet studied form of Broken Wing. On the other hand, the young lad was wary of Keats, spitting, cursing and swapping dirty stories with Mr Bowen and Mr Weyland.

Ben noticed Sam also discreetly watching over Emily across the flames, smiling at her giggles of pleasure, clearly proud of his little sister and how her ever-cheerful demeanour instantly charmed the other children and Mrs Bowen and Mrs McIntyre.

He cares for her more like a father than a brother.

It made sense. There was no father and Sam was now of an age where he was becoming the man of their small family. But there was a wonderful tenderness he had noticed between them over the last few weeks. They were certainly much closer to each other than they were to that cold, hard-faced mother of theirs.

'Sam, would you like a little coffee?'

He nodded. Ben poured and passed him a mug that he held tightly in both hands, savouring both the warmth and the aroma.

'Do you have any other family, Sam? Uncles, aunts, grand-parents, left back east?'

'The community is our family,' he replied. 'We aren't allowed any family beyond that.'

'Aren't allowed?'

'Outside of our church.' Sam cast a glance across at the larger cluster of wagons across the way. 'Outside of *his* minis-try. But they're not our real family. There's only us,' he said, looking back at Emily. 'I don't like it over there,' he continued. 'We're all alone, never supposed to talk to anyone else. Some-times it feels like we're the only people in the world.'

Ben nodded. 'It was a bit like that for me too when I was a kid. I was an only child, and my parents were always busy with other things. That's why I like books. Can you read, Sam?'

'Of course, but we're only allowed to read two.'

'I'll presume the Bible is one of them.' Ben sipped his coffee. 'And what's the other?'

Sam shook his head. 'No, not that, not the Bible! Preston says it's full of mistakes and has been corrupted by the Jews and the

Popes. We read the *Doctrine and Covenants*, and the *Book of New Instruction*.'

Ben looked puzzled. 'Never heard of those.'

'The *Doctrine and Covenants* and the *Book of New Instruction* are the only texts we're allowed to read any more. We're not even allowed to read the *Book of Mormon*.'

'Eh? But you're Mormons, surely . . .'

'No,' Sam replied quietly. 'Not any more. Preston won't have us call ourselves that now.'

'Why?'

'He believes the faith has gone wrong, been taken over by greedy men. He says that's what always happens with faith — over and over. That it's men who take God's message and change it to what *they* want to hear.'

Ben shrugged. 'I think maybe he's right.'

Sam glanced at the distant glow coming from the other campfire. 'Maybe. But it meant we had to leave Iowa and come out here.'

'Why?'

'The church, other Mormons, wouldn't allow Preston to preach the faith. And we had to go because he wanted to—' Sam hesitated a moment, a confused anxiety spreading across his face.

'What is it, Sam?' asked Ben.

'I shouldn't say. I'll get in trouble.'

'Then don't. I wouldn't want that.'

Sam was silent for a while before quietly turning to Ben. 'He wants to write a new *Book of Mormon*.'

'Really? Won't there be a lot of people upset by that? Angry?'

Sam was silent, his eyes wide. 'It's our secret.'

'Because it'll anger other Mormons?'

Sam nodded. 'That's why he's taking us all to the west.'

'Away from the Mormon church?'

Sam nodded again and then reached out, grabbing Ben's arm.

Ben noticed the boy's hand was trembling. 'I . . . I told you something I shouldn't have. You mustn't tell anyone, please.'

Ben shook his head. 'Sam, it's okay. I won't.'

'If they found out I t-told anyone . . .'

'They?'

'The Elders. Preston, Mr Vander, Mr Hearst, Mr Zimmerman, my momma, Mr—'

'Sam, I promise, I won't tell anyone.'

'You swear?'

Ben rested a hand on his. 'I promise. Listen, I'm not that much of a Christian, Sam. I'm not that much of a believer in anything, to tell you the truth. If someone wants to mess around with a religious text, then that's their business.'

Ben felt a tug on his sleeve and turned to see Emily standing beside him. She showed him a wooden-peg doll. 'It's Anne-Marie's,' she explained, pointing across the fire at McIntyre's daughter. 'She said I could keep her for the journey. Do you like her, Benjamin?'

He took it off her and looked it over with an appreciative frown. 'She's lovely. Do you have many dolls in your wagon, Emily?'

Emily shook her head. 'Not really.'

'None,' said Sam. 'Momma doesn't approve of the dresses they wear. Says they look like dirty ladies.'

'Can I keep her, Sam?'

Sam looked down sadly at his sister. 'Sorry, Em . . . if Momma sees it in the wagon, she'll know we've been over.'

Emily nodded sadly, and turned to take it back.

'I can look after her,' said Ben. 'I could keep her in my saddle bag. When we stop over for noon break, I could pull her out and let you play with her for a short while. Your mother needn't know.'

Emily swung a small arm around his neck and planted a kiss on his cheek. 'Thank you very much.'

At that moment, they heard the collective murmur of prayers coming through the still night.

'Prayer meeting will be finishing up soon,' said Sam. 'We should go back now.'

Emily reluctantly passed Ben the doll.

'Don't worry,' he said, 'I'll keep her safe. You can play with her tomorrow.'

Sam smiled gratefully at him. 'And thank you for the coffee, Benjamin.' He grabbed his sister's hand and they set off a few steps towards the other wagons before he stopped and turned. 'Can I bring Emily over again?'

'If you like. As long as you both don't end up getting in trouble.'

Sam nodded, and then they were gone.

Ben finished his coffee as he watched them go, quickly fading into the darkness, soon no more than a flickering silhouette against the distant glow of the other campfire. He bid goodnight to those still gathered around theirs for warmth, and headed back to where his two ponies were tethered and his bedroll lay. He unscrewed the lid of his inkpot and dipped his pen carefully in.

The people we are travelling with – I know nothing about the tenets of their faith. It seems so strict and very much apart from the churches I know. The women folk of Preston's curious style of Mormonism appear obliged to be bound head to foot in modest clothing, with only their faces revealed. The men are all compelled to wear beards, clipped from their mouths, but left untrimmed beneath their chin, long enough to hide a fist within.

And what a hold he appears to have on them. That he can throw away the Bible and their Mormon book and start over . . . and they will take whatever he decides to write, as gospel?

He looked up from his journal, across at the dark outlines of the Preston party's wagons.

I find that disturbing.

CHAPTER 11

cave iram Dei

M	T	W	T	F	S	S
				1	2	3
4	5	6	7	8	9	10
11	12	13	14	15	16	17
18	19	20	21	22	23	24
25	26	27	28	29	30	

Saturday
Blue Valley, California

Rose studied a scanned page from the journal on her laptop. 'It's so weird.'

Julian looked up from the diner's very short, single-sided menu. 'What?'

'He just seems so . . . I don't know, so . . . it's like this journal was written *yesterday*.'

'Because it's not all "yea" and "forsooth" and "verily"?'

Rose nodded. 'I suppose so, yeah.'

'Diaries and journals are informal. They're usually the most intimate of historical records. No one writes a diary thinking it's going to be read by anyone else, let alone some historian from the future. It's personal, and a much closer and more reliable record of a person's life than any census or public document.

'When I was a researcher for the BBC – Christ – ten years ago now,' Julian continued, looking down the menu once more, 'I went through loads of unearthed correspondence from Roman soldiers, dug out along Hadrian's wall – amazing stuff that could've been written by squaddies serving in Iraq; lads asking their mums for extra pairs of underwear, for soap. The language that normal people use and the things that fill their everyday lives, what concerns them . . . none of that ever really changes. I love that about history.'

The waitress came over with her pad flipped open and ready to go. 'What'll you have?'

Julian puffed and bit on his lip for a moment before looking up at her with a hopeful smile. 'I don't suppose you got anything along the lines of a lasagne or a—'

She sighed. 'Just what's on the menu, sir.'

He nodded, suitably chastened. 'Oh. Then, um . . . a Ranch Burger, please.'

Rose waited until she'd finished scribbling. 'And I suppose I better have the caesar salad,' she said.

'Another drink with yer meals?'

Julian looked at Rose. 'Another couple of beers?'

'Why not? The last lot went down easily.'

Rose watched her go before looking back at her laptop, perched on the small table between them in their cosy corner booth. 'We've got all the pages digitised now?'

Julian nodded. 'I flicked through and scanned them last night. The Lambert journal is now tucked safely away, sealed, dry and covered. Grace would approve, I'm sure. And very soon it'll make a nice exhibit for some local museum.'

'That's a relief. Knowing how clumsy you can be, Jules, I had visions of you spilling coffee all over it, or something.'

Julian grinned. 'The ole girl would skin me alive.'

Rose nodded. 'She would that.'

Julian looked around the bar, empty except for a couple of young men shooting pool on the far side, away from the booths. A TV behind the counter was on FOX News. They were covering the Reagan Presidential Library debate; six candidate hopefuls for the Republicans were slugging it out between them.

'I think he sounds really sweet.'

'Who?'

'This bloke, Benjamin Lambert.'

'Don't tell me you're falling for a *dead* guy?'

She smiled. 'He comes across as tender, sensitive. I like that.'

Rose had come across very few men in her life thus far that she could genuinely describe as tender and sensitive. None that had seen past her falsely confident cheeriness, and sensed the insecurity inside. Not even Julian, who seemed to know her so well; not even he sensed she felt like an ugly duckling amongst the glamorous production assistants and floor managers and other media muppets that swanned around their world.

Rose knew Julian thought highly of her. Respected her talent, trusted her judgement. In fact she was certain most of the male professionals she interacted with on a regular basis were quietly impressed with her techie talk and media savviness, but beyond that saw nothing more than a plain-Jane struggling to stay in a size twelve.

'I'm no glamorous Paris Hilton,' she'd moaned once.

'Sod that. You're *the* most talented filmmaker I've ever worked with,' Julian had replied sincerely.

Just what an ugly duckling needs to hear.

The waitress returned with their food and drinks, deftly dealing them out with a cheerless smile. 'Enjoy your meal,' she said in a flat tone, and was gone.

Rose speared a leaf of lettuce with her fork whilst looking at Julian's plate. 'God, I wish I could eat that sort of crap and stay whippet-thin like you.'

'I've got a fast metabolism – nervous energy. Actually, I thought hitting my late thirties would slow me down a bit,' he said and then swigged a mouthful of beer.

'God. What were you like at *my* age?'

'Twenty-five? Much the same, I suppose. Nature's been kind so far. You wait till I hit my mid-forties, then I'll age ten or fifteen years overnight.' He picked up his Ranch Burger, which dripped melted cheese and bacon fat.

She shook her head and smiled wearily. 'I guess I'll stick to eating rabbit food, drinking decaf and drooling over my George Clooney screensaver.' The only intimacy she shared these days was with things that came with an AC adaptor. Filming, editing, mixing. Filming, editing, mixing. And once in a blue moon she got lucky with a bloke wearing beer goggles. It always seemed to be a sound, lighting or camera guy, charmed more by her ability to talk *kit* than anything else.

They ate in silence for a while, both hungry after the afternoon's hike out of the woods to the park's camp site. Julian worked through his burger with his eyes on the TV over the bar, absent-mindedly regarding the suited, carefully groomed candidates slinging uninspired soundbites at each other.

'So okay then, Rosie,' said Julian, wiping his mouth with a napkin. 'Down to business. We need to plan out what we're going to do.'

'You're the boss,' she said dryly.

He put down his burger, wiped his hands and frowned – deep in thought for a moment. 'I think we could make something more out of this, much better than the usual docu-channel fodder. I think we could make a feature-length documentary, and we could try for something that's good enough for a theatrical release. There's no reason why we shouldn't, frankly. What do you think?'

Her eyes widened as she chugged a mouthful of beer from her bottle.

'There's beautiful scenery up here,' he continued. 'It's made for a larger screen. Those woods and peaks, swirling morning mist . . . the right background score?'

'God, yes,' she replied, grinning.

'Something you and I could be proud of,' he said, picking up his bottle and clinking it on hers. He finished it and wiped the suds from his lips. 'Nice drop of lager, that.'

'Jules, love. They call it *beer* here.'

He waved his hand. 'Beer, shmeer. You want another?'

62

'Go on then.'

He caught the waitress's eye and ordered two more.

'The thing is,' he continued, 'I need to head back to the UK. This was meant to be a quickie project, cheap and cheerful. Now it's something altogether different, we'll need a bigger budget and some investment partners. I want to pitch it to some more substantial players, not just the BBC.'

'Oh, God. This could really make us!'

Julian felt a little light-headed. He wasn't sure if it was the adrenaline rush or the Budweiser.

'What about me?' asked Rose. 'I need to get back to our studio to put everything we've got together.'

He looked at her. Her cheeks were pink with excitement.

'Maybe you should stay here, Rose. I'll be home for no more than a week, I guess, and then be right back to help. I just think someone needs to stick around and keep an eye on our turf, if you know what I mean.'

She nodded. 'Yeah, maybe you're right.'

'What's the broadband like at our motel? You tried it?'

'I think it's pretty good. Both our rooms have got a connection.'

The waitress brought the beers over. 'Get you guys anything else?'

Julian checked his watch. It was late and he knew he needed to be up early to make his way to Reno-Tahoe International airport to catch a flight to Denver and back to Heathrow. Once they had a few interested partners and some budget money to play around with, then he and Rose could celebrate properly.

'Just the bill, please,' he replied.

When the waitress had gone he turned back to Rose. 'Whilst I'm in London, could you knock up a short, tasty showreel and send it over?'

'Sure,' she said, pushing her fringe back out of her face, 'no problem.'

She realised he was looking at her for longer than was comfortable for either of them. Rose looked away awkwardly and started peeling the label off her beer bottle. Julian chugged another mouthful.

'Reno's about two or three hours' drive. I'll take our hire car there, if you can get another one arranged locally.'

She nodded as she finished the last of her beer, a careless trickle running down her chin as she set the bottle down on the table.

Julian leaned forward and wiped it away with his thumb. 'Lush.'

Rose felt it. She wondered if Julian had.

A little frisson. A momentary fizz of excitement.

He looked awkward, slightly embarrassed and withdrew his hand.

'We need to go to my room and check the bandwidth.'

Rose felt her cheeks colour. *I can't believe I just said that.*

'Sorry?'

'Of the broadband connection?' she quickly added.

The waitress came with the bill. He settled it and left a tip.

'Maybe we should test it,' said Rose quietly. 'Before you go and it's too late to know if it's good enough to upload a show-reel.'

Julian smiled hesitantly and pushed his glasses up the bridge of his nose. He sensed something in the invitation, something that stepped outside of their tight professional partnership. They were both high on the excitement of the story, and several beers each was helping to leverage the mood . . . but he knew where this had the potential to go and that in the morning they'd both regret it.

'Errr . . . I . . .' he stammered.

Rose quickly looked down at her bottle and carried on peeling the label.

'Or maybe not,' she replied uncomfortably.

'Maybe it's just fine. Yeah, I'm sure it probably—'

'Yeah, sure . . . it uhh . . . maybe . . . we should check it in the morning.'

'Sure.'

They both smiled and fidgeted for a moment, before reaching for their coats.

CHAPTER 12

23 September, 1856

Ben shivered, despite being wrapped up in his thick woollen poncho. The snow was coming down lightly; a fine dusting right now, but it had been coming down like that all day. Enough of it had settled on the ground that the wheels were slipping perilously on the sloping track.

He watched as a knot of men, a mixture from both Preston's and Keats's parties, struggled together with the jury-rigged windlass at the top of the rugged incline. Stout rope was wound around the inner hub of the rear wheel of a large conestoga, secured firmly at the top, and several lengths ran down the short, steep track to a wagon that was midway up and double-teamed with straining oxen. The men pulled on the ropes in unison, working in concert with the oxen to ease the cumbersome vehicle up the slope.

Ben eagerly wanted to be back in amongst the scrum of men working the wheel, if only to build up a sweat again and get warm. But there were only so many men that could fit a helping hand on the spokes without getting in each other's way. They pulled together with a synchronised grunt. With each twist of the wheel the wagon lurched upwards and the straining oxen staggered forward.

All but a few of the wagons had been manoeuvred to the top

of this steep section of Keats's trail – *the shortcut*. This was the route, the old man assured them all, that would get them through these wooded peaks to the pass faster than any other trail. It was a far quicker route but, he had cautioned, a much tougher one.

The process of winching the wagons up the side of the gulch had taken most of the day, slowed down by the increasing lack of purchase the wheels were having on the ground as the snow had begun to settle during the overcast and gloomy afternoon.

Mr Hussein stood beside him shivering too; his breath hung before him as he spoke. 'Is being . . . uh . . . much coldness today, Mr Lambert. Yes?'

Ben nodded. '*Very* bloody cold. I can't believe only two days ago I was walking on salt flats with my shirt-sleeves rolled up.'

Hussein's face knotted with concentration for a moment as he translated and then he nodded and smiled. 'Yes. Very sudden . . . is very coldness.'

The men heaved again and the wagon suddenly lurched forward, slewing alarmingly to one side of the trail.

'Shit!' Ben hissed quietly, as the wagon continued its uncontrolled sideways drift.

Mr Hussein held his breath as they watched.

The trail up which they were attempting to winch the wagon was narrow, flanked on one side by a steep bank strewn with boulders and small bushes and trees clutching tightly to the ground. On the other side, the trail dropped away, descending steeply to a rocky gulch through which a stream gurgled noisily below.

My God, it's going to go over.

The oxen were losing their footing, sliding in the churned-up slick of mud and powdered snow turning to slush. Ben recognised the woman aboard the wagon as the wife of one of Preston's council of Elders, Mrs Zimmerman. She was perched anxiously on the edge of the jockey board, coaxing the oxen forward. She let out a shrill cry of alarm as the wagon continued its slide towards the edge. The wagon finally came to a rest, the left rear wheel slotting into a worn groove on the track, carved by the previous wagons. Mr Hussein's breath gushed out, a plume of languid vapour that hung before him in the still air.

As it creaked ominously uphill, Ben realised it was the crippled wagon.

'Oh no, it's the jury-rigged one.'

'Beg pardon?' Hussein asked.

Ben's eyes darted to the improvised wheel, the round oak table-top, just as it was beginning to buckle and splinter under the lateral weight of the wagon. The wagon suddenly lurched at an angle, and the wheel cracked loudly.

Ben, along with several other bystanders, called out to her to jump off.

Mrs Zimmerman, perched on the jockey board, stared down at the gulch beside the wagon, and then glanced behind her through the pursed canvas opening of the cover behind her, drawn tight with a puckering string.

What's she doing? Jump, woman. Jump!

The wagon slowly slid in the mush, further over the edge, the fractured wheel creaking alarmingly. The oxen on the left-hand side of the doubled team, seeing the drop right next to them, began to panic, scrambling to the right, causing a spreading confusion amongst the others. The wagon canted still further and Ben could see there was an irretrievable momentum building up that was going to carry it over.

'For God's sake jump!' he shouted at her.

Mrs Zimmerman suddenly turned and clawed at the tightened canvas flap. She screamed something, a warning . . . as she tried to get inside. He remembered then that the woman had a young daughter, and that she must be inside the wagon. The woman managed to loosen the ties of the canvas flap and was half inside, desperately scrambling to reach for her little girl, when the improvised wheel suddenly shattered with a loud crack.

The top-heavy wagon lost its grip, toppling over the edge, throwing the woman out on to the ground. She landed heavily at the top of the slope only to watch the wagon roll over as it tumbled down the slope, crushing the hickory canvas bows and, undoubtedly, the poor girl inside. The oxen, dragged over the edge with it, followed in its wake, a squirming tangled mass of muscle and hide and flailing legs.

The wagon's tumbling descent, as one whole, came to a shuddering halt as it slammed into a tree trunk. The wooden vehicle shattered with an explosive force, leaving an avalanche of debris – torn and jagged planks of wood, barrels and boxes and tattered cloth and shattered pottery – to continue its rolling descent to the bottom of the gulch. The oxen followed the same path down, most of their limbs and necks already broken and flopping like lengths of ribbon.

Skittering down the slope a moment later came a length of rope and, attached to it, the axle ripped from the conestoga being used as a winch at the top of the hill.

Ben looked up the trail to see that the wagon had been pulled partway down and turned on its side, leaving a trail of damaged and battered possessions strewn behind it.

Mr Hussein whispered a curse in Arabic.

It was Preston who reacted before anyone else, throwing his broad-brimmed hat to the ground and beginning to scramble down the perilously steep slope, with little apparent care for his own safety.

From the top of the hill, where the men had been working together to winch up the wagon, Ben heard Mr Zimmerman bellowing with grief.

CHAPTER 13

cave iram Dei

M	T	W	T	F	S	S
				1	2	3
4	5	6	7	8	9	10
11	12	13	14	15	16	17
18	19	20	21	22	23	24
25	26	27	28	29	30	

Sunday
Flight UA176

Julian stared out of the window at the fluttering port wing of UA176 and the two very heavy-looking engines that wobbled precariously beneath it.

He hated turbulence — really hated it. The 'seat belts on' sign pinged.

'Great,' he muttered, gripping the armrest tightly.

The little girl sitting beside him looked up from the game on her phone. 'Are you scared?' she asked.

He pushed his glasses up the bridge of his nose and knotted his eyebrows sternly as he turned to her, hoping he was conveying both a relaxed lack of interest in the mild buffeting and the notion that right now, he really didn't need to be consoled by a maternally minded child.

'Just fine, thanks.'

She nodded, satisfied he wasn't going to need babysitting and returned to her game. He returned to focusing his mind *off* the fact he was riding a 350-ton kerosene bomb, 30,000 feet above the ground, kept aloft merely because they were travelling through air fast enough . . . for now. He turned away from the window and pulled down the blind. If he couldn't see those wafer-thin wings wobbling through the turbulence, it might help.

There was news playing on the small dropdown LCD screens; more on the still-distant US election, and the Republican party's continuing efforts to find a strong partnership to run against the Democrats. It was followed by a quick throwaway item on several independent candidates who had already thrown their hats into the ring. There was the usual array of attention-seeking nuts amongst them, Julian noticed. He decided to turn his attention to work, opening up a folder of printed sheets – the Lambert journal – but his mind swiftly drifted off-piste.

Rose.

What happened there?

In the last few years they'd spent literally thousands of hours in each other's company, and a few dozen of those, the worse for wear from booze. But nothing like that had ever happened before. On the one hand, there was a tingle of desire, on the other, it felt wrong – like looking at a sister or an auntie in a funny way.

Julian shook his head. Why, all of a sudden, after three years of working together, had this awkward situation cropped up?

Why now, for crying out loud?

Work, Jules . . . work.

He looked back down at the open folder and the scanned pages of the Lambert journal. The first entries had been few and far between, sometimes days, even weeks between them. The handwriting was measured, tidy, comfortably spaced and relatively easy to read. But, as he flicked quickly through the pages, they became longer, the handwriting more erratic, cramped, dense and much harder to decipher – like a child running out of space in a school exercise book, the letters were shrinking towards the end, and the ink grew fainter. He found himself squinting with the folder held up almost to his nose as he tried to make out a few random sentences on the last few scanned pages. There the writing was all but indecipherable – careless hurried scrawls.

A word here, a word there stood out of the dense pages. He wasn't sure if his tired eyes were deciphering the spidery handwriting correctly. But one word he thought he had picked out whilst digitising the pages a couple of days ago, he now saw again.

. . . *murder* . . .

He felt some instinct inside him twitch. He suspected there might be something more to this story than a wayward wagon train that had got lost in the mountains. As soon as he got back home, he planned to set up some meetings, but he was going to have to read through as much of this journal as he could in the meantime, then get the story transcribed and typed up for others to read more easily. More importantly, reading through this diary would help him make sense of the mystery he'd discovered at the very back of the journal – the ragged edges of three or four pages that had been ripped out.

Murder and mystery.

'This just gets better and better,' he muttered to himself. The girl beside him looked up from her phone for a moment before turning back to playing her game.

Then there was research. He was impatient to get back to his flat, fire up his computer and start the process of researching this Benjamin Lambert's background. He suspected it wasn't going to be too difficult. Even back in mid-1800s England, it was difficult to live a life without leaving behind a forensic trail of yellowing paper records.

First things first, though.

He flipped back several pages in his notebook and resumed transcribing the contents of Lambert's journal, stopping every now and then to interpret the faded ink scrawls, the gentle buffeting of the plane soon forgotten about.

CHAPTER 14

23 September, 1856

Preston emerged onto the track where Mr Zimmerman stared anxiously down at the tangled wreckage below, holding his sobbing wife in his arms and rocking her gently.

Mr Zimmerman looked up at him. 'William . . . is she . . . ?'

Preston, breathless from the exertion of pulling himself up the steep slope, ignored the father and looked around at the gathered faces. He spotted Ben.

'Mr Lambert?'

Ben nodded.

'Your trail captain, Keats, says you have some medical knowledge.'

'What? Just a little. I was training as a doctor before I . . .'

'Come with me, now.'

'Let me get my bag.'

'Quickly, please.'

Preston led the way back down, a treacherous descent made more difficult by an inch of snow rendering every foothold slippery and unreliable. Near the bottom, as the rush of the stream grew louder, they passed the oxen, wrapped around the base of a stout Ponderosa pine like some many-legged, many-headed beast. To Ben's surprise, amidst the mass of tan hide, one or two of them were still alive, struggling and bellowing pathetically.

They climbed down further, until Ben could see the tangled remains of the wagon, and the curious sight of modest undergarments and Sunday-best clothing dangling from the higher branches of several trees nearby, as if hung out to dry.

Lower down he could see Keats squatting over *something* near the stream. Preston stopped and turned round to face him. Ben could see tears in the man's normally stern eyes.

'I think young Johanna will not live . . .' He struggled to clear the emotion from his voice. 'She's down there.'

Preston led him to the floor of the gulch, strewn with boulders, shards of shattered and twisted timber and scattered personal belongings. The small, ice-cold brook energetically splashed and gurgled around them, carrying away with it the lighter things; letters, poems, dried flowers, keepsakes and mementoes sailed away downstream.

'This way,' said Preston again, leading him over to where Keats squatted, powder snow gathering on the floppy brim of his tan hat. To his credit, the grizzled old guide had managed to manoeuvre his scarred and pockmarked old face into something that resembled a tender smile for the poor child.

Ben looked down to see him stroking the ghostly white face of a young girl, stretched out across a wet boulder and bathed in the freezing cold water of the stream. Across her narrow waist lay a large section of the wagon's trap. The heavy wooden frame had crushed her, cutting her almost completely in half.

'My God,' Ben whispered and Preston shot him an angry glance.

'*If you cannot help her, at least let her think you can,*' he hissed at him.

He nodded and then knelt down beside her. 'Johanna, is it?'

She looked up at him, her blue lips quivering from the cold. 'I . . . I know you. Y-you're an *outsider*.'

Ben nodded and smiled. 'That's right, my name's Benjamin.

I'm a . . . a doctor. I'm going to have a little look at you. See what we can do.'

She smiled up at Preston. 'G-God a-always p-provides.'

Preston stooped down and held her hand. 'Yes, he does, Johanna, my love. God saw to it that Dr Lambert was to travel with us.'

'Where is m-my m-momma and p-papa?' she whispered, through flickering, trembling lips that were turning blue.

'Your mother is fine. She leapt free and is safe at the top.'

She sighed with relief and turned to look at Preston. 'M-momma t-tried to get me . . . d-didn't she?'

'Yes, she did. Because you're *special* to us, Johanna.'

Ben looked across at Preston; it was a tender thing to say.

She smiled faintly, shivering as she did so. 'I'm h-happy my m-momma is s-safe.'

Preston nodded. 'She's fine, just fine.'

Ben fumbled for her pulse; it was weak and fading. 'Johanna,' he said, 'we're going to get you out of here, then I'll tend to you shortly, up at the top of the hill.' It was a shameless lie to comfort her last few moments. He looked down at her separated body. The shattered timber had cut through her like a serrated blade, not a clean bisection but an untidy tangle of shredded organs, muscle tissue, skin and fragmented bone . . . messy.

'Yes, we'll have you out of here very soon. But first, let me give you something. You'll feel better.'

Ben reached into his bag and pulled out a bottle of laudanum.

'What is that?' asked Preston.

'An opiate. It will help her . . .' Ben's words faded to nothing. He uncorked the bottle. 'It'll make it easier.' He lifted the girl's head and poured a modest amount through her quivering lips. Almost immediately the trembling began to ease.

'There, there,' cooed Ben softly, stroking her face, 'there's a good girl. You're going to be fine.'

The young girl nodded dreamily, reassured by the soothing tone of his voice and the soft touch of his hand. She was slipping away now, mercifully, very quickly with the hint of a smile on her purple lips.

Ben glanced across at Keats, seeing, to his surprise, tears tumbling from narrowed eyes, and down his craggy cheeks into his beard. The guide chewed on his lip silently as Preston uttered a quiet prayer.

Looking back down at Johanna, Ben could see she had slipped away.

'I'm sorry,' he muttered, 'there was nothing I could do.'

Keats nodded. 'Nothin' no one could do.'

Preston turned to them both. 'I'd like a moment alone with her, if you please.'

Ben put the glass bottle carefully back in his bag and stood up. Together he and Keats made their way across the stream and a few yards up the steep hill.

'She must have been only eight or nine years old,' whispered Ben. 'Poor girl.'

'Yup,' Keats replied, his gravel-voice still thick with emotion. 'And these stupid sons-of-bitches will consider it God's will . . . just you see.'

Ben nodded.

They stood in silence awhile and watched as Preston knelt down and kissed the child.

'What you saw there, Lambert,' said Keats, 'was the elephant.'

He knew what the guide meant, and that was exactly how it felt; as if some huge malevolent entity had grown tired of watching from afar and decided to announce its presence.

'All of us seen the elephant today, Lambert . . . all of us. And that ain't no good.'

CHAPTER 15

```
cave iram Dei
M   T   W   T   F   S   S
                1   2   3
4   5   6   7   8   9   10
11  12  13  14  15  16  17
18  19  20  21  22  23  24
25  26  27  28  29  30
```

Sunday
Fulham, London

Julian was glad to be home in his modest flat. Junk mail was piled up against the inside of his front door, and the smell wafting through from the kitchen suggested some food in his waste bin had gone off. In the fridge there was nothing to grab — he noticed some paté had grown some blue hair, and a litre jug of milk had separated into curious layers of yellow liquid and pale gunk.

Otherwise, though, his flat was the tidy little *sanctum sanctorum* he had left behind a fortnight ago.

Though keen to hit the sack and catch up on the sleep he'd missed in the woods and on his uncomfortably hard motel bed, he called Soup Kitchen's part-time receptionist, Miranda, to grab a handful of phone numbers that he'd be calling later.

Then he turned his attention to finding some details on B.E. Lambert.

Three hours later he pushed himself away from the desk, wandered over to the phone and ordered himself a pizza. With twenty minutes to wait, he sat back down at the desk and reviewed the notes he'd printed out.

It appeared that Benjamin Lambert had come from a very

wealthy family. His father, Maurice, had made a fortune on property in the Square Mile, but accrued most of his wealth as a result of investments he'd made in America. Most of this information Julian had found on the website of Banner House Hospice (formerly Asylum). Maurice Lambert had donated substantially to the institution, funding the building of a wing – the Lambert Wing, naturally.

Maurice Lambert, knighted later on, had only one son with his wife Eugenie – née Eugenie Davies, a distant relative through marriage, Julian discovered, to the Duke of Westminster. Their son, Benjamin Edward Lambert, went to Westminster Boarding School and on to Oxford to study medicine, later specialising in the emerging discipline of psychiatry. Julian wondered if that was his father's aspiration – for his son to practise medicine in the hospital he paid for?

He also managed to find a short article in *The Times*' online archive, an article dated 1855 in which it was mentioned that Benjamin Lambert, son of Sir Maurice, had announced that he was preparing to extricate himself from polite London society and travel to the Americas to explore the wilderness of the west. He planned to write a study of the frontier, perhaps even a novel, which he would publish on his return. The paper wished him *bon voyage* and looked forward to serialising his work.

And that's where the trail of information dried up.

Julian chewed absent-mindedly on a biro.

That didn't necessarily mean Lambert perished out in those woods. There might be further biographical footprints from later on in his life, elsewhere. For example, he might have survived and stayed in America – in which case, there would be a trail somewhere.

But for now, there was nothing more he could easily find. Any further information on Lambert would require some digging.

The doorbell rang, and five minutes later Julian was sitting in his bay window looking out past rain streaks at the evening traffic on the road below, enjoying a glass of wine and tearing hungrily into a slice of pizza.

Idly, his mind kept drifting back to Rose and what might have happened last night if there'd been just a couple more empty beer bottles on the table between them.

Get a grip, Julian. You work together . . . it's best that nothing happened.

Outside a siren bounced off the block of flats opposite as a police car tore down the wet street. The noise broke the spell. And he figured, if it was a spell broken so easily, then perhaps it wasn't meant to be.

Back to work, slacker.

He wiped grease from his fingers and returned to the keyboard, opening up Google and typing 'Preston Party'.

He got the usual avalanche of irrelevant hits. 'Preston's Bar' in Chicago was having a party. There were photos of a Preston Macey's graduation and subsequent party. Preston Town's civic hall was hosting a question and answer session with their MP from the Labour Party. Preston Entertainment, an online DVD store, had a list of movies with Party in the title. And so on, and so on.

Julian sighed. There was so much tat on the web these days. He tried refining his search: 'Preston Party' + 'Mormons'.

He got several more pages of hits to wade through. The 'Mormon' tag was predominantly giving him loads of community and church pages, featuring chatty reportage about recent, wholesome family days out and pending prayer meetings. Lots of pictures of happy, shiny faces; pictures of church elders, respectable and smart – successful by the look of many of them – gathered at picnics and fairs and camps and tents. Pictures of sandy-haired kids in smart casual clothes, innocent and healthy, baring happy grins as they hugged each other and goofed around for the camera.

Julian wondered if any of these kids would one day walk into a high school dressed in black and packing an assault rifle in their shoulder bag ready to do *God's work*. Perhaps not. Whilst

Julian was not a big fan of religion he conceded that it seemed to hold communities like these together like a sturdy glue. It always seemed to be the loners, the kids who'd floated off into their own lonely parallel universe, who ended up blowing their classmates away.

He leafed through the printed pages of the journal, looking for something. Finding a reference to the preacher's first name, he tried again: 'William Preston' . . . and for good measure he added '+Missing Wagon Train'.

The search was too specific. It gave him only one hit. He was about to have another go when something about the brief thumbnail description caught his eye.

. . . account of a Mormon wagon train on their way to Oregon that went missing . . .

He hit the link and was immediately presented with a simple page, a black screen topped with a banner that read 'Tracing William Preston's Party'. Beneath that was a rather dry and blandly written block of text laid out in a small and tiresome font that described little more than the early history of the Mormon church. If Julian hadn't had a particular interest in the subject, this drab-looking web page would have had him clicking away very quickly.

The solid block of text started out by briefly describing how the Church of the Latter Day Saints was founded by Joseph Smith; then the subsequent troubles in Nauvoo; the unpleasant in-fighting of the church; the schisms; how the Mormon church was rounded on by non-Mormon Christians; the outbreaks of violence; and then, finally, describing the Great Mormon Exodus across the Great Plains.

Further down the page, there was a little detail on a minister by the name of William Preston who had formed one of many breakaway Mormon groups and was delivering his flock from the decadent United States into God's untamed wilderness to set up their own Eden. The short article concluded that Preston's party set out from a place called Council Bluffs, Iowa, in the spring of 1856 and stopped off at an outpost named Fort Kearny.

From there they set out into the wilderness, never to be heard from again.

Julian noticed an email address at the bottom. That was it; there were no other links for further reading, no hyperlinks to other related pages, just this one page of text written by someone who clearly needed to work on his writing style.

There was a comment beside the email address.

I am working on a book about this. If you have information, or wish to share information, please contact me at Arnold.Zuckerman@artemis.com.

Julian hovered over the link, tempted to bash out a quick email to see if he could pump the person behind this page for some quick and easy details. Maybe if he suggested he had some – loose – association with the BBC, the author would be flattered enough to open up and share everything with him.

He clicked the link and started to write an introductory email and then stopped.

Hang on. Maybe I should finish up on the Lambert journal first?

Yes. It would make a lot more sense if he knew *how* the story of the Preston Party was going to go before hooking up with anybody else. He decided this might be someone worth contacting at a later stage, if he needed to fill in some details. But not right now. Whilst this page was most likely authored by some retired old enthusiastic amateur, it might just be another journalist or, God forbid, another programme researcher with the scent of a story in his nostrils.

Instead of emailing the person, he bookmarked the page.

'We'll talk in good time,' he muttered.

He poured himself another glass of red, settled back in his bay window which was rattling with spots of rain, and picked up the pages of Lambert's journal.

CHAPTER 16

cave iram Dei

M	T	W	T	F	S	S
				1	2	3
4	5	6	7	8	9	10
11	12	13	14	15	16	17
18	19	20	21	22	23	24
25	26	27	28	29	30	

Sunday
Haven Ridge, Utah

William Shepherd looked out of the tall bay windows of his study, over the manicured lawns of the campus, kept a lush green by the regularly spaced sprinklers that stirred to life in synchronicity every evening.

Several classes were sitting in the warm mid-morning sun on the lawn, noisily debating scripture, or silent in prayer, all of them young and earnest people, radiant with purpose and God's love. Such a contrast to the surly groups of teenagers he noticed on every street corner these days – soulless, mean-spirited creatures with dead eyes, clustered together like cancer cells.

Shepherd shook his head sadly. There was a knock on the door to his study. 'Mr Shepherd, studio three is ready to record your mid-week sermon.'

'Thank you, Annie,' he called out. 'Tell them I'll be along presently.'

He heard the squeak of Mrs Wall's sandals on the wooden floor outside, dutifully hurrying off to inform the studio team.

I have things to think about.

He had almost missed it because it had been buried amongst all the other email he received daily. Shepherd had almost deleted it out of hand as a piece of spam mail. The message

82

was automated, mailed by 'SiteDog' software that monitored the accessing of a nominated web page and reported back on details of who and when and how long they had been studying the page. He got these notification emails very rarely, one every couple of months at most. The web page that SiteDog was set up to monitor had deliberately been designed to be as unappealing as possible, tedious for any casual surfer who might by accident stumble upon it. Only someone looking for something very specific would be enticed to stay a while.

He opened the notification mail.

One visitor, several hours ago, had loitered around the page for ten minutes and thirty-seven seconds and then clicked on the contact email link.

'Who are you, then?' asked Shepherd curiously.

Someone else interested? Or just a passing surfer?

Someone interested might just mean someone with a little information. If he wanted, he could find out more about this person who had stuck around on this page longer than anyone else had ever done, who had even clicked to send an email, but apparently decided against it. SiteDog presented him with an IP address. With a little – not entirely legal – effort he could get a postal address out of that, if he wanted to.

Be cautious.

Yes, he needed to be that for sure.

I can't afford to make any silly mistakes now.

Shepherd was beginning to become newsworthy, a candidate that some of the news shows were quietly predicting might be worth 'watching for the future'. Beyond his core audience of Latter Day Saints worshippers, beyond those that tuned in regularly to the Daily Message, his name was beginning to register; his message was beginning to hit home.

But, unlike the other running candidates, there was no party for him to hide behind, no ranks of fellow Democrats or Republicans to close formation around him like a Roman *testudo*, to shelter him from the sticks and stones of politics.

There was just his name, his reputation . . . and the message.

I have to be whiter than white. I have to be so careful. I cannot afford a single skeleton in my closet.

CHAPTER 17

29 September, 1856

Ben watched another of the heavy conestogas slide uncontrollably along the churned narrow trail, one wheel clunking and splintering against a jagged rock. It held, but even he could see it was a wheel now fit to break on the next stubborn boulder or sudden rut in the track — either of which could arrive unannounced at any time beneath the thickening carpet of snow on the ground.

The snowfall had started with a light dusting yesterday morning; a feathery weak-willed attempt by the winter to window-dress the peaks a fortnight too early. But it was enough, Ben noticed, to put the fear of God into Keats.

And he'd been driving them hard since — driving them relentlessly towards this pass of his, the one he swore would claw back for them days if not weeks and lead them out onto gentle valleys that sloped mercifully down the rest of the way towards the promised land.

Keats convinced Preston that a last hard dash was required, a run through the night by the light of oil lamps, and now, through an ever-thickening curtain of snow. A dash for the pass because, hampered by snow, the final assent would be impossible for the big wagons and more than likely be too much for the small traps as well.

They had pushed on almost thirty-six hours straight, with only two short stops for cold food. In that time, they had made painfully slow progress uphill, along a winding trail through dense woodland. Trees that had further down the trail held their distance either side of them now brushed against their canvasses, and stung their cheeks with swipes of needles and cones.

Not for the first time, Ben found himself wondering if the old guide had lost his way in the dark, and led them up a dead end.

He led his two ponies, the first bearing his personal things, the second his medicine box and several sacks of cornmeal and oats. He didn't trust their footing now to ride, instead choosing to feel his way forward through the three or four inches of snow to the uneven and rutted ground.

Keats likewise was on foot ahead, pulling his animal behind him with a vicious determination.

Have you bloody well lost us, Mr Keats? He wanted to call out. This trail of his seemed to be little more than a narrow artery of steeply ascending ground on which the trees had mutually elected not to grow. It certainly didn't feel like wagons had worn a path this way . . . ever.

Beside him, an ox lost its footing and stumbled, causing the beast behind it to step to the side, pulling the conestoga askew. It slid in the trampled mush and thudded into a sapling, splintering its trunk and sending a shower of snow down on the canvas. The oxen, and the man leading them, struggled to get the wagon on the move again, up the incline. Behind them, well . . . he could barely see the glow of the oil lamp of another man leading his team of oxen, through the thick veil of feathery snowflakes. The train was halted.

Ben looked uphill towards Keats. The old man was pressing on regardless.

'Keats!' he called out. 'Hey, Mr Keats!'

The guide glanced back, quickly noting the temporary snarl-up. He gestured forward, and said something that Ben failed to understand. Then he carried on, leading the other wagons with him uphill, until Ben could barely see the faint bobbing glow of the lamp swinging from the back of the rearmost wagon.

He wondered whether to hurry forward to catch them up, or remain with the wagon here, still struggling with the weary team of oxen.

'Keats!' he called out again, but his voice bounced back off the trees either side, and was quickly smothered by the heavy descending blanket of swirling snow.

'Are the others not waiting?' called the man with the wagon, one of the Mormons.

'It seems not, Mr Larkin.'

'What? They can't leave us all here.'

'Let me run ahead. He may not understand you've stopped.'

Ben tied his leading pony to Larkin's wagon, and then trotted forward, stumbling as he tried to catch up. As he made his way ahead, the lamp at the front of the wagon behind him grew faint, and within a dozen more faltering steps he found himself alone in complete darkness, and wary that not being able to see anything he might veer away from the grooves in the snow and become lost in the pitch-black wilderness.

'Dammit,' he whispered.

'Keats!' he called out, stepping quickly forward through snow that was ankle deep.

Up ahead, he saw the reassuring faint glow of light from the rear wagon, and puffed with relief.

As he approached, he sensed the incline of the ground lessening, each step growing easier. The light burned more clearly, surrounded by a bloom of illuminated tumbling flakes. The wagon had stopped, and beside it he saw the shadowy outline of several people.

Oh, what now? Another mishap?

He drew closer and recognised the outline of Keats and his Indian, Broken Wing. They were talking with others, the men from the wagons, gathered together in some sort of impromptu meeting.

'. . . up ahead. Not far,' Keats was saying.

Ben joined them. 'What's not far? The pass?'

'Nope,' Keats shook his head sombrely. 'Ain't gonna make the pass now.' He looked up at the dark sky, and squinted at the thick flakes settling on his face. He brushed them irritably away. 'No way we gonna get through that now. Broken Wing found us a space big enough we can camp up in for tonight.'

'We're stopping?'

He nodded. 'We're stopping.' He spat into the snow. 'Can't see for crap in this, anyhow. We'll see what kind of a mess we're in in the morning.' He turned to the men gathered around. 'Follow Broken Wing. It's just up ahead.'

As the men moved off to return to their wagons he stepped towards Ben.

'You head back down the hill, Lambert, and tell the others there's a big clearing up ahead, and we're makin' camp there right now.'

Ben nodded. 'I suppose this is it, then?'

Keats shrugged. 'Snow's come real early. Might just be a warning, an' it'll melt off in a day.'

'Or?'

'Might be the winter's gone an' beat us to the mountains. I'll see better in the mornin'.'

CHAPTER 18

30 September, 1856

It seems Keats was right. We should have left that crippled wagon behind and moved with greater haste.

Now with the morning I can see what sort of a predicament we are in. To my inexperienced eye, this doesn't look like snow that will melt away under a few hours of sunshine.

Ben looked up from his journal and out through the open canvas flap. The pale morning sun was a pitifully weak glowing disc in the white sky. The forest surrounding the clearing was uniformly white, the tall Douglas firs and spruces each bearing their own thick burden of snow. Against many of the wagons thick powdery drifts had piled up, almost completely burying their wheels.

Last night, as the snow came down in gusting diagonal streaks — enormous flakes the size of a child's fist — Ben had hurriedly tried to improvise a bivouac. It was too dark to hack branches from the trees around the clearing. The best he could manage was to roll himself up snugly in his poncho, inside his bedroll and canvas tarp, moisture-sealed with linseed oil, and shelter beneath the trap of Mr McIntyre's conestoga, whilst his two ponies shivered together out in the open. But McIntyre wouldn't have it when he heard Ben shuffling around beneath their cart and insisted he come in with them for the night.

The otherwise uncomfortable squirming of fidgeting children was pleasantly comforting and, more importantly, warm. The McIntyres were kind to have offered him a space, but with three children in the back of the wagon, the arrangement could only be for the one night.

There was a stirring in the wagon and a chorus of croaky 'good mornings' exchanged, amidst plumes of condensation. Outside, Ben could see there was already a flurry of activity. Keats was already up and taking note of the downfall. His flinty old face, normally frozen into its one and only expression of tired sufferance, was now drawn into a stretched scowl of concern. Ben watched him talking quietly with Broken Wing, both looking up repeatedly at the featureless white sky. Other people were rising, emerging from their wagons, pushing cascades of snow off their laden canopies, dropping out of the back into knee-deep drifts and yelping with surprise.

Keats nodded firmly, the discussion with Broken Wing concluded and a decision made. 'Goddamned snow's here now!' he bellowed angrily. His voice echoed back off the trees a moment later. 'There'll be no going anywhere now!' He stamped snow off his boots and deerskin britches. 'Damn it!'

Ben put away his writing things.

'C'mon! Everyone up! We've got work to do!' Keats was barking out orders to everyone, his people and Preston's, to get up, to get to work.

'That's it! C'mon! Everybody up! Your wagons ain't wagons no more. They gotta be turned into winter shelters!'

Ben thanked Mr and Mrs McIntyre for taking him in last night. Considering how deep the snow was, he realised he would have had to dig himself out – if he hadn't frozen to death in his sleep. McIntyre was already sorting through his tools. Mrs McIntyre flashed him a smile. 'Well now, we're all in this together, Mr Lambert, aren't we?'

'Everyone up! C'mon! There's work to do! Plenty of it!'

Keats's voice echoed around the clearing. 'Get up and grab your tools!'

Ben disentangled himself from the splayed limbs of the still-sleeping children and climbed out through the canvas opening, shuddering as a blast of freezing air enveloped him — a contrast to the warm fug of body heat built up in the McIntyres' wagon overnight.

He dropped off the trap, knee-deep into the snow, and found himself wincing at the bright, upward-reflected glare all around him. Looking around, he hadn't realised how big the clearing was. Last night, the wagons had limped into this place after dark, with snow reducing visibility to just a few dozen yards. There had appeared to be space enough to spread out off the track and corral the oxen together, and so they had, expecting that with first light, they would hitch up again and be moving on.

Ben watched as men obediently stirred from every wagon — Preston's people as well as Keats's — each brandishing a saw or an axe. They waded through the snow towards Keats. He saw the tall, slender frame of Preston amongst them, almost a head taller than most of the stocky men of his church.

'Gentlemen, join us here in the centre!' Preston's voice boomed across the clearing. 'With your tools, if you please!'

Ben made his way towards Keats. Broken Wing stood silently beside him, his head covered with a red woollen cap.

'Good morning,' said Ben.

'What's good about it?' spat Keats angrily.

Men gathered about him. Preston pushed his way through them. 'Mr Keats, it appears then that the weather has let us down.'

'You could say that,' the old guide replied dryly.

'Will this lot melt, do you think?'

Keats shook his head. 'Nope. This ain't a warning of winter . . . this is it for real. It just arrived last night, and ain't goin' nowhere till spring.'

'Could we not at least try for your pass?' asked Preston.

91

'Too goddamn steep. You want the ground clear, dry an' hard. An' sure as hell it ain't any of those right now.'

'So you're saying we're stuck here?'

'Unless we leave here on foot.'

Preston shook his head. 'No . . . no, that would be impossible. These wagons contain all my people have. Everything.'

Keats nodded. 'They'd lose it all, that's for sure. Anyway, you'd be a fool tryin' to make it out on foot through the winter. Not even Indians an' trappers'll do that if they can help.' Keats nodded to the people emerging from their wagons. 'An' you got women and little 'uns to worry 'bout.'

Preston nodded contritely. Ben sensed there was an unspoken apology in the subtle tip of his head. 'You are a man I presume who has experienced a winter in the wilderness.'

Keats snorted sarcastically. 'Reckon a few.'

'Then I shall bow to your greater experience. What are we to do?'

The old man sucked a lungful of chilled air in through his bulbous, pockmarked nose. Ben suspected that deep down, the guide was probably savouring a moment of *schadenfreude* at Preston's expense.

'Well, if we'd left that lame wagon, we'd have made it through. But I reckon winter's here now. So . . . best we can do, Preston, is think about turnin' this space in the woods into a winterin' camp. That means you gotta turn those wagons of yours into shelters.'

There was a ripple of consternation amongst the men nearby.

'Yeah, that's right. You're gonna break 'em up for lumber that you can use to build—'

'I can't do that!' called out one of the Mormon men. 'My wagon cost me the best part of fifty dollars!'

Other voices murmured in agreement.

'Should we not just wait for this snow to clear?' asked another.

Keats shook his head. 'Like I already said, this ain't clearing till March.'

'Would the wagons not be shelter enough?'

Keats looked at Broken Wing and repeated something in an Indian tongue. The Indian snorted with dry amusement.

'Gonna get a lot colder than last night. You gonna have to build yourselves proper winter-overs.'

Several more voices amongst the gathered men – now numbering about forty – were raised in concern. Ben noticed none of them, neither Preston's men nor Keats's party, were happy with the idea of admitting defeat so readily.

'Quiet there!' barked Preston.

There was silence.

'Mr Keats knows better than anyone here what winter in these mountains will bring.' Preston looked around at the men. 'We shall take his very good advice, and be thankful to God that he sent this man along with us.'

Preston turned back to Keats. 'Not a one of us has had to build a winter shelter in haste from a wagon. How do you suggest we proceed?'

'You gotta build yourself a sturdy frame from the lumber, to start,' Keats replied without a beat. 'Gotta be a good goddamn frame too; there's plenty of snow gonna drift up, and that weighs some.' He pointed to the nearest conestoga. 'Good solid planks there along the length of the trap will do fine. The canvas goes over the frame, then you gotta cut yourself as much pine as you can for warmth – pile it on top of the canvas, thick as you can. The snow that'll gather on top of that will keep you warmer still.'

Preston nodded.

'Frame's gotta be strong, though,' said Keats. 'Gonna be your home for near on six months, I'd say.'

CHAPTER 19

30 September, 1856

Ben stood back, exhausted by the morning's work and sweating profusely, despite having stripped down to his shirt and rolled both sleeves up. Faint vapours of steam rose from his damp, exposed forearms, and out through the unbuttoned neck of his shirt.

He watched Broken Wing working with several spruce saplings, bending their pliable length to form an onion-shaped dome, the tapering ends at the top bound tightly together, the thick bottoms wedged deep into the ground. Meanwhile Keats returned with another armful of pine branches and dropped them on a substantial pile beside the frame to their shelter.

'You helpin', Lambert? Or just gonna sit on your ass and watch?' he growled.

'Sorry.' Ben jumped.

Broken Wing finished securing the frame of their shelter and spoke in his tongue to Keats.

'He's asking for your canvas sheet.'

'Oh, right. I'll fetch it.'

Ben hurried over to where his two ponies were huddled together, and pulled out his tarpaulin from a saddle pack. He returned and handed it to the Indian. Broken Wing turned it over in his hands, studying it, and then looked up at Ben, flashing him a quick grin and a nod.

'Isss good,' he uttered in a chopped, guttural manner. It was the first time, Ben realised, that he'd heard the Indian speak in English.

'C'mon, Lambert, help me get some more of this. We gonna need to pile it high on top of the canvas.'

Ben followed Keats to the edge of the clearing, looking around him as he stepped through the snow. The clearing was alive with activity and noise. The hacking of axes and zipping of saws through lumber bounced and echoed around their little world, framed on all sides by tall spruces and firs that grew up gentle slopes surrounding their bare basin.

He saw a team of Mormon men bring down an entire tree. A barked warning, then a creak and crash as it swung down amidst a cloud of dislodged powder snow. Then the men swarmed upon it. Other men worked diligently on their wagons, easing out lumber nails, carefully cannibalising the precious planks to use for their frames.

'Here,' said Keats, pointing to a pile of pine branches ahead at the edge of the clearing. 'Take those back to Broken Wing.'

Ben bent down and scooped up as much as he could carry, the coarse needles and cones scratching his bare forearms. He stood up and looked into the thick tree line in front of him, an ascending gradual slope of tree bottoms, a world of only two colours – white, and the dark grey-green of bark.

'Move yourself, Lambert,' grunted Keats as he took an axe to a nearby fir and hacked another low-hanging and heavy branch from it.

Ben staggered back across the clearing with his load, nodding politely to Mr Bowen and Mr McIntyre, both working together on building their frames from the planks harvested from their traps.

He dumped his load of branches on the pile and looked at the progress Broken Wing had made with the canvas. It was already wrapped tautly around the sapling frame, and their shelter, for the moment, looked like a low, bulbous tepee.

'Will that be strong enough, do you think?' asked Ben.

The Indian looked up at him, his face a questioning frown.

'The frame?' said Ben, reaching over and running his fingers along one of the ridges beneath the tarpaulin. He gestured at the pile of pine branches. 'These branches are very heavy.'

Broken Wing nodded. 'Isss ssstrong.' He whacked the frame with one hand. It creaked alarmingly, but barely moved.

'It's fine, Lambert,' said Keats, approaching with another armful of branches that he dumped down on top of the pile. 'The weight of this lot, an' the weight of the snow, will make it stronger.' He grinned, a mouth with as many gaps as teeth. 'It's all in the shape, lad.'

Ben nodded. 'Yes, I suppose, like arched brickwork spreading the load.'

Keats shrugged. 'Reckon.'

At that moment, Ben spotted Preston approaching. The minister, like every other man in the clearing, had shed his long dark coat, his white shirt and dark waistcoat and stood in a vanilla cotton undershirt, circled with dark patches of sweat.

'Mr Keats!' he called out breathlessly, as he took the last few strides through the snow towards them. 'Mr Keats,' he said again as he drew up beside them, 'I suggest we have a clear plan for our camp, where things should be, if we are to winter here.'

Keats stroked his chin for a moment and nodded. 'Reckon so.'

'May I suggest the oxen be corralled centrally, in the middle of this clearing.'

Ben looked around. The clearing was roughly oval, about a hundred and fifty yards, maybe two hundred in length – an oasis of open space in an endless sea of unbroken woodland that continued all the way up to a horizon of bare, craggy peaks.

'You un'erstand the oxen will die, Preston? They're our food now.'

'Yes, indeed. I suggest if we corral them all together in the centre of the clearing, in the space between your shelters and ours, they'll keep each other warm and last longer.'

Keats pursed his lips. 'Make better sense to kill 'em all now. Longer they live, the thinner they'll get.'

Preston glanced towards the assembled herd of beasts – well over a hundred of them. For the moment, there was meat and muscle under their tan hides.

'I'd like to keep them alive a little longer, just in case this early snow is a passing thing.'

'It ain't passing.'

'Nonetheless, for now, I'd prefer to keep them alive.'

Keats shrugged. 'The cold'll get 'em before they starve, anyways.'

'We shall have to be sensible and fair with how we ration out the food,' Preston uttered thoughtfully. 'You say we're likely to be stuck here until spring?'

'Yup.'

'Hmm.'

Keats bent down and picked up his deerskin jacket. Now they were just standing, the cold was beginning to bite. 'Reckon we need to be careful with the food from now on,' he said, fastening the toggles. 'Start as we mean to go on.'

'Yes, of course.' Preston nodded. 'One of my people, Mr Stolz, is a butcher by trade. He might be best qualified to deal with each carcass as it becomes available.'

'I think Mr Bowen is as well,' cut in Ben.

'Then, I reckon, they can *both* be in charge of the ox meat. That good for you, Preston?'

Preston nodded, even managed a faint smile. 'That seems fair.'

'Also gonna need regular firewood comin' in.'

'Yes, I suppose we can arrange some kind of rota. Start a firewood pile in the centre and make sure that it's kept topped up each day.'

Keats grunted agreement. 'An' we need to 'rrange a night

watch. Never know what's out there in these woods, even in the winter.'

Preston looked surprised. 'Is there likely to be anything out there, Mr Keats?'

Keats glanced towards Broken Wing, and they exchanged a few words in his language.

'Broken Wing says it's possible some Paiute huntin' party might be aroun'.' Keats looked up at the trees. 'Hell, might still have a bear or two out there lookin' to fatten up, yet. Be worth havin' someone awake with a loaded gun.'

'Yes, I agree with you.'

Keats managed a laugh.

'What's the matter, Mr Keats?'

Keats looked at him and shook his head with bemusement. 'Seems like we foun' ourselves agreein' on a whole buncha things. Hell . . . never would've expected that.'

'Perhaps it's God's will, Mr Keats, that we are marooned here together,' Preston said, offering a genial smile, 'that we can learn a little from each other.'

Keats's expression froze for a moment. Ben half expected a caustic reply, but instead his craggy face split into a grin, his laugh a loose rattle. 'Well, you can put in a good word for me if you like, Preston.'

Preston nodded politely. 'We shall include you and your people in our prayers this evening.' He turned to observe the men in his group working vigorously with their axes on the thick branches they had hacked from the trees. 'And I will call a meeting amongst my people directly. As you suggested, we shall arrange things like the firewood and the allocation of meat from the oxen.'

'Good.' Keats nodded. 'An' mine'll do likewise.'

Preston turned to go and then stopped, his eyes turning on Ben. 'Mr Lambert?'

'Yes?'

'Would your knowledge of medicine be available to all of our . . . small community?'

'Good grief, yes . . . yes, of course,' Ben replied.

'We would of course pay for any medicines we consume, and your services—'

Ben shook his head. 'That'll not be necessary, Mr Preston. I believe we're all together in this now. I have a good supply of medicines in my chest, and I'll certainly have enough time on my hands to practise doctoring.'

Preston's long and normally severe face cracked with a good-natured smile. 'That's generous of you. My thanks.' He nodded politely at Keats and then turned away, pushing through the deep snow towards the nearest of his men.

Keats looked up at the darkening grey sky. 'Shit. Gonna start snowin' again,' he muttered.

CHAPTER 20

Sunday
Blue Valley, California

Rose watched the upload bar slowly creep forward.

'There you go, Jules,' she said, stretching tiredly in her chair. He was going to love it, she was sure. She'd edited together a three minute 'sizzle' — a montage of footage from the site, the surrounding woods, a couple of quick establishing shots of the Sierra Nevadas taken from a professional online image and video library, and some sepia portraits of emigrants ready to set out from Independence. Over this she had laid some of Julian's commentary, and some of Grace's comments — that earthy Midwest 'Marlboro' voice of hers played beautifully against the images.

In the background she had laid down a fantastically haunting and chilling piece of music she'd found on the net; a piece of traditional folksy *Americana* played on a guitar and a violin.

Having completed the editing and composited a final build, she had sat back and watched the short piece at least a dozen times. Every time, the hair on the nape of her neck began to tingle and rise.

He's gonna love it.

Rose checked her watch and realised it was three in the morning.

She looked around her motel room. It was a tip, littered with a couple of empty pizza boxes and soda cans, her clothes lying in a mouldering pile at the end of her unmade bed. The muted TV in the corner flickered with the images of a twenty-four-hour news station.

It reminded her very much of her student digs from a few years ago. Only back then it wasn't just her mess, it was the communal mess of half a dozen of them: ongoing-party mess — empty cider cans, unwashed dishes, overflowing ashtrays, and half-empty packets of cigarette papers . . . all very cool, very young, very groovy. Looking at the squalor around her right now in her silent motel room, this mess made by one lonely person just looked very sad.

Why the hell did I hit on him like that?

The thought came out of the blue. Rose winced. Keeping busy these last two days and nights, she'd managed not to think about it. But now, having got the job done, there it was: an awkward exchange of mumbled words clumsily loaded with a suggestion.

Check out my broadband.

She shuddered.

What was I bloody well thinking?

Julian had distinctly recoiled with embarrassment. She looked in the vanity mirror above the dresser.

Look at me. A twenty-five-year-old frump.

Her rat-brown hair was pulled back into a practical bun. Her red-rimmed eyes, fatigued from forty-eight hours of staring at a monitor, were small and unappealing. She hated her stubby nose and thin, uninviting lips . . . and out of view of the mirror was the one-stone-over, bottom-heavy figure she preferred to keep hidden beneath baggy jeans. On any normal high street, she looked average. But amongst the glamorous, waif-like media moppets that populated the world of digital TV, Rose felt like a sack of potatoes.

It was a sad state of affairs that Julian, a man fifteen years older than her, had politely turned her down. And Jules was hardly Johnny Depp, with a choice of fawning waifs to choose from.

She looked at a segment of digital footage on her laptop — Julian talking to camera. She smiled.

Not so much Johnny Depp as a downmarket Louis Theroux.

Again her mind drifted painfully back to that *maladroit* exchange, and she cringed.

'Forget it,' she muttered. 'Do some more work.'

She watched the loading bar on the screen near completion. Now that Jules had his sizzling trailer to show off at the meetings he'd arranged, she'd decided it might be a useful idea to research this story from the urban myth angle. This small town — Blue Valley — had more than its fair share of them, according to Grace. Rose wondered if they linked back somehow to this lost wagon train. Inevitably most urban ghost stories tend to originate from a root event, usually quite mundane. She wondered whether most of the interesting tales they'd recorded last week whilst interviewing the locals — stories of shrouded figures, walking skeleton-men and glowing lights in the woods — could ultimately be traced back to survivors of that wagon train.

It was a possibility.

There would have been survivors, surely?

Rose wondered if Grace was around in town tomorrow, or whether she was on duty at the National Parks Service camp site up in the woods. Maybe she'd just drive up in her rental and see, take some flapjacks or bagels up, have a natter and a nibble.

Rose liked Grace. She reminded her of a grumpy old chain-smoking aunt she'd had, before cancer got her.

CHAPTER 21

5 October, 1856

Ben could hear children further away in the woods, their voices echoing distantly through the trees.

'That's the Stolheim children,' said Sam. 'They're out collecting firewood too.'

Ben bent over, picked up a fallen branch and brushed the snow off it. 'There's a lot of dead wood and kindling in this forest. A hell of a lot easier than foraging for buffalo chips out on the prairie, eh?'

Sam grinned guiltily at Ben's casual profanity.

'So, where's Emily today?'

He turned and glanced back through the trees towards the camp. Several pale columns of smoke rose lazily up into the featureless white sky from within the clearing below. 'She's at a prayer meeting in the temple.'

Preston's people had put a lot of effort into constructing one shelter that was larger than all the others in the camp. From the outside, it appeared to be big enough to allow room for the Quorum of Elders, a committee of twelve, who met several times a day in there. They also used it for prayer meetings and scripture studies for the younger ones. It was their church . . . or *temple*, as they referred to it, as well as Preston's shelter.

'Vander, Hearst and Preston take turns teaching scripture to some of the children directly.' Sam picked up a branch then turned to look back down at the snow-covered mound of the temple. 'Vander's teaching her right now. Teaching her on her own.'

Ben detected something in his voice.

'I don't like that,' said Sam after a while.

'Why?'

Sam didn't answer at first, instead busying himself with searching for twigs and small branches.

'Sam?'

'Vander once taught me . . . alone,' he said eventually, more to himself than aloud to Ben, 'when I was smaller.'

There was an uncomfortable silence. Ben had once experienced a similar faltering conversation with a very withdrawn first-year boy at boarding school. Unpleasant things had happened there from time to time that were best left alone and not raked over. You endured whatever treatment came your way and didn't cry about it. That's how the best schools turned boys into men.

At least, that's what Ben's father used to say.

'Ben?'

'Yeah?'

'When we make it down from these mountains, in the spring, where will you go?'

'I shall head for Portland eventually. Maybe I'll explore a few other townships along the way. Then I fancy I shall spend some months enjoying the comforts of a hotel room in that fine-sounding town and write about the crossing and our adventure here in the mountains and see about getting it published.'

Sam smiled faintly. 'Will Emily and I be in your book?'

'Of course! How could you not be?'

Sam smiled. He liked that.

'And what will you do after that?'

'Then, I suppose, I ought to return to London. My parents expect me to one day come back, and if not become an eminent psychiatrist, to at least take over my father's business affairs.'

Ben was resigned to that ultimate fate. It was waiting for him eventually, in a few years' time. 'I would miss the freedom out here in the wilderness, though, miss it sorely; but I owe my parents on a promise I made, to come back soon.'

He turned to Sam. 'What about you?'

'Preston will lead us someplace where we're all alone, away from any other people, from outsiders,' he replied cheerlessly and returned to the task of foraging for firewood, dipping down to pull a long, crooked branch from the snow and brushing it off. He snapped the dry wood with several loud and brittle cracks, tucking the shorter lengths into his bundle of kindling.

Ben resumed foraging and they worked in silence for a while, accompanied only by the crunch of their feet on the snow and the distant sounds of movement and chattering voices elsewhere in the woods.

'You're not happy in Preston's church?'

Sam shook his head. 'He frightens me.'

'Frightens you? Why?'

The young man tightened his lips and shook his head. 'He just does.'

'Look here.' Ben stood up straight and adjusted his bundle of kindling. 'I suppose when you're grown up you could leave, though, couldn't you? If you're so unhappy with them, you could find your own way, couldn't you?'

Sam shook his head. 'Not without Emily. I'm all she's got.'

'She has her mother.'

Sam looked at him. 'They'd never let her go, anyw—'

They heard a raised voice ahead of them – an unmistakable cry of surprise or alarm, then other voices, including Preston's, calling out.

Something had happened.

Ben and Sam dropped their bundles and headed towards the exchanged shouts, Ben unslinging his rifle and Sam following suit. They pushed through a tangle of undergrowth and briar poking up out of the thick snow, dislodging clouds of powder from the low-hanging branches above them.

'This way!' said Ben, leading Sam up a steep incline, stumbling over buried knots of tree roots, rocks and sapling stalks. At the top the incline levelled off, revealing a small glade nestling below in a dimple of land in the hillside. The glade had been hacked clear of wood — from the look of the old, weatherworn tree stumps that poked up through the blanket of snow, a task carried out by someone many years ago.

In the middle there was a crudely constructed shelter, clearly not the work of any trained artisan; there was no carpentry to be seen. It was a ramshackle structure of stacked boughs, held together with hide strips and the gaps between them daubed with packed mud.

Ben and Sam made their way down the slope towards the clearing to get a closer look. The entrance to the shelter was a low, arched gap in the uneven, knobbly wall, covered over by a tattered buffalo hide. In the small clearing in front of the shelter, frames of wood had been erected. Ben noticed the dried and leathery carcasses of skinned forest hares dangling in an untidy row from several of them. They'd been dangling for a long, long time by the look of it. The hares seemed more fossilised than rotten.

Preston and three other Mormon men stood in the clearing before the shelter, surveying the scene. They noticed Ben and Sam as they emerged into the clearing.

'Mr Lambert . . . Samuel,' Preston called out. 'It appears we're not the only ones out here in these woods.'

Ben made his way over. 'What is this? Is it an Indian camp, do you think?'

Preston casually scratched the dark beard beneath his chin. 'Is it more likely a trappers' camp?' he replied, pointing towards a wall of the shelter, lined with an arrangement of different-sized skulls, their smooth yellow ivory boiled and scrubbed clean by somebody long ago, or perhaps merely worn away by the elements. Ben couldn't identify with any certainty what animals they had once been; one or two of them might have belonged to deer or stags, another might have belonged to a horse or a pony.

'Actually, it looks like it's been abandoned for a while,' said Ben.

Preston nodded. 'Yes, it would seem so.'

'Should we look inside, William?' asked Hearst, one of the men with Preston.

He nodded. 'Perhaps, to be sure.' He held out his hand. 'Your gun please, Saul.'

The man passed him his rifle and Preston pulled back the hammer to half cock and slotted a percussion cap in, the weapon now ready to fire.

'You men best stay back,' he said as he stepped towards the entrance. He lifted aside the tattered flap of canvas and called out. 'Is there anyone inside?'

There was no answer. Ben watched Preston stoop down low and step into the dark interior, admiring the confidence and courage of the man. The others stood in silence, their rifles held ready, listening to the whispering wind in the trees and the hiss of disturbed snow cascading down through shifting branches. From inside the shelter they heard a shuffling of movement, then after a few moments the canvas flapped to the side and Preston emerged.

'This is some poor soul's grave,' he uttered solemnly. 'By the look of it, quite a few years ago.'

Preston turned round to look at the shelter. 'He died in his cot, so it seems.' He shook his head sadly. 'A lonely death for this man.' Preston bowed his head. 'Let us pray for his soul.'

Ben watched the men and Sam remove their broad-brimmed hats and lower their heads. He took his own felt hat off out of respect, and listened to Preston's sombre words. He finished and the men chorused *amen*.

Ben nodded towards the shelter. 'We could use the wood.'

Preston shook his head. 'We'll not strip this place for firewood. Let it remain, to mark this unknown soul's grave. There's plenty enough kindling lying on the forest floor. Come on.'

He led them away from the clearing, up and out of the dimple. Standing for a moment on a small ridge of high ground and looking through a break in the trees, down the sloping hillside, Ben could see in the distance the large clearing in which their camp nestled. Amidst the churned dirty white of mud and snow, he spotted the small shapes of sluggish movement among the shelters, the tan mass of huddled oxen stirring in the centre and the pall of a dozen wispy columns of smoke snaking up into the heavy sky.

Ben turned to look back down into the dip at the long-dead hunter's shelter, a forlorn sight, and wondered how it must feel to die alone, and not be missed by anyone.

CHAPTER 22

10 October, 1856

I share this small space with Mr Keats and Broken Wing. I have to admit they have built a very robust and surprisingly snug shelter. There is no room, of course, to stand upright. One enters on hands and knees, and at best, in the very centre of the shelter, may stand, but only if stooped over. At the top, where the saplings converge in a knot of coerced boughs, there is a small gap that frequently needs a stick poked up through it to clear the snow. This small hole in our roof allows for us to burn a modest fire inside, the smoke being very efficiently sucked away through this improvised chimney. Not every shelter, I notice, anticipated this luxury, and I have often seen less fortunate people spilling out of their shelters coughing and spluttering.

I have much to be thankful for, having such experienced and knowledgeable shelter companions. However, I do find many of Keats's personal habits quite repulsive at such close quarters. His incessant ritual of snorting and spitting, whilst tolerable outside, is utterly unforgivable inside. So much so that I gifted him with one of my own fine linen handkerchiefs — a present from mother. I imagine she would be mortified at the unimaginable material that gets deposited into it every hour of every day. But as a small consolation, now at least my hands are less likely to find congealing, tar-stained globules of mucus on the floor of our shelter.

Ben looked up at them. Broken Wing was absorbed in carving an intricate pattern of criss-crossing lines into the bark of a log. Keats was smoking his pipe silently. Ben wondered how much tobacco the man had brought with him, since he seemed to be always either at the point of filling his pipe or emptying it.

Keats looked his way and took the stem of the pipe out of his mouth. 'What the hell you scribblin' 'bout in there anyway? I seen you doin' it enough. Been meanin' I gotta ask.'

'My journal. I . . .' Ben shrugged self-consciously. 'I have always aspired to be a writer.'

'Thought you was a doctor.'

'I am, at least . . . I was studying anatomy before I changed to psychiatry.'

'Si— what?'

'Study of the malaise of the mind. But to be a writer of tales, like Charles Dickens – that's my dream.'

'Never heard of 'im.'

The fire in their shelter had died down to little more than a bed of embers, which every now and then sprouted a flickering flame.

'That's why I came across to the Americas. To explore the wilderness, to have an adventure to write about.'

Keats chuckled. 'Reckon you got more 'venture than you bargained for, eh?'

Ben smiled. 'I console myself with the thought that my journal will turn out to be far more interesting than I could have hoped.'

'Aye,' grunted Keats.

'I think I've used enough candle tonight.'

Ben closed the lid of his inkpot, noting as he did that it was approaching half-empty and that he'd need to weaken the mix with some water to let it stretch further. He snuffed out the small candle beside him, instantly throwing the shelter into complete darkness save for the occasional guttering flame from the middle that illuminated them with a staccato amber light.

It was then that they heard the first sound of disturbance. A moan that was a note deeper than the wind. Then they heard the muffled scream of a woman.

'The hell was that?' growled Keats.

Another, more intense scream.

'Come on!'

The flap to their shelter swung open, letting in an icy blast. Keats scrambled out, followed by Broken Wing. Ben reached for his poncho and crawled outside. A gusting wind was carrying small, stinging, powdery granules of ice.

The scream came again.

'Over amongst them Mormon shelters!' said Keats, immediately setting off across the clearing, pulling out his hunting knife. Broken Wing followed, instinctively pulling out his *tamahakan* from a sheath strapped to one thigh.

Ben looked down at his hands.

And what did I bring? A bloody writing pen.

He shook his head, chastising himself for not reaching for his gun, then set off after them.

They scrambled through knee-deep snow, around the huddled mass of oxen baying pitifully in the cold, towards the more congested end of the clearing – almost a village-worth of ramshackle shelters clustered around the only construction that looked remotely like a building: their church.

Ben could see movement in between the shelters. The glow of their communal campfire provided enough light to see a confusing melange of fast-moving silhouettes but nothing he could make sense of yet.

They heard the deep moan, and even Ben's untrained ears identified what he had heard.

'Bear!' shouted Keats. 'Goddamned bear!'

They saw it, reversing out of a shelter, its powerfully muscular hindquarters back-pedalling, its head and shoulders angrily

111

shaking off the pine branches and snow that had tumbled onto its back as it probed inside through the low entrance.

The shelter shook violently as it pulled out and turned round to face the gathering circle of people. Immediately it reared up on its back legs, bellowing furiously and waving two enormous paws in front of itself, claws protruding and glistening like knife blades.

'Anyone with a primed gun?' shouted Keats.

There was a confusion of panicked responses from those gathered. Already a dozen men had emerged, most clasping a rifle, but none, it seemed, loaded and ready to fire.

The night was alive with cries of alarm, dancing half-light from the nearby campfire, shadows darting in fear, and the towering form of the bear in the midst of it all. Ben saw Preston's tall frame emerge from their church and quickly join the crowd.

'Who's the night watch?' Preston called out.

'Aye!' a voice called out from the growing cacophany.

'Can you fire?'

'Yes.'

'Then do so!'

Ben saw a man emerge from the confusion and take several fearful steps towards the bear. He saw the long barrel level horizontally, wavering for only a moment before discharging with a deafening boom amidst a cloud of powder smoke.

The shot missed.

The bear dropped down onto all fours and then, with terrifying speed, charged across the snow towards the man, who remained frozen to the spot with fear. Too late he gathered his wits and turned, but the bear was on him, swiping both legs from beneath him with a casual blow of his forepaw.

The man fell on his front and flipped round onto his back to fend off what he knew was coming, his hands held out before him — a pitifully futile gesture. The bear's jaw snapped open and closed on one hand. The man's voice became a scream of terror as the bear swung its muzzle ferociously from side to side, snapping bones and tearing off the man's hand and forearm, leaving a tattered and ragged stump at the elbow.

The man showed surprising prescience by taking the fleeting opportunity to try and escape as the bear mauled for a moment on its prize. With his one good arm he hurled the spent rifle at the creature, then attempted to pull himself to his feet.

There were screams of encouragement from those gathered. Short-lived.

The bear again swiped at his legs, and this time collapsed its heavy weight onto his back, driving the wind out of him – more than likely crushing his ribcage. Without any hesitation this time, the bear's long muzzle closed on the man's head with a sickening crunch.

It was then that Ben noticed Preston stepping quickly forward from the crowd, a smoking branch in one hand.

'Get away!' he roared angrily, charging the last dozen yards forward and poking the smouldering end of the branch into the bear's flank. It let go of the man's head and turned to face Preston, roaring with wild rage at the intrusion and swinging a claw at the branch.

Get back, you fool, Ben found himself urging Preston.

'Away!!!' shouted Preston, taking a step forward and jabbing the creature in the flank again. The second jab was enough. The bear abandoned the man on the ground who, Ben was surprised to see, was still moving. It advanced on Preston, rearing up on its hind legs and baring teeth red with blood, from which dangled tatters of flesh.

'Can anyone fire?' Preston called out over his shoulder, his voice broken with fear.

Ben looked around to see at least half a dozen men frantically and shakily priming their guns with powder and shot.

The bear dropped down on to all fours.

'Can anyone fire?!' Preston shouted again, backing up slowly. There were screams of alarm, people begging Preston to turn and run while he still had a chance. But he stood his ground, bending his knees in readiness, holding nothing but a smoking, fragile branch.

Then the bear charged.

One paw swiped aside the pitiful stick. The other swiped across Preston's chest, hurling him a couple of yards across the snow, where he landed heavily and almost immediately began to stain the snow dark.

The bear was astride Preston when another shot rang out, this time punching the bear heavily in the side. It reared up in rage and agony, losing its balance and tumbling over. It recovered its footing, but the shock of the wound seemed to have been enough to change its agenda. With surprising speed, it raced away on all fours from the baying crowd, out of the pall of light from the fire and into the darkness.

Ben looked around to see where the shot had come from, and saw Keats still squinting down the levelled length of his rifle and a cloud of blue smoke languidly rolling away from the muzzle.

Ben rushed towards Preston, lying on the ground and clutching his side painfully, gasping short little breaths that peppered the snow with dots of blood.

He looked up at Ben and managed to rasp, 'I'm fine, man. You tend to James first. I'll wait.'

CHAPTER 23

cave iram Dei

M	T	W	T	F	S	S
				1	2	3
4	5	6	7	8	9	10
11	12	13	14	15	16	17
18	19	20	21	22	23	24
25	26	27	28	29	30	

Monday
Blue Valley Camp, California

Rose found her easily. She was serving in the convenience store on the camp site.

She had enjoyed the half-hour drive up the twisting mountain road from Blue Valley. It was a steep incline all the way that taxed the hire car's modest engine so that it whined like a fly in a tin can, but also a spectacular drive with thick firs to her left and a drop to her right, revealing a sweeping and breathtaking picture-postcard vista of a broad valley and a gently winding river.

The camp site, set alongside a small man-made lake, was all but deserted this time of year. Most of the family cabanas were empty, just one or two occupied by hardy folk who obviously enjoyed hiking National Park sites all year round. She imagined that in the middle of summer with a clear blue sky, bathed in welcoming sunlight and alive with smoking barbecue pits and children charging into the crystal-clear lake water, it was the kind of camp that holiday brochures are made for. But right now, with the wan light of autumn and a bland Tupperware sky, abandoned and silent, it looked a somewhat cheerless place.

The door to the convenience store opened with a quaint small-town *ding* that reminded her of Mr Godsey's corner shop on Walton's Mountain. Grace was perched behind the counter in her National Parks Service uniform, stuck into a sudoku puzzle.

She looked up and her weatherworn face creased into a smile.

'Hey, Rose.'

'Hi,' Rose replied. 'I must have taken down your cell number wrong. I tried to call you.'

'Problems?'

'No.' Rose shrugged. 'Just getting a bit lonely, I suppose. Jules has shot back to London for a few days, and I'm taking a break from messing around with my cameras.'

Grace put down her paper. 'How're things going with your little film?'

'Very well, I think. I haven't heard much from him. He sent a text saying he's already got some good meetings lined up.'

Grace nodded and then leaned forward, lowering her voice slightly. 'Louise Esterfeld, the Park Manager, asked me about you guys. How the field trip went.'

'Oh?'

'Wanted to know if *her* camp's going to end up in your film,' she snorted, 'whether you guys goin' to give her an interview and such.'

'I suppose we could do that if you think it'll buy us a little good will.'

Grace shook her head. 'Screw that. Silly woman just wants her face on TV. Anyways, told her you were wanting another trip up into the woods sometime soon.'

Rose smiled coyly and winked. 'And that's when we'll discover a very interesting find?'

Grace nodded. 'Can't leave it too much longer, though.'

'I know.'

It was Jules's suggestion that they give her a little 'thank you' money. There were ways and means of doing that. Rose imagined a proud and hardy woman like Grace would find a wad of notes in a plain brown envelope distasteful – although she could probably well do with it. It had taken no more than a dozen mouse clicks on the internet for Rose to find how little the

National Parks Service paid their wardens; a pittance. They seemed to rely more on the dutiful enthusiasm of their staff to keep things running than on a properly managed budget.

Grace leaned back on her stool and pulled a mug out from a shelf beneath the till. 'Wanna coffee?'

'Thanks. Look, Grace. I've got a couple of days to kill. I thought I'd fill the time with a bit of research and gather up some local flavour for our story.'

The older woman filled the mug from a Thermos flask and placed it on the counter. 'Comes already with cream and sugar,' she said.

'That's fine, thanks.'

'What sort of research?'

She passed a steaming mug over the counter to Rose, who took a sip. It was sickeningly sweet. 'Well, I suppose I could start with the various ghost stories we've heard from people in Blue Valley. There do seem to be a lot of them.'

Grace nodded. 'Yup, and all very different.'

'But I wonder whether it's possible to trace their roots back to something that did actually happen.'

'You're thinking some of them might have something to do with that find out there?'

Rose nodded. 'That's usually the case, though, isn't it? I mean, maybe some of the people who ended up stuck in those mountains made it down okay, into this town. They'd have stories to tell, possibly some quite gruesome stories . . . particularly if they ended up like that Donner party.'

'It's possible, I s'pose.'

'I can imagine that over a hundred and fifty years those could eventually become the basis for the local ghost stories that Julian and I recorded people talking about last week.' Rose sipped her coffee. 'I mean, there was one bloke who said – you know how it goes – a friend of a friend was camping up in those woods and saw a walking skeleton . . .'

Grace laughed. 'Oh yeah, the Rag Man story. I've heard about a dozen versions of that one from my boys over the

117

years, and now my grandchildren scare each other in the play-ground with the same old thing.'

'Ooh, let's hear it.'

'Not much to it, really. It's just the name for our local boogieman. The Rag Man, a walking skeleton, sometimes in a monk's cowl, sometimes in rags, sometimes he's an escaped lunatic, sometimes a drug-crazed serial killer. Some stories have him hacking up lonely teenage girl campers, some stories have him wandering around in town stealing little girls.' Grace shrugged. 'Kids round here regurgitate all sorts of rubbish from the crappy movies they watch, and then replace Freddy Kruger with the Rag Man.'

'Hmmm . . . what about older ghost stories? Ones that aren't Hollywood inspired. Do you know of any?'

Grace looked up at the ceiling of the store, trawling for some long-forgotten fireside tales from her youth.

'What about Blue Valley?' Rose asked. 'There'll be some sort of local archives in the town, right?'

She shrugged. 'I s'pose. There's a one-sheet free local news-paper that runs only during the holiday season. You know the deal: a few local-issue stories, some local flavour for the visitors, and a bunch of adverts. An old boy runs that pretty much on his own. *Blue Valley Bugle*, it's called.'

Rose sipped her coffee again. 'Do you know who?'

'Yeah, Aaron Pohenz. He owns one of the motels in town. Valley Lodge. Know it?'

She nodded. It was a little further down the street from hers. Looked a lot nicer, too.

'He's got a printing press in the basement, does it all from there. You could start with him. I'm sure if he can't give you any more details, least he can do is point you in the right direction.'

Rose made a note of the name, and then finished up the treacle-sweet brew in her mug. 'Thanks, Grace, you've been a great help,' she said and turned to go.

'Hey, Rose.'

Rose turned back.

'You told him yet?'

'Told who . . . what?'

The old woman smiled knowingly. 'How you feel.'

Rose felt her cheeks colour. 'I . . . you're talking about *Jules*?'

Grace nodded. 'You know, it's pretty obvious, even to an old stick like me.'

Oh shit, am I really that obvious?

'Tell him,' she said. 'There was a man I once let go without sayin' a thing. Long time ago. Hell, he probably would've said no. On the other hand' – she looked out of the store window at the wooded peaks – 'might have said yes.'

Rose felt her cheeks flush. 'Oh, you're mistaken, Grace. There's nothing between me and Jules; we're work-mates is all. Seriously, that's all. He's not my type – too old.'

Grace studied her and then shrugged. 'Oops, I'm sorry. I thought I detected a little chemistry there.'

Rose managed a smile. 'Nope, no chemistry.'

She bid farewell and closed the door behind her, heading back across the deserted camp site towards the road leading back into town. A fresh breeze played with her hair and sent a chill down her neck as she cast a glance around at the empty cabins and the sail dinghies lined up on trailers parked a few yards away from the lake's edge. Their nylon halyards clattered against the masts with a rhythmic tapping.

119

CHAPTER 24

13 October, 1856

James Lock lived for three days. I was surprised he lasted that long — the wounding to his head was so severe. The bite crushed the right-hand side of his face and skull, destroying an eye in the process. It would have been merciful for him and his family if the bear had bitten down that much harder and finished the poor man then and there.

Preston, however, appears more promising. There were a series of deep lacerations around his waist, requiring that I sew them closed. My fear is that fever will set in. I cleansed the wounds as best I could with alcohol, and checked that the claws had not proceeded any deeper than opening his skin and had not damaged his organs. It does appear that he was lucky not to have suffered a greater injury. Nonetheless, only time will tell whether the wounds were properly cleaned.

I have been tending to Preston within their church. It is perhaps a tribute to how much I am trusted, or more likely, how much they value him, that I'm allowed in there. These people of Preston's seem completely lost without him, unable to make the simplest decisions. He seems to be their compass in many ways. Without him they are directionless and frightened. Each time I approach their temple there is always a gathering of people outside the entrance eagerly enquiring as to his condition.

Despite my earlier reservations about the man, I have to admit to admiring his strength and courage standing between his people and the bear armed with nothing more than a stick, whilst I recall myself trembling with fear and rooted to the ground. I envy a man who can stand firm in the face of terror and not yield.

Sitting in their church, I feel I have a clearer understanding about how the affairs of these people are run. Preston has a council, a Quorum of Elders, amongst whom decisions are made. Senior amongst them are two men: Eric Vander and Saul Hearst. It seems whilst Preston remains incapacitated, these two have assumed responsibility for running things on their side of the camp.

Neither man, however, seems to command the same kind of respect and reverence that is freely given to Preston.

Ben leaned over and felt his forehead.

'Fever?' asked Dorothy Dreyton.

'A slight one,' he replied. Preston's face felt hot and damp with sweat. He was in a restless sleep, stirring and murmuring.

'Will he live, Mr Lambert?'

'He's strong, I'll say that for him. A very strong and fit man.'

'But?'

Ben offered her a tired smile. 'But, there is infection in his wounds. His body will fight it as best it can.'

Mrs Dreyton's face crumpled with poorly contained grief. 'We would be lost without him. I . . . would be lost without him.'

She stroked one of his hands affectionately. 'He's our saviour, in so many ways.'

Ben studied her genuine fondness for him. Absolute devotion. He suspected she would happily surrender her life in a

121

heartbeat, if it would guarantee saving his. And by the look of concern etched on the faces of those gathered outside in a night and day vigil, so would any number of them.

'How has he saved you?'

She looked at him with an expression halfway between hostility and bemusement. 'How? From following the wrong path, a path that would have led us to darkness and desolation. Like so many others of our church.'

'Mormons?'

She nodded. 'We departed from that faith, as we departed Council Bluffs. The message from God was corrupted by greedy men, who even now are fighting for control of the Mormon faith.' She looked at Preston, lying still and breathing deeply. 'William warned us that the faith was all wrong. That it would eventually turn on itself. God told him directly.'

He looked at her.

'Oh, yes. William talks with God. He does so . . . through Nephi.'

'Nephi? Who's that?'

Dorothy closed her mouth. But her eyes momentarily darted to a metal chest lying beyond Preston's cot.

'He talks with God directly,' she said again. 'There are no other holy men who can honestly say that.'

'But doesn't every preacher say that?'

'Only William does for real,' she replied with a whisper. 'Actually *hears* His voice. I would surrender everything just to hear what he hears.' She stroked his face. 'He's so special.'

They sat in silence for a while, listening to the mournful gusting wind play with the flap of material over the entrance.

'Why has Preston led you out west?'

She sighed. 'We couldn't stay in Council Bluffs. We had to leave everything behind. A storm is coming.'

'A storm?'

She looked at him and gently smiled. 'Perhaps being with us, there'll be mercy for you. You'll be safe.'

Ben shook his head. 'I'm not sure I understand.'

'A judgement is coming. A judgement on this wicked world. William says it will soon be upon us, and the earth will be swept clean so that God might start over.'

'God will destroy everything?'

'Only the people. His creatures need no cleansing.'

'Everyone?'

She nodded sadly. 'I grieve for the many people with good hearts who will die. But it's necessary. William was told this, and that we must make ready for it. There is work for him to do,' Dorothy whispered, glancing once more at the metal chest. 'Please, Mr Lambert . . . be sure to do all you can to help him.'

He nodded. 'Of course I will.'

She placed her hand on his and squeezed it affectionately. 'We are so grateful to you. You're a good man, Mr Lambert. Maybe I am at fault for not seeing that sooner.'

Ben shrugged. 'I have a doctor's training. It'd be a waste for me not to use it.'

Preston stirred, his deep, commanding voice a pitiful whimper.

Dorothy winced in sympathy. 'He's in pain.'

'Those wounds will be extremely painful as they heal.' Ben opened his medicine bag and pulled out a bottle. 'I have some laudanum for the pain.' He pulled out the stopper and poured a small cupful. 'I'll leave this with you to administer to him. A couple of sips now to settle him, Mrs Dreyton. No more than that. This is a strong medicine.'

She nodded.

'If, later on tonight, the pain stirs him again, you may try another dose. Will you be sitting with him tonight?'

'Yes. Mr Hearst or Mr Vander may relieve me come midnight.'

'Good, then advise them about the medication. It is not to be over-dosed. I'll expect for some to be still in the cup when I return in the morning.'

'I understand.'

He closed up his medicine bag.

'I think he'll be fine in due course, Mrs Dreyton. He's a fighter.'

CHAPTER 25

13 October, 1856

The campfire, placed centrally amidst the small circle of shelters at the Keats end of the clearing, burned noisily, crackling and hissing as it feasted eagerly on the needles and pines that had been tossed onto it.

'Never been so bleedin' scared in all me life,' exclaimed Mrs Bowen. 'Such a big thing it looked like. I could see it from all the way over 'ere.'

Ben nodded.

You should have seen it up close.

'Do you think it'll be back again, Mr Keats? My little 'uns are terrified to sleep.'

Keats wrinkled his nose and snorted. 'Unlikely. Scared it off good, an' I reckon the wound will kill it eventually.' He spat into the fire.

Weyland tossed a small branch on. 'Am I mistaken then in thinking that bears should be hibernating this time of year?'

Keats shrugged. 'The snow's come early. Maybe it caught the bear out. Maybe the bear ain't fattened himself up enough to go sleep yet.'

Broken Wing muttered something in his language and Keats laughed.

'What did your Indian say?' asked Bowen.

'He said the woods sent the bear to frighten us white-faces away.'

'The woods?'

'The Shoshoni — Broken Wing's people — believe the wood has a spirit. Like everythin' else . . . rivers, mountains . . . all got their own.'

'That's ridiculous,' said Mrs McIntyre.

'Ain't no more ridiculous than believin' there's devils beneath the earth waitin' to prod us with their little pitchforks.'

Mrs McIntyre shook her head sombrely. 'God help us . . . you'll bring trouble on us all talking like that, so you will.'

Keats smiled.

'So your man, Mr Keats, believes the woods would like us to be gone?' said Weyland.

Broken Wing spoke up. 'Thisss' — he gestured to the dark hem of trees beyond the pale moonlit snow on the ground, beyond the warm glow of the fire — 'not for white-face. Thisss Paiute, Shoshone land.'

'Indians reckon we belong in our dirty cities, livin' on top of each other an' turnin' the sky grey with our smoke. Not out here in the wilderness.'

Broken Wing cocked his head listening to Keats, then nodded a moment later. 'Yah.'

'Hmm,' growled Keats, 'reckon the bear came down 'cause he could smell food cookin'.'

The group sat in silence for a while, listening to the light wind teasing the trees. All of Keats's party were huddled around the fire; Bowen and his family, McIntyre, Hussein and their families, Weyland and his Negro girl, Keats, Broken Wing and Ben — eighteen people, hugging woollen blankets around themselves and gazing into the comforting, flickering light of the fire.

'Hey, Benjamin,' muttered McIntyre, nodding, 'looks like your wayward friends have come to join us again.'

Ben turned round to see Sam leading Emily by the hand towards them. They approached furtively, Sam looking back over his shoulder, past the huddled oxen towards the distant campfire glow coming from the other end.

'Benjamin,' Sam whispered hoarsely. 'Can we sit with your group awhile?'

Ben waved them over. 'Here, squeeze in.' He smiled.

Emily shuffled in close beside Ben. Sam found some space on his other side. They held their hands up to the warmth of the fire, savouring it.

'Momma's sitting with Preston,' said Sam quietly.

'Yes, I left her with him earlier. Oh . . .' Ben reached round and pulled something out of his leather satchel. 'Here you are, Emily. Would you like to play with the doll?'

Her face lit up and she grasped it. 'Thank you, Benjamin.' She cast her eyes around the gathered group and, spotting McIntyre's daughter, Anne-Marie, offered a shy wave to her across the fire.

Keats tapped the bowl of his pipe onto the snow at his feet. 'Reckon we wanna keep a little more watchful at night, people. Though it ain't likely we'll see another bear any time soon, better we be ready for it if we do. Night watch should always have 'least two guns good to shoot from now on.'

'That seems a sensible precaution,' added Weyland. 'And perhaps, ladies and gentlemen, we should consider doubling up on the watch?'

A discussion stirred to life over the matter – whether there were enough men to sustain that kind of rota indefinitely. There were several varying opinions chorused at the same time.

Ben settled back, uninterested in the exchange. 'You all right there, Sam?'

The young lad nodded and smiled. 'Yes. Emily and I like coming over here. Emily likes those children,' Sam replied, nodding at McIntyre's daughters.

'What about the other children in your group?'

He shook his head. 'Stolz's won't really play with anyone else. The others don't really play at all. Poor Em only has me.'

'I'm sorry not to have seen much of you these last few days.'

'Momma says you've done a wonderful job caring for him.'

Ben hunched his shoulders. 'I do what I can, which I'm afraid isn't much. I'm sorry there was nothing more I could do for Mr Lock.'

Sam nodded, gazing at the crackling sparks from the fire lifting up into the ink-black sky. 'I wish I were like you, Benjamin,' he said presently.

'Like me? Good grief, why?'

'You got education. You know things like medicine and science.'

Ben pulled a face. 'I don't know enough. If I'd stayed on a few more years, I could have become a senior doctor. But instead, I'm just a travelling journeyman doctor, hoping one day that I'll do better as a writer.' Ben tossed a loose cone into the fire. 'I wish I was a little more like Mr Preston.'

Sam looked up at him sharply, the good-natured smile wiped from his face. 'Why?'

'It takes courage to do what he did. He stood before that bear to save Mr Lock.' Ben turned to Sam. 'And me? Well, I was too damned frightened even to move.'

Sam shook his head. 'It wasn't courage.'

'It was an incredibly brave thing to do.'

Sam didn't reply for a long while, his gaze long and without focus.

'I'm glad you're not like Preston,' he said eventually. 'Or those others.'

Anne-Marie McIntyre came around the campfire and sat next to Emily. After a faltering, self-conscious start both girls were soon chattering together and passing the doll between them. Ben sat back, watching Sam. The boy seemed at ease, content, watching over his sister – her eternal guardian. He admired the young man's relentless devotion to her.

Later on, Sam turned to him quietly and asked an awkward question.

'When we leave these mountains, would you take Em and me with you?'

'What? I couldn't do that, Sam. I'm . . . your mother would—'

'Momma will never leave Preston,' muttered Sam, 'not ever.'

Ben felt an overpowering sympathy for them both, destined to be locked into the isolated, small world that Preston was promising his people in God's great wilderness, as they patiently awaited an end that would never come.

'Sam, I couldn't take Emily from her mother. You . . . you're seventeen?'

'And a half.'

'Then you're old enough to find your own way, Sam. But Emily is still just a small child – your mother's child.'

Sam nodded sullenly. 'I know.'

Ben placed a hand on his shoulder. 'Come the spring, when the snow melts, who knows how your mother will feel? Hmm? Perhaps she'll see things differently.'

Ben sincerely doubted that. But it was all he could think to say at that moment.

CHAPTER 26

Monday
Blue Valley, California

Aaron Pohenz looked at Rose quizzically for a moment then smiled. 'Oh yes, Grace called and told me to expect a visit from you. You're the English lady who's making a movie?'

'A documentary about local folklore, that's right.'

He waved his hand. 'Come on in.'

She stepped inside the motel. It smelled strongly of varnish and she wrinkled her nose.

'Whilst it's quiet season and I'm closed up I thought I'd work on the wooden banister up to the rooms. Needed tidying up,' he offered by way of an explanation.

Rose looked around the entrance hall. It looked *homey*; old sepia portraits hung on the wall alongside a few hunting trophies, and a cheerful rug was spread across a wooden slat floor. In the corner, beside an open doorway that led into what looked like the kitchen, was a rocking chair made from a rich, dark wood.

'It's lovely,' she said.

He batted the compliment away with a hand. 'It's what the summer season guests expect; a slice of traditional.'

She nodded. 'You've got that all right.'

He gestured for her to follow and led her through the open

door into the kitchen. The *slice of traditional* motif had spread into there as well. Pine cupboards lined the edge of the square room and in the middle, a large, sturdy, pockmarked and stained oak dining table surrounded by half a dozen breakfast stools beckoned them to sit down.

'Take a seat,' he said and then went over to the counter and poured a couple of cups of coffee from a cafetiere. He sat down opposite her and slid a cup across the table.

'Thanks.'

'So,' he said, 'I'm not real sure what it is you're after. Grace mentioned something about the old wives' tales that get told round here?'

She nodded. 'Yes. That's what brought us here originally . . . the number of spooky tales, UFO sightings, the Bigfoot sightings that seem to be floating around the area.' She took a sip of the coffee. It was black and strong as hell – just how she liked it. 'I'll be honest, there's a quirky internet site called DarkEye that deals with all things strange and Fortean; they listed this region as one of the most sighting-rich areas of America. So' – she hunched her shoulders apologetically – 'that's really what brought us here.'

The old man's eyes narrowed suspiciously. 'Hmm . . . see, I trust Grace. She's a rock in this community. Not that she was born here, mind. But she's been living here long enough that we look at her as a valley girl. If Grace said you're all right, I guess that's good with me too. But,' he said, raising a finger, 'we've had a few news and TV people come here from time to time, especially when someone starts up with a new ghost story. They come up, film a little, interview one or two people and then go away. When it comes on the TV, they make us look like a bunch of simple-minded idiots.'

Rose shuffled awkwardly on the stool. That was exactly the sort of crap she and Julian had originally come here to make.

'You get a lot of news people?' she asked.

'No, once every couple of years, when one of 'em stories

crops up, is all. Ain't all bad I suppose, though. Brings us a little extra motel business.'

She looked around the kitchen and noticed a corkboard with hooks in, and about a dozen sets of keys dangling from them.

'You run this motel by yourself?'

'No, my sister comes up from Fort Casey during holiday season and helps out. Rest of the year, when it's closed . . . it's just me here, rattling around like a pea in a tin can.'

'Grace said you run a town newspaper of sorts as well.'

He nodded. 'That's right. Hardly a newspaper, though, sometimes just a page, sometimes maybe I get five or six sides with some local stories, a bit of history and a bunch of adverts for local businesses. The paper's free and the ads don't barely pay for the print.'

'It's a labour of love, then?'

He smiled, showing several gold teeth. 'Could say that. Used to be a bigger paper, but then, it used to be a bigger town. I sort of inherited it . . . the paper, that is.'

'Grace suggested you had some sort of archive and a lot of local historical knowledge.'

Aaron nodded dismissively. 'I guess you could describe me as an amateur historian.'

'I'm after some details about a thing that might have happened back in 1856. I know this'll sound silly, but Grace mentioned Blue Valley has its very own boogieman. She called him the Rag Man.'

Aaron smiled. 'Ah yes, that ol' chestnut. Yes, just about all the local stories use him in some way or another.'

'Could there be a grain of truth to the Rag Man? I mean, was he once based on a real person?'

'Oh, yes,' Aaron said. 'Yes, it was, once upon a time, a very real person. He was a man that emerged from the mountains, nothing more than skin and bones, who was nursed back to health in Blue Valley. He then took himself off, never to be seen again.'

Rose smiled. 'That sounds promising.'

132

'Of course, back then this town wasn't called Blue Valley. It was referred to as Pelorsky's Farm, after Jacob Pelorsky who had built up a trade store here — trading for beaver pelts with the trappers and the Paiute and Shoshone.'

Rose scribbled the settlement name down and then sipped her coffee.

'There's a bit more to that particular tale.'

'Really?'

'This man emerged from those woods on the point of death, see. Somehow he managed to hang on and survive. As they fed him and tended to him, he recovered his strength, but he didn't immediately take himself off. He stayed on for about half a year; a very troubled period of time that was too.'

'Troubled?'

Aaron nodded, swilling a mouthful of his rich, aromatic coffee. 'The man seemed to bring all sorts of bad karma with him. He was very disturbed by something. The family that took him in described him waking them all up repeatedly at night with his screaming. Anyway, apart from being a very mentally disturbed individual, there was a growing feeling amongst the small community around Pelorsky Farm that he was in some way cursed.'

'Cursed?'

'I use the term *cursed* in preference to the term *possessed*. I think, thanks to that movie, the term comes with a lot of unnecessary baggage.'

'Which movie?'

Aaron shook his head. 'I'm guessing, looking at you, you're probably way too young to remember it. Horrible movie. Horrible. Gave me nightmares.'

She looked at him, pen poised.

He sighed. '*The Exorcist.*'

Rose knew of it; she'd seen the film once years ago and thought very little of it. The flying goo and the spinning heads had amused her and her fellow room mates, certainly not frightened them.

133

'So, they thought this man had some sort of devil possessing him?'

'Well, like I say, I'd rather use the term *cursed*, it's less provocative,' he said, sipping his drink before continuing. 'So . . . they thought this man was cursed in some way. There were those who thought it was some kind of Indian thing, thinking the man had trespassed on burial grounds or something. Anyway, the point is, whilst he was with them, bad things happened.'

'Bad things?'

'Bad things,' he echoed with no elaboration. 'Then it finally came to a head when a child went missing. The next morning the man was gone. Never saw him again.'

'That's pretty creepy,' she whispered.

Aaron nodded. 'The man was evil; well that's what they thought – that he had evil in him. And just maybe he picked it up in those mountains.'

'What do you think?'

Aaron finished his coffee with several quick gulps as he pondered an answer. 'I'm not a churchgoer, you understand? Nor am I some dumb sap who'll believe any old conspiracy or ghost story doing the rounds. I think Ouija boards are a load of crap. I think mediums and spiritual healers and their type are a bunch of crooks. Okay? I'm telling you this just so's we can be clear that I'm not some sort of whacked-out small-town hokey. Are we clear?'

Rose nodded.

'But, I think there is stuff out there that we don't have the tools to measure and explain and quantify.' He looked at her with grey, keen and intelligent eyes. 'And, yes . . . I think maybe there's something out there in those woods that can do something to a man. Change him somehow.'

'Change him?'

He shrugged. 'Turn a good man bad.'

She finished her coffee. 'Tell me, Mr Pohenz, is there any record of this man's name?'

'Because it started as a verbal tale, no one really remembers if he did give a name. The Rag Man is the only name people remember. It's kind of catchy,' he said with a smile.

'And would you know roughly what year that happened?'

He smiled. 'I know exactly; it was the spring of 1857.'

CHAPTER 27

17 October, 1856

'I heard it again!' said Zimmerman. He lowered the bundle of kindling in his arms to the ground and reached for the rifle slung across his broad shoulders.

The group stopped dead in their tracks. Keats swung his long-barrelled Kentucky rifle down, gently half-cocking the hammer and readying a percussion cap. He turned to Zimmerman.

'Same thing?' he muttered under his breath.

The man nodded. 'Whispering again. I'm sure I heard whispering ahead of us.'

Keats looked to the others. 'Anyone else hear that this time?'

Bowen and the other Mormon, Hearst, shook their heads in silence.

'I'm certain I heard someone whispering ahead,' said Zimmerman again with a hushed voice. 'There's definitely somebody here, besides us.'

They remained frozen, listening to the subtle rustling of the snow-covered forest. Echoing from the far distance, they could hear a metal cooking skillet being banged and the steady rap, rap, rap of someone's axe on wood, noises from their camp . . . but no sounds from close by, except for the rasping, fluttering sound of their breathing.

'I ain't hearing nothing,' muttered Keats uneasily.

'I believe he's right,' said Weyland, nodding at Zimmerman, 'there *is* most definitely something or someone out there. It's been following us for a while.'

Ten minutes earlier, Weyland had set them on edge by claiming he thought he'd seen a pair of eyes staring out at him from low down in the undergrowth.

Now Zimmerman.

'You sure?' asked Keats.

The man pointed to the trees ahead of them. 'I'm sure I heard it come from over there. Quiet talking . . . whispering.'

Keats swivelled his Kentucky towards where the man was pointing, squinting down the long barrel at the low-hanging, snow-covered branches ahead. The others fixed their attention on the same place. He looked beneath the trees, thick with ferns and bracken poking through the deep and lumpy carpet of snow. His eyes picked out nothing untoward, no movement at all.

And then he caught a flash of pale brown – the colour of cow-hide; a colour out of place in this twin-hued world of white snow and dark green pine needles. He stared intently through the dark web of branches, his keen sight picking out another incongruous detail: a dark horizontal strip and two pale ovals within.

The ovals blinked.

Eyes!

'I see it now,' Keats whispered over his shoulder to them. 'Nobody do nothin',' he hissed. 'Remain . . . completely . . . still.'

He studied the eyes, staring out at them, perfectly motionless until they blinked again and then vanished. He looked from side to side, beneath the low branches, trying to find them again.

And then spotted another pair of eyes.

And another . . . and another.

'Others . . . see 'em?' hissed Keats quietly.

Zimmerman nodded.

'Reckon I owe you a 'pology there, Zimmerman.'

Zimmerman swallowed nervously. 'Uhh, don't worry.'

The eyes glided smoothly behind the fir trees a dozen yards in front of them.

'God preserve us,' muttered Hearst, his voice trembling, 'what devils are these?' His hold on his rifle tightened.

'We're bein' stalked,' Keats said quietly.

'They're *demons*,' whispered Hearst. 'Satan has tracked us down out here.'

Keats's eyes narrowed. 'Ain't demons, Hearst. It's worse than that.'

All of a sudden one of the low-hanging branches was yanked to one side, dislodging a cascade of powder snow from the tree. Through the momentary blizzard something emerged, crouching low, coiled with enough energy to launch forward onto them at a moment's notice: a dark face, painted still darker around wide unblinking eyes, and grasping in one hand a *tamahakan*, a war-club with a vicious-looking hooked blade, in the other a short bow.

'Far worse . . .' Keats muttered.

There was movement to the left and the others turned to see several more emerge from the trees and foliage, and more to their right.

'They're Paiute.'

Weyland leaned forward. 'Would they be the—?'

'Yeah . . . the ones you *don't* want to run into,' Keats replied evenly and quietly, his eyes locked on them.

Some of the Paiute carried older flintlock muskets, acquired hand-me-downs from another era. Others carried bows — but all of them held in the other hand hunting knives, or war-clubs of one sort or another, ready to be used with lethal efficiency at close quarters. Keats counted six of them. Six he could see, that is.

Even if the other men with him were all loaded, ready to fire and managed each to bring down a target with their first and only shot, he suspected there'd be more who would be in amongst them within seconds, wielding the serrated edges of their *tamahakan* to lethal effect. It would be a bloody and brutal fight that Keats suspected would be over even before their powder smoke cleared.

'Look at their skin,' muttered Hearst. 'Scorched by God . . . they're demons!'

'Shut up and be still!' Keats hissed through clenched teeth.

Dark skin — Keats had heard the Mormons refer to that as the mark of evil.

He studied the Paiute, coiled and perfectly still. The bone piercings and the shrivelled leathery tokens that dangled from their necks served to make them look more demonic.

The Indian who had first emerged from the trees spoke. The language was sharp and guttural, but one Keats recognised as the common tongue loosely shared by the Paiute, the Shoshone, the Bannock . . . he was speaking *Ute*.

'*Trapper, you lead these white-face here?*'

Keats nodded. '*I lead them through only*—'

The Indian frowned and cocked his head curiously at Keats's poor pronunciation.

'*White-faces bring evil spirit with them into mountains. Must leave.*'

'*Snow stops us*—'

'*They must leave.*'

'*Snow stops us.*'

The Indian studied them, his eyes drifting from Keats onto the others, slowly scanning each of them in turn, drinking in every small detail from head to foot.

'*The evil spirit will bring much bad before snow is gone.*'

And then barking a command to his men, he turned round to step back through the undergrowth from which they had emerged. The others followed, backing up very slowly through the branches, keeping their eyes on the white-faces. They were all young men, very young and keen to prove their courage. Keats realised the encounter might not be over just yet.

'What did he say?' asked Bowen as he watched them warily withdraw through the thick veil of frosted foliage.

Keats shook his head. 'Later . . . listen,' he said, quickly turning round to face the others, 'put your guns down *right now*.'

Weyland shook his head incredulously. 'Are you mad?'

Keats placed his rifle gently on the snow. 'Do it! Before—'

At that moment there was a shrill cry from ahead and one of the Paiute charged out into the open with a ferocious speed and agility, crossing the distance between them as a frightening blur of motion.

The Indian singled out Hearst, his eyes locked resolutely on him as he snarled a vicious war cry. The Paiute scrambled across the deep snow, his raised hand holding high his war-club.

'Hearst! *Drop* your gun!'

The thickset Mormon froze, his face a static cast of panic. The Indian swooped down on him, swinging the blade of his *tamahakan*, missing Hearst by no more than a foot, and lightly, almost tenderly, tapping his shoulder with the handle of the club. He whistled past Hearst with a whooping cry of victory — goal achieved — and raced for the safety of the trees beyond.

Hearst spun round and shakily levelled his gun at the retreating Indian.

'No! Don't shoot!!' cried Keats.

But his words were lost amidst the deafening report of the rifle.

In the silence, they heard the crack of gunfire rattle around the forest and the startled flutter of feathered wings in the trees above them. Keats quickly scooped up his rifle again.

'Damn! You've fuckin' done it now,' he spat at the man, dropping to one knee and shouldering his weapon ready to fire. 'I told you to drop your gun.'

'He . . . I thought . . .'

'He was *countin' coup*, you fool! That's all!' Keats looked around at them. 'Close up and ready your guns.'

The others adopted Keats's stance, dropping to one knee and shouldering their rifles. Hearst was unready, fumbling to pour a measure of powder into his gun with shaking hands, then dropping his lead shot in the snow.

'Hurry, Hearst,' said Keats. 'Hurry, you fool!'

The faint peel of gunfire was still echoing around the woods as the man finished ramming the shot home with a rod, readied a percussion cap and shouldered his weapon.

Then it was quiet.

The silence stretched out for half a minute, all five of them waiting, holding their breath trying to keep the long, heavy barrels steady with hands that were trembling and arms that were tiring.

'Where are they?' Weyland whispered.

There was no answer. They were gone.

'Anyone see any of them?' muttered Keats.

'No.'

'Check to the sides, an' behind,' said Keats. 'The bastards may try and surround us.'

Weyland obeyed the guide and turned to face towards their rear, taking a few cautious steps back until he nudged up against one of the others.

'Keats, what the hell are we supposed to do now?' he asked.

'We sit tight an' wait is what we'll do.'

Several minutes passed, with all of them straining to detect the slightest rustle of movement amongst the trees. Keats glanced down to his left and saw the body of the Indian lying on its side. A single small hole was drilled into the back of the young man's head. His face, by contrast, was spread out over the snow. One of the young Indian's hands moved involuntarily, slowly balling into a fist, then opening, then closing, then opening again.

Keats turned and hissed angrily at Hearst. 'That's why I told you to drop your fucking gun!'

'I thought his axe had struck me!' complained Hearst. 'I thought—'

'It's done now.' The old guide shook his head. 'Some young men amongst them, I knew one of 'em would try an' count coup.'

Bowen looked up from the twitching hand. 'Count coup?'

141

'A test of manhood, courage. He touched him on the shoulder is all. Nothing more.'

Several tense minutes passed before Weyland whispered. 'Mr Keats, what did the Indian say to you? You know, before he turned to go?'

Keats shrugged. 'Hell if I know . . . strangest goddamned version of Ute I ever heard.'

'You must have an idea.'

Keats wondered how much to share with the others. The Paiute hadn't directly threatened them; in fact his words had carried the cadence of a warning, more than a threat. Although, Keats reflected, that might change now that Hearst had killed one of theirs.

'We ain't welcome here, was the best I can make of it,' replied Keats. Not exactly the truth, but close enough.

CHAPTER 28

17 October, 1856

Preston's wounds seem to be healing well, with only small indications of infection. There is some inflammation around one of the wounds, and a little weeping, but one would have expected far worse from the unclean claws of a wild animal. There are some signs of a mild fever — the man's skin is hot to touch — but his greatest discomfort seems to be pain from the wound. Inside which, regarding the lacerations, the bruising must be quite considerable. I have given him more laudanum, to which he responds well. It is a potent solution, which I prefer to prescribe sparingly.

Too much can lead to a reliance upon it.

Dorothy Dreyton is with me now. As a matter of fact, she lies asleep on the floor. Her vigil is almost constant. She must be at the point of exhaustion to allow herself the luxury of an hour or two to sleep. I wonder if she has the slightest notion that her children have spent more time during the last few days at our end of the camp than they have in theirs.

Preston stirred restlessly in his sleep and muttered, his deep voice thick with cloying mucus. Ben guessed that the recently administered opiate was doing its work and had entirely banished the pain for now. But it was also weaving a darker magic.

On an unconscious mind it conjured the most lurid nightmares. He had seen first-hand the poor wretches that had found themselves admitted to Banner House Asylum by way of over-using laudanum and other such soothing tonics, tormented by visions and delusions that hounded them in their sleeping and – for the less fortunate – waking hours.

Ben leaned over and stroked his forehead, feeling the warmth and dampness of his pale skin. Lying on a cot in this sorry condition, there was still something very impressive about William Preston, Ben decided; he exuded an air of authority even as he slept. A man like that, in the right place with the right message, could lead a people to do anything.

Preston's murmuring continued. Beneath the thin parchment skin of his closed lids, his eyes jerked from one side to the other rapidly. Then with a gasp, they snapped open.

'Mr Preston?'

He licked his lips dryly – thirsty.

Ben put away his inkpot, pen and journal and reached for a cup of water. He placed a hand behind Preston's head, the man's long grey-blond hair lank with sweat, and lifted him to take a drink.

'Here, some water,' he said quietly.

Preston's glassy eyes focused away from the low canvas ceiling, bulging with the weight of snow, and onto Ben's face. By the flickering light of the oil lamp, it looked like the elder's irises were fully dilated.

The laudanum.

'M-my G-God . . . they . . . they . . . they know!' gasped Preston.

'Shhhh,' Ben comforted him. 'Drink some water.'

Preston refused. 'Th-they know!' he rasped again, grabbing Ben's hand tightly with one of his own, squeezing desperately.

Ben leaned down closer to him. 'Mr Preston . . . William, it's okay.'

'W-what if . . . they know! They s-see . . . they can see . . . see what I am!' His voice was dry and soft, a keening whisper that sounded like the wheezing rattle of an old man. Preston stared wildly at him, intently, but Ben wondered what exactly his eyes were seeing – whom he thought he was talking to.

'I . . . I . . . hear nothing from it! N-nothing!'

Preston's head jerked round to look at the dark space behind his cot, towards the metal chest nestling amongst sacks of oatmeal. 'Nothing!' he cried, his voice cracked pitifully.

He turned back to face Ben. 'Eric! What if they know? What if they know we took it . . . that we stole it!'

Ben could have replied that he wasn't Eric. But he decided not to.

'Eric, what if they know the angel sh-shuns me? What . . . what'll I do?'

Preston slumped back in the cot, his head resting once more against the pillow.

'Just words . . .' he wheezed quietly, his voice softening, spent. 'They're just words . . . just *my* words.'

His eyes closed again. 'My words,' he muttered, slipping back into a restless and troubled sleep, 'not *God's* . . .'

Ben sat and watched over him for a while, fidgeting in his sleep, several times murmuring, but nothing Ben could understand.

He knew the stronger tonics could do that – take the small whispering voices at the back of a person's mind and turn them into a deafening scream. He was wondering what was troubling Preston in his sleep and had a mind that the answer might lie inside the metal chest just beyond him, when he heard Dorothy Dreyton stirring on the floor and begin to rise.

'Did he wake you, Mrs Dreyton?'

She said nothing, sitting up and staring wide-eyed at Preston. There was something about her manner that troubled Ben.

'Mrs Dreyton?'

Her eyes were distant. Without a word, she got to her feet and, stooping low, she pushed the flap aside, letting in a gust of freezing wind that set the flame on the oil lamp dancing, and stepped out into the cold day.

Above the rumpling wind, he thought he could hear distant raised voices; a commotion from across the clearing, and a ripple of disturbance and questioning from the Mormons standing nearby. Something was going on.

Ben stood up, and stooped as he swept the flap aside, squinting at the brilliant all-white glare of the day.

'What is it?'

A man standing dutifully beside the entrance, Mr Hollander, with a dark beard almost down to his belt, pointed across the clearing. Ben could see Keats and several others moving quickly down-slope and emerging from the tree line onto the open ground of the camp, their guns unslung and held ready, anxiously looking back over their shoulders.

'Thought I heard someone shout something about *Indians*,' said Mr Hollander.

CHAPTER 29

cave iram Dei

M	T	W	T	F	S	S
					1	2	3
4	5	6	7	8	9	10
11	12	13	14	15	16	17
18	19	20	21	22	23	24
25	26	27	28	29	30	

Monday
Central London

Julian found a number of books on the subject in the library's index. The librarian helped him locate them amongst some shelves towards the back. He thanked the young man and sat down at a table to work his way through them.

He realised he knew absolutely nothing of the Mormon church. He hadn't even realised that they were otherwise referred to as the Church of Latter Day Saints. It had quickly become evident to him that if he was going to be pitching this project to a commissioning editor or two, it wasn't going to look good if he hadn't at least done some token research into the faith of Preston and his followers.

At an instinctive level, he wondered if there was another angle to this story; an angle other than a simple survival story.

What if this was some kind of Jonestown thing?

The idea was as intriguing as it was chilling; that a community led by some charismatic religious nut had been steered into a remote wilderness – by accident or design – and there, every last one of them was talked into taking their own life for some bizarre theistic rationale.

There were several books he'd pulled up on Amazon that

looked interesting and he had quickly printed out the details of them, before taking the District Line tube into town.

Here in the library they had copies of three out of the eight titles he'd listed. Not bad, considering how obscure some of them were. To be fair, it wasn't as though Amazon was likely to have all of them in stock either.

He started by flicking through a recent edition of the *Book of Mormon*, quickly becoming irritated with the confusing language and woolly, meaningless terminology. He moved swiftly on to the second book: *Mormonism, and Departure from Christian Convention*. Without drawing breath, it jumped straight into a detailed theological discourse comparing the tenets of Mormonism with those of conventional Christianity.

He sighed and pushed it to one side.

The third book was called *The First Mormon* by one J.D. Pascal. The opening prologue of the book dealt with the Mormon church's founder, Joseph Smith, and the story of how the *Book of Mormon* came to be written.

An atheist for pretty much most of his life, Julian had never had much time for what he considered the incomprehensible, paradoxical rambling of most writing on religion. A classic example of nonsensical theistic nit-picking being the eternal debate over the daily miracle that was said to occur with every communion; the debate over *when* the bread actually became Christ's flesh, whether it occurred in the priest's hand or on the recipient's tongue . . . or, in fact, whether it was now meant to be considered merely a metaphor – downgraded from being taken as a *literal* miracle – because by today's standards it was too far-fetched.

For Julian, the discussion, at best, was a waste of everyone's time, up there with 'How many angels can dance on the head of a pin?'

However, despite his irritation with that kind of nonsense, he found this particular account of the birth of a brand new faith utterly fascinating. Joseph Smith's was a tale of divine inspiration, and profound discoveries in the wilderness of Utah of religious relics and seer stones, of ancient angels from bones, and sacred golden scrolls delivered from God in a long-lost language.

It was pure theatre.

'My God, this is priceless,' he muttered, scribbling down notes in his jotter as he leafed through the prologue.

This stuff is fantastic.

He read on with a growing sense of astonishment at the tale, affirmed regularly by the author as Joseph Smith's *direct testimony*, and not enhanced or exaggerated in any way.

When he had finished he looked at his watch to find the afternoon had slipped away from him and that he had to make tracks to his meeting with Sean. He returned the books to the librarian to file away and stepped out onto Basinghall Street, to be greeted by the jostling hubbub and rush of pedestrian traffic, flowing like a human river towards Mansion House tube station.

But his mind was on what he'd just spent the last few hours reading – and one circling thought kept bubbling up over and over, making him shake his head with incredulity.

And . . . this is the fastest-growing faith in America?

CHAPTER 30

20 October, 1856

The 'others' — I call them that instead of referring to them as Mormons now. Sam has made it quite clear to me that they don't think of themselves as members of the Church of Latter Day Saints, nor have they since they left Iowa with Preston. They view themselves as quite apart from anyone else.

The others, whilst Preston is still convalescing, have been prepared to take instruction from Keats with regard to the setting up of night watches around the clearing. There is a great concern throughout the camp that the Paiute hunting party encountered three days ago might just return and seek revenge for the Indian shot dead by Mr Hearst. I suspect fear of those Indians has driven them all some way towards accepting Keats's way of doing things. Although Mr Vander and Mr Hearst, being the two most senior members of the quorum, Preston's trusted lieutenants, are nominally in charge, neither carry the authority of Preston, and on this matter are more swayed by Keats's greater experience.

Preston continues to recover. A surprisingly strong man for his middle years, this morning he sat up in his cot and managed to eat a bowl of oat stew. When Mr Vander relayed the news of this to the small gathering outside, I heard a hearty cheer. He complained, however, that the wounds were still extremely painful for him with every move. I prescribed another modest dose for the pain. But I'm reluctant for him to take too many more measures of the laudanum.

Preston asked me why Dorothy Dreyton has not been to see him these last few days. I had no answer.

Ben looked up from his journal across the heat shimmer of the campfire. This morning the skies were heavy and dark and promised a new inches-thick carpet of snow to rechristen the ground. The women – Mrs Bowen, Mrs Hussein and Mrs McIntyre – were preparing a gruel of stewed oats flavoured with some strips of pemmican, taking turns stirring the contents of a large, steaming iron pot suspended over a bed of ash-grey logs. By the pallid light of this morning the fire looked lifeless and spent, the flames all but invisible. The same fire at night, though, would look like a furnace, casting a reassuring amber glow across their end of the clearing.

Beyond the heat shimmer, his eyes drifted onto the now utterly still mass of tan hides.

The last of the oxen froze last night. That is it now; they're all dead. Which is a merciful relief, for us as well as them. The occasional pitiful bellowing in the freezing cold of night was an awful sound that I was struggling to ignore. The oxen froze from the outside of the herd in. One imagines if they were human, or perhaps more intelligent, they would have taken turns, shuffling those on the edge to the middle to recover some warmth. But they didn't. The last one to freeze to death was at the very centre of their huddle.

No doubt he'll also be the very last one we butcher to eat.

His eyes focused beyond the carcasses – to the rounded snow-covered hump that was the Dreytons' shelter, and he wondered what was wrong with Dorothy. Sam and Emily had spent some time around the campfire with Ben last night. Sam had talked about his mother, how worried he and Emily were about her.

She had sunk into some kind of stupor of despair, unwilling to step outside, unwilling to talk, unwilling to eat.

Ben wondered if she'd managed to hear Preston's drug-induced outburst. He wondered if she'd been troubled by what she'd heard. It was quite clear that, for Dorothy, for many of these people devoted enough to leave everything, risk everything to follow him out into the wilderness, Preston was the very centre of their universe. To hear him talk like that . . . what was it he'd said?

They're just my words, not God's?

Ben didn't believe for one moment that God came down every night to have a chat with Preston. He looked at the half a dozen men and women gathered outside the church shelter, stamping their feet and rubbing their hands to stay warm.

But these people undoubtedly do believe that.

They believed in him completely, that every stricture, every instruction, every word he had thus far penned in what Sam had referred to as the *Book of New Instruction*, were words directly from God's mouth.

What else had he said?

What if they know? What if they find out what I am?

In the minds of these strictly faithful people, Ben knew there was a special place in hell for someone who might lead them astray – for a false prophet. And yet, given what he knew of Preston, the genuine courage he'd demonstrated, the genuine compassion he had for people, Ben didn't believe for one moment that the man's motives were suspect, that he was a charlatan.

Those drug-induced words were nothing more than a momentary crisis of faith, a hallucination, the babbling of a feverish man. He wondered whether it might help if he were to pay Mrs Dreyton a visit to explain this to her; that it was just the laudanum she had heard talking.

CHAPTER 31

22 October, 1856

Ben stared out into the moonlit darkness. The snowy carpet on the ground and the pillows of snow on every laden branch seemed to glow phosphorescently by the quicksilver light. He was relieved that his turn on watch was made easier by a clear sky and an almost full moon. Beside him the bowl of Keats's pipe glowed as the old man pulled on it.

'Hmm,' the old man's voice quietly rumbled. 'So what'll you do with all them words you been writin' down?'

Ben shrugged. 'I'd like to get them published back in England.'

Keats laughed quietly. 'You mean like a proper book?'

'Perhaps.'

'You s'pecting to get rich with this book o' yours?'

'Oh, probably not,' he replied with a faint smile. 'It would just be nice to see my story printed. Perhaps even in a newspaper.'

Keats was quiet for a while. Ben watched the glow of his tobacco floating in the darkness, bobbing gently. 'You got the bear in yer book?'

'Of course.' Ben smiled.

Keats laughed quietly. 'Bet you writ about yerself bringin' it down like some big ol' hero, eh?'

'Hardly. I wrote about how terrified I was,' Ben replied with shame in his voice. 'I wrote about how all I could do was stand frozen to the spot, like a fool.'

'You writ 'bout me shootin' it in yer book?'

'Yes.'

'You made me sound all brave an' heroic?'

Ben nodded.

'Good. I ain't never been in a book before. The ladies'll like that,' he snorted.

'Do you think it's dead?'

'The bear?' Keats grunted. 'Ain't no bear worries me. It's 'em Paiute out there.'

'You think they're still out in those trees somewhere?'

'Reckon so.' Keats pulled on his pipe and the embers glowed and crackled gently. 'One way or 'nother, they're certain we're all going to die. I reckon they'll be waitin' on that so's they can come scavenge what they can find.'

'Were you scared when you and the others ran into them?'

'Scared?' Keats considered the question for a moment. 'Well now, my blood was up. Don't want to die just as much as you, Lambert.' The pipe glowed and Ben caught the aroma of tobacco smoke wafting past him. 'Thing is,' he continued, 'them Paiute ain't afraid to die. Hell, they can't *wait* to die an' join their ancestors in some milk an' honey land.'

'It makes a man dangerous, that.'

'Why's that?'

'Belief in a paradise after death. The stronger your belief, the more dangerous you are.' Ben shrugged. 'Or at least that's what I think.'

Keats digested that for a moment. 'I guess I'd have to agree with you on that, son. A man should value life enough that he's *always* afraid to die.'

They listened in silence to the sounds of the woods; the creak of laden branches and ancient swaying trunks, the hiss of a gentle breeze through the tops of the trees.

'That mean you don't believe in the Almighty, Lambert?'

Ben often wondered if he did. 'I don't know. The more I learn of the mechanics of this world, the less room I can see in it for something like the hand of God, if you see what I mean.'

'Not sure I do.'

'I have a book in my trunk, a medical textbook. I bought it in London before I set off. You can see, looking through it, that we know how the body works now, what each organ does for us. But before we knew these things, we believed our bodies were simply clay that God had breathed life into. Do you see? It takes just a small amount of knowledge to undo so much of what we've been told to believe for centuries and centuries.'

'I dunno . . . seen things in my time that no medicine book gonna explain.'

'Of course, not *everything* can be explained. But it seems to me, every week in the medical and scientific journals I used to subscribe to back in London, there is more and more of God's mysterious work that we can unravel and discover the hidden cogs and gears within.'

Keats thought about that for a moment. 'Hmm, mebbe so.'

'To answer your question, though,' Ben continued, 'I'm not sure I do believe in a God, not any more.'

'Shit,' Keats cackled, then slapped him on the back. 'You see that bear 'gain, bet a nickel you'll start praying, eh?'

I probably would.

He smelled another waft of tobacco smoke and then Keats hawked up and spat. 'Guess I better go and check in on our other watchers,' Keats grunted. 'I'll be back shortly,' and the glow of his pipe and the outline of his form disappeared into the darkness.

Alone, it was quiet save for the rustle of a fresh breeze through the trees, and the hiss of shifting powder snow. His eyes combed the tree line, a dark wall of foliage just a dozen yards away, drawn instantly to every little rustle of movement out there.

Hurry back, Mr Keats.

It was funny. Back home in West London, in the fashionable and affluent area of Holland Park where his parents had purchased a considerably generous town house for him, he would have turned his nose up in disgust at the sight of the grimy, gaunt and bristly old man. He would have considered him as something less than human; part of the sea of urban misery that loitered suspiciously amongst the back streets and tradesmen's entrances of Soho, Covent Garden and Piccadilly Square. He had the same grime-encrusted and weathered face that filled the pungent main thoroughfares of the East End.

But right here in this clearing, in the middle of this dark and forbidding mountain forest, he trusted the man with his life.

Ben heard the light crunch of snow underfoot coming from behind him. He spun round to see a dark form standing a few feet away.

'Who's that?' he whispered.

The dark form took another step closer and then stopped. Then he heard the softest whisper. 'It's Mrs Dreyton.'

'My God, what're you doing out at this time, Mrs Dreyton?'

'I . . . I . . . need to talk to someone.' She took a step closer to him. By the wan light of the moon, her face appeared almost as pale and luminescent as the snow, her eyes dark pools of torment. 'You were there. You heard him.'

'Preston?'

She nodded. 'I . . . I've been to see him.'

Ben smiled. 'That's good. He was asking after you today.'

'I told him what I . . . what I know now.'

'What?'

Her voice broke and she sobbed. 'I gave him everything. My life, my love . . . my body, my children.'

'Mrs Dreyton?'

'I thought, through him, God was touching me. Touching Emily and Sam.'

156

'Dorothy, what you heard him say the other day was nothing more than the product of the medicine, of a fever—'

'No.' She shook her head solemnly. 'I see now his lies have led us to this place. He's no prophet.' Dorothy's hands went to her face. 'Oh, God, forgive me for following him.'

'Dorothy, what did you say to him?'

'That I know he is a liar . . . and a thief.'

'A thief?'

She looked up at him. 'What he has was not *gifted* to him, it was *taken*.'

He held out a hand to comfort her. But she shied away.

'What? What is it he *has*, Mrs Dreyton?'

'God will punish him for that,' she cried. 'God will punish him, and punish us all for following him.'

'What is it that he has?'

She ignored him. 'We have to leave here, Mr Lambert. We have to leave soon, before it's too late. My children trust you. I trust you. Will you help us?'

'What? We can't leave here now. We'll freeze, or starve, or—'

'God's vengeance will come down on us.' She reached out and grabbed his arm tightly. He could feel the steel grip of her hand through three layers of clothing. 'Do you believe in eternal torment, Mr Lambert?'

'What? No . . . no I can't say I—'

'Because that's what awaits Preston, in the very depths of hell.' She looked back at the other camp. 'Or maybe it'll come to us . . . here in this forsaken place.'

'Mrs Dreyton, you're not making much sense to me.'

She shook her head. 'Maybe . . . maybe, if I tell the others, warn the others,' she muttered, turning away from Ben, 'I'll be forgiven.' She stepped away from him, crunching back across the snow.

'Mrs Dreyton?' he called to her softly, but she was gone.

Had she really accused Preston of being a liar and thief?

157

Ben wondered for a moment how Preston would react to his most devoted follower denouncing him as a false prophet. And realised, with a shiver of unease, that it would lead nowhere good. Not for anyone.

CHAPTER 32

```
cave iram Dei
M   T   W   T   F   S   S
                1   2   3
4   5   6   7   8   9   10
11  12  13  14  15  16  17
18  19  20  21  22  23  24
25  26  27  28  29  30
```

Monday
Munston, Utah

Shepherd smiled at the people out in the basketball court, waving to them as a rousing rendition of 'Abide With Me' was being belted out by the Munston Homes Choir for God, stepping as one from side to side and clapping their hands to the infectious rhythm.

Booking them had been a good idea. His campaign co-ordinator, Duncan, had said, 'You can't beat a good ol' Baptist choir for feel-good factor.'

He was right, of course. The rally had gone spectacularly well. Originally it had been booked into a local school. But support was growing for the campaign so fast that Duncan's team had quickly needed to upgrade the venue to the sports hall of a nearby college.

Shepherd noted, with satisfaction, a bank of cameras at the back. Not just local press photographers, but some network camera crews too. The town of Munster, home to one college, a cereal processing and packing plant, one shopping mall and at least seventy churches of different denominations, was just the third stop in his tour of Utah.

The state was easy territory. Everyone knew him now, and it was obvious already that neither Republicans nor Democrats were going to get their foot in here. His message was a fresh message that was coming right out of the blue and wasn't tainted with the tit-for-tat baggage that the other two parties were burdened with. His message didn't have the shrill sound of a party frantically hanging onto power, nor the hectoring 'Doubting Thomas' tone of a party impatient to get *into* power.

Shepherd knew that he didn't sound like the other candidates, and more and more polls were beginning to show that was going to be just about enough to cajole tentative support from the soft conservative centre.

Shepherd bowed again to the ecstatic audience's delight, and then strode defiantly off the podium, flanked by a pair of security men from his ministry. They walked him briskly through changing rooms that reeked of body odour and the sort of cheap aftershave that young men like to douse a little too liberally. They led him out of a rear door to where a dark-windowed Humvee waited patiently for him, engine already idling.

The door was opened for him and Shepherd slid inside. One of his minders slipped into the front passenger seat; the other climbed into the limousine waiting behind.

Alone, Shepherd opened the laptop on the seat beside him and accessed his mail.

There it was — a message he was expecting, a no-questions-asked favour from a sympathetic face in the department of Homeland Security.

As requested,
The ISP number was traced to an address in London,
England. The address is 59 Lena Garden Road,
Hammersmith, London, W6. The name against the ISP
number and the address is Julian Francis Cooke.
    Cooke is/was a minor media personality presenting some
current affairs programmes, investigative programmes. His
media profile is lower than it used to be, but he is still a
recognisable name and face. He runs a small production
company called 'Soup Kitchen Studios' that makes low-cost

160

documentaries. Recent programmes made by them include one on a radical Islamic imam, Mohammad Al Bakti, released from US custody a few years ago. The association with this Muslim cleric was for a period of two weeks. For some reason, this has escaped a Homeland Security flagging. (By the way, I can have this guy, Cooke, pulled in. It's something I can easily do for you if he's causing you any problems.)

You might want to know, fifteen days ago he passed through immigration at Denver International. The same day he connected on a flight to Reno. He then flew back from Denver to London thirteen days later and is currently at his home address in London.

You should also know that he flew over here with an associate, Rosemary Whitely, who also flew on to Reno with him, and has not returned to the UK. So she's still in the US.

As requested, I've authorised a tap on Cooke's phone and an intercept on his internet connection. Not difficult justifying that because of his past association with Al Bakti, and it's relatively painless burying the paperwork since we're only dealing with British intelligence, and those guys will bend over backwards for us.

They'll ask . . . but I don't need to give any reason.

All intercepted emails will be copied to your encrypted account. All intercepted calls will be recorded and uploaded to the secured ftp site you listed.

Hope this helps.

Your friend in the Big Building

Shepherd looked out through the smoked glass of the window. The town of Munston, little more than a highway flanked on either side by big-box retailers fronted by acres of tarmac parking, slipped past forgettably.

It was useful information. Useful to know exactly who was sniffing around. Perhaps he had nothing – perhaps he'd found something.

The thought triggered a tingle of excitement.

Perhaps he's discovered them?

Maybe there was some sort of mutual exchange he could do with this Mr Cooke; information for information.

CHAPTER 33

23 October, 1856

I have slept poorly, worrying about Sam and Emily's mother. I can understand, for certain types of people, their faith is everything. Hers has been shaken. I have no idea what Preston's story is . . . whether he genuinely believes he is on a mission for God. I suppose that's irrelevant. What matters is what Mrs Dreyton believes.

Or should I say, believed. Past tense.

What worries me more is whether she will sow seeds of doubt amongst the others. Whilst I am no fan of peculiar and strict religious sects like Preston's, it is their faith in him that seems to hold them together. And thus far . . . I have myself found Preston to be a rational and reasonable man.

I am troubled by this situation.

Ben put down his pen and rubbed his hands vigorously together. Even with a woollen scarf wrapped tightly around his writing hand, it was stiff with the cold.

The usually sullen grey sky was broken today, allowing the heartening sight of scant patches of blue — a dash of colour to their monochrome world that he much missed. A weak ray of sunlight speared down from the scudding clouds, dappling the clearing momentarily before racing away across the trees.

His gaze fell upon the pitiful sight of their dead oxen. Under Keats's supervision, the first few of the dead oxen had been towed a short distance away from the others and butchered for meat. The well-trodden snow around their carved-up carcasses was pink and, amongst the exposed ribcages, a pile of inedible purple and grey organs was steadily growing. Ben wondered how long it would be before that offal was no longer considered inedible.

For the while, food was not going to be a problem. But the collective mouths of over a hundred and twenty people made short work of each carcass as it became available. The mathematics of the situation was inescapably obvious to him already. There weren't enough oxen to keep them all going through the winter and into spring. At some point, they were going to have to find other food to subsist on to supplement the oxen. Or perhaps reduce their numbers.

It occurred to him that he might not be the only person already making that kind of calculation.

He blew on his hands, cursing the aching stiffness of unrelenting cold. Around the campfire and tucked up in his shelter at night, with the flap sealed tight and the shared body heat of Keats and Broken Wing building up a fug of warmth inside, it was tolerable. But outside, away from any cooking fire, the bitter chill, compounded by the occasional icy gust, was a miserable experience. Ben vowed to travel to warmer climes come the spring and the end of this unfortunate ordeal, and to never again stray from a temperate latitude.

He gazed at the small world of their clearing, like an island amidst a dark, forbidding ocean. There were a few people stirring. Several meagre fires were heating water for a morning bowl of stewed oats. Most families still had barrels of cornmeal and oats previously used as packing insulation for fragile family possessions, but now gratefully being consumed each day for breakfast.

Giles Weyland was offering to share with him a special treat this morning; the last of his coffee beans. There was enough, he said, for a canteen of it. Enough for him and Ben and his girl. They would savour it together, then fill their tummies with stewed oats. Weyland had only himself and his Negro girl to feed and had many boxes of fragile china stuffed with cornmeal packing to get through.

Ben put away his writing things, slipping them back inside his travel trunk in the shelter. He wrapped his poncho around himself and squeezed out again into the scudding sunlight, enjoying a fleeting moment's warmth on his shoulders and back as a sunbeam raced over him, then up through the trees, towards the craggy peaks above them.

Making his way towards Weyland's shelter, he noticed that the Negro girl was up already building their campfire, whilst Weyland was spreading out the last of his coffee beans to be roasted and cornmeal to be stewed.

The question had yet to be asked by anyone, and Ben was surprised that no one yet had the answer . . .

. . . *Is this girl your property?*

It was something Ben felt he should have already asked on principle, but had yet to find the right moment and the right way. Whilst he admired Weyland's southern charm and his unflappable manner, Ben doubted he could, in all good conscience, sit down and eat with a man who believed in the institution of slavery.

As he crossed the ground between shelters to join Weyland for breakfast, and was working out the wording for this delicate question, he caught sight of Emily and Sam on the far side of the clearing.

Both were being led by Mrs Dreyton up into the tree line. By the look of the small canvas sack slung over Sam's shoulder, they were off to gather firewood together. But there was something about their manner that caught his eye. It seemed to be a furtive departure, Mrs Dreyton and Sam looking back over their shoulders. A terrible thought occurred to him.

They're not leaving, are they?

They'd die out there, for certain. He stopped in his tracks, and half turned to race across the clearing to them, to plead with Mrs Dreyton to stop this craziness, when he realised neither she, nor Emily were carrying anything and Sam had just the small sack and his gun slung over one shoulder.

Mrs Dreyton might have been quite mad enough to head out into the woods with nothing but the clothes on her body and the shawl around her head, but Sam was quite sensible. At the very least, Sam would have called over to talk to Ben first.

Relax . . . they're after some firewood, that's all.

He watched them as they climbed up the slope into the trees. Just before they were lost from sight behind the dense firs, he saw Sam look anxiously back towards the camp. Ben wondered what Sam was glancing at when he noticed Preston and Vander standing side by side just outside their church, silently watching the Dreytons go.

It was an odd tableau that had Ben puzzling over it as he arrived beside Weyland, squatting over a foil-lined wooden box in which nestled no more than a fistful of dark coffee beans. The rich aroma of the box wafted across to him seductively and his mouth moistened in anticipation. Savouring it with a deep breath, the odd scene was for the moment pushed far from his mind.

'Morning, Mr Weyland.'

'Ah, Mr Lambert,' said Weyland, looking up. 'A promise is a promise. Take a seat and I shall roast us these beans.' He turned to the Negro girl, 'Violet, bring me the skillet will you, my dear?'

Violet was busy nursing the first flames of their cooking fire. She shook her head. 'Giles, get it yo'self, you lazy man. Cain't you see I got my han's busy tendin' to this?'

Giles turned to Ben and shrugged with a world-weary flicker of his eyebrows. 'Pfft, women, eh?'

Ben smiled with relief, glad that he could sit down and join them with a clear conscience. Violet was no slave; that much was for sure.

CHAPTER 34

23 October, 1856

The sun was on the way to its zenith, shining through a gap in the grey sky when he heard the scream. The young man was unsure of the noise at first. Unsure because it was not a sound he normally associated with these woods; a woman's cry, or a child's cry in this place was as strange as a bear's call out on the plains. These wooded peaks were not a place for womenfolk, nor children, nor the old — especially not in the dead of winter.

He heard it again. This time he was certain it was a woman's cry, not a child's. The first time had been a sharp shriek of surprise; the second was protracted and drawn out and made the fine downy hair on his forearms rise. The scream endured, a terrible blend of pitiful agony and abject terror, causing him to grimace and adrenaline to instantly flood his body, entreating him to flee like a startled rabbit or stand firm.

A woman.

He heard a third scream, higher pitched this time.

A child.

The young man knew the only women and children in these woods were the 'white-faces', the ones that had lost their way in the mountains. Black Feather said their fate was sealed now; none of them would last until the snows melted. If cold and hunger didn't kill them all, then the dark spirit they had brought into the woods with them would.

His first instinct was to drop the hare that he was gutting, go find Black Feather and the others, and tell them what he'd heard. But the second cry, the child's cry, alerted some deeper instinct in him. He couldn't ignore the innocent cry of a child, not even a white-face child.

His thinking went no deeper than that. He dropped the hare, cleaned the blade of his knife with a wipe across his sleeve and strode swiftly in the direction from which the screams had come. He moved with the athletic agility and speed of a young man whose feet knew the terrain well, intuitively judging from the gentle undulations in the snow, where lay the dips, the bumps, the twisted roots that could snap an ankle.

The woman's scream came again from up ahead.

This time he knew, from the abrupt and gargling way it came to an end, that it would be the woman's last scream. He made an approximate best guess from which direction it had come, making allowances for the acoustic tricks the forest could play. He redoubled his pace, his feet flicking lightly through the shallowest snow, stone-stepping across the mounds of firm ground, from one boulder to another, vaulting with graceful agility over the fallen limbs of long-dead trees.

Up ahead he glimpsed, between trunks, spears of weak sunlight lancing down into a small glade and he detected, amidst this world of only two colours, virgin white and deep wooded green – an unmissable splash of bright crimson.

He slowed down the pace to ensure his arrival would be in complete silence, darting forward another dozen yards and then abruptly settling to the ground beneath the boughs of a fir tree. Catching his breath in quiet, controlled gasps, he looked out through the needles at the clearing beyond, trying to make sense of what he was seeing.

There was a lot of blood.

Too much blood for whoever had lost it to live. That was immediately obvious to him.

Then he saw her.

Stretched over a fallen trunk, he could make out the body of a white-face woman, her dark clothes stained almost black with the blood spilling from her torso. Beside her, curled up in the snow on the ground, was a child, a little girl, hugging her knees and shuddering — convulsive twitches that racked her body in ebbs and flows.

She was alive — her eyes were wide. But he could also see her mind was gone. Shock had rescued her sanity, taken it someplace else.

He scanned the small clearing, looking for a trace of the creature that had done this.

A bear?

It was possible. Although they slept through the winter, Black Feather frequently cautioned that they could be very easily disturbed and enraged.

He noticed the smooth snow was trampled and flattened across the glade and stained dark with splatters and smears of blood.

Three distinct foot profiles — possibly four — mingled across the glade; a child, a woman, a male, and perhaps another. The story he tried reading in the snow was too complicated. But it was clear that a body had been dragged from the clearing whilst bleeding, leaving a trail that disappeared into the foliage on the far side.

An older mind would have advised caution at this point; he should back away and leave this scene behind him. This was the evil spirit Black Feather spoke of — he could sense it, smell it . . . the white-face evil. Only *their* evil could be so careless with its bloodletting, so uncontrolled, so savage.

But the young man was alone and too confident and curious to know better. In any case, he couldn't leave this child — no older than his own sister — to die in the same brutal way as her mother appeared to have done.

The long, crooked blade of his hunting knife balanced ready for use in one hand, his other hand easing out the finely crafted flint-bladed *tamahakan* tucked into his belt, he rose with one slow, fluid movement and stepped out from beneath the tree into the clearing.

He listened carefully as he moved soundlessly. In the distance, echoing noisily through the forest, activity coming from the white-face camp could be heard. The *thak-thak-thak* of wood being chopped. A gentle breeze disturbed the snow-laden pine branches overhanging the clearing, and powder snow sifted lightly down with a gentle hiss from one bough to the next.

Approaching the shuddering child and the body splayed across the log, he could see more clearly how much damage had been wrought on the woman's torso. Several deep gashes had opened her belly exposing ripped organs, and tatters of those same organs were draped out across the bark of the tree trunk. The gashes reminded him of the sort of wound a bear *could* make with one of its powerful front paws. But looking at the spacing and the length and depth of these gashes, it would have to have been a very large bear.

The girl was only a few feet away from him, shuddering and rocking. She didn't see him; her eyes and her mind were far away.

He slowly reached one hand towards her, not sure how she would react to his touch.

It was then that he heard it.

A deep rasping of breath coming from the edge of the clearing and circling around beyond sight. In the silence of this sound-insulated glade it was deafening, echoing from all sides, a deep, pulsing, hoarse rattling . . . like that of a male buffalo, cornered and exhausted at the end of a hunt, blowing foam out of each nostril.

He noticed a long gun on the ground beyond the girl. He knew how these weapons were used, but not how to *feed* one. There had been no loud thunder before the screams, and he realised the white-face weapon would still be ready to use, still deadly.

The third white-face, the one that had been dragged away,

must have dropped it. Which told him something useful about this creature.

It is a very fast creature. The white-face had no time to fire.

The breathing grew quiet now, as if awaiting his next move, daring him to reach out for the weapon and try using it.

CHAPTER 35

23 October, 1856

Ben heard a voice cry out in alarm, then another. There was a commotion going on outside.

Broken Wing glanced up at him. 'What isss?'

Ben shrugged. He leaned forward and poked his head out through the flap of their rabbit-hole-like shelter to see what was going on. He saw Mr Bowen's head poking out from the shelter next door, and, further away, Mr Hussein's — like curious prairie dogs.

He heard another cry of alarm and the challenge of a couple of male voices. The disturbance was coming from the far end of the camp.

Broken Wing kicked Keats, who was napping. 'Keatttt!' he shouted.

Keats grunted unconsciously.

Ben, meanwhile, reached for his medicine box, pulled himself out through the flap and quickly stood up, craning his neck to see what was going on. He could make out a gathering group amongst the far shelters, milling around something or someone. Ben automatically began to head towards them.

'What's going on?' Mr McIntyre shouted out through the flap of his family's shelter as Ben strode past.

'I don't know. I'm just going to see.'

Weyland pulled up alongside him as they crunched across the compacted snow and waded through ankle-deep drifts of fresh powder. The Virginian's usual measured voice carried a tone of uncertainty as they approached the knot of people.

'Thought I heard one of them Mormon gentlemen shout something about an Indian.'

They passed the oxen carcasses, entering the Mormons' camp, weaving their way through the snowed-covered humps of shelters and pushing their way forward through the crowd.

Weyland made his way to the front and stopped dead. 'Good God,' he gasped.

Ben followed his gaze. The first thing his eyes registered was Emily, coated from head to foot in blood. She was cradled in the arms of a young Indian man. Ben presumed he was one of the Paiute hunting party encountered a week ago. He looked about the same age as Sam, seventeen or eighteen. The Indian was on his knees, holding as tightly to Emily, it seemed, as he was to life. From a deep, ragged gash that angled down from his left shoulder, across his chest and stomach to his groin, a tangled nest of his entrails had spilled onto Emily's blood-soaked lap.

He gasped, short and shallow percussive breaths, his eyes glazed.

Mrs Zimmerman knelt down in front of him and reached out for Emily. The young Indian, wide-eyed and in shock, looked uncertainly at her. The woman offered a reassuring smile and nodded.

'Let me take her,' she said quietly.

The Indian glanced down at Emily before reluctantly releasing his tight hold of her. Mrs Zimmerman scooped Emily into her arms and stepped back.

'Thank you,' she uttered.

The Indian swayed momentarily before collapsing onto the snow, calling out something loudly. To Ben's ears the words were unintelligible, but he noticed they were the same, over and over.

174

Keats noisily pushed through the crowd, barking at people to get out of his way.

'The Indians are still out there,' somebody in the crowd gasped.

The old guide emerged from the throng and knelt down beside the prone body of the young Paiute. Ben stepped forward to join him, crouching down quickly to examine the wound but knowing – as he had with the Zimmerman girl – that there was too much damage to save the young man. He looked at Keats and shook his head.

The Indian was still chanting something.

Somebody in the crowd muttered, 'Those dark demons've killed the Dreytons,' and there was a ripple of reaction through the crowd, followed by an outbreak of muttered, whispered prayers amongst them. Whether they were praying for Emily, her family, themselves or for the Indian, he couldn't tell.

Keats grunted irritably at the growing cacophony of noise behind him. The young Paiute had stopped chanting and was now whispering. Keats crouched down close to the young man, who looked now to be only a few moments away from death, placing one gnarled cauliflower ear close to the Indian's lips. Ben noticed tiny flecks of dark blood dotting Keats's cheek as the Indian panted, and desperately whispered something.

'What's he saying?' Ben asked quietly.

'Can't fuckin' hear,' Keats hissed. He turned to face the crowd. 'Shut up!' he barked angrily at them. The praying and hubbub of noise immediately settled down to a gentle rustle of breathing.

He dipped down again to listen to the dying Indian. The Paiute seemed to rally enough strength for his tormented and distant eyes to focus for a moment on Keats. He grabbed the old man's arm and gasped something to him; a quick rattle of Ute that Ben wasn't confident the old guide entirely understood. Then the young Indian's eyes rolled, showing just the whites, and a last fluttering breath came from his mouth, flecking his lips with sprayed dots of blood.

They heard the distant caw of a murder of crows circling high above the trees some way into the forest, and the sibilant whispering of someone still praying amidst the crowd.

Ben reached out and closed the Indian's eyes; even in death, the look of them unsettled him.

He turned to Keats. 'So are you going to tell me what he was saying?'

Keats looked at him and shook his head, confused. 'Didn't seem to make much sense.'

CHAPTER 36

cave iram Dei

M	T	W	T	F	S	S
				1	2	3
4	5	6	7	8	9	10
11	12	13	14	15	16	17
18	19	20	21	22	23	24
25	26	27	28	29	30	

Tuesday
Shepherd's Bush, London

'So,' said Sean Holmwood, tucking a fork into his pasta carbonara, 'that sounds like an intriguing find.'

Julian returned a wry smile. Sean always calmly understated things. That was probably what made him such a good commissioning editor – he never gushed praise or approval; instead, he exuded it cautiously behind a poker face.

Julian nodded. 'It's not just the story of a bunch of settlers caught out by a particularly bad winter either, Sean. There's a lot more to this.'

Sean's fork stopped midway from his plate. 'Oh?'

Julian leaned forward and lowered his voice. The corner of the bistro in which they were sitting was far enough away from the other patrons that it was an unnecessary precaution, but nonetheless he felt the need to keep it down.

'This guy leading the larger of the two parties,' he said in a conspiratorial whisper, 'Preston . . . he's like, I don't know, like some sort of a David Koresh figure.'

'Koresh? Koresh . . . I know the name.'

'The Waco siege.'

Sean rolled his eyes. 'Of course, yes.'

'This guy, Preston, he seemed to have a hold on these people;

a really unhealthy hold over them. Lambert – the guy whose journal I have – has written an incredibly detailed account of what happened up in those mountains. And I'm telling you, Sean, it's really good stuff.'

Julian took a sip of wine.

Sean nodded. 'Go on, Jules, you've got me interested.'

'This Preston bloke appears to have led his congregation into the wilds with the intention of setting up his own small community, with their very own version of Mormonism. Do you know much about the Mormons – the Church of Latter Day Saints, Sean?'

Sean frowned. 'Aren't they like the Amish or something? Wear funny hats and beards?'

'Uhh, no . . . they're not really anything like the Amish.'

'Maybe I'm thinking of Quakers.'

Julian shook his head. 'Nope, not even close.'

Sean shrugged. 'Well, which Christian sect are they then?'

'I'll be honest with you, Sean, I'm not even sure they're Christian.'

Sean looked confused. 'Not Christian? What the hell are they?'

'They're one of a kind. I suppose you could think of them as nineteenth-century scientologists.'

'A cult.'

Julian nodded. 'I don't know where you draw the line between a cult and a religion. But, yes, I suppose back then it was more like a cult. Their religious texts are really quite incredible.'

'Not the Bible then?'

Julian laughed. 'Nothing like the Bible. Hang on,' he said, opening his satchel and pulling out a wad of foolscap, covered with his handwritten notes. 'Let me read you a little on the founding of Mormonism. It's great stuff.'

He flicked through the pages. 'Ah, here we are. Okay . . . so yeah, the whole thing was founded by a guy called Joseph Smith in the 1830s.' He looked up at Sean and grinned. 'You simply couldn't make this stuff up. This guy, Smith, wasn't anyone special: son of a local farming family with acres and acres of grazing land in some rural area just outside of New York. Anyway, there was a craze going round at that time for treasure hunting. Apparently everyone suddenly suspected their small-holding might contain ancient Native American treasure hordes. Well, this Joseph Smith got bitten by the treasure bug, and really got into it, digging little holes all over his family's land. Then all of a sudden, he announces the find of all finds.'

Julian paused, teasing Sean into splaying his hands impatiently. 'And?'

'Smith claimed he had found the word of God.'

'What do you mean *word of God*? Are we talking stone tablets?'

'No, Smith wanted to go one better than that. Not stone . . . gold. He claimed he'd found the word of God on several golden scrolls.'

'Just like that, eh? Started digging and found these scrolls?'

'Oh no, it gets better. He claimed it wasn't just blind luck. He added to his story by claiming he was guided to a remote hillock on his family's farm by an angel that came to him at night, and spoke inside his head, giving him directions to this place.'

'Ah, yes . . . the classic prophet story.'

'Well, yes, it is. Arguably it's no more credible – or incredible – than all the others. But this one gets crazier and crazier. Smith claims he was guided to this remote place, dug up an ancient stone box containing these golden scrolls, the remains of the guiding angel, and some things called seer stones. From this point on, the story reads a bit like David Icke on a bad day.'

'Go on.'

'At about this time, like I say, 1820s, early 1830s, another craze doing the rounds in England and America was a fascination with Ancient Egypt. There were a lot of fanciful theories going around amongst hobbyist historians. One, for example, being that the Native Americans were descendants of the Pharaohs. So guess what?'

Sean shrugged in response.

'Making his magical find sound even sexier, he announced it was written in a holy language of the angels, otherwise known as Reformed Egyptian.'

'Reformed Egyptian?'

'Sounds vaguely legitimate, though, doesn't it? It certainly helped to sex his story up back then. Smith claimed the angel was resurrected with an elaborate ritual and made flesh so that he could help him translate the scrolls. And so, the story goes, night after night, he spent time out on this hill, alone with this angel, translating the scrolls, which were meant to be the *actual* spoken words of God. The angel also told him the complete correct history of man, from the Egyptians onwards.'

Sean smiled wryly. 'The *correct* history?'

'The angel told Smith his name was Nephi, or Moroni, depending on varying early accounts by Smith and his first followers. He explained to Smith that several ancient tribes sailed for the Americas a couple of thousand years before Christ came along, back around the time of the Tower of Babel. These people sailed for the Americas, settled there and built themselves a huge, advanced civilisation – which perhaps might be a nod to Atlantis, who knows. Anyway, this civilisation did very well for itself for several hundred years until a war amongst them destroyed everything.'

'Leaving absolutely no archaeological traces behind it.'

Julian smiled. 'Yup, leaving no traces because, according to Nephi, it was a ferocious war. There were two groups, Nephites and Lamanites. Only one of these people survived this war: Nephi – this angel. With God's help, he transcribed the history of his people and the new commandments of God on these golden scrolls writing in his language – this Reformed Egyptian – and then buried these scrolls in a hill.'

Julian forked up a mouthful of his cooling dinner. 'Which, many centuries later, would end up being a hill in the middle of Mr Smith's farm.'

'Wow.'

'And this history, this story I've just told you, is pretty much what the original *Book of Mormon* contains. Smith wrote it all down, published it and began selling copies. He revised the book over the ensuing years, adding to it from further sections of the scrolls that he claimed he'd yet to translate fully.'

'With this Nephi guy?'

'No, not after the initial translation. The angel was never seen by anyone. After his initial moonlit sessions on the hill, Smith claimed that he no longer required Nephi's assistance, as the angel had taught him how to use the Seer Stones to translate the Reformed Egyptian. So now he could do it all by himself, the angel Nephi presumably became dusty bones once again, and vanished in a puff of make-believe.'

'So, did anyone ever see these scrolls?'

'There were written testimonies by his first followers that they had seen the scrolls first-hand, albeit briefly. But Smith was always careful to guard them closely, allowing his early followers to see them only for a moment, and from afar.'

'So, these scrolls – where are they now?'

'No one knows. Smith claimed that when he'd finished transcribing the symbols on them, the angel returned and he handed them back, and they, and the angel, all vanished.'

'Convenient.'

'Well, there were rumours that he buried the scrolls back where he found them beneath a hill on his family's farm, rumours that they and some of the other relics were stolen from him, possibly by a follower, or someone out to discredit him. But they never did resurface, so it makes sense that he just folded that into his story – that the scrolls were returned to God, the angel returned whence it came . . . and voila, we have the origins of the *Book of Mormon*.' Julian sipped some of his wine. 'Well? What do you think?'

Sean nodded. 'It's wacky.'

'And here's the thing, Sean. There's thirteen million people in the States who are Mormon, who actually believe in this stuff as an article of faith.'

'So this Preston bloke was a Mormon, then?'

Julian shook his head. 'Once, perhaps. The church went through a schism after Joseph Smith was killed, something of a power struggle. I suppose it's not unlike the Shi'a-Sunni split over who should rightfully succeed Mohammed. The Latter Day Saints splintered into several groups with different ministers claiming authority. Brigham Young was the name of the guy who wrested control of the mainstream Mormon faith. But amongst all this unrest and confusion, Preston emerged, and won over a small flock of devout followers. He must have had something – a compelling manner, a unique message – enough that the mainstream Mormons turned angrily on him, and he and his congregation had to quickly leave Iowa for the west. That's how the poor buggers ended up in the Sierra Nevadas.'

'Did any of these Preston people survive?'

'Well, here's the thing. There's no knowledge of it. I mean, literally nothing. Nada. No one at the time noticed they'd vanished. So I can only guess they all died up there, because there were no newspaper articles, no eye-witness accounts.'

'Perhaps it wasn't newsworthy. I'd imagine quite a few of those wagon trains came unstuck, went missing somewhere across America.'

'Not really. I mean every group lost *some* people to sickness or malnutrition, but the only other group that actually went missing was the Donner Party. That event happened a few years earlier, about a hundred miles further south of where we found Preston's party. But you see, the Donner Party made news back then, simply because there were a few survivors who could talk about it. I mean, it became a story written about in every paper of the time all over the States.'

'Donner Party . . . I've heard of that. There was cannibalism, right?'

Julian nodded. 'That's probably one of the main reasons it became such a huge story. But it probably would never have been a story at all if there'd been no one who survived. Now, this Preston party . . . absolutely nothing, not a single thing about it. So that's what makes me think absolutely *no one* walked out.'

Except that one . . . very odd web page, Julian reminded himself. *Someone else knows about it.*

Sean nodded, his pasta forgotten for now. 'So any ideas how it all ended?'

'I'm working on it. I'm still trying to make sense of this journal. They may have just starved, might have been attacked by Indians . . . I mean, there's a mention of an encounter with Indians called Paiute. Or who knows, it might have ended up as some bizarre cult suicide thing – you know, another Jonestown.'

Sean's eyes widened. 'That would be quite a horrendous tale.'

Julian nodded. 'I'm heading back out there at the end of the week. We have a small window of time to scoop what we can, then this site has to be called in. At which point, I'd imagine various American heritage agencies will boot us off.'

Sean smiled cautiously, chewing on his food in thought.

Julian reached for his wine and sipped. 'What we have here is an interesting relationship between a charismatic cult leader and his ultimately doomed followers. It's a strong angle to play on. The danger a religion can pose when it's twisted, *radicalised.* That's a very relevant theme to discuss these days, isn't it?'

Sean hummed in agreement. He pulled out a pad and began scribbling some thoughts, whilst Julian finished his dinner in silence.

'And you've read through all of this journal?'

'It's quite a thing to translate.'

'Why, is it written in code or something?'

'No, just a combination of things. The handwriting's hard work and gets a little more wobbly on each successive page. The ink fades towards the end, which makes me think the author was watering it down to make it last. It gets almost illegible in places.'

'Was the author . . . do you think this Lambert started losing it?'

Julian looked out of the window at the bustling foot traffic passing the bistro's fogged window. 'No, I don't think so, Sean. No, I don't think he's losing it.'

'Well then, let me ask you this. Do you think the author is reliable?'

Julian had considered that possibility. 'You can never know for sure. But I'll say this: he comes across as very level-headed. I know it sounds like an odd thing for a researcher to say, but I think I trust him.'

Sean picked up his fork and started tucking into his pasta once more.

Julian watched him in silence. 'Anyway, have I snagged your interest?'

Sean placed his fork down and clasped his hands thoughtfully. 'Yes, I think I might be interested,' he replied softly. 'It might be an idea to keep it to yourself for now, though. I'll consider putting this on a fast-track footing within our editorial group, assuming of course it's us you want to deal with?'

'Well, Rose and I want to deal with you, Sean. We worked well together on *Uncommon People*. There's no reason to think we wouldn't work well together again.'

Sean looked up and smiled. 'Yes, we did, didn't we? It was fun.' He gazed out of the window at a passing bus. 'Look, I'll make some discreet calls tomorrow, and maybe we'll meet again later in the week?'

'Sounds good to me. I'm flying back at the weekend. So if you want to meet again before I go . . . well, you've got three more days.'

CHAPTER 37

23 October, 1856

'Are you certain that is what the Indian said?' Preston asked again quietly, light from the oil lamp suspended from the cross-beam making his gaunt face look like a skull draped with fine silk.

Keats shook his head. 'Nope. But it's the best I could make out.'

Midday was gone and the low, sleepy sun already yearning again for the horizon by the time a meeting of the quorum was convened in the church. Ben was surprised to find himself and Keats asked to attend – although not surprised that Broken Wing, whom Keats insisted come along too, was stopped at the entrance and sent away.

'Dark skin's a mark of evil,' Mr Hollander had grunted, standing like a sentry beside the flap.

'The evil spirit took them? That's what the Indian said?'

Keats shrugged. 'Hell, he could have said that . . . other hand, maybe the words could've meant somethin' else. The Indian was speakin' all kinds of crazy.'

'What other things did he say, Mr Keats?' the minister pressed him.

Keats shook his head. 'Said somethin' about an evil spirit

185

reaching out from the trees. Wasn't makin' any goddamn sense to me.'

'The Indian was in a state of shock,' said Ben. 'His mind and his eyes were playing tricks on him. The wounds across his front could have been from some wild animal. Ragged cuts like . . . like a claw, not clean like a blade. Perhaps the bear?'

Keats shook his head. 'Ain't no bear.'

They sat in silence for a few moments. Outside the temple they could hear the muted sound of wood being chopped and cooking fires being prepared. The routine of survival went on, despite the traumatic event earlier in the day.

Preston winced painfully as he shifted his position, holding a protective hand over the linen binding around his torso.

'And where is Mr Hearst?' asked Jed Stolheim, running a tired hand through his thinning auburn hair. 'He's not been seen since this morning.'

'I don't know, Jed,' replied Preston. 'It's been long enough that I'm fearful for Saul.'

'It's them Indians out there did it,' someone muttered from the back.

'I'm not even sure they are Indians,' replied Vander. 'Me and Mr Zimmerman saw 'em up close in the woods. Dark as the Devil himself, they were.'

Keats snorted. 'If they ain't Indians, what the hell are they?'

'Demons, Keats . . . Satan's imps sent to torment us.'

There was a sharp intake of breath amongst the quorum.

'That's enough, Eric,' snapped Preston. 'We have God on our side, so we have nothing to be afraid of.'

Ben heard a tremulous note of uncertainty in the elder's voice. Or perhaps it was his weakness, or the pain, that robbed his voice of authority. Preston turned to Ben.

'How is Emily Dreyton?'

'She's in deep shock. Her mind has gone for now.'

'Has she spoken of what she saw?' asked Vander.

'She has said nothing. Nor do I imagine she will for some

time,' replied Ben. 'So terrified was she at what she saw . . . her mind is gone, and it may never return.'

'Poor girl,' muttered Preston. 'Poor Dorothy, poor Samuel,' he added with genuine remorse etched across his face.

'Who's with her now?' asked Vander.

'Mrs Zimmerman.'

There was a murmur of approval amongst them. The woman had lost a daughter, Emily had lost her mother. Mrs Zimmerman was the best person to sit with her.

'They may still be alive,' said Ben. 'All we have is Emily and some blood – most of it I'll wager came from the Indian boy. They could still be out there.'

Preston nodded thoughtfully. 'Yes, you're right, Lambert. We should send out a search party to—'

'We ain't headin' out tonight, Lambert,' Keats cut in, 'and that's final. I ain't riskin' the lives of anyone else lookin' for dead people. First light tomorrow we will look.'

Ben turned round to him swiftly. 'What? We can't leave them out there overnight!'

'I ain't leadin' out a party in the dark!'

'They'll die of the cold!'

'Reckon them to be dead anyways,' muttered Keats. 'We go at night, we'll miss the tracks and we'll not find them.' He looked around at the others. 'Sky's clear tonight. Don't expect no snow, so we go at first light. That way we can follow the blood up to where whatever happened . . . happened.'

Preston nodded. 'That seems sensible, Mr Keats.'

Ben shook his head, knowing the guide was probably right that poor Sam and his mother were gone and there was nothing they could do about it but try and find their bodies. The small, unlikely hope that Sam might be lying somewhere wounded and pleading for help was nothing more than a wish that he knew was going to torment him through the night.

'And I shall come with you, Mr Keats.'

Vander turned to him. 'Are you well enough, William?'

187

'I'll be fine, Eric.' Preston offered Ben a courteous nod. 'Mr Lambert has strapped me up well.'

'First light, then,' said Keats. 'Reckon we want to have at least two dozen men with guns readied to fire. Might want to be ready if we bump into 'em Paiute. They're out there nearby for sure.'

There were murmurs of agreement amongst the gathered men.

'What are we going to tell the others?' asked Mr Larkin. 'About what did this to the Dreytons?'

'Reckon we'll tell 'em it's a bear for now,' growled Keats, 'till we know better.'

Preston cocked his head. 'You may tell your party what you wish.'

'So what're you goin' to tell yours?'

'It was the work of those demons out there!' snapped Vander.

'You forget,' replied Ben quietly, 'that one of those *demons* died bringing Emily back to us.'

'The Devil likes to play games with the innocent, Mr Lambert.' Preston spoke softly. 'There's sport in that for him. For now, until we know a little more, we shall tell our people to pray for Dorothy and Samuel. We shall assemble a party in the morning.'

Preston stood up, his head dipped beneath the low ceiling. 'This meeting is done now.' He uttered a short prayer, then dismissed them. The men filed out into the weakening sunlight. Vanilla rays lanced through the tree tops, bathing their small world in cream where they landed, and leaving violet shadows where they didn't.

Preston touched Ben lightly on the arm as he followed in Keats's wake.

'Mr Lambert.'

'Yes?'

'Might I have another dose of your medicine tonight, for the pain?'

Ben studied his pale features. 'Is it that bad?'

Preston nodded. 'It gives me a merciful release from it.'

He thought about it for a moment. 'A small dose then.'

'Whatever you think is correct.' Preston smiled.

'I'll return with the bottle after I have checked in on Emily,' he said and then turned to catch up with Keats.

Preston watched them go, then stepped back inside the church, shuddering at the transition from bitter cold to the pleasant warmth left behind by the accumulated bodies.

'I'm worried about Saul,' said Vander from the gloom inside.

Preston's eyes slowly adjusted and found him sitting on the cot. He sighed sadly.

'William, you know it was necessary. She would have spread doubt amongst the others about you.'

Preston slumped down wearily beside Vander. 'I know. They need me now, more than ever. But I wish in my heart it had been anyone other than Dorothy who was troubled with doubt. She was so devoted.'

Vander nodded.

'And now we have to wonder what has happened to Saul,' said Preston. 'Perhaps it might have been the bear, perhaps the Indians.'

'And Emily? What did she see?'

Preston nodded regretfully. 'What might she say?' He turned to Vander. 'I love her too, like all my children.'

'God needs you strong, William.'

'I know.'

Ben ducked down and entered the shelter. Its frame was sturdier than the one he shared with Keats and Broken Wing. The Mormon men had constructed, for Dorothy and her children, a firm lumber frame from their wagon, large enough for three or four people to sit together in, but only tall enough to kneel in.

By the light of a single candle he could see Emily huddled away from the entrance, wrapped in several blankets, her knees pulled up to her chest, and staring blankly into space. Lying beside her was Mrs Zimmerman, sadly stroking the girl's forehead and singing a lullaby. She stopped to look up at him.

'Mrs Zimmerman,' Ben said politely, nodding. 'How is she?'

'She's gone far away from here.'

He knelt down next to the girl. 'God only knows what she witnessed.'

Ben looked closely at her face, moving his hand to and fro in front of her dilated pupils, with no reaction.

'She's not spoken?'

'Not a word. Not a single word,' she replied, studying Emily's pale face. 'Truth be, Mr Lambert, I have never seen fear so bad as that in my life.'

He shuffled closer to her, unwinding his poncho and draping it over Emily's blanket-covered body.

'I've seen shock like this before: industrial accidents brought into the London hospital where I was studying. Shock . . . the mind closes down to shut out the pain, and yet can still function amazingly well. I once witnessed a man walking in carrying his own arm under the other. Machinery had wrenched it out at the shoulder.'

Mrs Zimmerman made a face.

'The point is, the mind is very resilient. Emily's has shut down for now . . . from what she's witnessed. I can only presume it was something quite horrific. And now, her mind is in a dormant state, hiding . . . hibernating somewhere safe.'

'But she'll come back to us eventually, won't she?'

Ben nodded. 'Eventually.'

'What happened, Mr Lambert? Do you know?'

'Eric Vander thinks it was the Indians did this. Keats says it might have been a bear.'

Mrs Zimmerman nodded tiredly.

'Tomorrow morning there'll be a search party and we'll find out all that we need to know,' he said.

Ben knew it would be a hard find, chancing across their bodies. Hard, in as much as he would see Sam in a horrible way. If it had been a bear, their bodies would be horrendously disfigured. It was not a final image he wanted to have in his mind of the lad.

I'm so sorry, Emily. So sorry.

He stroked her pale cheeks, remembering a cheerful face around the campfire, delighted with the loan of a doll.

'I'll look in on her again soon,' Ben said to Mrs Zimmerman. 'Will you be with her tonight?'

Mrs Zimmerman nodded. 'All night.'

Ben smiled. 'Good.'

CHAPTER 38

cave iram Dei

Tuesday
Fulham, London

The phone rang only a couple of times before a deep voice answered it. 'Dr Thomas Griffith.'

'Tom, it's Julian Cooke.'

A moment's hesitation passed. 'Julian . . .' Then, 'Julian! How the hell are you?'

'I'm well, Tom, very well.'

Julian had worked with him a few years ago on their series *Uncommon People*. Dr Griffith was a forensic psychologist who freelanced for the Met, on occasion for the Crown Prosecution Service and, more often these days, he also found himself contributing the foreword to books on hard-case East End gangsters and the criminally insane. His last collaboration had been with a crime novelist, co-writing a book on Harold Shipman.

The book was doing very well. Julian had noticed it piled high on the centre tables of Waterstones and Borders, and spotted Thomas on daytime TV shamelessly plugging it. Thomas was made for TV; a gregarious character, a large and generously covered frame and an enormously deep voice finely tuned to deliver a Welsh accent.

It was all going very well for Thomas, right now.

'What are you up to these days, Julian?' his baritone voice boomed down the line.

Julian sucked on his teeth. He knew the call was going to involve eating a small helping of humble pie.

'Not as much as I'd like. Business is still coming in, but you know what it's like; a lot less money sloshing around the TV business these days.'

'Indeed.'

'I saw your book. Doing very well, I see.'

'Yes, isn't it? I'm quite taken aback. There'll be more, I hope.'

Julian smiled. 'Oh, I'm sure there will be. Publishers love to keep backing a winner.' Actually he was pleased for the lucky bastard. Good fortune couldn't have fallen into the lap of a nicer bloke.

'Tom, look, apart from wanting to hear the melted-chocolate tones of your voice again, there's another reason I rang.'

Griffith chuckled. 'Go on.'

'It's something I sort of stumbled upon by accident over in America. Before I go into too much detail, this is between us and no one else, do you understand?'

'Of course.'

'I'm not going to need to send you a confidentiality agreement, am I?' Julian asked cautiously. He trusted the man more than most. Thomas's word had been good in the past when they'd worked together. But it would be reassuring to hear him make a verbal promise.

'On my mother's grave, Julian.'

'Okay.'

Julian explained what he and Rose had found, careful not to tell him exactly where it was. Only Grace knew the precise location, and for now he wanted to keep it that way. He described the Lambert journal, and summarised the tale he had transcribed thus far. Dr Griffith patiently listened in silence as Julian talked through it for nearly three-quarters of an hour.

'Well now, Julian, what're you asking for? A diagnosis over the phone?'

'Yes, but I'd like to back it up with a meeting. Perhaps, if you're interested, involve you in the documentary somehow.'

'Well, I'm . . . I'm—'

'Sorry, Tom, I didn't mean to put you on the spot like that. I know you're busy right now promoting the book—'

'No,' he cut in, 'no . . . I'm interested, Julian. I'm fascinated. I'd very much like to be a part of this. I mean, to all intents and purposes, if we're ruling out Indian wood spirits and giant grizzly bears, it sounds very much like you have a reliable account of an interesting mystery.'

'Yes. That's what I thought.'

'And this journal sounds like wonderfully detailed material to work from.'

'It *is* very detailed. I mean, the author obviously had a lot of time to fill, waiting to die up in those mountains. So look . . . I presume we're both thinking it's the same person?'

'The religious leader chappie.'

'Uh-huh, Preston.'

He heard Griffith shuffling position, the sloshing of water in the background, and remembered the large Welshman kept his phone by his side, even in the bath.

'A fascinating character by the sound of him. A classic cult patriarch, isn't he?'

'Yeah. Look, Tom, I can email you what I've transcribed already of the journal, and attach a load of jpeg images of the other pages I've yet to work through, if you're interested in taking this further?'

'Yes, please do.'

'And then when you've had a chance to look through, per-haps we can arrange to get together for lunch and talk about it?'

'That would be marvellous,' Griffith boomed back.

'Great. Your email address – still the same?'

'As always.'

'I'll put "*Preston*" as the subject heading so you don't miss it amidst all the spam.'

'Very good.'

'How long do you want to have with the material? Thing is, I'm here in the UK for another three days, then I'm heading back out to the States to rejoin Rose. We've got to move quite quickly.'

'Why's that? It's sat around a century and a half already.'

'We've got a grace period of a couple of weeks, courtesy of a kind old park ranger who's sitting on it before she calls whatever US heritage department covers this kind of find. So, we're scrambling around to get as much virgin footage of the site as we can.'

'I see. Well, hmm . . . you've caught me at a good time. I could do with a break from the current routine. Give me a day with the notes, and then we'll talk.'

'Thanks.'

'Oh, and Julian?'

'Yup?'

'Do you know how it ends? What do you know of what happened?'

'As far as we can surmise, no one survived. There's no record of it anywhere.'

'Oh that's good – somewhat chilling,' he said, the water sloshing again. 'I like that.'

Julian smiled. 'I thought you would.'

'Well, send me what you have, and then we'll do lunch later on this week. I'll make sure my publicist keeps Thursday and Friday lunchtimes free.'

'I will. It's been good to speak to you again, Tom. Been a while.'

'And you.'

Dr Griffith hung up abruptly and the line purred. Julian was about to set his phone down when he heard the faintest click over the earpiece. The purring sound cut out momentarily and he thought he could detect, if only for a second or two, the rustling sound of movement picked up by an open microphone. Then another click, and the purr resumed.

He put the phone down, still looking at it.

'That's . . . that was odd,' he muttered.

And not the first odd thing, either, is it?

Returning from a visit to the Soup Kitchen office earlier today, he had an inexplicable feeling that his flat had been entered. Not quite able to put his finger on the tiny, intangible details that made him think that – a book out of place, the mouse cable coiled differently around the back of the keyboard – he hadn't been certain enough not to dismiss it as some sort of creeping paranoia.

But now this.

He looked again at the phone, long enough to convince himself that all he'd really heard was a digital gremlin on the network or, quite possibly, his line crossed with another for a fleeting moment.

He shook his head reproachfully. 'Come on, Julian, get a grip.'

CHAPTER 39

24 October, 1856

A light downfall of snow during the night had not managed to fully conceal the trail left by the Indian; there were enough dark patches of almost black blood that had soaked into the snow and were now a frozen part of it.

Keats led the way up through the trees, his keen eyes squinting and watering from the dazzling upward reflection of sunlight off the snow. The sky was a clear blue, combed with one or two unthreatening clouds, and the sun beat down a welcome warmth on their backs and shoulders as they went uphill, moving between the trees from one splatter of frozen blood to the next.

A search party had not been painstakingly chosen; the old guide had simply emerged from his lean-to as soon as the sun had breached the tree line, and bellowed out with his foghorn voice that he was ready to go and wanted some volunteers.

Within a few minutes every single man and boy old enough to carry a gun had mustered in the centre of the camp around Keats and Broken Wing. Preston joined him promptly and then they dismissed roughly half the men to stay behind and guard the camp. The other half, eighteen men including the two trail captains, set off swiftly from the clearing and up the shallow bank of the forest floor, through saplings stripped bare for kindling and into the deep foliage of older trees.

They followed the trail for only about ten minutes, just long enough to lose sight of the camp below, climb a small spur and descend the other side towards a small glade beyond, when Broken Wing suddenly raised a hand and shouted out something in Ute.

Keats pulled his pipe out of his mouth and muttered, 'This is where it happened all right. Jus' up ahead.'

They emerged from the trees. Even dusted with snow and no bodies to be seen, it was clear a butcher's blade had been hard at work here. A log, lying across the clearing, was slick with glassy frozen blood and beside it on the ground was what looked like a small heap of offal.

Ben took a few tentative steps towards it, knelt down and inspected it more closely. It reminded him fleetingly of the regular invitation-only demonstrations carried out, *sectio cadaveris*, in the lecture theatre off Threadneedle Street, on the illegally obtained cadavers of the hanged – the organs removed one by one, discussed, then discarded upon a growing grey and glistening pile.

'I'm afraid these are human,' said Ben. 'I'm certain of that.' He looked at the guide. 'So, we know that, at the very least, one of them is dead,' he added sombrely, feeling his voice thicken with emotion. He swallowed and steadied himself.

I can grieve for Sam later . . . but not now.

Keats hunkered down beside him and prodded the pile with a stick. It was frozen solid. 'Guess this little guttin' job must've been done yesterday,' he said quietly.

Ben nodded.

'Bear don't gut his food before eatin' it, not that I know of anyhow.'

Broken Wing, squatting on his haunches nearby, perfectly still, was reading the ground. His eyes traced a narrative out of the disturbed snow, his lips moving silently, telling him the tale. All of a sudden he stood up and strode across the glade, past Preston and the other men.

'What is it?' the minister asked.

In the middle of the glade, the snow had been trampled and disturbed more noticeably, and a curved arc of spattered blood was inscribed brightly across it.

'Issss fighting here,' he said, pointing to the blood. 'Cut bad.'

Keats joined him. 'Someone got cut bad all right,' he said. The splatter arc was a grisly curl of dark crimson. 'Fatal bad, I reckon.' He looked around. 'I guess it was that Paiute boy.' He nodded in the direction they had come. 'It's his blood we been following up here.'

Broken Wing walked towards the bloodied log, stooped down and studied the ground. He spoke in Ute to Keats.

'He says the Paiute boy picked your girl up over there, beside the log, an' ran into the woods with her in his arms.'

Keats turned to Preston. 'Brave young lad.'

He offered no response, his eyes locked on the confusing tapestry of blood and suggested movements written in the hard snow.

The guide squatted down and studied the ground near the log for a moment, his teeth clamping noisily on the stem of his pipe as he sucked a meagre mouthful of smoke from fading embers in the bowl.

Something caught Broken Wing's eye and he brushed aside this morning's light dusting to reveal twin grooves of compacted snow, stained dark and now as solid as ice. He nudged Keats and pointed.

Keats brushed more of the snow away. 'Hey, Lambert, look at this,' he said.

Ben took a couple of steps over, stepping past the men who had gathered closer to see what Keats was so interested in. He knelt down beside him and looked at the grooves.

'What is that?'

Keats pointed with the long stem of his pipe. 'Heel marks. Reckon a body was dragged away.' He pointed to dark stains smeared along the ice-hard grooves. 'Still bleedin' like a stuck pig whilst it was dragged, I guess.'

Ben inwardly winced at the thoughtless choice of words.

Broken Wing brushed aside more of this morning's light powder, standing up and following the parallel grooves across the clearing towards the edge of the glade. Ben followed him and joined him there, looking through the foliage in front of him. He could discern a clear path of dislodged snow, the crushed stems of brambles and briar, flattened fern leaves and broken twigs, spotted here and there with dots and splatters of blood.

The others joined them and stared intently at the unmistakable trail left behind.

'Whoever it was left tracks a blind man could follow,' said Ben.

Preston stroked his bearded chin. 'Whoever?'

'Reckon we're past lookin' for a bear now,' Keats nodded. 'That leaves us, Indians, or demons . . . whichever you prefer. Ain't made no effort to hide their trail, neither.'

Broken Wing pointed to another pair of faint parallel grooves, and spoke in his tongue.

'Second trail there,' said Keats.

Ben could see it. A second path through the undergrowth out of the clearing, but along this one there were no evident spots of blood.

'Came back a while later an' dragged another body away. Only I reckon this one was frozen up by then.'

Ben nodded and his heart sank when he realised what it meant. 'They both died here then,' he uttered.

Keats offered him a rare gesture, placing a hand on his arm. 'Maybe not. There's the other fella still missing. Seems like we only got two bodies so far.' He knelt down and studied the flattened path through the foliage. 'Maybe some hours passed 'tween taking the first body and comin' for the second.'

Bowen stepped forward. 'Are you sure this is no bear, Keats?'

Keats shrugged. 'Carryin' food away like this is jus' what a bear does. They do that . . . store their food, pack it in a nook somewhere like a goddamn pantry. But' – he turned to look up

200

at him – 'they sure as hell don't gut an' clean their kills. Them organs back there is just as good for a bear as the rest.'

'We should press on,' said Ben quietly.

'Yeah.' Keats turned round and barked over his shoulder. 'We'll follow this trail.'

'Gentlemen,' called out Weyland from the back, 'what if there *is* a bear up ahead?'

Keats shook his head, looked at Ben, exasperated. 'Reckon 'tween our eighteen guns we might jus' bring it down,' he shouted in response.

'What if it's them Indians?' asked someone else.

'Then reckon we got us a fight on our hands.'

'And what if they are demons sent by Satan?' asked Levi Taylor, one of the younger fathers amongst Preston's church. 'What if they're here to get us?'

There was a murmur of assent amongst the Mormon men.

Preston quietened them down with a wave of his hand. 'We should proceed and have no fear of the Devil's impish tricks. Trust me. We're on God's mission.' He turned to Ben and Keats. 'And it is right that Dorothy and Sam have a proper burial, when we find them.'

'I agree,' Zimmerman piped up from the back. 'There's no way we should leave them out for the forest animals to pick at.'

Keats stood up. 'Well? We gonna sit around like a bunch of lady folk,' he grunted, 'or we gonna go find 'em?'

Preston nodded firmly. 'Lead the way if you will, Mr Keats.'

Keats glanced round at the group of anxious men. 'Just remember, folks, we got them goddamned Indians out here in these woods still.'

Ben looked at the snow-frosted tangle of branches, ferns and long-fallen trees ahead of them and wondered whether he would shame himself if they happened across these Paiute.

'Keep your guns nice an' handy,' Keats grunted loudly, 'and don't be bunchin' up right behind me, neither. If I need to turn an' run, don't want to be runnin' smack into one of you fools.'

There was a ripple of hesitant, nervous mirth from one or two of the party as the old man nodded to Broken Wing to lead the way, stepping out of the glade and pushing his way into the foliage, his beady eyes locked onto the frozen dabs of blood that marked the way ahead.

Ben followed him, a few yards behind.

CHAPTER 40

24 October, 1856

As they made their way down a shallow incline, Keats ten yards ahead of them, Broken Wing ten yards further, the Shoshone suddenly dropped down onto one knee and waved for everyone behind to do likewise. The men did so obediently.

Broken Wing studied the scene intently for a couple of minutes before silently shuffling back to Keats and relaying what he'd seen.

Ben suddenly got his bearings and recognised the lay of the land, the dimple in the hillside . . .

The trapper's shelter.

Around them, the forest was utterly still and completely silent save for the distant and knowing cry from a cowbird he could see through the winter-stripped branches of a spruce, flying impatient circles high above the trees. Huddled low amongst frozen ferns and twisted thorny briars, Ben's breath hung before him – anxious clouds of steam that floated lazily up like smoke from the muzzle of a musket. He shivered in the knee-deep snow, partly from the seeping cold, partly from the anticipation.

Whatever had done for Sam and his mother had dragged their bodies up here to this forlorn place. He dreaded what he *knew* they were going to find.

Keats finally waved an arm for the men to make their way forward and join him.

Ben shuffled forward with the others and presently they knelt beside him, looking out past shoulder-high undergrowth down a shallow slope at the crudely constructed shack, more of it concealed by drifts of recent snow than the last time he'd seen it.

'Trapper's place, by the looks of it,' whispered Keats. 'No sign anybody been using it recently, though.'

'It's abandoned,' said Preston.

Keats turned to him. 'What?'

'We came across it some days ago. It's not been used in years.'

'You didn't think to goddamn well mention it to me?'

Preston frowned indignantly. 'It's a man's grave.'

'Why the hell ain't you told me 'bout it?'

'I'd rather people didn't come up here and strip it for firewood. The dead man inside deserves at least that.'

Keats shook his head, hawked and spat. 'Didn't occur to you that them Paiute might be camping in it now?'

Ben expected Preston to thunder an angry response to save face in front of his men. But instead he was impressed to see the minister nod humbly. 'You're right, Keats. I should have mentioned it.'

Keats scowled at him. 'Yeah, perhaps you should've.' He turned to look back at the shelter. 'Preston, have your men spread out and along this ridge and ready their guns. We got a good field of fire on 'em if they're inside.'

Preston nodded and issued the word quietly to his people.

Keats stood up and handed his rifle to Ben.

'What're you doing?'

'If them Paiute are inside . . . gonna go talk to 'em first.'

Keats strode down the incline casually, Broken Wing beside him, and called out in Ute, making enough noise to ensure his approach would be clearly heard by anyone inside. At the bottom of the incline he walked across the clearing, between the old wooden hanging frames a few yards away from the small entrance, and called out again loudly.

From inside the shelter came a sound of startled movement. Ben instinctively flexed his finger on the trigger and lined his sight on the small rounded entrance at the front. A moment later the dangling tatters of canvas that hung down from the door-frame fluttered to one side as several crows emerged, their wings a frantic confusion of dislodged feathers and panic. He watched them flap noisily away, strings of crimson dangling from their beaks.

Battlefield scavengers.

That was how his father used to refer to these birds. As a much younger man, a junior officer in the British army, he had witnessed the morning-after carpet of battle. He had described to Ben seeing the ground undulate with the shimmering beetle-blue of crows' feathers as they worked on the bloated bodies, and the sky darken with their startled wings – swarming like flies at the sound of a discharged gun, only to return moments later with a renewed vigour to feast on the soft faces of the dead.

Ben waited anxiously along with the others, his rifle braced against his shoulder and aimed at the entrance.

'If there are Indians in there, they must sleep like the dead,' muttered Weyland, one eye squinting down the barrel of his gun.

'Maybe Indian dead too,' whispered Hussein in reply.

Weyland took a deep breath and let it out in a cloud. 'I'm not sure I'd find that entirely reassuring, Mr Hussein.'

Broken Wing called out, his sharp voice cracking with the effort. It was the first time Ben had heard the Indian speak in anything other than a soft murmur.

There was no further sign or sound of movement from inside. With a casual hand gesture to Broken Wing, Keats stepped forward. One hand resting on the hilt of his hunting knife, he pushed the tattered canvas flap aside and then cautiously stepped inside and out of sight.

'The old boy's got balls of iron,' whispered McIntyre beside him. 'Walking in like that.'

Hussein nodded. 'He has much . . . kuh . . . cour . . . ?'

'Courage?' offered Weyland.

'Yes. Is much *courage* inside him. Much.'

'That's for sure,' McIntyre whispered.

A full minute passed in silence before the flap finally jerked aside and Keats emerged, stooping low through the entrance and then standing erect. Ben watched him breathing deeply for a moment, hands on hips, like someone mustering something from inside. He leaned over and spat . . . or maybe he was heaving — it was hard to tell.

What's he seen in there?

Keats wiped his mouth, his cheeks puffed and a languid cloud of vapour rose. Then he turned towards them and silently waved at them to come down and join him.

They rose as one and clambered down the incline, stumbling carelessly on the snow-blanketed branches, twigs and roots, dislodging little cascades of powder that sifted with a gentle hiss down the slope towards the clearing.

Preston approached Keats. 'You found the body of the trapper in there?'

'The trapper? Oh, yeah. I noticed him as well.'

Ben regarded Keats's weather-worn face and saw something in those narrow eyes he'd never seen before.

As well?

'Preston, you better come look inside with me.' He turned to the rest of the men, gathered together in front of the entrance. 'Rest of you spread out an' keep your eyes wide open.'

He took another deep breath before stooping down, pushing the canvas aside and leading the way in. Preston looked around for a moment at his men and nodded. 'Do as he says,' he said curtly. He turned to Vander. 'Eric, you come with me,' he said and then followed Keats inside.

Outside, the men spread out in no particular pattern, gazing uncertainly at the wooden hanging frames and the bones of animals dangling from them, the macabre decoration of the row of animal skulls nailed to one of the shelter's walls.

Weyland sauntered over to where Ben and Broken Wing stood a few yards from the doorway.

'Can't say I've ever been amidst so many trees and heard it as quiet as this,' he almost whispered. 'Can you hear, Ben? No birdsong at all.'

Broken Wing frowned for a moment as he processed Weyland's drawl, then nodded. 'Bad spirit ssscare birds.'

'It's unnatural,' Ben heard himself reply, and then immediately cursed himself for sounding like some superstitious old crone.

'That it most definitely is,' Weyland said nervously, stroking the handles of his moustache. 'Very unnatural.'

They heard footsteps coming from inside the shelter; a rapid scraping of feet and then Vander emerged with a face as white as the snow on the ground. He took several staggering steps away from the shack before vomiting.

'Lambert!' he heard Keats calling from inside.

Ben exchanged a look with Weyland and Broken Wing and then headed towards the entrance. He shot one last glance at Vander, emptying his guts onto the snow – a steaming puddle of bile that quickly sank down through the fresh powder and out of sight.

Let it not be Sam . . . please.

He took a final breath of crisp, cold air, suspecting the next breath he took would be tainted with the fetid odour of . . . something. He ducked down and pushed his way past the canvas flap.

CHAPTER 41

24 October, 1856

For a moment he stood stock still. It was too dark to make sense of his cluttered surroundings. He allowed a moment for his eyes to adjust.

'Lambert,' he heard Keats's voice growl quietly, 'over here.'

Soon he could pick out the dark shapes around him. He shuffled his foot forward, finding, to his surprise, two very steep steps taking him down.

The floor of the shelter was dug out of the ground.

Of course, that made sense. The shelter was more protected from the elements this way and that much more insulated. Ben had expected to be stooping uncomfortably as he made his way through the interior. Instead, having taken two steps down, he was standing erect. He reached a hand up and found a foot clearance above his head before his fingers brushed against branches and dried mud, crumbs of which rattled down through his fingers.

Thin beams of light speared down through slender cracks in the roof and front wall, dappling the uneven earthen floor with pin-pricks of light.

His eyes adjusted, he could make out some things he expected to see: bales of dried and compressed beaver pelts, traps hanging from hooks on the wall along with a few simple tools with which to work wood, and a bag of long iron lumber nails. On a crude workbench he saw skinning and gutting knives, a tub of salt . . .

He heard the shuffling of feet nearby. 'This way, Lambert,' Keats grunted again quietly.

He looked towards where the voice had come from and saw the shack was divided by a flimsy partitioning wall – no more than a row of stout branches standing vertically side by side from floor to ceiling, and a wattle of strips of bark woven through them. Keats stood in a gap in the middle of the partition staring impatiently at him.

'In here,' he said. 'We found one of 'em.'

Ben felt his heart sink. 'Which one?'

Keats offered him a weak smile. 'It ain't Sam,' he reassured him quietly.

He made his way towards the opening, but Keats remained where he was, blocking his way. He leaned forward so that the bristles of his beard almost tickled Ben's face. 'You done a bunch of doctorin' . . . so I guess you'll be readier than Vander was. It's the Hearst fella.'

Ben felt a small rush of relief and then felt immediately guilty. 'What condition is the body in?'

'Well, it ain't pretty,' he whispered.

Ben nodded, took a deep breath and vowed silently that he'd remain calm and composed in front of the other two men. Keats stepped to one side and allowed him through.

This second half of the shelter was smaller. It was where the trapper once slept. There was a small gap in one wall, a deliberate hole – a window of sorts – that was almost entirely plugged by the snowdrift outside. It allowed enough diffused light in to the dark interior that he could immediately discern what he'd been called in to examine.

'Oh my God,' he whispered.

Nailed to the wall with several of the long lumber nails he'd seen on the workbench, was the naked body of Saul Hearst. He was pinned upside down in a parody of the crucifixion posture, his arms splayed, one nail through each wrist, and his feet crossed, a single nail through both of them. From his pelvis to his chest, a knife had been at work. He had been comprehensively gutted, and hung against the wall like a carcass of prime beef in a butcher's shop. There was surprisingly little blood there, and no sign of the removed organs.

Keats looked at him quizzically.

Ben nodded. 'Yes, I presume those organs would have to be his.'

For the first time he registered Preston. He was standing with his back against the partition wall and staring at the man, his deep eyes locked in a silent expression of fear. His lips moved soundlessly.

A prayer.

Over and over.

Ben took a reluctant step closer to the cadaver. And as he did so, his eyes registered something written along one of Hearst's pale thighs. Closer still he realised the words were not written on the skin – they were carved into it . . . letters formed from the small, precise slashes of a sharp blade.

'You can read it?' asked Keats.

Ben nodded. He glanced at the left thigh. '*For all his dirty sins.*'

'Anyone know what the hell that means?' growled Keats.

Ben shook his head. They both turned to look at Preston. 'You're a preacher,' said Keats, 'an' that sounds to me like *God talk*. Mean anythin' to you?'

Preston's eyes flickered off the corpse to look at them. He was about to say something, and then shook his head. 'No, I have no idea what this could mean.'

Ben studied the intense stillness of Preston's face, a rigid mask concealing a head full of secrets that clearly he was unprepared to share with them right now.

'Well, one thing's for sure,' grunted Keats, 'reckon it ain't them Paiute. Not less they learned 'emselves to read an' write all of a sudden.'

Preston's eyes turned back on Hearst's body. He looked like a condemned man taking the last few steps up a scaffold and catching his very first sight of the hangman's noose.

The bastard's holding something back.

Ben was about to ask Preston again what those carved words meant, when they heard raised voices coming from outside the shelter. Keats was the first to react, leading the way as they stumbled clumsily through the cluttered interior up the two deep steps and emerged outside.

McIntyre was striding towards them. 'We found the others!' he shouted breathlessly. 'Through the trees over there,' he said, pointing past the wooden hanging frames. They made their way there, McIntyre leading them around a thicket of twisted and tangled brambles and presently they stood before a recently dug grave. Poking through last night's light snowfall could be seen the dark peaty colour of a mound of freshly turned soil. There had apparently been no attempt at concealing it – quite the opposite. The burial mound was topped with a cross; two short lengths of branch crudely lashed together with twine. The entire party of men crowded around the grave, as Preston, Keats and Ben pushed to the front.

'So where's the other grave?' asked Keats.

'Just one grave,' said McIntyre. 'They're both in it together.'

Ben looked at him. 'Both?'

McIntyre nodded. 'Sorry, Ben.' He pointed to the grave where two holes had already been dug into the freshly turned soil. 'We had to dig to be sure who was here.'

Ben stepped towards the grave and saw what he recognised as the dark pattern of Mrs Dreyton's shawl and the pale lace bonnet. Beneath the flowery trim of her bonnet he could see that her face had been slashed, dried blood caked her cheeks and the eyes, nostrils and mouth were plugged with soil.

Another hole had been dug on the other side of the mound and already he could see Sam's forearm, his white shirt dirty and stained, one of his strong young man's hands curled up like an old man's arthritic claw and discoloured a dark brown by death.

Ben recognised that as the inevitable pooling of immobile blood beneath the skin.

'Please cover them over now!' snapped Preston.

Ben nodded. He'd seen enough too.

McIntyre, using the butt of his rifle as a spade, began pushing the dislodged soil back into the holes.

'Gentlemen, we also discovered the body of Saul Hearst in the shelter,' announced Preston, more for the benefit of his men than Keats's people. 'There is now, I'm certain, an evil at work in these woods. The misfortune of our wagon, the early snow, the attack of the bear, the dark savages nearby . . . these are agents of the Devil, sent here to test us, to torment us.'

There were murmurs, whispers amongst the men. Ben saw several of them bow their heads in prayer.

'You must trust me. God has a mission for us, a destiny for us, and the Devil does not like that. He has found us, and now tries his tricks and strategies. We will return to our camp and pray for the Dreytons. Tonight I will talk with God and seek his guidance.'

Preston waved at his men to move out. They turned away from the grave and headed across the clearing towards the shallow slope.

'What about your man, Saul?' Ben called out. 'Don't you want to bury him?'

Preston turned round. 'We'll not return here again. This is an evil place. Do you not feel it? We're leaving. You're best coming too.'

'What about Saul?'

'Saul is in the same place as Dorothy and Sam now, Lambert – a much better place than this.' Preston turned back round and led his men up the slope, pushing knee-deep through the snow.

'I . . . I'm leaving with them,' said McIntyre. 'I can feel it too. This is no place to hang around.' He set off after the others.

Broken Wing nodded and muttered to himself, looking at the thick apron of foliage around the small clearing, then followed McIntyre.

212

'What did he say?' asked Ben.

Keats shook his head. 'Damned superstitious Indian.'

'What did he say?'

'He said he could feel the white-face spirit watching us from the trees.'

Weyland grinned nervously. 'If you'll excuse me, I think I might join them.'

Keats snorted and spat. 'Might as well. Ain't nothing we can do for 'em now.' He headed off after the others, leaving Ben alone.

Ben turned to look back at the grave. 'I'm so sorry, Sam. I would have taken you with me come the spring. You, your mother and Emily.'

He turned to leave and then stopped and turned back round. 'I'll take care of Emily for you. She'll come with me. I promise you that.'

CHAPTER 42

cave iram Dei

M	T	W	T	F	S	S
				1	2	3
4	5	6	7	8	9	10
11	12	13	14	15	16	17
18	19	20	21	22	23	24
25	26	27	28	29	30	

Tuesday
Claremont, Colorado

Shepherd watched the soccer match with feigned interest, smiling, clapping and cheering at all the right moments – as far as he could tell. The young boys playing on the pitch before him in no more than flimsy nylon shirts and shorts looked under-equipped and too willowy to his eye to be playing a proper sport. A strong gust of wind would carry them all away like a bundle of red and blue twigs.

He preferred a good wholesome all-American sport like football, where sheer brute willpower, strength of heart and tactical guile normally won the day, unlike this peculiar game that seemed to turn on the mere lucky bounce of a round ball.

He sighed.

A sign of the times.

It seemed just about every boy and girl wanted to play this imported game these days. No doubt because it looked like an easy sport to play and master, unlike football.

The referee blew his whistle at some minor infraction.

The Mayor leaned towards him. 'Offside,' he muttered. Shepherd nodded politely, none the wiser, as he watched the young boys waiting for play to resume, all of them gasping clouds into the cool winter air. It was a heartless grey day with a wintry bite on the breeze. A light mist veiled the edge of the sports field, but the strong turnout of parents and church friends on this distinctly autumnal Sunday afternoon spoke of a strong local community.

Good Christian people, all of them, he thought with a smile, *despite liking this ridiculous game.*

Duncan, his campaign manager, had briefed him that the statistics team was reporting strong grassroots support here in this part of Colorado, almost as strong as it was in Utah. The people here liked what they'd already seen of him on the main cable stations, and the prominent coverage he was beginning to get on FOX. Perhaps even more encouraging was the fact that not many of them were members of the Mormon faith. His appeal was beginning to hit a wider vein.

'That's incredibly important,' Duncan had said. 'Thirteen million Americans, all members of the Church of Latter Day Saints, are votes in the bank for you come polling day. But that isn't enough. We've got just over eighteen months of campaigning to broaden your support beyond the Mormon community into the soft conservative Christian Right.'

Shepherd clapped along with the rest of the assembled parents at a narrowly saved shot at the goal.

It was a big task for an independent to try and pull off. However, it seemed both of the other parties – up to their necks in sleaze and allegations of corruption and nasty, dirty backbiting between their leading candidates – were doing most of the hard work for him.

Of course, if things continued on their current trajectory, sometime soon the Democrats and the Republicans were both going to realise they were leaking votes to him and would start working hard, perhaps even together, to dish the dirt on him.

They were going to come up empty-handed.

William Shepherd wasn't distracted by bubbly blonde interns, or lithe young call boys; his hands had never wandered where they weren't wanted. Nor had he ever felt the need to roll a joint or snort a line of coke, defraud a pension fund, buy

215

shares with inside information, bribe a court official or involve himself in any spurious land deals. They could dig all they liked; they were going to find no skeletons in his cupboard. No foul-smelling crap was going to stick to him.

His old-fashioned message gave him the air of some character out of a Norman Rockwell painting, made him sound like someone from another century, but that was just fine. The politically correct liberal media might wince at his unfashionable values and the rabid right-wing radio jocks might scoff at his naive aphorisms, but his voice was hitting all the right notes with an ever-growing audience of frightened Americans. Their world was sliding towards increasing instability; a weakened dollar, punitive interest rates, a plummeting jobs market . . . a simple and reassuring message that promised redemption was all they were after; a message delivered by someone who didn't reek of bullshit.

The large crowd of eager parents and local civil dignitaries around him in the stalls cheered jubilantly as the ball flew into the back of one of the nets. Shepherd nodded, applauded and smiled, his mind elsewhere.

There was something, though, something that he'd never confided to Duncan. Shepherd smiled. If Duncan only knew . . . if his campaign supporters only knew . . . they'd run a mile. His sights were set somewhat higher than the Oval Office.

It's out there somewhere . . . in the Sierras.

He could see it in his dreams, buried somewhere in the deep woods, perhaps in a secure travel chest; seasons changing above it like the seconds on a ticking clock, years, decades drifting by, and there it sat, waiting to be found.

Shepherd had tried and failed. As a younger man with a lot more time on his hands there had been quite a few hikes taken into those mountains, going on whatever hunch was driving him at the time, listening to the inner whisper of divine guidance. But, there was a lot of wilderness to cover out amongst those wooded mountains. It wasn't like trying to locate a downed plane — at least something like that left a noticeable impact and burn scarring. The Preston party's camp would now, he surmised, be little more than barely detectable humps on the forest floor.

He sighed.

Somewhere out there.

And now, it seemed, like Bilbo Baggins ill-deservedly happening across a certain ring, there was one *Julian Cooke* who had stumbled across the place where they lay buried. He knew it would happen one day; a hiker, a party of drunken hunters, a bunch of teens goofing around in tents . . .

Something of a conundrum, this man Cooke: someone he needed badly, and at the same time someone he needed like a bullet in the head. It seemed from his email traffic that this Cooke could lead him directly to the place where Preston's people had vanished. Which made him someone he very much wanted to sit down and talk with. On the other hand, this British guy was talking to other people now. If he kept doing that, talking to many more people, he could become something of a liability. The collection of meetings he'd been holding with his media buddies over in London wasn't good news. He suspected that none of them would probe any deeper than an intriguing survival story set during the days of the old west. But there was always the possibility that someone might be clever enough . . . *intuitive* enough, to join together some very obscure dots.

The call that concerned him the most was the long one Cooke had had with the forensic psychologist, focusing on Preston.

It was a little too close for comfort.

Something like Preston's story was the one and only thing that could come and bite him in the ass when he least needed it.

'Politics is about nothing more than nuance . . . finesse.' Another of Duncan's very true maxims. 'Something as trivial as a badly timed facial boil, the tiniest speech fumble or a badly behaved distant nephew can lose you a million votes.'

To be associated, in any way, with what had happened out

there, albeit over a century and a half ago, could be damaging, very damaging.

He wondered if it wouldn't be prudent to deal with Cooke sooner rather than later. This Julian Cooke, a man with a modest level of success in the past, something of a fading star now, was running what appeared to be a failing business – a single, middle-aged man with no close family. Shepherd could imagine he was probably a very lonely, very discontented, disillusioned person. A man like that might easily have one drink too many, might have a dark night of the soul and wonder if it was all worth the effort. A man like that might look down at the busy street below his apartment and decide to find out what it would be like to fly for a few precious seconds.

No. I need him.

Just a while longer. It was clear from the email exchange with his colleague, Rose, that the man was returning to the States in a few days, and then, hopefully, one way or another, Shepherd was sure he could talk him into leading him there. Money usually did the trick.

The crowd erupted with a good-natured roar as the ball flew past the goalkeeper's hands and tangled with the net. Shepherd smiled and clapped. He knew he wanted this more than he wanted the White House.

I have a higher calling.

CHAPTER 43

Tuesday
Fort Casey, California

The librarian, a bespectacled, plump lady with permanently flushed cheeks and ham-shank arms, looked back at Rose with eyes as wide as Starbucks cookies. 'You're from the BBC? You mean from *England*?'

Rose smiled self-consciously. 'I work for them, indirectly.'

The woman seemed not to care too much about the distinction. Her friendly face broadened with a welcoming smile.

'Oh goodness, I love all your TV shows and your World Service. My husband loves your *Fawlty Towers* and all those Python programmes.' She offered Rose a hand. 'I'm Daphne Ryan . . . pleasure to meet you.'

Rose reached for her hand and shook it. 'Rose Whitely.'

'We don't get many visitors from so far away here in Casey,' she continued, her voice rising from a whisper with the excitement, 'especially not from England. Do you live in London? Near that Nottingham Hill place?'

Rose smiled and shook her head. 'No, sadly not. I live in a place called Clapham. It's in London, but not near Notting Hill.'

Daphne shook her head in wonder. 'I'd love to live there; all those quaint little book shops and Buckingham Palace and the Big Ben . . . it must be lovely.'

Rose nodded and smiled. 'It's okay,' she agreed.

'Not like Fort Casey,' she continued, the enthusiasm quickly draining from her face. 'Ain't much going on here. There never is.'

Rose shrugged. 'It's a sleepy town. I really like that.'

Daphne lit up again, obviously as proud of her town as she was fed up with it. 'You do?'

'Yes, it's a lovely place, really,' she replied, managing a sincere nod.

Fort Casey might have been a picturesque frontier town a generation ago, with a square and a gazebo, a town hall, a corner store selling ice-cream sundaes and every home fronted by a white picket fence — all of it perfectly framed by the distant purple peaks of the Sierra Nevada mountains. But now it looked like every other small town: a single through-road flanked by homogenous chain stores and acres of parking tarmac. Unlike Blue Valley, thirty miles east towards the mountains, there was no tourist trade here. No need to worry about appearances.

'I'm interested in the history of this town.'

'Oh, you've come to the right place!' she said, her voice beginning to carry across the small library. 'We have an extensive local history section. History of our town, archives of our paper, the *Report*, a section on the old army fort and garrison . . .'

'I'd like to look at that,' said Rose. 'Your paper, how far does it go back?'

'Oh, golly, it goes back ages and ages. As far back as the town does. We have the archives, every page of every issue on our DVD.'

Rose had already done some homework on the town. It dated from the 1840s when land was purchased for a song by the army, on Paiute territory, to build an outpost and oversee the trickle of settlers emerging from the pass and heading north-west on the final leg towards Oregon. Being directly on the most travelled route from Emigrant Pass, it had developed more quickly than Blue Valley. By the late fifties the small military outpost had been swamped by a bustling town full of traders, merchants and craftsmen looking to resupply and tend to the unending procession of weary overlanders streaming out of the wilderness.

Fort Casey was an unavoidable next stop for anyone heading for Oregon. Rose was curious where this apparently real Rag Man had disappeared to. Presumably his journey would have taken him away from the mountains from which he'd emerged.

That meant north-west. That meant passing through here.

'Can I look at this DVD?'

'Sure, I can fix you up on our internet station,' Daphne said, pointing towards the library's solitary PC, sitting in an ill-lit corner and currently being used by a sullen teenage lad. 'Lemme sort that out for you,' she said, heading out from behind the counter. She approached the boy on the computer, muttered something quietly to him and pointed Rose's way. He turned to look at her, a dark mop of hair covering his face except the pout of a bottom lip. He shrugged a *whatever*, closed down the MSN chat box, and shuffled towards the graphic novels and *manga* section of the library.

Daphne waved her over.

'All yours,' she cheerfully whispered as Rose sat down at the machine. 'That's Craig, my nephew.' She nodded towards him. 'Better he hangs out here, where I can keep an eye on him, than elsewhere. Library's a good place for him; all these books and learning around him.'

Rose nodded, but wondered if there was a great deal of learning going on there.

Daphne left Rose and returned a moment later with a shimmering gold disc in one hand. She slotted it into the PC and a title page popped up on the screen.

The Report: Archives 1842–1939

'We got two discs of material,' she said. 'Now, our recent history, from the war right up to, well . . . yesterday, I guess, is on the other disc. You want that one as well?'

'Just the first disc'll be fine, thanks.'

'Okay, well then, if you click on this,' she said, moving the mouse over a search dialogue box, 'you can enter a date here or an issue number, or you can even do a word search. Now' – she clasped her hands together – 'what specifically can I help you to look for?'

Rose felt awkward. Daphne Ryan had been exceedingly nice, but right now she needed a little space in which to think. She really didn't know *specifically* what she was looking for, not yet.

'I'm just going to browse a little.' She looked up at her. 'If that's all right?'

'Sure.'

Daphne hovered, waiting to be of further assistance. Rose was thinking how she was going to politely ask Daphne to give her a bit of room, when an old boy sidled up to the counter with a small stack of Clancy novels to check out. Daphne placed a hand on her shoulder. 'You shout if you need anything else, okay?'

Rose nodded. 'Thanks, Daphne,' and watched her head back to the counter. She faced the screen again.

Right.

Aaron Pohenz said the Rag Man left the town of Blue Valley, then known as Pelorsky's Farm, in the spring of 1857. He left on foot. If he headed north-west, then Fort Casey was only a week or so away.

So . . . from perhaps February 1857 onwards?

She typed a broad window of time into the date fields; February of that year to February of the next.

But what am I looking for?

She typed 'Rag Man' into the word search, hoping for an early hit. The DVD drive whirred but the search threw up nothing. Which was what she expected. The Rag Man was a Blue Valley myth – unknown here.

She decided to think things through from another angle. A paper like this, a town like this back then, would have focused its attention on the people passing through; the overlanders coming from the east. That's how news travelled back then, not over some twenty-four-hour news network, but from the mouths of travellers on their way through. Every new wagon train of people stopping to resupply, to repair damaged or weakened wheels, reshoe horses and oxen, would have a tale to tell of their journey, of any Indian encounters, of the latest news and fashions from Europe, the latest political manoeuvrings back in Washington.

She wondered if a lone traveller, no doubt still gaunt from a winter of malnutrition, a troubled man with little to say to anyone, would have attracted the curiosity of this small town.

A search for 'loner' produced an article about a local farmer who had decided to introduce sheep to graze on his land, arousing the anger of local cattlemen who viewed the creatures as un-American and had hounded the poor man out of town.

Perhaps the Rag Man had talked of his experience in the hills?

'Survivor' yielded a dozen eye-witness accounts of Indian raids, undoubtedly exaggerated to sound more heroic for the paper. Rose also stumbled upon a heartbreaking story of three small children dying of thirst and hunger and found clinging to the bodies of their parents. A whole party of seven wagons had been stranded on the salt flats of Utah after their horses had perished from drinking foul water. The children, two young sisters and a baby brother, were picked up by the passing emigrants, but died one by one over the following week.

'Cursed' spewed out hundreds of printed sermons from the town's lay preacher, Duncan Hodgekiss, who it seemed spent more time admonishing the wicked and godless from the offices of the paper than he did from the pulpit of his church.

Rose bit her lip with frustration, suspecting the twenty-minute drive down the interstate from Blue Valley, and the last half-hour in the library, had turned out to be something of a wild goose chase. The odds of tracing a nameless man from a hundred and fifty years ago amongst the spurious tales printed in a local rag were long, to say the least. In all likelihood, this weakened, troubled man . . . this *cursed* man, most probably had died by the wayside traipsing north-west on foot.

She wondered if he had been one of the names she'd picked out of the journal: Keats, Preston, Weyland, Vander, Hussein . . . or perhaps even the author himself, Lambert? There was no telling. This survivor might have been one of them, or one of the other Mormon men.

Or nothing at all to do with the Preston party?

She indulged the thought for a moment and then dismissed it. The Rag Man had wandered out of the very same mountains in the spring of the following year. Given the remote location off the beaten track, it was unlikely the two events *weren't* linked.

She sighed, frustrated. 'Which one of them were you?'

Searching randomly with tag words was getting her nowhere. She noticed once a week there was a regular column in the paper entitled 'What the Wind Blows In'. It was penned by the same author each time, one Theodore Feillebois, the paper's editor. It was a gossipy column that catalogued the more interesting arrivals of the week. Rose decided to focus her attention on those.

She was into May editions when she finally hit upon something that stirred the fair hair on her forearms.

. . . came into town on the dawn like a ghostly phantom. This intrepid reporter, always the keen hunting dog for the exciting tales that can be told by these courageous citizens who have braved the elephant's tail and the deadly Indian savage, I approached the man.

He was, I found, the most curious of passers-through that I have encountered in the service of this paper of ours. A tall, gaunt, silent man, with eyes that appeared to have seen things that this reporter would be unable to commit to paper for fear of frightening the fair ladies of this town.

A pilgrim crossing this untamed continent of ours alone is either very brave or very foolish, and I have no doubt that he must have experienced much that would blanch the faces of even the brave troops who garrison our fort and protect our souls day and night.

224

When I asked him for the story of his crossing, the man's response was a silence and an intense stare that I can only describe as haunted. I persisted in encouraging this man — whom I shall refer to hereon in as The Pilgrim, as I have no name for him, unwilling as he was to provide me with one — to tell me something of his adventurous crossing. But alas he declined.

He was dressed in ill-fitting clothes that appeared borrowed from another, better-nourished man, and with not a single possession in his hands. The Pilgrim, whoever he was, is a face this scribe will never forget.

When I asked this mysterious traveller where he was headed, his reply, dear reader, was one enigmatic word. A word that perhaps sums up the single-minded, dogged spirit and will-power of these brave, hardy folk.

He said to me, 'Oregon.'

He then shuffled away from me, little more than a crow-scare in tattered clothes and not a single thing to call his own. I soon lost sight of him amongst the busy throng of traders and over-landers that fill our main thoroughfare on any given day of the week . . .

'Oh my God,' Rose whispered. 'I think I've found him.'

CHAPTER 44

24 October, 1856

Preston turned to Vander. 'You saw it?'

He nodded. 'Yes I did, William.'

'For all his dirty sins,' he said, lowering his voice. Outside, Preston could hear the muted voices of his people. They were gathered around the men that had returned, hearing various versions of what had been discovered. Uneasy rumours would be spreading amongst them, the men scaring their wives, their wives terrifying their children.

He was relieved that only he and Eric from their party had gone inside and seen poor Saul's body. To some degree, it was better that the awful things done to him were not common knowledge. As only he and Eric had seen, he could control what his people were allowed to know.

Preston clamped his lips tightly and swallowed. 'Someone knows.'

Eric nodded, ashen faced. 'My God! What if it's *not* one of our people?'

'What do you mean?'

'What if we're being punished?' Eric's voice trembled. 'What if He's angry with us, William?'

'What we did was His will. It was all wrong, his Church, all wrong. Our founder took something sacred and made a mockery

226

of it. Joseph Smith should never have been led to it. It was right that he was killed. That, Eric, *that* was God's anger right there.'

'But we took them. They were not given to us!'

'No . . . if the Lord hadn't wished for me to take them, I would not have them with me now.' Preston turned and nodded at the metal chest. 'They're here with me because He wishes that to be so. And Joseph Smith is dead, beaten to death by a mob, his church split amongst greedy rivals. Again, that would not be so unless the Lord wished it.'

Vander looked unconvinced.

'We are the light, Eric. The good. Be certain of that. If this was not what God wanted, we would have known about it a long time ago.'

'Then who killed Saul?'

'Someone who knows.'

'But who, other than Dorothy?'

Preston sat down heavily, wincing from the sharp tug on his bound wounds. He cast his mind back to the night before last.

Dorothy comes to me, enraged and heartbroken.

'You took me in when I had no one,' she cries. 'I abandoned my faith for you.'

'Dorothy, listen to me—'

'I gave you my heart, my soul . . . my body. I gave you my children.'

'Please, listen to—'

'We trusted you. We trusted your message from God. You told lies, William. You told us lies! You led us away from God. You've led us here to this forsaken place . . . me, my children, and all the others.'

'Why are you saying these things to me, Dorothy?'

'Because in your sleep, it came out. The truth. One night after the next, fever made you tell the truth. Fever pushed the truth out of you, as it pushed sour liquid from your wounds. You and Saul and Eric, the three of you . . . are evil!'

'Whatever I must have said was feverish nonsense.'

Dorothy shakes her head. 'No, I . . . I've suspected some of these things before. Even punished myself for letting the Devil put doubts in my head. But you . . . you are doing what you claim our founder did — taking the words of God and making them your own!'

'Dorothy!'

'Your words . . . not God's!'

'William?'

Preston looked up at Eric. 'Yes?'

'If she knew, because of what she heard you say in your sleep . . . then who else might she have told?'

Preston shook his head. 'I don't know. Perhaps the important question should be who else might have heard me.'

'Only Saul, Dorothy and myself sat with you.' Vander turned to look at him. 'And that doctor, Lambert.'

Preston took a deep breath and nodded slowly. 'Yes . . . yes, he was with me a few times.'

Vander's eyes widened. 'Do you think he might have done this?'

'I don't know.'

'But he would not know of your work. Our Book.'

Preston considered that for a moment. He had seen Lambert become close to Dorothy's children over the last few months, particularly Samuel. The lad might have shared with Lambert what their mission was. He might have explained the Book of New Instruction. He might even have shown him a copy. It was possible that Dorothy went to Lambert and told him everything she suspected. But he couldn't imagine the man killing with such ferocity and anger. He couldn't imagine Lambert carving those letters into Hearst's skin with the tip of a knife.

Preston looked up at Vander. 'I sent Saul to reason with Dorothy not to upset the others with her doubts.'

Vander nodded. 'Maybe Saul went too far?'

Preston shook his head gravely. 'Perhaps.'

'Dorothy could have undone everything with her doubts and suspicions. He must have decided he had no choice.'

Preston sighed. 'Might be that is so.'

'Is it possible, William, that Lambert came upon them dead and found Saul there . . . ready to deal with Emily.'

'And killed him in anger?'

Preston nodded. It was a possible scenario, but one he could only imagine if some greater presence was at work.

'Eric,' he said after a few moments, 'it is quite possible that the Devil is acting through this man to get to us. To stop our work.'

Vander trembled with fear, or rage, or both. 'The Devil is all around us, isn't he? He's in Lambert, the others in that group, the savages out there . . .'

'Yes, that's what I sense. We have in that chest what the Devil fears the most: God's true message waiting to be heard for the first time. And we *will* make His words known, one way or another.'

'We should kill Lambert.'

'No. I'll not have any more blood shed. I would never have sent Saul if I had known he was going to take a knife to them.'

'Maybe that was God's will?'

Preston sighed. 'I don't know. I need to rest, and pray. God will talk to me tonight. We shall discuss this further in the morning.'

Vander nodded. 'All right.' He turned to go. 'Will you take some broth, William? Mrs Lester is cooking some on the campfire.'

'I'm not hungry. I just need some rest for now.'

'As you wish.'

Vander pushed aside the drape and stepped out, letting in the flickering glow of the nearby campfire. The cloth flapped back down, shutting out the light and leaving Preston in the gloom of a single guttering oil lamp.

He settled back on his cot and reached for the ceramic flask tucked behind it. He pulled the stopper out and sighed with relief. He could feel the onset of trembling, a cold sweat and light-headedness, but he knew these unfortunate symptoms would be washed away with this last dose of Lambert's medicine.

He drank the bitter tonic.

I must ask Lambert for some more tomorrow.

'She's unchanged?'

'Yes,' whispered Mrs Zimmerman, 'she's as she was. Not spoken a word, nor moved at all.'

Ben knelt down beside her. She was curled into a foetal ball, her knees pulled up, her hands clasped together between them and her chin, her blue eyes lost, some place far away. There were still dark spots and smudges of dried blood in the creases of her skin that had resisted being sponged away. He wondered how many of those dark flakes of blood had come from her mother and Sam.

Her long blonde hair was still clotted and tangled, although the dress she had worn yesterday, stained appallingly with the Indian's blood, had been replaced with another. Mrs Zimmerman had done her best to wash the dark spatters from her face, leaving it clean but ghostly white.

'My husband told me you found the others?'

'Yes.' He looked at her, wondering how much her husband had told her – probably she knew of the graves, but nothing about Mr Hearst. Clearly Preston didn't want the awful scene to be relayed to the others. It would spread a dangerous panic amongst them, and more than likely distrust and enmity would be misdirected at Broken Wing.

'They were all dead,' he replied.

'Was it the savages, do you think?'

No, of course it wasn't. Indians don't bury the dead. Nor are they likely to read and write.

'I don't think so,' he replied. But that left him considering two very unsettling alternatives. Either it was something he couldn't accept . . . something beyond science, something that belonged to a time of darkness and ignorance — something supernatural.

Or?

Or it was somebody from the camp.

He recalled the words inscribed into Hearst's pale flesh.

'Mrs Zimmerman?'

She looked up at him; her hand stopped stroking Emily's hair.

'Will you be with her tonight?'

'Yes. I'll stay with Emily as long as she needs me,' she replied. 'My husband and I have no children to care for now . . . not any more.'

The trace of bitterness in her voice was almost fully concealed, but still detectable and unmistakable. He could hardly imagine the pain of losing an only child — something far beyond any other kind of loss. He wondered whether, beneath her carefully contained, tight-lipped grief, she silently blamed someone for losing her little girl.

Her husband? Preston? Perhaps even God?

'I'll bid you goodnight. I shall come back in the morning to look in on her.'

Mrs Zimmerman nodded.

Ben reached out and stroked Emily's face. Her eyes stared blankly ahead of her.

'Goodnight, Emily,' he said quietly.

CHAPTER 45

24 October, 1856

From up here, I can see them all.

The camp is quiet. The sky has opened up and unleashed a silent flurry of heavy snowflakes that cascade and land without a noise. Down below, the communal campfires have been left to burn out, and all of them are tucked into their shelters, except four of them in two huddled pairs.

The night watch.

I see you, though. I see you, William Preston, in your shelter. What are you thinking now? Are you afraid yet? You should be.

Long before the snow melts, they will all know about you, William Preston. They will know that you are a pretender, a false prophet, a charlatan, a liar, a thief . . . and a murderer. And when they discover this, they will turn on you . . . for leading them to this. They will turn on you, and burn you like a witch.

An idea suddenly occurs. An ingenious way to torment Preston before this happens.

'I'm coming down there tonight.' The voice is nothing but a whisper.

'I'm coming to take something from you.'

CHAPTER 46

24 October, 1856

Why do you not speak to me?

Preston stirred uneasily on his cot, not quite asleep, but not awake.

Why? Everything I've done, I have done for you.

But neither God, nor his emissary, the angel, spoke.

He felt hot and restless beneath the layers of blankets over him, kicking them back in his restless half-sleep.

The angel would only come to those he trusted . . . those God trusted. A truth he knew. The words of God were so precious, so very fragile, so easily taken and corrupted by those with ambition, by those self-appointed to speak on His behalf. The Bible, written by a succession of men with selfish agendas — greedy men, arrogant men. The *Book of Mormon* written by Joseph Smith, a man who hungered to escape anonymity, to author his very own religion from nothing. The Torah, the Qu'ran . . . an endless procession of pretenders.

I'm not like these men. I don't do this for myself. I do this for you, God. So that finally it is YOUR words that people will hear, not mine. Nor any other man's.

The silence was deafening.

Something was wrong. That was why Nephi was not coming to him, to translate the language of angels to one that his humble human mind could comprehend. Something was keeping Nephi away.

Perhaps Vander was right. Perhaps it was the Devil keeping him away. There was evil all around them. The dirty-faced savages out amongst the trees; the others in the camp; amongst them a Catholic family, a Muslim family, a Negro with skin scorched by sin, Keats – profane, ugly, crude – and his Indian partner.

And Lambert, of course, an atheist who tried to insinuate his way into Dorothy's family like a snake, whispering dirty lies to both Samuel and Emily.

His thoughts, disjointed and fleeting as they were, were abruptly halted by a powerful, certain knowledge that he was not alone in his temple. He thought he heard the whisper of movement beside his cot, something that stirred inside his metal chest. The soft squeak of unoiled hinges opening, the gentle clink of fragile bones.

'Is that you?' he muttered breathlessly in the dark. 'Have you come?'

William.

The voice, a quiet whisper, materialised in the pitch-black emptiness just above his cot.

'Nephi?'

Yes.

An overpowering, euphoric surge of relief pulsed through Preston. He felt dizzy and lightheaded. 'Oh, thank the Lord . . . thank the Lord! I was afraid that I'd done something wrong.' Preston sat up. 'Are we to start God's work this night? To translate his message from the scrolls?'

He sensed movement in the dark, the brush of something passing by.

No.

The answer confused him momentarily. 'Then what are we to do first?' he asked.

I am leaving you, William.

The words hung in the air before him, incomprehensible for a moment. Words he never expected to hear. '*Leaving*? But . . . but why?'

There was no reply.

'Why?'

Preston felt another gentle draught of movement coming from the pitch-black space in front of him, and heard the soft tinkle of the bones in their canvas sack.

You disappoint me.

'How? How do I . . . what have I done wrong?' Preston cried.

The angel left the question unanswered.

'What have I done wrong?' Preston cried again, his voice raised, his sweat-damp cheeks moistened further with tears. He felt a sudden cold blast of air from outside, chilling his damp body.

'No!' he screamed. 'No! PLEASE NO!'

He jerked on the cot, suddenly fully awake and trembling like a mongrel left outside on a frozen night. But he was lying down, not sitting up as he thought he had been, and covered once more with his blankets, cold and damp with his sweat.

Was I dreaming?

Preston realised that he must have been. But it had felt so real, so dreadfully, painfully real. He felt his heart pounding in his chest and a wave of relief wash over him. Just a dream, then – a nightmare, in fact. The angel hadn't spoken to him after all. With that realisation there was disappointment, but it was more than compensated by the relief that he'd not been judged and found wanting.

He reached for some matches, struck one and lit the wick of the oil lamp that sat on a small wooden crate beside his cot. It caught, flickered and glowed softly, pushing the darkness back through the wind-teased flap and out into the cold night.

He turned in his cot, the wooden frame creaking with the weight of his body, to see the metal chest sitting wide open.

'Oh . . . n-no . . . no,' he whispered.

235

CHAPTER 47

cave iram Dei

M	T	W	T	F	S	S
					1	2	3
4	5	6	7	8	9	10
11	12	13	14	15	16	17
18	19	20	21	22	23	24
25	26	27	28	29	30	

Wednesday
Fulham, London

Julian sat in what he was beginning to think of as the 'waiting room'. Dr Thomas Griffith's offices in Fulham consisted of a couple of rooms: his office and another, larger room in which his personal assistant sat behind a desk facing a sofa and a coffee table. Last time Julian had worked with him, his office had been a small study in his home.

The book was obviously doing well.

The phone had been answered at least four times since he had arrived and he half-listened to one-sided conversations whilst flicking through the Media pullout in today's *Times*. From what he could hear there was a steady traffic of public appearance requests.

His eyes drifted onto a copy of *USA Today*.

On the cover was the image of a face he vaguely recognised. He reached across the coffee table and picked up the magazine. Then he managed to place him: it was the American business-man who had recently thrown his hat in for the presidential election. It was an item on the news show he'd caught during the flight back home; an outsider many were calling a fool because he was campaigning so early and was bound to peak and wilt before the final showdown in about eighteen months' time.

He recalled the man was some kind of a religious figure . . . *Shepherd*, that was it, that was his name; a lay preacher of some kind with a lot of money to burn, and a lot of friendly, mostly religious, sponsors gathering around his campaign. Skimming through the article inside, he discovered Shepherd owned a regional media network in Utah, and ran a string of small *spiritual* colleges that, in the eyes of the journalist, were vaguely reminiscent of the Islamic madrasas in northern Pakistan.

The door to the office swung open to reveal Dr Griffith's wide frame. He had put on even more weight since the last time Julian had seen him. At a glance he guessed he must weigh sixteen or seventeen stone.

A lot of good living.

'Julian!' his rich voice boomed as he thrust out a hand towards him. 'Fantastic to see you again.'

Julian reached for his hand. 'Good to see you too, Tom. Things are looking good, eh?'

'Very good. I should be writing more and doing less television, really. I'm becoming like those media tramps I despise.'

Julian grinned. 'Or *ex*-media tramps in my case.'

Tom grinned. 'You were never a tramp, Jules. Come on in,' he said, gesturing to the study beyond. He turned to his assistant. 'Judy, don't put any calls through for the next half-hour or so, okay?'

'Of course, Dr Griffith.'

Julian stepped into the office and sat in a winged leather seat opposite Tom's expansive dark wood desk. 'Very nice *sanctum sanctorum* you've got here,' he said, looking around at the tasteful decor and the glistening sheen of polished wood.

'I've always loved quality office furniture,' said Tom as he pulled his seat out and sat heavily down. 'It's one of my weaknesses. The timber for this desk is reclaimed Indonesian teak – reclaimed from the hulls of fishing vessels. There's no way to get your hands on that kind of wood without bribing the right official.'

'My desk, by contrast, is a flat-pack from Ikea.'

Tom laughed, not unkindly. 'I don't recall you being as vain or materialistic as I am, though.'

'No, I suppose not,' said Julian with a wry smile. 'Be nice to be able to put that to the test, though.'

Tom offered a conciliatory nod. 'Things will turn around for you, Jules. You're smart and you're tenacious. That girl you worked with . . . Rose, was it?'

'Yes, Rose.'

'You're still partners in crime?'

He nodded.

'She's an incredibly good film-maker. I really liked what you did with that series. And . . .' said Tom, reaching across the vast expanse of his desk and pulling out a lined pad of paper from the pile in his in-tray '. . . I really think you two will be on your way back out of the wilderness with *this*,' he said, flourishing a page of notes written in his spidery hand.

Tom reached for an inhaler on his desk and took a hit. Julian remembered the man suffered with asthma.

'Bloody fascinating stuff this, Julian, absolutely bloody fascinating.'

'You've had a chance to go through some of the stuff I sent over?'

'I've been through *most* of it, Julian. I couldn't put the damn thing down, even though I should be working on the foreword to a colleague's book.'

'So? What do you make of it all?'

Tom settled back into his chair and pursed his lips in thought for a few moments. 'What I think you've got there, my friend, is a very detailed account of a serial killer going about his business.'

'That's the obvious conclusion, isn't it?'

238

'But here's the big question. Which one of them is it?'

'Maybe it's more than one of them?'

Tom shrugged. 'Could be.'

'So?'

'So from the account written by this Lambert character, it looks very much like the most likely culprit is the Mormon preacher, Preston.'

'Yeah.'

'He appears to exhibit all the obvious traits of a narcissistic messianic complex.'

'A narcissistic . . . a what?'

'A dyed-in-the-wool sociopath of the very worst kind. I'm not sure how this little tale ends up, Julian—'

'I'm still working my way through the journal.'

'But,' Tom continued, 'I'd be prepared to bet bloody good money it ends with the death of most of these people. In particular, most, if not *all* of his followers.'

Julian looked at him. 'What makes you so certain of that?'

'He's a classic Reverend Jim Jones figure. You recall the Jonestown incident, right?'

'Of course.'

'A strong-willed, charismatic sociopath, driven by a delusion of some messianic destiny. The pattern I'm seeing in this Lambert journal is very similar: a religious patriarchal figure leading his devoted followers out into an isolated wilderness away from the interference and prying noses of authority; in Jim Jones's case it was Guyana. In Preston's case, I'm presuming, he was heading for some unclaimed tract beyond the reach of the US government to set up his own little kingdom. Away from the rule of law, away from the established Church of Latter Day Saints.'

Julian nodded. 'That's about the size of it.'

Tom got up from his office chair and walked over to the door of his study. 'Fancy some coffee?'

Julian nodded, and Tom cracked the door open and asked

239

Judy to rustle up a cafetiere of Kilimanjaro Fairtrade for both of them. He closed the door gently.

'To what end, though?' Julian asked.

Tom smiled. 'Like Jim Jones, like David Koresh . . . or to pick a few secular examples, like Idi Amin, Robert Mugabe . . . even Adolf Hitler – to realise his manifest destiny. To appease the particular malevolent imp inside him.'

Julian's brows arched.

'Imp?'

Tom spread his hands apologetically. 'Forgive me. It's a characterisation I'm using way too often right now. I'm consulting on a TV drama, a supernatural version of *Cracker*; the scriptwriters have been using that phrase, that metaphor in their dialogue, and I'm finding myself doing it now. It's like catching someone else's cold,' he laughed. 'No, I mean the *delusion* that's driving him. Like I say, a classic dyed-in-the-wool sociopath.'

Julian had heard the term many times, but had never been given a concise definition of it that made sense.

Tom seemed to pick up on that. 'It's an over-used word these days, Julian. One bandied about a bit too readily by screenwriters, crime novelists and daytime TV shrinks. It's similar, in a way, to autism, an inability to comprehend the feelings of others; a total absence of the ability to empathise. But autism is an example of the brain misfiring, not working properly. It's a *dis*order. On the other hand, the sociopathic tendency, I believe, is . . . for the sake of a better word an *enhancement*. It's designed.'

'Designed?'

'Darwinistically speaking, of course.'

Julian grinned with relief. 'I thought for a terrifying moment there that you were going all creationist on me.'

Tom laughed. 'No, I've seen enough of how the mind works to never be in any danger of suddenly finding God. No, by *designed* I mean the sociopathic tendency has evolved amongst a minority of people. Every serial killer is a sociopath; you'd

240

need to be able to do what they do. The inability to perceive the feelings of others, the suffering of a victim, gives a killer an advantage . . . the competitive edge, if you like. Which, of course, in Darwinistic – one might even say Dawkinsian terms, these days – makes a hell of a lot of sense, if you think about it.'

The door creaked open and Judy brought in a tray of coffee and biscuits. Tom thanked her then waited until she had left before continuing.

'You'd be surprised how many sociopaths are out there.'

Julian's dark brow arched. He reflexively pushed his glasses up. 'Uh, how many?'

'It's a trait that's really quite common. Perhaps about one in ten people exhibits sociopathic tendencies to some degree.'

'What? Surely the streets would be awash with blood.'

'Well, you know where there's an absence of a controlling mechanism – law and order – that's exactly how it is,' sighed Tom. 'You only have to consider Baghdad, or Darfur, or Sarajevo, or Kenya.'

He dipped his biscuit, swilled it around and then carefully lifted the soggy thing to his mouth.

'But listen, it's a mistake to think that violent behaviour is always a natural follow-on for those who have this inability to pity, to empathise. You ever watch *The Apprentice* on the telly?'

Julian nodded guiltily. 'Yeah, I hate to admit I got sucked into the last series.'

'No one got sliced open or garrotted with piano wire, at least not that I'm aware of. But I'd say a very high proportion of those contestants had a sociopathic tendency of one sort or another, prepared to do anything to anybody just to be the winner.'

'There now,' said Julian, half joking, 'I always knew there was a reason I didn't like *suits*.'

'Well, that's a fair comment. The corporate world is an ecosystem that rewards the most sociopathic competitors and punishes the most altruistic. Even the phrases commonly used in the business world – dog eat dog, it's a jungle, who dares wins, hostile takeover – are all very aggressive. The business language

241

is a very predatorial language. By logical extraction, it's likely that the most successful businessmen – the CEOs, the senior executives, the city traders, captains of industry – are the most ruthless of them.'

'The most extreme sociopaths?' said Julian.

Tom nodded. 'Yup.'

Julian sipped his coffee. 'Kind of puts a different spin on the whole Thatcherism thing, doesn't it?'

'Of course it does. *There is no such thing as society any more.* Spoken like a true sociopath, eh?'

'Yes,' Julian chuckled.

'If you believe that she sent this country of ours to war in order to stir up the patriotic vote and win herself another term, resulting in the deaths of over two hundred and fifty British servicemen, then, in my book, that puts her serial killer's scorecard up there above Harold Shipman's.'

'And Tony Blair?'

Tom smiled. 'There you go, arguably another cold-blooded bastard. In fact the world of politics is an even more fertile place for them to flourish; more so than the world of business. Even the worlds of sport, fashion and celebrities attract sociopaths to the very top, like bees to honey. I imagine, flipping through the glossy pages of *Hello!*, *Heat* and *OK!* magazines, the majority of those perfect, sun-tanned, smiling faces have got where they are by happily trampling on the shoulders of others.'

Tom leaned forward. 'Let me put it to you this way, Julian. I wonder how many of them would be prepared to quietly stick the knife into someone in their way? Hmm? A competitor, a rival . . . a particularly nasty critic?'

Julian nodded. 'Sure, I suppose.'

'How far would they go to hang on to their fame and success? Here's a question for you. How many celebrities do you think would actually *kill* to keep their status or climb further, if they knew they could get away with it? Hmm?'

Tom's voice had begun to grow wheezy. He reached for his inhaler and took another puff whilst Julian dwelled on that idea for a moment. The thought of those endless supermarket celebrity magazines being populated by a procession of potential serial killers left him feeling decidedly uneasy.

'Let me ask you,' Tom continued, 'whom would *you* kill to ensure you hung on to this particular story?'

'What?'

'Would you kill me if I threatened to pick up the phone on my desk here, ring the editor of the *Mirror* and totally blow your scoop?' Tom's beefy hand reached teasingly across towards his desk phone and picked it up.

'No, of course I wouldn't. But I'd be really flippin' pissed off with you if you did!' Julian answered testily.

Tom's laugh filled the small office as he put the phone back down in its cradle. 'There you go then. You're not one of them. You lack the killer instinct, my friend.' He smiled. 'That's what makes you one of the good guys.'

'Very funny,' Julian mumbled irritably.

Tom gestured at his pad full of notes. 'This chap Preston strikes me as the type who would easily kill to see out his goal – which, from what Lambert writes, seems like an attempt to rebrand the Mormon faith in his own way, casting himself in the role of prophet.' He stroked his chin in thought. 'A man like that would kill again, and again, and again. Maybe by his own hand but, just as likely, by getting into the heads of his followers and having them do his dirty work.'

'You're not a big fan of the religious type, are you?'

He laughed. 'You kidding? The underbelly of religious fanaticism is thick on the ground with narcissistic freaks. Rasputin, Tomas de Torquemada, most of the early popes, the crusade-era popes . . . Innocent III, who decreed a crusade against other Christians, never mind Muslims; the imams who groom children to blow themselves to pieces. If ever you wanted a definition of hell, Julian, it's the inner landscape of minds like these.

'A *messianic narcissistic sociopath*.' Tom smiled. 'My phrase, by the way. You can use it in your documentary if you want. Just make sure to attribute the quote to me.'

Julian nodded. 'I'll make certain.'

'Yes,' added Tom, looking back down at his notes, 'very nasty, very manipulative and very dangerous people.'

CHAPTER 48

Wednesday
Wimbledon, London

Sean Holmwood tossed the stick for Watson out across Wimbledon Common and watched the labrador chase after it, kicking up flecks of mud behind him as he tore across the well-tended grass towards the spinney — an acre of mixed trees, most of them bare and patiently awaiting winter, a few of them hanging on to the last of their golden leaves.

Normally, taking Watson for his evening walk was a daily chore that his wife was happy to do, but this evening he had volunteered as soon as he came home, grabbing the lead and setting out with Watson eagerly pulling all the way.

Sean needed some thinking time. Julian Cooke's project sounded intriguing.

Watson returned with the stick wedged in his teeth, flecks of saliva across his muzzle. He dropped it at Sean's feet and sat obediently.

'Good boy,' Sean muttered perfunctorily as he scooped it up and tossed it as far as he could towards the spinney.

It seemed Julian had landed on his feet with this find. From what Sean had been told of the story, and from the compilation of fantastically moody footage he had seen on the laptop, there was easily the makings of an hour's worth of fine-looking documentary. But Julian was quite right to be thinking bigger. This could also be written up as a docu-drama; there were film rights and book rights that could be sold on the back of it. The Mormon angle of the story was also very intriguing. With increasing media attention being focused on the wildcard Mormon independent presidential candidate, William Shepherd, there was a topical relevance to this story.

He looked up at the darkening sky. It was near six, and the dull glow of a drab October day was fast fading.

Watson's walk was going to be a short one this evening. Sean wanted to get back and put together some notes. If he wanted to fast-track an editorial decision, he needed to sell the project internally. Tonight he'd put together a sales pitch, which he would float across a few desks first thing in the morning.

Watson returned with the stick, and this time Sean tossed it hard into the undergrowth of the spinney.

Let him work off some energy rooting around for it in there.

The labrador hurled himself in amongst the trees in hot pursuit, kicking up fallen leaves and twigs in his wake.

Sean pulled a small plastic freezer baggie out of his pocket and shoved his hand in, pulling it back over his wrist so it was like a glove. He grimaced slightly, still not entirely used to the unpleasant task of scooping up a warm one.

Watson should be just about ready to deliver the goods.

He heard the dog scampering around in amongst the trees and bushes, cracking twigs under-paw and gruffing and growling with frustration looking for the *correct* branch.

Sean felt a tingle of excitement at the prospect of taking off with this project. Julian's pitch had sold it, but then seeing Rose's showreel — moody footage of thick and dark woods, mist undulating through the trees, the haunted feel of a clearing in the woods, the moss-covered humps, the slow and steady zoom-in on the rotting wood of a wagon wheel . . .

'Marvellous stuff,' he muttered to himself.

Up ahead, deep amongst the undergrowth, he could hear Watson still scampering about like an idiot.

He laughed quietly – a truly thick dog.

Come on, dummy, one stick's just as good as another.

Yes, tomorrow morning Sean would get the ball rolling and return to Julian with a firm offer within a day. They needed to be quick. Whilst there was a good working relationship between them, he was certain Julian wouldn't walk away from a better offer, elsewhere. After all, money's mon—

Watson yelped.

'Watson? Here boy!' Sean called out.

It was silent across the manicured lawns, except for the rustling of a light breeze through the branches and dry leaves, and the distant rumble of traffic around the three distant sides of the common.

'Watson?' he called out with a sing-song timbre that usually brought the daft dog to him. 'Here boy!'

Nothing.

Sean felt a prickling of concern. Watson never, *ever* ignored him like that. He half walked, half jogged over towards the edge of the spinney and looked inside for the telltale flash of his chestnut-coloured coat in amongst the foliage.

There was no sign of him.

'Watson?'

He took several quick steps forward, off the well-clipped grass onto a thickening mat of dead, crispy leaves, twigs, acorn husks and conker shells. Sean wasn't terribly keen on stepping too much further inside. He turned to look back out at the common. There were a few people around; a couple roller-blading along one of the tarmac paths, another two or three dog owners walking their dogs, a group of teenagers chatting on a bench several hundred yards away.

He wasn't exactly alone, but in the gathering gloom of early evening, he might as well be.

'Watson! Dammit! Come here!'

Shit.

It was on Wimbledon Common not so long ago that a woman had been stabbed to death by a care-in-the-community type, a lost and tormented man who'd been convinced that every blonde-haired woman was an agent of Satan, coming to extract his soul and take it down to the underworld.

Sean instinctively reached down and fumbled for a twig big enough to call a branch and grabbed hold of it. It felt reassuring in his hand.

Just in case.

Emboldened, he advanced further in, pushing through a thorny bush that effectively obscured him from view to those few people out on the common. Something must have happened to Watson if he wasn't answering. Perhaps he had found a rabbit hole and taken a tumble, or run headlong into a tree trunk and stunned himself; he was that stupid a dog.

Or maybe he'd found a bitch willing to take the silly old bugger on.

'Watson!' he called out again.

There was a rustling to one side of him and the dull, muffled crack of an acorn underfoot — it sounded very much like someone shifting weight from one foot to another.

'Okay, who the fuck's in here?' Sean called out, hoping his polished boardroom voice sounded more menacing than it did to him.

The rustling ceased immediately, but somehow that made it seem a million times worse. Sean sensed that this was the moment he ought to back quietly out of the trees, past the bush and onto the common and walk away without his dog.

'Watson!' he called out once more, 'I'm going, you stupid hound!' He had turned round to head out of the undergrowth towards the open green when he heard movement in front of him.

His eyes picked out a dark silhouette against the edge of the spinney and the darkening grey sky beyond. Any further detail was lost to the last of the early-evening light, but unmistakably it was a man wearing a hood.

'Yes?' he said, and then as an afterthought, 'Can I help you?'

The silhouette remained perfectly still.

'You after some money?'

'No,' a dry voice answered.

Stay calm, Sean cautioned himself. *Control the situation.*

'My dog came in here. Did you see him?'

The man advanced a step forward. 'You spoke with someone I've been watching.'

Sean shrugged. 'I've spoken to a lot of people today.'

'You spoke to him about a story in America.'

Playing dumb probably wasn't going to help. 'How do you know about that? Who are you?'

The silhouette was silent. 'What the hell do you want?!'

'I'm here to tidy things up,' said the man.

CHAPTER 49

25 October, 1856

This morning, for the first time, I sense the others looking at us with distrust. I don't know whether they have collectively discussed who or what killed Dorothy, Sam and Mr Hearst, and decided it is one of us, or whether they each privately harbour that suspicion, but I can see it in the quick, wary glances, the shortest possible exchange of pleasantries with us.

Keats spoke of Mr Larkin, their butcher, not wanting to work alongside Mr Bowen. And visiting Emily's shelter this morning, I was silently watched by a group of five men gathered around their breakfast fire; watched intently. Moments after entering and talking with Mrs Zimmerman, Mr Vander stuck his head in and made it clear I was to check on her as quickly as possible, then leave.

I do wonder whether—

A buffeting wind shook and rattled the creaking wooden framework of their shelter, whilst the flap over their entrance, tied down against the gusting wind, rustled and whipped, complaining like a tethered dog. A blizzard was coming down almost horizontally, small, dry, sand-like beads of ice that stung against bare skin.

Above the rumpling thud of wind, he heard a muffled voice.

'Mr Lambert?'

He recognised it as Preston.

'Yes?'

'A word, if you don't mind.'

'Uh, yes, of course.' Ben closed his inkpot and put away his journal before readying himself to step outside.

'I'll come in,' said Preston. Ben saw fingers work on the tie, and a moment later the wind whipped it open. Snow hurled in, chased by a vicious, biting blast of freezing air. Preston stooped down low, pushed his way through the flap and settled down on his haunches inside, securing the flap once more.

'Are we alone?' he asked quietly, squinting in the dark interior.

'Mr Keats and Broken Wing are foraging for wood with some others.'

'Good. I wished to speak to you in private.'

Ben felt his skin run cold, realising he was alone with someone who might just be capable of violent murder and barbaric mutilation.

He'd not do something to me here, now, surely?

Unlikely as that was, he found his hand subconsciously reaching for the handle of his hunting knife, tucked away under his poncho in his belt.

'What do you wish to talk about?'

'I . . . find the discomfort of my injury is continuing to be unbearable and I would like to take with me a complete bottle of your medication, that I need not keep bothering you to personally administer it.'

'Well, it is no bother,' Ben lied, his mind recalling the openly hostile glances he had drawn earlier this morning, approaching the Dreyton shelter.

'That's as may be. However, there are those amongst my people who would rather your party remain, from now on, on your side of the camp.'

'Mr Preston, I think I should advise you that this medication is really best only prescribed a few times. There are unfortunate side-effects that can occur when used repeatedly.'

Preston's face hardened. 'Make no mistake, Lambert, I *do* need this medication. The discomfort is such that I am unable to lead prayers and services. My people need me to be strong more than ever now. Not for me to be laid up as invalid.'

Ben nodded. 'Yes, well, I can continue to give it to you, but I think it's best that I measure it out for you.'

'I can manage well enough with the measuring.'

'But it requires a steady reduction in measure, to ensure—'

'Lambert!'

Ben hushed. There was a brittle anger in his voice that sounded like the fracturing of dangerously thin ice over a deep rushing river.

'I will have a bottle . . . if you please.'

Ben could see something in the stern glare of his deep-set eyes.

'You understand, I could return here with several of my men, and help myself to all of your medicines . . . don't you?'

'Y-yes, I . . . I suppose you could.'

'There are those who think the butchering of our people was *your* handiwork, Lambert. They know you have training as a doctor and would have skill with a surgeon's tools.'

'What?'

'There are those who think you were becoming *unnaturally* close with young Samuel.'

'Unnaturally?'

Preston managed a humourless, predatory smile. 'That's what some of them are saying.'

'But . . . but, what are they . . . what do they mean by tha—?'

'I've overheard some of my men suggest you might have been rejected by Samuel. That you became enraged.'

'And what? I killed him?'

Preston nodded. 'And his mother. That Mr Hearst intervened, and that you took your surgeon's knife to him too.'

252

'That's crazy!'

'As for myself' — Preston's smile softened slightly — 'I don't see that kind of evil in you. You are godless and arrogant; for that you are eternally doomed. But what I don't see before me is a murderer.'

'Then you must tell the others that!'

'And I must have my medicine,' he replied.

Preston stared in silence at him, whilst outside the wind buffeted and whistled impatiently, eager to get in.

'I see,' said Ben.

'Good.'

The understanding was passed in silence. Ben turned around and rummaged in his medicine bag, a moment later producing a stoppered dark green glass bottle. 'I have only this last bottle of the laudanum. That's it.'

Preston reached for it, but Ben held it back.

'Mr Preston, do please be aware of what this tonic can do. In some it can stimulate alarming visions, and an increasing dependency—'

'I have had many visions before now.'

'Visions of God?'

'Yes. He comes to me, talks with me.'

'Only he doesn't, does he?' whispered Ben, immediately regretting it.

Preston looked sharply up at him — a look that chilled Ben to the core.

That was very, very stupid.

'You heard the things Dorothy heard?' he asked.

Ben nodded. 'Dorothy came to me, the night before she died.'

'And what did she tell you?'

He wondered how much more to reveal. 'That she had lost her faith in you.'

'I see.' Preston's jaw set. 'And you think I saw to it she was killed?'

Ben refused to respond. He found his hand tightening around

253

the handle of his knife once more. Whether he'd be able to use it was another matter.

'I loved her, Lambert. I loved her more than any of my followers. And I loved her children, too. They were mine.'

'You . . . you mean, what? You were Sam's father?'

Preston nodded. 'And Emily's. In fact, many of the children in my church are mine. I would never allow any of them to be hurt. My people know that.'

'The other men, the "fathers", they know this?'

'Of course. They understand this as our way. I am the closest to God – on this evil world – the closest living soul to God. Who else would you rather have seed your child?'

Ben shook his head. 'They . . . they would turn on you, wouldn't they? They'd turn on you if they knew.'

The ice-cold façade slipped for a moment from Preston's face, revealing, for only a second, fear.

'If they knew *what*, Lambert?'

Don't push him into a corner.

'What exactly are you talking about, Mr Lambert?'

He realised it was already too late to back away now. 'That you are a . . . a fraud.'

The word hung for too long on its own in the space between them before Preston spoke.

'I don't know what you know, or what you *think* you know. But you are no longer to visit our camp. None of your group, in fact, will be permitted to step beyond the dead oxen in the middle. Is that understood?'

'What of Emily?'

'She is being cared for well enough by Mrs Zimmerman.'

'I must look in on her. Surely you'll let me do that?'

Preston leaned closer to Ben, his long, slim nose only inches away from Ben's face. He could feel the tickle of the man's stale breath. 'If I hear of you visiting Emily,' he whispered, 'who knows what will happen to you? Perhaps you will find yourself gutted and hung like so much butcher's meat?'

Ben struggled to contain the trembling that coursed through his body. 'M-my God . . . it . . . it *was* you, wasn't it?'

Preston reached for the bottle. 'We are two separate camps now. Be sure to tell Keats that. Be sure to tell him none of your people are to talk to mine.'

He pushed his way out through the flap, letting in a small blizzard of hale that veiled his exit.

CHAPTER 50

cave iram Dei

M	T	W	T	F	S	S
				1	2	3
4	5	6	7	8	9	10
11	12	13	14	15	16	17
18	19	20	21	22	23	24
25	26	27	28	29	30	

Wednesday
Blue Valley, California

The call connected and Rose heard the ringing tone. It was gone three in the afternoon here; it would be gone eleven in the evening back home in London. She wondered what he was up to.

'Julian Cooke,' he answered crisply.

'It's Rose,' she replied. An awkward pause followed, the memory of the other night's momentary *frisson* still vivid for both of them.

Julian broke the silence. 'All right?'

'Yeah, fine. And you?'

'I'm good . . . you know, keeping busy.'

Rose fiddled uncomfortably with a tress of her hair. 'You asked me to call.'

The email had come through an hour ago; two perfunctory and polite lines from Julian suggesting they should quickly hook up and update each other on their progress.

'Uh, yeah. I just wanted to see what you're up to and let you know how things're going from my end.'

'Uh-huh. So . . .'

'So shall I go first or do you—?'

'No, er, fine. You go first and update me, if you like.'

256

Julian coughed. 'Okay. Well, good meetings so far. We've got Sean on board. He's putting together a deal as we speak. And with the BBC signing on, it'll make it a shitload easier to sign up another partner.'

'That's great.'

'So, money soon shouldn't be quite such an issue. What else? Oh yeah, I spoke to Dr Griffith. You remember Tom?'

'The shrink we interviewed for *Uncommon People*?'

'That's the fella. He's doing very well with his book, by the way.'

'Lucky Tom.'

'He's really hooked by this. Wants to do something with us.'

'Okay. He's not going to hijack it, is he?'

'No. But he may be a useful, authoritative talking head. It really depends whether we do a straight documentary, or a docudrama, which is what Sean is suggesting. Anyway, Tom's convinced Preston is some kind of whacked-out religious nut-job.'

'That's hardly a difficult diagnosis.'

Julian laughed. 'Nope. But he made some very interesting comparisons with other similar whacked-out nuts from history. It'll make for a good angle to play around with. Plus his reputation carries some authority. If he's happy to say Preston's a sociopathic killer prepared to murder all his followers just to satisfy delusions of destiny, then—'

'He said that?'

'Yup.'

Rose felt the skin on her arms tingle. 'Oh my God.'

'It *is* kind of creepy, isn't it?'

She wondered whether to confess to Julian exactly how spooked she was beginning to feel about the whole thing.

'What we may have, according to Tom, is one of the earliest, most detailed accounts of a serial killer going about his business, courtesy of our good friend Lambert.'

'Julian?'

'Yeah?'

'It gets better.'

Better or . . . weirder?

Rose didn't like the fact that the story was beginning to get to her.

'How so?'

'I'm almost certain one of the Preston party emerged from the hills,' she said.

'What?'

'I've been following up on some of the Blue Valley folklore. There's an account of a survivor who emerged the spring after Lambert's diary entries, emaciated, at death's door, and quite out of his mind by the sound of it. '

'Who?'

'Well, that's the mystery. It was a man. They called him the Rag Man. He never gave a name. They nursed him back onto his feet and he left Blue Valley early April 1857. Then I picked up his trail in a town called Fort Casey, about forty miles north-west, where he attracted some attention. He entered the town and a curious reporter tried to collar him for an interview.'

She read the article to Julian.

'That's really quite weird,' he said.

'Isn't it?'

'But how can we be sure it's someone from the Preston party?'

'We can't. But Blue Valley, Pelorsky's Farm, was well off the beaten track for emigrants. The only people back then that they encountered were trappers and traders and occasional Indians. It's too big a coincidence that a starving white man emerged from the mountains a few months after those people got caught by the snow, don't you think?'

'Hmm.'

'And that article was dated mid-April. So it would fit the timescale of someone making forty miles westward on foot.'

'You know, having a mysterious survivor emerge from the mountains and into enigmatic obscurity would really add a lot to our story.'

'It certainly would,' she replied.

'Whoever it was.'

'Yeah.'

'If that person survived . . . what if that man had children?'

'It would be one helluva coup to track down a descendant and interview him or her.'

'Yes,' said Julian. 'Look, we've got quite a few names from Lambert's journal: Keats, Weyland, Preston, Bowen, Larkin, Zimmerman, Stolz, Stolheim . . . to name just a few. It would be worth a shot, if you're up for it, to comb through the archived press of the time, like you did in Fort Casey.'

'That'll be like looking for a needle in a haystack.'

'Maybe. But we could filter this down a bit. If this Rag Man was headed north-west, there were only a few destinations for him back then, weren't there? I mean, you had Portland, Astoria and Fort Vancouver. None of those settlements would have been that big back then, perhaps only a few thousand. If we ran all the names mentioned in Lambert's journal through their local press archives, their parish records, we might get a hit.'

'True.'

'And I'll help you with this, as soon as I join you out there. Meantime, I'm going to follow Preston's trail. I mentioned to you there's a guy out there on the internet who's set up a page on Preston?'

'Yeah, I saw your mail.'

'There's an email address on his page. I'm going to see if we can squeeze him for some detail.'

'Be careful, Jules,' Rose blurted.

'Uh?'

'Well, you know, don't sound *too* interested. Who knows? It might be another journalist who's on the same story.'

Julian chuckled. 'I'll be sure to sound extremely casual about everything.'

Then the conversation came to an unexpected halt. This time Rose stepped in. 'So when are you coming back?'

'I booked a flight back on Friday. We should arrange with

Grace to have another visit up to the site. See what other bits and pieces we can dig up.'

'She won't like it if I say it like that.'

'Well, obviously we're not going to run a JCB across the place — just a little trowel work, that's all. Actually, having read most of the journal, I think I understand the layout of that clearing. I think it'd be a cinch, for example, to locate Preston's shelter.'

'Yes?'

'And' — Julian let slip a nervous chuckle — 'who knows what crazy stuff we'll find if we do, hmm?'

Rose shuddered. 'Spooky stuff.'

'Oh, that's for sure.'

CHAPTER 51

26 October, 1856

He listened to the howling wind outside, knowing that it was bringing with it many inches of snow that would be covering the entrance to the shelter. But it was a warm shelter, so much better than the hastily erected lean-tos down the hillside in the clearing. A good place from which to do work.

Yes.

A good place to become something more. He looked around at the tools hanging from lumber nail hooks; sharp tools, unused for many decades. On the floor beneath them nestled an ancient-looking flintlock weapon, from another time, perhaps even a previous century — no good to anyone now. The tools, however, he could use.

You are strong.

The voice inside him made him shiver with delight.

I hope so.

He looked down at the canvas sack of bones; daring to pull open the threaded mouth of the bag, he glimpsed the small cluster of dark-coloured, almost black bones inside.

You came to me.

Yes. I chose you. The other was wicked.

Preston.

You are a good man.

I try so hard to be.

He resumed his work with the sharp tools – the dry brittle scrape of metal on dry bone. Rasp . . . rasp . . . rasp.

You will help me?

I will.

We can help each other, can't we?

Yes.

He resumed his work, shards of bone gathering on the dry earth floor at his feet – his work at *becoming*.

CHAPTER 52

28 October, 1856

It has been some days since the split. I am losing track of how many days now. I think I might be wrong on today's date, but how would I know?

We are like two tribes now, warily regarding each other across a rapidly diminishing island of ox meat. The others will no longer take Keats's supervision on the sharing of the meat. They help themselves too readily to what's there, and even I can see that this store of food will be exhausted long before the snow clears.

Keats and Broken Wing have attempted to forage for additional food, but there is little that one can feed on during the winter.

What we fear now is that the others will decide not to share the oxen any longer. That surely is a matter of certainty.

Ben shuddered with the cold seeping relentlessly through his poncho, seeping into and tightening his fingers so that it made holding his pen difficult.

We are posting our own guards now, as much to keep an eye on the others as to keep an eye on the woods. I share the early watch this morning with Mr Hussein.

He studied the stocky brown-skinned man standing next to him and staring out into the featureless misty grey before them. Ben found him to be an interesting man, from an exotic world far away. Through the still, early hours of the morning they had talked in quiet whispers, as long a conversation as Ben had yet had with the man. Hussein told him how he and his family had travelled here from Persia to discover for themselves this new world. They had come, he said, because several years ago, Hussein had read a book about the war with the British and had read a translation of the Declaration of Independence in Arabic. The words had proven so powerful and so moving to him that he resolved, then and there, to sell his businesses and home, gather his family and come to this faraway place that promised freedom and tolerance for all, regardless of creed or colour.

Ben was curious about Hussein's faith. It was a religion of which he knew precious little. Hussein had shown him a small, beautifully decorated book, his Qu'ran, and told him of the articles of faith, the pillars of Islam. Listening to the man describe his faith, it occurred to him how *practical* it sounded compared with the doom and gloom of sermons he'd heard from so many school chapels that harked back to a medieval past of bloodshed and brimstone; depictions of hell and demons and raging fires stoked to sear the souls of those not worthy enough of God's dominion.

By contrast, Mr Hussein's description of his faith sounded refreshingly forgiving, peaceful, tolerant. Perhaps the thing he was most taken aback by was the profound elevation of women as almost sacred, to be protected and revered.

Ben closed his journal and tucked it away into his satchel. 'Tell me, do you believe the Devil is out there?' he asked quietly.

Hussein's eyes remained on the wall of mist as he considered the question. 'My book, tell of many evil. The most evil is *Shaitan*. But I believe is much more evil, is more *haram* in hearts of men,' he replied, talking quietly. He turned to look at Ben. 'And you?'

Ben looked out at the mist, managing only to detect the faint outlines of the tree tops surrounding them. 'I don't believe in such things, Mr Hussein.' The image of Hearst's gutted, suspended body flickered across his mind. 'But yes, I think I believe an almost limitless evil can dwell in the hearts of men.'

'You are think, is *man* did those thing? Kill woman and boy?'

He shrugged, unwilling to speak aloud the tangle of suspicions and thoughts in his head. Preston truly frightened him. There was a chilling ruthlessness in the man's eyes on his last visit. And yet he struggled to imagine the same man, who'd been prepared to place himself between his people and the bear, being able to kill his own so brutally.

His own son, Sam, and Dorothy, his lover.

None of it made sense to him.

'I honestly don't know,' he replied and looked at him. 'I can't believe in a Devil. I just don't. But perhaps the evil we carry in our hearts, if it's strong, if there's enough of it, can take some sort of physical form?' Ben shrugged. It sounded unconvincing even as he gave words to the thought. 'It's just an idea.'

Hussein's eyes narrowed as he briefly struggled to make sense of what he'd said. 'I see.' He nodded after a few moments, considering the idea. 'Shaitan is the *haram* of heart of man – evil in our heart?'

Ben nodded. 'Perhaps.'

Hussein's eyes suddenly widened. Ben thought that the man had a further thought on the subject, but then Hussein swiftly raised his gun and pointed.

'Look!' he said, a finger jabbing out of the camp towards the blank and pale wall of freezing mist before them.

Ben turned to look at where he was pointing and saw absolutely nothing. 'What is it?'

'I see . . . moving.'

Ben scooped up his musket, placed the weather-worn butt against his shoulder, slipped a percussion cap in place and cocked it. Then he continued to study the formless mist in the direction the man was pointing.

'Are you sure?' he whispered.

'Yes.'

They watched and waited in silence. The only sounds Ben could hear were the thumping of his heart and the fluttering rustle of his breath. The mist was a deadening blanket wrapped around the woods, killing every natural sound beneath its weight. He only hoped the freezing moisture in the air hadn't percolated down the barrel and dampened the compacted charge of powder inside.

His eyes picked out nothing. And then he heard the crack of a branch; its brittle snap echoed through the mist. Beyond the edge of the clearing, in amongst the trees, something was moving.

'Do you see anything?' he whispered.

Hussein shook his head. 'Not see nothing now.'

He wished Keats was standing alongside them, charmless and vulgar with his revolting snorting and spitting, but unflinchingly steady with his gun. Even the rancid smell of his cheap tobacco seemed vaguely reassuring.

He heard more movement, further along to their right.

'Did you hear that?'

Hussein nodded silently.

Something's moving out there. Circling the camp.

He brought his gun up again, shouldering the butt and continuing to search for a ghostly outline of movement beyond its long barrel. Directly, he could pick out nothing, but then his peripheral vision detected the faintest flicker of movement to the right. He swung his aim in that direction, and for the briefest moment thought he saw the faint silhouette of some tall, lumbering, tusked or horned creature moving slowly between the trees.

Then it was gone.

266

'Oh my God, did you see it?' he hissed through clenched teeth.

'See nothing.'

'I thought I saw . . .'

Thought you saw what, exactly?

'Damn . . . I don't know what I saw.'

There was another crack of a branch, louder and closer — much closer, perhaps only a dozen yards away. Hussein grunted some foreign curse under his breath and his aim swung round towards where the noise had come from.

'Is near,' he said.

Then Ben caught an outline again, a darker smudge of grey that was moving directly towards them. His eyes struggled to discern the shape, but it very quickly became distinct. It looked vaguely crucifix-like — a short vertical and a longer horizontal cross bar that drooped and flapped as if broken in several places.

Ben lined his aim up on the thing and gently applied pressure to the trigger. With a *clack* the hammer came down. The percussion cap ignited, sending a puff of acrid blue smoke and a shower of sparks towards his face. A mere fraction of a second later, the weapon boomed deafeningly, punching his shoulder hard as it kicked upwards, obscuring his target with a thick pall of powder smoke.

As the smoke cleared and the shot echoed off the trees around the camp, he realised Keats was standing right next to him holding the end of his barrel up and to one side.

'What?'

The old man called out a sharp challenge in the harsh, percussive language Ben now recognised as Ute. There was no immediate reply. As the last tendrils of smoke from his gun drifted up and out of sight, he noticed that the dark cross-shaped smudge remained before him.

It stood perfectly still now.

He noticed another dark smudge to the right of it, and another.

Keats called out again. And this time, after a moment's

hesitation, a reply echoed back, a young man's voice with the brittle sound of fear in it. There was another, much longer reply from someone further away. Keats listened with his head cocked, and then replied.

He turned to Hussein and Ben. 'Lower your guns. Them Indians we met last week? They're comin' in.'

CHAPTER 53

28 October, 1856

The Paiute emerged from the mist like half a dozen ghosts. Ben watched the nearest of them step cautiously forward, becoming gradually more defined through the thinning wisps of cold air.

He held a weapon in each hand; a *tamahakan* in one, a knife in the other.

Keats barked something out, and the Indian stopped where he stood in the snow. The other five joined him and Ben noticed two of them struggling with something held between them. As they drew nearer and their outline became more distinct, he could see it was a body.

The sound of Ben's shot and Keats's barked challenge was drawing others from around the camp. He could hear the crunch of feet on snow and the smothered sound of questioning voices emerging from the mist.

'Tell the Indians I'm a doctor. I can take a look at their man,' muttered Ben, shouldering his rifle. Keats nodded and uttered a phrase in Ute. The nearest Paiute to Ben seemed to be the one to whom the others deferred. He appeared to be no more than eighteen or nineteen – a man, just. The others, closer now, he could see were a few years younger.

They struggled to understand Keats, the leader cocking his head and frowning.

From a few feet behind him, Ben heard Broken Wing call out sharply, making the language sound far less ugly than the guide had.

Ben pointed to the body. 'Can you tell them I can look at him?'

Broken Wing nodded and spoke at length to them. There was an exchange amongst the young men, and then the eldest nodded. The others stepped back from the body as Ben warily approached. He knelt down and by the wan light of early morning, most of it lost behind the carpet of mist, he quickly inspected it.

An older man, much older. He was dead, his skin cold and clammy.

Ben looked up at Keats and Broken Wing. 'Dead.'

Blood, congealed and sticky, had flowed down out of his grey-streaked hair and across his face and neck. Ben carefully probed the matted hair and found a jagged section of bone held by a flap of scalp, and a hole.

'A blow to the head, a small penetration. I suppose something like a pickaxe, or,' he said, gesturing at the *tamahakan* held by the nearest Paiute, 'one of those might have done this. I would say he died several hours ago.'

'Ask them what happened,' said Keats to Broken Wing.

The Shoshone spoke briefly, and the eldest Paiute spoke at length, making up for the gap in their shared vocabulary with elaborate hand gestures that seemed to tell as much of the story as the words. Keats had told Ben that Ute was a universal language shared by the Paiute, the Shoshone, the Ute and several other tribes west of the Nevadas, but they each spoke their own language, a bastardised hybrid of their shared tongue; consequently there was plenty of room for misunderstanding.

Broken Wing turned to Keats. 'He sssay, white-face demon, it hunt . . .' He struggled to find words in English, then finally relayed the rest to Keats in the version of Ute they seemed to share well between them. The crowd was growing; one huddle Keats's party, another Preston's people, warily emerging from their end and suspiciously regarding the others. Keats nodded, digesting it all before turning to Ben, stroking his beard distractedly for a moment.

'What did he say?'

He spoke quietly, for Ben's ears only. 'He said somethin' about a *white-face demon* has been . . . well . . . huntin' them. *Playin'* with them, last few days.'

There was a ripple of disturbance amongst the gathered people as Preston pushed through to the front. He took one look at the body, his face frozen, expressionless.

The Paiute spoke again with Broken Wing, who translated for Keats.

'He said the white-face demon's been watchin' them for the last two days, and then this morning, as they were spread out foraging, it attacked their elder, White Eagle. They found him already dead.'

There was a murmuring amongst those close enough to hear what was being said. Ben looked up at them to see women and children, their faces all radiating fear as they stared at the young Indian men.

Keats pointed to the one who'd done the talking. 'They're afraid of the demon. He's askin' if we'll let 'em in.'

Preston's gaze fell on the Paiute. 'To stay amongst us?'

A ripple of unrest stirred the crowd.

Keats nodded. 'They're scared of what's out there.'

The Indian gestured with his hands. The message was clear enough that Ben had the gist of it before Keats began translating. 'He says they fear what is out there more than they distrust us.'

'They can't stay in this clearing,' said Preston firmly. 'That is out of the question.'

Keats didn't bother to translate that for the Indian. Instead he turned to Preston, speaking quietly.

'Look, we need 'em more'n they need us. They know how to survive in these mountains better 'n we do. And,' he said, nodding towards the dwindling pile of oxen carcasses, 'what we got there ain't gonna last us much longer.'

Preston glared at Keats. His eyes widened, a damp sheen of sweat on his pale face.

'You don't understand, Keats. Those . . .' He looked over Keats's shoulder at the nearest Indian. There was a manic undercurrent to the way he spoke, an edgy fidgeting in the way he moved. 'Those creatures cannot stay with us.'

'Damned lick-fingered fool, they're not a *danger*. They're more scared than we are!'

Preston shook his head. 'They cannot stay. Not here! Not in this camp!'

Keats hawked, spat and turned away from him. 'Fuck it! They're staying with us.'

Preston cast a glance towards Ben, and then to Mr Hussein and one or two other faces in the crowd that were not of his party, and shook his head.

'We foolishly allowed ourselves to mix freely with you, to share food and comfort with you. And this after God came directly to *me*!' he said, thumping his chest with an open palm, '*To me!* And told me I must lead my people away from the contamination of outsiders. Look at us now,' he said, sweeping them all with his dark eyes.

'My people are living cheek by jowl with papists,' he said, directing his gaze at McIntyre, and then down at Ben. 'Atheists' – he looked at Hussein – 'and infidels.'

He then turned to study the six Indians, their dark, tattooed skin, their heads shaven like Mohawks, the shrivelled and dried totems of a long-ago raid dangling from leather thongs making them appear grotesque.

'And now we are to add Satan's gargoyles to the list.' Preston's voice drew quiet and ragged, for the benefit of Keats only. 'It's not a demon out there, fool. It's something far more frightening.' He smiled. 'For you, that is.'

'What're you talkin' 'bout, Preston?'

'A force you can't begin to imagine: God's rage. It's out there now, in those trees, looking down upon us all. Your people will all die badly, Keats! Mark this warning! A force you can't

272

begin to imagine will come for these demons, and rip to shreds anyone it finds with them.'

'They're not demons!' Keats snapped. 'Goddamn Indian savages maybe, but they ain't no demons or gargoyles or nothing!'

Ben glanced at the Paiute standing silently, bewildered as they watched the heated exchange.

'You welcome evil into your home and you *become* evil. Do you understand that?'

Both men remained silent for a moment, their eyes locked on each other.

The guide turned his back on Preston and took several steps towards the eldest Indian. He spoke in Ute and gestured and the Indian replied, but Ben's attention remained on Preston, who looked on in silence, taut muscles working beneath his gaunt cheeks as he bit down on his anger.

Ben wondered how much of his bottle of laudanum was left.

Standing behind Preston, he noticed a small group of the Mormon men, amongst them Vander, Zimmerman and Hollander, had brought guns and held them ready, undoubtedly loaded and primed to fire.

This isn't good.

Just a nod or a word from Preston and he suspected every one of them would open fire on the Paiute, perhaps on them, without a second thought. Of that he had no doubt. *And that's what Preston's considering right now, isn't it?*

The exchange in Ute between Keats and the Indian continued, both of them, it seemed, oblivious to the growing current of tension and whatever conclusion Preston was silently and very rapidly approaching. Zimmerman cocked the hammer on his rifle; the click sounded deafening even through the deadening wisps of mist that were swirling about them.

'Keats!' Ben shouted out, automatically swinging his own gun up from the ground. Hussein, standing beside him, also armed for guard duty, did likewise. Weyland stepped forward, pulling a Colt revolver from beneath his long winter coat.

The guide stopped, turned and saw the hesitant stand-off, guns readied on both sides, raised, but not quite aimed . . . not yet. The threat of an immediate exchange of gunfire was implicit; it remained just a few badly chosen words away. He laughed – a wheezing convivial campfire cackle that instantly made the frozen tableau look ridiculous.

'Oh dear,' he said, grinning and shaking his head. 'Well, this ain't a smart way to go now, is it? Goddamn stupid, if you ask me.' He looked at the half-dozen rifles held ready amongst the men standing behind Preston. 'See . . . reckon it would be you and me, Preston, who'll be the first to get a lead shot, eh? Don't make no sense, that.'

Preston said nothing, grinding his jaw in silence.

'How 'bout we all lower our guns an' we put this down as a little misunderstandin'?'

The men standing behind Preston looked to him for a sign, a word of command.

'See, we *all* need each other. Biggest thing we need to be considerin' now ain't no demons or monsters, but this winter and makin' do 'til spring.' Keats turned to look out at the faint outline of the trees. 'An' whatever's out there in them woods, the more eyes we have' – he nodded towards the Paiute – 'keepin' a watch out, the better for everyone, right?'

Ben noticed some murmurs of agreement amongst their people, but a stony silence from Preston and the gathered crowd behind him.

Keats slowly stepped forward, stretching out a hand. 'Preston? You know I'm talkin' sense here. Them Paiute can stay with us, on *our* side. An' we'll keep it like it is . . . ain't none of my people, nor these Indians, goin' to step beyond them oxen. How's that sound?'

Ben was close enough to Preston to see he was trembling; subtle repeated tics on his face and hands that shook gave him the air of a badly stacked lumber pile ready to tumble.

Preston shook his head almost imperceptibly. 'A storm is coming, Keats.'

He turned away from them towards his people and spread his hands. He spoke quietly to the armed men standing next to him and gently ushered them away. The crowd, men, women and children, drew away into the mist, heading back towards their side of the camp. The rumpling sound of boots on compacted snow slowly diminished as they faded into the grey.

Ben thought he saw Preston's tall frame lingering on in the mist as his people trooped back, and thought he heard whispered words, perhaps intended for his ears, perhaps not.

He will come for you all, and soon.

CHAPTER 54

```
cave iram Dei
M  T  W  T  F  S  S
            1  2  3
4  5  6  7  8  9  10
11 12 13 14 15 16 17
18 19 20 21 22 23 24
25 26 27 28 29 30
```

Thursday
Palo Cedro, California

'Can I top your coffee up?'

'Yes, please,' she answered, eyes still locked on the laptop's screen and the lengthy email she was tapping out.

'Real good brew,' the waiter added. 'Ground the beans myself, just for you.'

Irritated at her train of thought being broken, she looked up . . . and caught her breath.

'Here you go.' He poured a rich dark blend into the dregs of her cup.

She figured he was three or four years younger; at a guess, still at college. *Gorgeous* didn't do justice to his sculpted cheeks and warm Travolta eyes beneath a floppy fringe of dark brown hair.

'Thank you,' she said.

His eyes narrowed curiously. 'You British?'

'Yeah, well . . . uh . . . English, actually.'

He grinned. 'God, I love that.'

Rose's cheeks burned, caught off guard by such intimacy. 'What? What do you . . . ?'

'The way you guys say that: *act-u-all-y*. That's just s-o-o-o British.'

'Oh, God, that's embarrassing,' she muttered self-consciously. 'I'll remember not to use that word again.'

'No way, I love it,' he said. 'You staying in town?'

She shook her head. 'No, I'm just passing, really.'

'Where you going?'

'Where I'm going you probably haven't heard of, but I've just been up to Portland.'

'Cool,' he said, 'that's where I go to college. Linguistics and media.'

Rose smiled and nodded, wondering what to say to that.

'So . . . are you, like, on holiday?'

'Um, no, not really, it's work. I'm doing some research.'

'Yeah? Cool,' he said. He glanced over his shoulder quickly. 'Look, uh, my shift manager would kick my ass if he heard me, but are you, like, in town tonight?'

She felt the colour drain from her face as she looked up at him – a lean young man with the chiselled contours of a Calvin Kline model.

What? Is he actually hitting on me?

'Umm, I'm . . .' She looked out at the mid-afternoon sky. It was still several hours' drive back to Blue Valley, and whether she grabbed a motel room here, or booked back into the room she had been occupying for the last fortnight, it was still thirty-nine bucks out of the dwindling slush fund.

'Only, I know a nice bar nearby,' the waiter continued. 'Nice food, nice place. Just a drink and a burger. I'm buying.'

'I, uh, I really, I'm . . . I wasn't . . .' she stammered awkwardly.

Dammit, Rose, get a grip. You sound like a retard.

The young man shrugged apologetically, realising he'd caught her on the hop. 'Sorry, there's me diving in like that,' he said quietly. 'I just fell in love with that accent when you asked for a table earlier,' he added, taking a step back with the coffee pot in his hand. 'I finish up here at six, if you wanna go get something?'

Rose managed a composed smile. 'I'll think about it.'

She watched him head back to the counter, irritated with herself for being caught off balance and coming across as a gibbering idiot.

She slurped a mouthful of her coffee and sneaked a discreet glance at him.

Gorgeous though, isn't he?

He was. But she reminded herself that she was just a frumpy plain Jane, and that after he got over the novelty accent and got his cookies, he'd be off just like every other bloke.

Back to work, girl.

There was an email that needed writing and sending ASAP. What she'd uncovered this morning was rich pickings, very rich pickings indeed.

Julian,

I've just driven back from Portland, Oregon. I got a hit on Benjamin Lambert.

You won't believe what I found. Okay, let me do this in order so it makes sense. My thinking was that if it was Lambert who survived, he'd turn up at some point in their press. He's English, a posh guy, an aspiring writer – let's not forget, a writer with one hell of a story. At the back of my mind, I was thinking that maybe, at some point, he might have taken his story to the penny press.

Now, you said you researched UK records up to the point he set sail for the Americas, right? And then that's it. According to you he vanished. I'm guessing you let the trail go there because you've been too busy to take it any further, what with shmoozing with the suits for money, but here's the thing, Jules . . . Lambert's story continues.

Oh boy does it continue. Let me give it to you as best I can make it out from the paper archives I've been rummaging through.

It most definitely was Lambert who got out alive. There may have been others, but I'm almost certain that Lambert was the 'Rag Man'. Apparently, he made it all the way to

Portland, and stayed there for a long while. A very long while. It seems like he managed to recover from his traumatic experience in the mountains. He settled there and made a life in Portland. He found God, by the way, which is interesting given how much of an atheist he sounds in the journal.

Mind you, perhaps it's also understandable, given what he went through?

Anyway, local archives show he became a lay preacher. He also became something of a successful local businessman, making money from property. He also wrote articles from time to time in the papers, some preachy stuff, and become a local civic leader, a councillor.

He married, had kids, and made more money.

The Lambert family exists today as a very wealthy family. They own a lot of property around Portland, and have a lot of money in various big companies – but it's all very discreet, like the Barclay brothers – there just isn't much out there on the family. You might do better than me.

Point is, Ben survived. And if we approach it right, we might get a chance to interview some reclusive billionaire and hand over the journal to him, filming his reaction, of course.

Rose nodded, happy with that, checked her laptop was still getting a decent wi-fi link and then hit 'send'. She knew Julian would be jumping up and down with excitement over this.

She smiled, pleased with her legwork up in Portland. It would be satisfying to show Jules she could do just as well as him at trawling for facts. Maybe he might start thinking of her as more than the technology geek in their partnership.

She looked up and caught sight of the waiter, gracefully weaving his way between some tables to deliver an order to a table of truckers. He handed out several plates of food and tossed the men some false small talk before heading back to the counter. He caught her sneaking a glance and offered her a snatched, coy smile as he rounded the counter and headed into the kitchen through swing doors.

Rose felt an uninvited tingle of excitement and a momentary stab of guilt.

Just a burger and a beer, then I'm heading off . . .

CHAPTER 55

28 October, 1856

Snow cascaded down; giant feathery flakes that tumbled from the heavy sky above and settled with a whisper. The afternoon was almost as dim as night, the weak and lethargic sun hidden away from sight behind the surging grey blanket of cloud.

The gathering around the fire in the middle of the Keats party camp was well attended, the flames licking high, pushing out an undulating envelope of warmth that embraced the small gathering. The flickering light of the fire glinted in the eyes of everyone, intense and wide with anxiety, as they listened to the burning crack of damp wood and fir cones, and considered what needed to be discussed.

In silence they stared at the six Paiute who, in turn, warily stared back.

'So, their leader, the older-lookin' one' – Keats gestured towards him – 'is called somethin' like Three Hawks. That's if I was understandin' him right.'

Mr Bowen regarded them unhappily. 'See, 'ow do we know we can trust 'em? I got a wife and little 'uns to worry about. These 'ere bastards were going to do for us last time we ran into them.'

'But they didn't, though,' said Ben, 'did they?'

Bowen curled his lip uncertainly. 'They'll do us in our sleep. Take what we got and disappear, just you see.'

'Fact is,' said Keats, 'they're here because somethin' out in those trees scared 'em into our camp, Bowen. Maybe they're wonderin' whether they can trust *us*, eh?'

Bowen said nothing.

Ben looked at Broken Wing. 'Can you ask them whether they've actually *seen* what's out there?'

Broken Wing asked the question. Three Hawks listened and then nodded and conferred quietly for a moment with the younger ones sitting either side of him.

'Mr Keats, can you tell us what they're saying?' asked Weyland.

'Dunno, they're talkin' too fast. Wait a minute . . . let 'em talk it out.'

After a few moments, it seemed some consensus was arrived at. Three Hawks turned to Broken Wing and Keats, speaking slowly and signing at the same time.

'None of them have seen it clearly,' Keats translated. 'But one of them' – he nodded towards one of the younger Paiute – 'said he caught a glimpse of it in the woods. He was the one who found their elder, White Feather.'

Three Hawks spoke again with Broken Wing. Keats waited until they'd finished, then asked Broken Wing in Ute what the man had said.

'He ssssay . . . demon, large . . .' said Broken Wing, his hands gesturing around his head, 'isss . . . like bone . . .'

'A skull?' offered Ben.

Broken Wing nodded. 'Ya! Ssskull, large ssskull. And, bonesss . . .' Broken Wing's hands mimed protrusions all over his body. 'Like ssspines.'

Keats spoke quickly with Broken Wing in the Shoshone dialect, scowling with disbelief before he repeated what he'd heard. 'They said it is a giant, three men tall. Yet moving silently like a spirit.'

Ben shook his head. 'I can't believe he saw that.'

Keats waved a hand dismissively. 'Hell, you're right not to. Damned Indian folk have a habit of exaggeratin' everythin'.'

Ben remembered reading the journals of an explorer in Africa. He had made the same observation of tribes he'd encountered. It was not that these savages were deliberately exaggerating their tales, it was simply that they didn't have an agreed metric for measuring and comparing. *Big* basically meant anything bigger than the storyteller. Big could mean any size. And stories that passed from one teller to another had a habit of inflating.

Keats was listening to Broken Wing again. Then, when the man had finished, he relayed what had been said.

'They believe it's a white man's devil. A devil that came into the woods with us.' He looked across the clearing at the shifting silhouetted figures on the far side of the camp. 'He believes it came from amongst the others.'

Ben nodded and muttered. 'That, I can believe.'

Keats pulled on his pipe, sending up an acrid puff of tobacco smoke. 'Fact of the matter is, I don't think it's no demon. One of them people's gone bad in the head. That's what it is, I reckon.'

'Not *bad*,' said Ben, 'but *mad*. Quite insane.'

Keats wiped his gnarled nose. 'Reckon you're talkin' 'bout Preston?'

Ben nodded. 'Yes, maybe.'

Keats shrugged. 'Same difference. Could be him, could be any other. It's one of 'em Mormon folk.'

'What worries me most,' said Ben, 'is what Preston's telling his people. Their devotion to him is *fanatical*.'

Weyland nodded gravely and tossed a branch on the fire. 'They sure looked ready to use their guns today. If he'd told them to, they would have fired. Of that I'm sure.'

'Not necessarily just on these Indians,' added Ben. Everyone around the fire looked at him. 'I think if there'd been shooting, those guns would have been turned on us just as soon as these Paiute had been dealt with.'

'Yup,' muttered McIntyre, 'that's how it looked to me, too.'

It was quiet for a moment, the crackle, pop and hiss of burning twigs and cones filling the silence.

'Something's changed in Preston,' said Ben. He wondered if it would be wise to tell them that the minister had most probably been pushed over the edge by the laudanum he'd helped himself to. That it was his fault for allowing him enough doses to become addicted to it. 'He's become unstable. His mind is playing tricks on him. The bear attack, the fever he's been through, the burden of leading his people; I believe these things have combined to send him quite mad.'

'These Indians,' said Bowen. 'He said they was evil demons.'

Keats shook his head. 'Preston been lookin' at us different since them people was killed. We're *all* outsiders to 'em, all *evil* to 'em – including these Paiute.'

'It's not just about survival, fear of what they think's out there,' said Ben. 'It's about manifest destiny. Preston and his people are out here for a reason.'

'What reason?'

'They weren't just travelling west for a new life. They're on a mission. Preston's led them on what he believes is a divine mission.'

'I have to admit, I've never come across religious folk as peculiar as these,' uttered Weyland.

'They're *Mormons*,' said McIntyre with distaste, 'what else do you expect? That's no form of Christianity I recognise.'

'They're not Mormons,' said Ben. 'They're something else. Something of Preston's creation.'

The others looked at him.

'That's what's happening. He's led them away to write a new faith, a new book of God.'

Mr Hussein shook his head and spoke quietly in Farsi to his family.

'What're you saying there, Mr Hussein?' asked Bowen.

He stopped and turned to the others around the fire. 'I say . . . man cannot rewrite words of Allah.'

284

The words hung on a silence, broken only by the spit and hiss of a log in the fire.

'I'm not sure I'm happy with the idea of some madman so close to us,' said Weyland, glancing at the distant glow on the far side, 'conjuring up his own religion from nothing.'

Keats grunted in agreement. 'Well, whatever crazy *hokum* that Preston's come up with, reckon we gotta now consider them folks as somethin' of a problem for us.' He tapped the embers of his pipe out into the fire, sending up a shower of sparks. 'Them oxen lyin' between us and them will be gone long before spring, long before any one of us can think of makin' our way out of here.' He locked his gaze on them all. 'There'll be fightin' long before then, I can assure you.'

He looked towards Three Hawks and the five other young men sat with him, watching the discussion dispassionately. 'Hell, that's why we need these Paiute folks with us 'cause if . . . *when* . . . the fightin' comes, we'll need every able-bodied man we got.'

Mrs McIntyre grasped her husband's hand tightly. 'Mr Keats, will it really come to that? A fight between us and them?'

The old man's wrinkled face softened with pity. He could see the woman, and the children whose arms were wrapped around her, were trembling. 'Fear makes people do some terrible things, ma'am. It's what folk like Preston *use* to make the rest of us do exactly what they want.'

Ben turned and looked towards the distant flames of the other campfire, and the indistinct silhouettes of people moving around it.

'You frighten a bunch o' people enough,' Keats continued, 'I mean really, really put the fear of God into them . . . reckon they'll do just about anythin' for you.'

'If you're right, Mr Keats,' said Weyland, 'then we should be asking ourselves what it is Preston might ask them to do.'

285

CHAPTER 56

Thursday
Over Utah

Shafts of autumn sunlight shone across the Oval Office, dappling the thick rug with light and shade. He could see it was a glorious afternoon out there on the White House lawn.

'Mr President?'

He stirred, drawing his eyes away from the explosion of rust-coloured leaves on the elms and maple trees to the dim interior of the office, and matters at hand.

'Mr President?' his aide-de-camp pressed him. 'We need a decision.'

Shepherd looked up at him. 'I'm afraid I really can't let this slide any longer, can I?'

'The people need to know where we go from here, Mr President.'

He nodded. Yes, these uncertain times required a strong leader and a clear message to those who would stand in the way of God's will.

'You've already threatened the use of the ultimate deterrent, sir. Perhaps it's time to—'

Shepherd cut in, smiling. 'To use the words of the Washington Post, *time to shit or get off the potty.'*

His aide made a face. 'That's putting it in unnecessarily

blunt terms, sir. There is still room for negotiation with these people.'

Shepherd shook his head. 'No, I don't believe there is. What we're looking at, Duncan, is a clash of faiths. These people will not listen to God's message.'

He stood up, flexing his tired and aching back. 'And what can you do to those who continue to refuse to sit at God's table? Beyond the light of His love, it is cold and dark and barbaric. These people, these . . . non-believers . . . burn in torment there, Duncan, and they know no better.'

'Sir?'

'I've extended the hand of friendship and love, opened the doors of our church for them to enter. What more can I do?'

'Yes, Mr President. But you understand, escalating this situation now would be very dangerous. There's a delicate geopolitical balance around the middle—'

'Duncan.' He turned to him. 'This is where faith in God comes into the equation. We will have a world under His new dominion. By hook or by crook, mark my words, He will unite us all under one faith . . . or He will leave ashes.'

He looked out at the carefully manicured lawn and beyond that at the gathered protestors bearing placards, held at bay by a cordon of marines. Above, the pure blue sky was dotted with helicopters and the smudge of smoke columns rising from the distant city riots.

'Now is not the time to walk away from destiny.' He turned round. 'If they won't open their eyes to His love, then let them feel His wrath.'

'Sir?'

'We'll send the missiles.'

'Mr President? We can't do that!'

'Send the missiles, Duncan.'

'Mr President!'

Shepherd felt the warmth of the sun through the bay windows on his cheeks and closed his eyes, and imagined he could hear

287

the roar of a thousand propulsion systems stirring to life in their silos.

'Mr President!'

'Mr Shepherd?'

Eyes still closed, he heard the rumble of the jet, a steady monotonous whine, and in the background the trill of some- body's cell phone several rows of seats further back – one of his entourage of campaign workers.

'Mr Shepherd, sir? I'm sorry to disturb you, but we need to review the figures ahead of the meeting this afternoon.'

He opened his tired eyes, blinking back the glare coming in through the round window on his right. Duncan was leaning forward in the seat opposite. 'I'm sorry, but we do need to go over the projected spending again for the next six months before the meeting.'

'Duncan?' said Shepherd.

'Yes?'

'You *do* believe in God, don't you?'

He looked confused. 'Of course.' He gestured towards the other workers dotted around the seats of the commercial airliner, most of them industriously tapping away on laptops or speaking animatedly on their phones. 'Everyone on this plane believes in God, Mr Shepherd. Everyone's behind you. And, if the polls really are giving us a true picture, millions more every day,' he added with a reassuring smile.

Shepherd nodded and smiled. 'I'm sorry. Forgive me.'

'You helped me see His light, brought me across to *your* ministry.'

Shepherd smiled. He could see the words were coming from Duncan's heart. 'I've never once looked back, sir. I'd follow you anywhere, Mr Shepherd.'

He smiled. 'You're a good man, Duncan.'

'But, uh . . . if I can press on. We're looking' – Duncan consulted his PDA, tapping the small screen lightly with the tip of his pen – 'at about two hundred million dollars media spend on campaigning for the next six months. That's if we want to stay in the game with the big two parties.'

Shepherd gazed wearily out of the window as his campaign manager began a tedious breakdown of fund allocations, and what additional funding support they would need to secure to stay the distance. But Shepherd's focus drifted off piste.

'. . . We're getting a lot of support pledged from churches outside ours, a broad spectrum of Christian right. I think both the Republicans and Democrats really damaged themselves through the primaries with all that back-biting and bitching between candidates . . .' Duncan's voice droned on.

I've been waiting so long for this. Waiting so long to find them.

The recorded cell phone conversation between Cooke and his female associate, Whitely, indicated they were both heading out once more into the wilds very soon. Shepherd needed to ensure he could find a way to locate the site. Nothing short of exact GPS co-ordinates would do. He knew what it was like up there. In those thick woods he could be fifty yards away from those mouldering remains and quite easily never find them. Cooke and Whitely were going to lead him straight there, but only if he played his cards right.

'. . . We're poaching a lot of support from both of them right now. But that's theoretical support, protest support. The trick will be turning that into genuine card-carrying support for your campaign, and sustaining that loyalty through the next eighteen months . . .'

Shepherd realised he was going to have to find an opportunity to slip away for a few days.

Prayer time.

That's what he'd call it. A little sojourn away from the seedy world of politics to find communion with God, to seek guidance. That would play well with his audience. He decided he'd announce that tomorrow on his next *Faith TV* broadcast.

This needs to be handled so carefully.

His special man sent over to the United Kingdom, Carl, was

doing a very thorough job, as always. Julian Cooke's first business contact, the BBC editor, had already been dealt with effectively. According to Carl, the bumbling British police were baffled by the motiveless stabbing and were already investigating a local suspect with a previous conviction for a similar offence and a history of violent mental illness.

The other contact Cooke had made, however, might be a bit more of a problem. He had more of a public profile. He trusted Carl to handle this intelligently.

'. . . in total, though, we're going to need to chase down at least another six or seven hundred million dollars in campaign funds to take us through to the finishing line next year. I've lined up several meetings this afternoon in Austin, Mr Shepherd. They're all interested in getting behind your campaign, but you'll need to assure them that yours is not exclusively a Mormon message, but a Christian message. That means you're going to have to equivocate a little on the abortion issue . . .'

Shepherd nodded absent-mindedly and settled back in his chair. He looked out at the patchwork of farmland, a chequerboard of olive and yellow squares, passing below. Iowa, Utah, Ohio . . . all those bioethanol-corn states were lining up nicely. He could sense that momentum was building already, carrying him forward to an inevitable appointment with destiny. He smiled and turned to his financial co-ordinator.

'Are you ready to serve your country in office, Duncan?'

Duncan Hope looked up from his PDA. 'I think so, sir,' he replied, hesitantly adding, 'Do you think we can really do it?'

Shepherd's gaunt cheeks creased with a winning television smile. 'This is where faith in God comes into the equation, my friend.'

CHAPTER 57

cave iram Dei

M	T	W	T	F	S	S
					1	2	3
4	5	6	7	8	9	10
11	12	13	14	15	16	17
18	19	20	21	22	23	24
25	26	27	28	29	30	

Thursday
Hammersmith, London

Julian was still playing the news through his head as he let himself in through the glass doors of the small industrial unit that was Soup Kitchen's office.

Sean dead?

He'd seen on the local news last night that a man had been stabbed to death whilst walking his dog on Wimbledon Common and, like every other viewer at home, he had sighed at yet another sign of the times; this was the result of allowing Britain's troubled and tormented souls to wander the streets at will with no one supervising their care and medication.

Then this morning he'd emailed Sean at his work address for an update on how things were proceeding, only to get a response from a harried colleague that *Sean* was the unfortunate man who had been attacked.

Miranda came in for only a few hours every other day. Today wasn't one of them, which was just as well. He wasn't ready for a cheerful *good morning* and some bright and breezy banter. He flipped on the dim overhead lights of their front office, filled up the coffee maker and put it on, then booted up his PC as he waited.

His mind raced with conflicting threads of thought.

On the one hand he was surprised at how shaken he was. Sean and he went back quite a few years, and the poor bastard was leaving behind his wife and a little girl. Sean had been an all-round good egg, and now, out of the blue, he was gone.

Shit like that always seemed to happen so quickly – death just sneaked in and changed lives in the blink of an eye. He made a mental note to order a wreath, and write a few words to Sean's wife before he headed to Heathrow tomorrow.

What is wrong with this evil fucking world?

He reluctantly pushed his mind onto other matters and felt like a mercenary bastard for doing so.

There was now no fast-tracked contract with the BBC being steered through the decision process. With Sean dead, the deal was dead too. Even if whoever replaced him finally got round to dealing with the in-tray and liked the sound of the project, it would probably be far too late to be of any use to Julian and Rose. Money was running out and they'd both need to go scare up some other work to keep the business going. He was halfway through a mental stocktake of clients they could tap for some quick tide-me-over work when another, unwelcome thought fluttered into his mind and settled like a crow on a telegraph pole.

You told Sean about the find and now he's dead.

He shook his head. 'Oh, come on.'

And was there not a click on your phone?

The coffee maker burbled and steamed that it was ready and he poured himself a cup, black.

. . . and someone was in your flat, weren't they?

'Oh for fuck's sake, Julian,' he muttered, 'now really isn't the right time to start becoming a paranoid twat.'

His old office PC finally finished choking on Vista and connected to the internet to pick up his mail. Thirty-three spams chased each other into his in-box, one after the other, most promising to turn him into a sexual leviathan. But there was one email that attracted his attention.

He clicked on it.

Mr Cooke,

Yes, I would be interested in exchanging information with you. I am fascinated by the untold, unheard story of the Preston party. It remains a profoundly interesting mystery. What happened to all those people? It's a story that has intrigued me for many years. And in all this time I have encountered no one else who has heard of it, let alone is actively investigating it. So it was very exciting for me to receive your email yesterday.

I am based in America. I have business that takes me back and forth between the east and west coasts on a regular basis. If you are planning a trip to the States any time soon, I'm sure I can co-ordinate my travels to coincide with yours, so that we can meet somewhere and discuss what we both have.

For my part, I have more biographical detail on William Preston than I have presented on the web page.

I look forward to hearing back from you.

Very best

Arnold Zuckerman

Julian sat back and sipped his coffee. Now that was something he really hadn't been expecting. The web page he'd stumbled on at the beginning of the week had looked like a dead site, something put up by someone long ago and forgotten about. Perhaps it would be something of a consolation if he could tie in a meeting with this Zuckerman whilst returning to pack things up. It might help fill a hole in the research. To Julian's chagrin, he'd been unable to come up with anything at all on Preston. The man's background was a gap they'd need to fill whether they made a documentary or a drama, especially if, as Dr Griffith had suggested, they were looking at a psychotic cult leader who had led his people to their deaths.

He hastily typed a response.

Mr Zuckerman

I'm due to fly out to the States tomorrow. Whilst I'm researching this story, my base of operations is a small town called Blue Valley, north end of California. It's a quiet place where people go for camping and hiking holidays these days. It's the nearest settlement to the site I mentioned in my previous mail – a day's hike from it.

I'll be honest with you: I won't reveal the exact location of the site, as it's a site of historical importance and it would be inappropriate for me to share that information willy-nilly. However, I'd be willing to share with you the story of what happened out there. We have recovered a detailed account of the events, a journal written by one of the party, almost perfectly preserved and for the most part legible.

I will be in Blue Valley for three or four days if you wish to arrange a meeting.

Julian Cooke (Documentary Maker)

CHAPTER 58

31 October, 1856

It has been snowing constantly for three or four days now. Several feet of it has covered the old trampled snow. The gutted ribcages of the oxen now lie mercifully beneath a thick carpet. The remaining untouched carcasses were hauled away by Preston's people at some point during the last few days. As we shivered in our shelters listening to the buffeting wind, they must have all been out there working in conspiratorial silence to drag them to their end of the clearing.

There were those in our group who suggested we march across, en masse, to reclaim a fair share of the meat. But Keats was not amongst them. He advised caution.

I must say I agree. They number more than a hundred; thirty or more of them, men able to wield a weapon of some sort. We, however, including our new guests, the Paiute, number less than a dozen who could fight. We still have packing oats to eat, and the Indians have managed to bring in small amounts of foraged food: hares, a few birds, some root bulbs that are barely palatable after being boiled interminably. It is hardly enough. Without the meat, I believe we will eventually starve.

Ben looked at the ominous words he had just scribbled on the page. The diluted ink was a pale blue and hard to read against the page by the flickering light of the small fire inside. Broken Wing placed another small branch thick with fir needles on, and almost immediately the fire crackled and roared to life, the smoke sucked effectively up through the hole at the top by the wind gusting outside.

Three Hawks shared the warmth with them, there being just enough squat room for the four of them.

Keats worked his knife on the inside of his pipe's bowl, scraping away a residue that was building up and blocking the stem. Ben could tell he was doing his best to catch one word in ten as Broken Wing and Three Hawks talked fluently in Ute, but by the frustrated frown on his face, was failing miserably.

'*Grey hair trapper called Keeet*,' answered Broken Wing.

'*You travel with him?*'

'*Yes. Two seasons.*'

'*Why?*'

'*White-faces pay dollars.*'

Three Hawks nodded. He knew dollars were much better to trade with than beaver pelts. '*Grey hair is friend?*'

Broken Wing regarded Keats silently for a while. '*Yes.*'

Three Hawks studied the old man, his eyes drawn to his bushy salt and pepper beard, and then to Ben, his chin framed by a dark blonde fuzz of hair.

'*Why do white-faces grow tails on their mouths?*'

Broken Wing shrugged. '*The Great Chief gave them only to white men.*'

'*Ah, I think I know why.*' Three Hawks raised his finger. '*So they can tickle their bossy wives.*'

Broken Wing looked at him, confused, then Three Hawks stuck his tongue out and waggled it. Both Indians dissolved with laughter.

'What's so funny?' asked Ben, roused from his writing by their snorting.

Keats shook his head. 'Some dumb-ass Indian joke,' he muttered grumpily.

He watched them both rocking on their haunches, their dark

faces split with carefree schoolyard grins. There was an *assurance* about them he envied, a cool fatalism in the way they squared up to face death that he wished he could emulate.

They don't fear it.

That was something Keats had told him — that they didn't have a concept of death. To them it was a journey, just a transition to another place. In their minds, it was a much better place. Ben supposed that kind of belief could make any man brave.

'I've not seen a single one of the others for a while now,' said Ben. Snow had been coming down heavily since the Paiute had arrived, a heavy blizzard that had reduced visibility through the thick, silent curtains of flakes, to a distance of yards.

Keats nodded. 'I can see their fires at night. They're still there, all right.'

'It's been three days since we've had any kind of contact with them.'

The guide nodded solemnly. 'That ain't so good.'

'What do you think is going on over there?'

'Hell if I know.'

'Maybe Preston's writing his new faith, his new bible?'

'Sonofabitch is as mad as a mongoose.'

Ben nodded. That much was for sure.

'That kinda crazy ain't what you need out in the wilds.'

'Keats?'

The guide looked up from cleaning his pipe.

'What are we going to do? The food we have won't last us until spring.'

'We sit tight for now, Lambert. Whatever killed 'em folk gonna come back an' do it again, I reckon.' He smiled. 'An' if it's happy killin' them, not us, I ain't complainin'.'

Broken Wing translated for Three Hawks. The Paiute said something and Broken Wing nodded.

'What's that he said?' asked Ben.

'Three Hawks sssay . . . white-face devil came with others. Will kill others.'

297

As the fire settled to embers, Three Hawks left to rejoin the Paiute, no doubt to exchange bemused observations on the white-faces. Broken Wing and Keats wrapped themselves tightly in blankets and hides and were soon asleep, Keats with his thick and irritating nasal rumble, Broken Wing soft and even like a woman.

Ben lay awake, troubled by what the Indian had said.

Whether a devil or, as Keats said, craziness, he knew somehow that Preston was going to bring death to this clearing. And he realised with certainty that there was perhaps only one way it might be prevented. If he wasn't already too late, that was.

Ben stepped out into the gusting night, immediately blinking back soft, clotted flakes of snow blown across the ground and into his face. He could hear the clatter and whack of something loose amongst their shelters being bullied by the wind, and the muted roar of trees around the clearing sounding very much like a restless sea as they swayed in unison.

He could see virtually nothing, just the next few yards in front of his feet, which disappeared through the new snow, down to the older, compacted and ice-hard layer below. Ben oriented himself and headed for the far side, stooped low and leaning into the freezing blasts, tears welling in his eyes and freezing on his cheeks. He decided to give the oxen's graveyard a wide berth, wary of tangling his feet amidst the ribcages and creating a commotion that might be heard above the restless weather.

He suspected they would still have a man or two on watch at night, but with visibility down to little more than the stretch of an arm amidst the swirling flurry, it would be for no more reason than to guard the appropriated meat.

She's up ahead. Not far.

Ben was familiar enough with the lie of the land, perhaps more so than any other person camped here, having made plenty of visits across this no-man's-land to care for Preston and Emily.

The first of their shelters lay ahead of him; a hummock of snow, the entrance marked only by a corner of tarpaulin flapping noisily like a pennant. Beyond it, another and another — all looking like identical mole hills.

If she can talk . . . tell them whom she saw . . . who killed her mother and Sam . . . ?

Ben wondered if that would be enough, though. He had no idea, for sure, how tightly they were holding on to the idea that Preston might be some prophet — that only by his side lay salvation and the way out of this wilderness.

I can tell them about the laudanum, the fevered confession, Dorothy coming to me.

Even as he considered that, he knew the odds were against him, especially if there had already been suspicions voiced that he might have been responsible for killing the Dreytons.

The thought filled him with an intense anger and revulsion. There had been nothing inappropriate in his friendship with Sam. He had merely seen himself in the boy; a younger version of himself, a curious young mind questioning the world, yet being suffocated inside Preston's bizarre religious strictures.

Even if he could not get Emily to talk, he resolved to take her away from these people. Perhaps if he took her with him tonight, and Preston arrived on their side with a posse in the morning to reclaim her, he could quietly do a deal with the man. It would be one less mouth for his people to feed, and should she begin to talk about what she had seen . . . better for him, maybe, that she be talking to outsiders instead of to his loyal flock?

Crouching low in the snow, his poncho fluttering around him, he looked from one shelter to the next, watching for any signs of movement. He could see no one. Ahead of him lay the hump he recognised as the Dreytons' shelter. He took several quick, loping strides towards it, kneeling down and preparing to lift aside the canvas flap.

He hoped to find only Mrs Zimmerman inside. The woman had seemed just about the only one of these people he could reason with. Perhaps she'd come with him too.

'I thought you'd return,' a voice hissed over the rumple of wind.

Ben turned to see the broad and stout outline of a man.

'Who's that?' he whispered.

'You know who,' said Vander, leaning forward. He held a long-bladed knife in one hand. 'And you have no business here.'

Ben stood up. 'I thought I should look in on Emily.'

'William told you, all of you, that you are to stay to your side.'

'I know. But listen.' *Perhaps I can make him see.* 'She must know who killed her family. We have to try to bring her out of this shock.'

Vander didn't immediately respond and Ben allowed himself to hope the short Dutchman was considering that seriously.

'She's witnessed the face of God's rage, Lambert. You think anyone can come back from seeing that? Her mind is completely gone.'

Ben shook his head. 'She's in shock.'

Vander stepped forward, his knife held in front of him. 'I see the Devil in you, Lambert. You should leave now, before someone guts you like a pig.'

'It's Preston, isn't it?' Ben blurted.

'What?'

'It's Preston who killed them. He did it to convince you all that—'

Vander reached out and grabbed him angrily. 'God's rage will be visited on you next,' he spat, 'if you say that again. And if not God's, then mine.'

He pushed Ben away. 'Back to your side . . . and keep your sick poison over there. You have Indian boys to befriend now.'

'Vander, listen to me. This will end in all of us dying, unless Emily talks to us and tells us what she saw. I think Preston has gone insane.'

The man reached out with frightening speed, grabbed the gathered layers of clothing around Ben's neck and pulled him forward. He could feel the tip of Vander's knife pressed into one ear.

'I could push this in and kill you, just like that.'

Ben felt his bladder loosen. A warm trickle that quickly cooled.

'I could cut the tongue from your mouth, Lambert. But . . .' He smiled. 'I'd much rather watch you starve with the others.'

He pushed Ben away.

'The storm is coming and it'll wash you away like so much shit.'

Ben took a step back.

'Go!' Vander hissed.

Ben turned and headed back to his side of the camp, wondering if Vander would run along and tell Preston of this incursion. He could imagine Preston marching over in the morning, accompanied by an armed guard, to make some punitive example of him. There would undoubtedly be a stand-off once more. He wondered if it would go beyond that and turn into a bloody massacre.

He cursed his bad luck at being discovered by Vander, and wondered if he'd made things worse by attempting to sneak across under the cover of night and the gusting wind.

There'll be consequences tomorrow.

Ben decided he was going to sleep with his gun loaded and right beside him tonight, if he slept at all.

Vander waited outside the shelter until he was sure the Englishman had gone. Then he stooped down, pushed the fluttering canvas flap aside and entered the muted warmth of Emily's shelter.

Mrs Zimmerman stirred. 'What was that? I heard whispers outside.'

'It was nothing,' he said, pulling the flap down and weighting the bottom of it with a log. He knelt down beside the huddled form of the girl. 'You can go now. I'll mind her.'

She looked at him. 'Emily has not eaten again today. I keep trying her with broth.'

Vander shook his head. 'She is already dead. Her body just hasn't learned of that yet.' He shuffled to one side to allow Mrs

Zimmerman to squeeze past. 'Go on and be with your husband tonight. I'll watch over her.'

She nodded obediently and manoeuvred passed him. Then she stopped, an expression of concern on her face. 'You're not planning to—?'

'Planning to what?'

Mrs Zimmerman swallowed nervously. 'She'll be all right come morning? Won't she?'

'That's up to the Lord now, isn't it?'

She studied him uncertainly.

'Go now,' he said, 'she will be fine.'

She nodded and then, after affectionately stroking Emily's still face one last time, she left the shelter, securing the flap behind her.

Vander sat perfectly still for a while, listening to the sound of the moaning wind, waiting to be sure Mrs Zimmerman had gone. He looked at the sleeping girl. Awake, her small oval face was just as expressionless, those eyes of hers locked into an unmoving gaze that never broke or wandered.

'Well, Emily? What did those eyes of yours see? Hmm? Enough that tongues may start wagging.'

Her breathing remained regular and quiet.

There's no longer a human soul there, he decided, looking down at her pallid skin and along the length of her huddled form, covered by several thick blankets.

You're just an empty shell now, aren't you, Emily? Something that looks like a little girl, but no longer is.

A guilty, tickling urge stirred inside him, an urge he had promised himself not to allow out again. A promise he had also made to Preston, some years back – not to *play* with the children in that way any more.

He lay down beside her so that his face was only inches away from hers. He could feel her short breath on his cheeks at regular intervals.

'Emily Dreyton?' he whispered.

Her sleep remained deep and undisturbed.

'Uncle Eric is here,' he said softly.

There's no harm in this. Just once more, before I smother her.

Preston knew about the particular . . . *interest* . . . he had in the children; both Eric and the late Saul Hearst shared different preferences of that same interest. Preston knew what went on, on rare occasions, and disapproved. It wasn't spoken of, provided they both kept their *playing* with the children discreet and out of his sight.

He looked down at her and knew she was going to be dead very soon. Preston would be none the wiser if he took his pleasure with her first.

He reached out and grasped the edge of the thick blankets, slowly pulling them down to reveal her pale woollen dress.

There's no harm. I'm just playing, is all.

He pushed the blankets down to her booted feet, and then his trembling, excited hand wandered back up to the top-most button of her dress, just beneath her chin, and was working it open when he felt a chilled draught that sent the oil lamp beside her head guttering and spitting.

It went out.

'Who is that?' Vander snarled angrily, quickly withdrawing his hand.

There was no answer. It was probably Mrs Zimmerman, he decided, having forgotten something. He reached for the box of matches beside the glowing wick of the lamp and shuddered from the chill as he fumbled for a match.

'You've let too much cold in,' he snapped irritably as he struck the match. It flared brightly for a second, throwing the snug shelter into sharp relief. He turned to scowl towards Mrs Zimmerman, only to find himself staring at two dark holes for eyes.

The match flickered out.

303

CHAPTER 59

1 November, 1856

Ben heard the very first scream from the other camp only a short while after he'd noticed the grey light of dawn stealing into the womb-like shelter. The scream was shrill and feminine and followed shortly after by the cry of several children.

He grabbed his gun, already carefully loaded and ready to fire – something he'd done quietly last night whilst the other two slept. His head throbbed from weariness, not certain whether he'd actually managed any sleep last night or not, since climbing back inside after his encounter with Vander.

Another piercing scream shook away the last of the fatigue. He wrapped his poncho around his head and shoulders and struggled to push the snow away from his opening, like some small rodent emerging from its burrow.

Clambering to his feet outside, he noticed the wrapped-up heads of several others emerging, pushing aside drifts of fresh snow as the screaming continued. The six Paiute had already climbed out of the shelter they had made, their blades drawn. Keats squeezed out of the shelter and joined them.

'What the hell's goin' on?' he muttered irritably.

'Coming from their side,' replied Ben.

Ben took a step up a drift of snow, gaining just a few inches' height as it squeaked and compacted beneath him. He craned his neck to look towards where the screaming was coming from. There was plenty of activity on the other side; a milling crowd of men, woman and children, agitated, pacing, praying.

'Something's happened over there,' uttered Ben.

Keats called out to Broken Wing. The Shoshone nodded. He turned around to look for the others – McIntyre, Weyland, Hussein, Bowen. 'All of you, come with me and bring your guns,' Keats barked loudly.

They converged as they rounded the smooth nodules of white that marked the oxen boneyard below, then spread out warily as they drew closer, guns cocked and ready, but, under Keats's instruction, barrels aimed downward.

Ben could hear no more screaming as they drew nearer. Instead there was a keening moan from several women, rocking back and forth on their knees, and amongst the others the frantic, whispered rattle of prayer. Above them, he had noticed from the far side of the clearing, was what he presumed was a shank of meat, suspended from a tree to keep it from scavenging animals.

Keats led them forward, stepping through them. 'What's goin' on?' he barked out loud. None of them seemed to notice Keats or the others, their attention directed towards the carcass dangling above them.

As they drew closer, Ben's eyes made sense of the gently swinging object.

'Oh my God,' he whispered.

He recognised the man, despite some disfiguration of the face and dried blood caked around his mouth – it was Eric Vander. His naked body suspended from a noose strung up to the over-hanging bare branch of a large dogwood tree. The body swung with the creak of the rope, twenty feet off the ground. A blade had worked on his bowels and, beneath the tangled string of intestinal cord that dangled down from his gut, almost to the ground, lay a small pool of blood and offal, frozen solid during the night.

'Oh, God, help us,' muttered McIntyre, his voice muffled through the woollen scarf wrapped around his head.

Ben could see a blade had also been at work on the man's groin. His genitals had been removed. Looking up at Vander's face, he realised where they'd been placed.

'For Christ's sake, someone cut him down!' Keats shouted angrily at the muttering, praying crowd.

Mr Zimmerman emerged and climbed up into the tree, his boots slipping perilously on the frosted branch that stretched a couple of dozen feet over the clearing from the forest's edge.

Ben watched the man hunker down halfway along the branch and produce a knife. He swiped a couple of times at the rope cinched around the branch. With a crack of twine snapping, the branch lurched upwards several inches, freed of the dead weight as Vander's body tumbled down. There were cries and whimpers at the appalling sight of his stiff body buckling on impact with the ground and lolling over at an awkward angle, a rigid arm pointing to the sky, one leg snapped and twisted like brittle firewood by the fall.

The crowd drew back from it instinctively.

Ben moved forward into the cleared space, Keats quickly beside him as he knelt down beside the body. Vander's eyes stared lifelessly back at Ben, wide and terrified and milky from death. He leaned forward, studying them closely.

'What're you doin', Lambert?' Keats muttered.

'The eyes. I believe sometimes they can capture an image, like a photograph, of the last thing a victim sees.'

'Really?' Keats sounded impressed.

Ben nodded, leaning closer still. 'Something I read before I came out. Scotland Yard police routinely photograph the eyes of the dead.'

He studied them intently but could see nothing in the clouded iris. The expression on Vander's face told him more.

'What's that stickin' out of his mouth?' asked Keats.

'See if you can guess.'

The guide's eyebrows locked in thought for a moment, then he looked down at the jagged wounds around Vander's groin, and nodded.

306

His own genitals in his mouth?

Ben was wondering what the hell that meant — it had to signify something, surely — when he heard a commotion coming from the back of the crowd. He heard a woman's voice, shrill and sobbing. It drew closer. The crowd parted and he saw Preston leading through a woman, his arm around her narrow shoulders. He saw the body, and calmly turned her around so that her back was facing the ghastly sight.

'Sophia . . . again, tell these people here what you told me,' he said gently.

She nodded. 'I . . . I . . . saw . . . the angel,' she muttered between sobs, 'last night . . . I saw it.'

Ben saw eyes widen and lips move amongst the gathered faces.

'I . . . I . . . was out . . . to relieve myself. I saw it.' Her small voice crumpled into a mewling whimper.

Preston rubbed her back encouragingly. 'Go on, Mrs Rutherford. Tell them.'

She nodded again, and took a breath. 'It . . . it . . . was . . . made of bones.' She shook her head, trembling as she struggled to recall what she'd seen. 'I th-thought I was having a nightmare. Tall . . . tall, it was . . . m-moving through our camp.' She looked up at Preston and shook her head. 'Please . . . please, don't let it come for my ch-children,' she pleaded with her hoarse, broken voice.

Preston nodded, whispered an encouragement, then held her tightly for a moment before letting her step back through the crowd towards her husband.

The minister turned and took in the sight of Vander's crumpled body: contorted, twisted and brittle. For the briefest moment there was no reaction on his face — a dull, lifeless response that seemed at odds with the tender reassurance he had offered the woman a moment earlier. Then his face darkened and he turned to address his people.

'Another judgement on us! A second judgement! This is His

307

warning!' Preston spun round to look at Ben and Keats. 'And it is *you* He is warning us of!'

An uneasy murmur stirred through the gathered people like an autumn draft through dry leaves.

'The *outsiders* are poisoning this place like bad water,' he spat angrily. 'And here they are, bringing those evil demons right into the heart of our camp' – he pointed to his shelter – 'within just a few yards of our sacred place!' He took a step forward. 'You've walked the Devil's servants, his eyes and ears, his scouts, right up to our door. Don't you see what you've done?' He pointed at Broken Wing. 'Don't you see the face of the Devil in his eyes?

Broken Wing defiantly returned Preston's glare.

'Don't you see him looking out at us, mocking us, enjoying the spectacle?'

'That's enough!' shouted Keats.

'You've tainted us with those devilish creatures,' he said, thrusting a finger towards the Paiute, standing back from the crowd, 'that you've foolishly embraced into our camp.' Preston gestured towards the crumpled cadaver in the snow. 'That, I fear, will be the last of our warnings! All the outsiders must leave this place today!'

Keats stood up. 'Don't be a fool, Preston!'

'You must leave before night!'

'No one's leavin' here. We'd die without shelter and food.'

Preston strode forward until his face was only inches from Keats's.

'Don't you see, Keats?' Preston muttered quietly so that only Keats could hear. Ben could see that his eyes were intense, bloodshot and dilated with fear, anger or excitement – it was impossible to tell. Flecks of spittle dotted his dark beard. 'My God, don't you see? I'm doing what I can to *save* you.'

'Save us?'

'If you and your people stay another night, you'll test the Lord's patience too far. He'll come like a storm. His angel will descend and rip you, perhaps even us, into bloody coils of flesh!'

'What goddamned angel?'

Preston ignored him. 'My people have a mission that cannot be started with you here. You have to leave!' For a fleeting moment, his face softened and he spoke quietly. 'I'm sorry, but that is how it is.' He shook his head with regret. 'I have been foolish and far more tolerant than I should have been. Your people are not welcome here any longer.'

Keats's face darkened angrily. 'My folks have every right to winter here. You can't make us leave.'

'You have to.'

'We try an' make our way outta these mountains whilst winter's on us, we'll die out there.'

Preston took several steps back from them and raised his voice. 'They must leave our side of the camp now!' he commanded, then, pointing towards the Indians, he added, 'Take those dark creatures with you. I can no longer ask my people to tolerate them near this place.'

Mutterings of agreement rippled across the crowd and one of Preston's men pushed his way to the front, shouldered his rifle and aimed it squarely at Keats's head.

'I'll not let you bring God's anger to my family's door!'

'Mr Stolz!' called out Preston. 'Hold your fire! We need no more blood spilled this morning!'

Another couple of men stepped forward, each holding a rifle, and from the stern expression on their faces, they were prepared to use them.

'You must return to your side and prepare to leave, before God decides to make an example of you right here and now!'

Ben stood up. 'Come on, Keats,' he spoke quietly. 'We should go.'

The guide nodded. They both backed away from Vander's body and began to pick their way through the gathered crowd. Ben could sense the cold, steely gaze of their eyes on them as they made their way through to join the rest of their group, waiting in a small huddle, their weapons held ready.

My God, thought Ben, *this is a hair-trigger away from being a massacre.*

As they drew up beside the others, the silence was broken by one of the younger Paiute who suddenly began shouting. Ben turned to see what was going on. The young man was pointing towards the gathered Mormons and hurling a stream of Ute at them.

'What's he saying?'

Keats shook his head. 'I ain't getting' it all . . . too fast.'

The Indian took several threatening steps forward, his *tamahakan* raised threateningly, and pointed once again.

Ben followed the direction of the young man's glare and saw that it was Zimmerman he was addressing with another screamed release of anger.

'*I sssee you.*' Broken Wing hastily translated the Paiute's words out of the side of his mouth. '*Killer of Lazy Wolf.*'

Keats shook his head and muttered to Ben. 'It was *Hearst* shot the Indian, not Zimmerman. The boy's mistaken.'

The Paiute took a dozen intimidating steps forward, and then tossed his weapon into the ground, the handle sticking up out of the snow. He screamed in Ute again.

'*Lazy Wolf hold no weapon.*'

He took another couple of steps forward until he stood opposite the man. Mr Zimmerman aimed his gun. 'Stay where you are!' he yelled.

The Indian understood and stopped in his tracks. Then, he spoke loudly. The gestures that came with it weren't hard to decipher. But then the Indian finished, turned round and headed back towards his *tamahakan*. Zimmerman called out. 'What the hell did the thing say?'

Keats bit his lip.

'I said . . .' Zimmerman swung the long barrel of his musket towards Keats. 'What the hell did it say?'

'The Indian said . . . when the fighting starts, he will find you, and cut your heart out.'

Without hesitation, the musket in Zimmerman's hands

swung back towards the Paiute, and then a plume of blue smoke erupted with a deafening boom.

A large star-shaped exit wound erupted from the top of the Indian's torso, hurling out on to the snow tatters of deer hide, skin and blood. The Indian staggered a foot forward, reaching out for the handle of his war-club, sticking up out of the snow, then collapsed.

A second deafening boom erupted from behind Ben. He turned and saw Three Hawks with his ancient flintlock raised and a ring of gunsmoke rolling away from the tip of its four-foot-long barrel.

Zimmerman fell backwards amidst a puff of crimson.

Another shot rang out from amongst Preston's men and a lead shot hummed between the Paiute and the others like a hornet.

'Stop!' Keats bellowed angrily.

Bowen and Weyland both discharged their weapons, one shot failing to find a target, the other clipping the arm of a woman. She dropped to her knees and screamed.

In the momentary lull before another shot could be fired Preston strode forward in front of his people. 'Stop this!'

Keats echoed that by turning round and knocking McIntyre's barrel up in the air. The gun boomed noisily and another pale blue cloud of smoke erupted to dissipate amidst a thinning strata of powdersmoke hanging above them.

As the peal of gunfire faded, a stillness descended over both groups. The woman was moaning in agony on the ground, her two children whimpering pitifully by her side.

'Go! Now!' barked Preston. 'Before it's too late,' he shouted, enraged.

Ben stared down at the white snow, criss-crossed with fresh and dark splatter marks.

'Now!' shouted Preston.

Keats turned to face the others. 'Let's go.' Broken Wing nodded, echoing the command to Three Hawks and the other Paiute. They began a slow retreat across the clearing, Hussein and Ben keeping their loaded guns ready, Bowen, McIntyre and Weyland attempting to clumsily pour powder from their horns as they walked backwards, spilling it in dark trails.

'Save it, you idiots,' muttered Keats, 'you're wastin' yer powder.'

We're going to need it, thought Ben.

Ben kept his eyes on Preston and his men. There were more of them mustering, spreading out in a long line, muskets being loaded — the metallic clattering of ramrods and rolling lead shot filling the air.

Shit, they're going to fire a volley at us.

Ben counted about two dozen of them, spreading out either side of their leader in a scruffy, irregular line that looked chillingly like a firing squad. Ramrods being tucked away, several of the muskets were levelled out ready to fire once more.

'My God, they're going to fire!' Ben cried.

'Goddamn it, keep moving!' Keats shouted, turning and breaking from a steady plodding retreat into a jog. 'Keep moving!'

Most of Preston's men had levelled their muskets by now and patiently awaited his say so to fire. Instead Preston raised his hands and cupped them around his mouth.

'Be gone from this place!' His words echoed off the tree line around them.

As they retreated around the lumpy carpet of snow-covered bones in the middle of the clearing, Keats slowed down, satisfied they were far enough away that most shots would fall wide.

'We ain't leaving, folks.'

Ben turned to him. 'But we have to.'

Keats ignored that. 'We have work to do — every man, woman an' child.'

CHAPTER 60

Thursday
Notting Hill, London

Dr Griffith turned the hot water off and settled back in the bath, enjoying the tickle of bubbles against his skin and the soothing sound of water gently sloshed by his movements, echoing back off the expensive granite tiles.

His home was modest; a nondescript terraced house in a quiet mews in a village-like enclave a minute's walk from Notting Hill High Street. He had considered moving to something more prestigious, but he'd made the place comfortable over the years, particularly his bathroom, on which he'd spent at least fifteen thousand pounds getting it exactly how he wanted it.

He spent a lot of time in there. His asthma, aggravated by the airborne particles of city life, meant every day ended in a hot and steamy bath to settle his chest, his inhaler resting on the soap tray at the side along with the TV remote and his cordless phone.

It would be fair to say this bathroom was the most used room in his home.

He picked up the remote and muted the small plasma TV hanging on the wall and then picked up his phone. Since speaking with Julian earlier in the week and reading further into the journal, there were some more thoughts he wanted to pass on before he got sidetracked with other things.

He dialled and Julian answered almost immediately. 'Hi.'

'Hello, Julian it's Tom. Listen, I thought I'd talk with you a bit more about this story of yours. You got time?'

'Sure. What's on your mind?'

'Well, I've read a little more of that journal and I'm increasingly certain that Preston's a — sticking strictly to medical terminology — a monster. A very dangerous individual capable of, well, frankly . . . anything.'

'Yeah, I think we're both agreed on that.'

'Anyway, there's something worth taking a moment to consider here.'

'What's that?'

'Whose toes you might be treading on.'

'What do you mean?'

'I mean that there may be descendants of Preston's who might not take too kindly to having their great-great-granddad portrayed as some kind of Charles Manson figure, a serial-killing cult leader who, very likely, murdered his entire parish. You could quite easily find yourself in some legal tangle over there on the grounds of defamation. Apart from anything else, you'll want to be careful that you define a very clear line between the Church of the Latter Day Saints and whatever Preston was preaching to his people, otherwise you'll have them on your back pretty quickly. And believe me, they have money to burn on lawyers.'

'Yes, that's true.'

'Seriously. For example, I would be careful in your use of the word "cult" in favour of the word "faith". There are significant implications over in the States, least of all tax implications, which faith groups will defend with a certain . . . *ferocity*. You quite often see that kind of issue being fought aggressively in court by very expensive lawyers on behalf of the Church of Scientology.'

'Yes, I can do without that kind of hassle.'

314

'Something else.'

'What?'

'Just something I was theorising about in a column recently.'

'Go on.'

'That sociopathic tendencies are a Darwinian strong suit.'

'Meaning?'

'Meaning, it's very likely a hereditary hand-me-down, like being left-handed, artistically inclined, having a musical ear.'

Tom reached for his inhaler and took a wheezy pull before continuing. 'Anyway, the point I want to make is this: just be careful what sort of people you piss off over there with your story, okay?'

'Well, it's not like we've had any real luck digging up anything on Preston. He remains something of an enigma. I've certainly not got any great-great-grandchildren lined up to do a door-step interview.'

Tom nodded. 'Well, that's probably for the best. You might end up getting a bloody nose.'

Julian laughed.

'So, you're heading back to the US tomorrow?'

'Yes.'

'Okay, have a good flight and say hi to Rose for me.'

'I will.'

'Oh, Julian, by the way, I'm away for a couple of weeks. My agent's flogging overseas rights to some European publishers, so I'll be part of the dog and pony show; meet-and-greet, then some talks, some signings. But we'll hook up again when you get back?'

'Yes, for sure.'

'Because whether you manage to put a production together or not, I'd dearly love to work with you on this as a book. We could co-author if you like, or you write and I'll consult, whatever. Want to talk about that downstream?'

'Yeah, sounds good.'

'Excellent. Happy flying, then. I'll speak to you soon.'

'Thanks, speak soon.'

Tom disconnected and placed his cordless phone back on the soap shelf, then settled back in the bath. 'Yes, a book,' he muttered to himself, his deep voice resonating off the granite tiles and around the bathroom.

He was reaching for the TV remote when he heard a noise from downstairs.

CHAPTER 61

cave iram Dei

M	T	W	T	F	S	S
				1	2	3
4	5	6	7	8	9	10
11	12	13	14	15	16	17
18	19	20	21	22	23	24
25	26	27	28	29	30	

Thursday
Notting Hill, London

It was a soft *clack*.

He froze for a moment, then realised that it was probably the wind playing with the letterbox flap. Outside, through the top, unfrosted panel of his bathroom window, he could see the tip of the solitary withered and miserable-looking inner-city poplar that grew outside the back of next door's house, uplit by the amber glow of street lights, swaying gently.

He watched it gently undulating from side to side, and listened to the pleasing tinkle of a wind chime.

He left the TV muted. Not that he was the twitchy sort, but there had been several burglaries along their cul-de-sac in recent months. In any case, it was relaxing listening to the hiss of a breeze through the leaves, and the gentle random musical notes. Despite being so central in London, and so close to the high street, he was constantly amazed at how quiet their little piece of backstreet Notting Hill was. In the distance a police siren wailed and a dog barked in reply . . . but other than that, so peaceful.

Another noise.

It sounded like the slightest scrape of one of his kitchen stools across the parquet floor. That was all it was . . . a *nudge*. Not a sound that could be mistaken for the central heating coming on, or any of the other plethora of tickings and creakings a house will make in the night.

It was the sound of someone else in his house.

Shit.

He felt the first cold prickle of anxiety, and a quickening of his breath. He reached out and took a pull on his inhaler.

Just a kid . . . a chav looking for something easy to swipe and run.

He knew from past dealings with young offenders that they were at least as frightened as the people they robbed or mugged. If there was someone down there, a confident *boo* would have him running like a startled rabbit.

'YOU HAVE EXACTLY TEN SECONDS TO PISS OFF BEFORE I CALL THE POLICE!' His voice boomed out of the bathroom. He listened intently for the sound of trainers skidding on his waxed floor, the clatter and slam of a door or window being opened and the diminishing slap of running feet outside on the pavement.

But he heard nothing.

'ALL RIGHT, SCREW IT. I'M CALLING NOW,' he bellowed again. This time there was a wheezy signature to his baritone voice.

He picked up his cordless, dialled all the nines, held it to his ear waiting to hear the trill of the call ringing through. But there was nothing, just a rustle and crackling and then something that sounded very much like a breath being taken.

'I can hear you up there,' a voice muttered out of the earpiece.

'Whuh?!' he blurted, dropping the phone onto his wet belly.

He heard footsteps across the downstairs hall.

'What do you want?' Tom called out, his troubled breathing beginning to rob his voice of its natural authority.

The lights upstairs suddenly went out, leaving the bathroom illuminated only by the flickering glow of his plasma screen. Some light spilled up the stairs from the kitchen and hallway lights, and he thought he caught the momentary fluttering of a shadow cast up the stairway and onto the wall outside his bathroom. Then it darted out of sight.

Oh fuck, fuck, fuck.

The lights downstairs went out. And finally his TV winked off.

'Please! Take what you want and go!!' he gasped in the darkness, his eyes struggling to adjust.

He heard the creak of weight settling on one of the stairs.

Oh God, oh fuck.

'Look,' he puffed between laboured breaths, 'my wallet is in my jacket down in the kitchen. There's at least a couple of hundred pounds in there.'

No reply.

'There's a cash card in there too,' he said and sucked quickly from his inhaler. 'The PIN is one, four, six, six.'

He heard creaking again on the stairs and knew that was the other wonky step near the top.

'Please! Take what you want and go!'

His eyes began to pick out some details around him, lit by the diffused amber glow of the street light outside.

'I've come to kill you, Tom,' a voice whispered from just outside his open bathroom door.

'Who are you?' Tom replied.

'Not that important who I am now, is it?'

He pulled himself with some difficulty up out of the warm, soapy water.

'Stay in the bath!'

'O-Okay.'

Play along, Tom. Play along.

He desperately searched his memory for someone who might have a reason to come after him like this. He'd contributed to the arrest and conviction of perhaps a dozen murderers in some small way. But he couldn't imagine how they could have—

'I'm afraid you know a little too much about things right now.'

'W-what? I . . . I know what?'

'Sorry, I'm not here to discuss that. I'm here to kill you.'

'What? P-please . . . I have money . . .' he stammered, struggling with difficulty to find his breath. 'If you t-tell me how much—'

Then his eyes detected something shifting. It was low down, squat, in the doorway, swaying from side to side. A rocking movement – compulsive. Tom trawled his memory for the most likely criminally insane candidates. There were one or two over the years whom he had written notes on, interviewed, but not necessarily been instrumental in putting away. No revenge motive he could think of.

'What's your worst fear?' the voice whispered.

'My . . . my worst . . . why? What? Why are you—'

'Come on. What do you fear the most?'

'I . . . p-please . . . don't—'

'Let me guess, then.'

Tom felt his lungs clench like a fist and a wave of light-headedness caused him to sway. He sat down heavily in the bath. Water splashed noisily out of the tub and onto the floor.

'I hear you wheezing,' whispered the voice. 'You're asthmatic, aren't you?'

Tom refused to answer.

'Hmm, I had a cousin who was. Worst thing she feared was suffocating. She used to have nightmares about that, night after night, screaming . . . gasping.'

'Oh God, please no!' he pleaded, subconsciously fumbling in the dark for his inhaler.

The voice laughed. A dry, brittle rattle that sounded sly and childlike.

'So, I'm afraid that's how it has to be, Dr Thomas Griffith.'

Oh God Oh God Oh God.

'This can be very quick. I've done it a few times before.' The voice laughed softly. 'They call it *water-boarding* . . . sounds like something fun, doesn't it?'

'Please, not drowning! Please!'

'Shhh. Listen, I can make it easy for you. I'll hold you under

320

while you breathe in that water. Thirty seconds of thrashing and it's over. The longer you hold your breath, the more your body will fight it.'

'Oh fuck n-no!'

'Or I guess you can struggle . . . and this'll take us both a lot longer. It'll be harder on you.'

Tom pulled himself unsteadily up onto his knees in the bath and suddenly felt his bowels open wide. Above the roar of blood in his ears and the deafening rasp of air struggling through a pinhole gap in his throat, he heard the tumbling of his own shit into the bath water.

'Decision time. Do I have to wrestle you under? Or are you going to lie down like a good man?'

Tom's vision clouded and the world skewed sideways.

He toppled over into the water, banging his head against the porcelain. He felt the impact and saw stars. Warm water rolled over his face and he snorted as water ran up his nose. Dazed and light-headed, he was still lucid enough to instinctively pull himself back out of the water.

He suddenly felt a heavy weight on his broad chest, holding him under. Through the turbulent, swirling veil of bath water, as his arms and legs scissored desperately, he thought he could just make out the pale face of his killer.

He held the man under for a full five minutes after the movement had ceased. Enough to satisfy himself that the man was dead.

He nodded with satisfaction. There would be little noticeable bruising on the man's body; he'd been careful not to hold him down under the water with his hands around the neck – instead he'd applied the weight of his body across the chest – no telltale thumb or finger marks.

He'd been taught by the best.

He fumbled in the water for the man's inhaler, fished it out and then held down the dispenser button, listening to the rush of medication whistling out. It took a solid minute before the thing exhausted itself. He then tossed it casually on the floor of the bathroom.

Make it look natural.

He went downstairs, flipped all the fuses back on and returned to the bathroom. He studied the scene with the bright bathroom spotlights on; the pools of water that had splashed out of the tub, the dark clot of blood on the edge of the bath, the empty inhaler tossed angrily aside. He was looking at the scene of an overweight and unhealthy man who'd had an asthma attack, found his medication had run out, panicked getting out of the bath, slipped, fell, hit his head and drowned.

He smiled.

Good enough.

The British police were amateur enough to read this as an unhappy accident. He doubted whether the two murders would be linked anytime soon. If some bright young go-getter in the CID intelligence office did eventually get round to noticing they both shared an acquaintance by the name of Julian Cooke, it would be too late to haul him in for questioning, because Mr Cooke was about to become a statistic; another poor, unfortunate, ill-prepared trekker who had vanished in the wilderness of the Sierra Nevadas.

He unmuted the TV, recessed expensively in the granite wall. A news programme was on. He stopped for a few seconds to watch, intrigued by how differently news appeared to be presented and packaged here in the UK.

The British like their presenters ugly and old.

He was bemused by that, contrasting the pair of presenters on screen with the tanned and well-groomed young studio-brats he was used to watching back home.

Interesting.

He wandered downstairs, checking that he'd left no telltale signs of intrusion, then went back through the lounge into the kitchen, to the window he'd eased open, out into the yard, over a fence and was gone into the night.

CHAPTER 62

Thursday
Palo Cedro, California

Rose smiled and slurped on an iced Becks. 'So, I'm not exactly sure what Forensic Linguistics is. It sounds impressive.'

The young man grinned. A chiselled dimple in each cheek made him look like a youthful Brad Pitt. 'Yeah,' he said, 'it's real interesting. They're just beginning to use it more in other countries. The FBI's been using it for years.'

Rose smiled. Lance, the guy from the diner, was good-looking, pretty smart too, but already she was finding him a little on the self-absorbed side.

Let's talk about me . . . me . . . me . . .

'They use it in corporate security too, filtering emails for phrases and communication patterns that are suspicious.' He nodded his head. 'That's where I wanna be at. Big dollars in corporate security, fuck yeah.'

'Wow,' she offered.

'It's really clever shit though, Rose,' he said, chugging his Becks from the bottle. 'The way people communicate, the choice of words they use when they're, like, talking the truth and when telling a lie. Going through a bogus email, or a fabricated suicide note, when you know how it works, how the brain processes stuff . . . it's so obvious.'

He leaned forward, putting his feet up on the rungs of her bar stool either side of her legs and casually planted a hand on her thigh. 'Take a faked suicide note. We studied one taken from an actual real crime. This husband knew his wife was cheating on him, so he decided to kill her 'cause he was pissed about it, but also because he had a big ol' life insurance policy on her. So one night, when he had an alibi covering his ass, he sneaked home and forced her to write her own suicide note, before blowing her brains out with the family shotgun.'

'Nice.'

Lance grinned. 'He went out again, then came home from his alibi, found her body and called the police. This guy nearly got away with it. The police were sure they were looking at a suicide until the note was run past the Feds. And this is the cool bit,' he said, nodding. 'They didn't find any tissue, fibre or prints to link to her husband. The handwriting was hers, of course. There was nothing there they could get him on, except . . . the language she used in the note.'

The language? Rose was intrigued. 'How do you mean?'

'It wasn't suicide language.'

'Uh?'

'Well,' he said, 'the language was, like, *too* depressed to be genuine.'

'Too depressed?' Rose shook her head. 'Er . . . she supposedly shot herself. Surely depressed is exactly how she'd sound in her note?'

'No, see, that's the common mistake. Most people think a person about to take their own life is miserable as shit. But that isn't the case, because they've found a way through what's troubling them. See? They've found a solution, so it's, like, all right now – everything is, you know, cool . . . I got myself a way out.'

'The *solution* being suicide?'

'That's right! So, when they're writing the note, it's full of, like, positives, it's optimistic, happy even.' He grinned that winning, sexy smile of his, inches away from her face.

'And *that's* a genuine suicide note. This husband guy forced his wife to write a doom-n-gloom, I-hate-this-evil-world-and-I'm-gonna-end-it-all-right-now kind of letter.'

He sat back and laughed. 'Dude was a dumb-ass. That's how the Feds got him.'

She looked at him, an idea germinating. 'So, you're telling me you can look at the language of a written piece of work and tell whether the writer is telling the truth, or making it up?'

'Sure. Like I say, Forensic Linguistics is the future.'

He took another swig, planting the bottle heavily on the counter. 'See, somebody lying will use one of two or three deception strategies. It's just a case of spotting which strategy is being used, counting the ratio of adjectives to nouns . . . stuff like that. Simple when you know how it works.'

'All right then,' she said, delving into her bag. She took out a folder, flipped through a dozen pages, settled on one and then pulled it out. 'Would you have a look at this?'

He looked at the sheet of paper, bemused. 'Now? Here?'

Rose looked around the bar. Being early evening, it was relatively quiet. She imagined in a small nowhere place like this, it wasn't likely to get much busier tonight. 'Yeah, why not?'

He smiled and shrugged. 'Yeah, okay. I'll take a look at what you got, if you like.'

She passed him the sheet of paper, and immediately he frowned as his eyes scanned the page. 'What is it?'

'It's transcript taken from a diary that I'm busy researching. I'd love to know whether the author was writing what he saw or' — she looked at him — 'whether this might be made up.'

Lance nodded. 'Just this page, right?'

'If you're game for it?' she said, smiling sweetly.

'Right . . . take me about five minutes, at a guess.'

'Okay. I'll order us another beer whilst you're at it.'

He asked the barman for a pen. 'Need some quiet. I'll be there,' he said, pointing to an alcove away from the bar and the noisy television sitting on a shelf behind it. She watched him go, sit down and begin to examine the words, underlining one every now and then with the pen.

Rose felt a further twinge of guilt, watching him. The kid clearly thought he was going to score tonight, but Rose had decided at least an hour ago that this had been something of a mistake. He was after a novelty notch to put on his bed – that was all.

She had been on the point of deploying a polite exit strategy when he'd moved on from regaling her about his frat-boy life-style to discussing his course on linguistics.

And that had most definitely piqued her interest.

She turned back round to the bar and ordered another two beers, as promised. Her attention drifted to the TV behind the bar. *Report Card* was on, a satirical news show that featured a couple of vaguely recognisable comedians as news anchors.

'. . . and in a surprising announcement this week, William Shepherd, the Mormon independent candidate from Utah, decided to take time out from his early campaigning to talk with his strategy team: God.'

There was a ripple of laughter that Rose recognised as canned.

'That's right, Steve. It seems Shepherd's taking a rest between rounds like Rocky Balboa and grabbing a little coach time.'

The image on TV changed to show the corner of a boxing ring and one of the comedians, sweating and gasping with the iconic Rocky bruised-and-battered make-up job. A well-groomed silver wig on his head and a Bible under one arm signalled that they were spoofing Shepherd. Into shot appeared the other comedian, sporting an impossibly bushy white beard and monstrous Old Testament eyebrows beneath a grubby woollen hat. He vigorously worked on 'Shepherd's' shoulders.

'Ya gotta get out there again, Sheppy!' he barked with a grizzly Philly accent. 'Them big bastards'll drop like a sack o' grain if you land 'em one on the kisser.'

'I dunno, God,' gasped Sheppy, 'they're killin' me out there, man.'

God held a spittoon out and Sheppy spat. 'Ya got's ta hit 'em where it hurts, Sheppy? Ya unnerstand? Hit 'em where it hurts.'

'But where's that?'

God shrugged. 'Hell, I don't know. Use ya damned brain, fool. Dat's why I gave ya people one.'

A bell rang and Sheppy disappeared out of shot. God watched and winced at the sound of heavy blows being traded. Another bell and Shepherd limped back into shot, even more battered and bruised.

'They're big sons-of-bitches, God. They're kickin' my ass.'

God scratched his bristles for a moment. 'Sheee-it. Wan' me to tag for ya?'

Sheppy nodded. 'I gotta rest up.'

The bell rang and God climbed through the ropes. 'Wish me luck.'

Out of shot, for a few seconds there was the sound of blows being traded, then a blinding flash flickered on screen followed by the sound of thunder. A waft of smoke crossed in front of Sheppy's face.

God walked back into shot with smoke rising from sooty boxing gloves.

'Bunch a' pussies.'

Canned laughter mixed in as the image cut back to the two comedian anchors.

'Sheeeesh, Steve. You get God pitching on your side, you just can't lose, eh?'

'S'right. God, and about two billion pledged campaign dollars.'

The image on the screen cut to footage of Shepherd talking at a rally earlier in the week, camera flashes popping and strobing. Shepherd talked energetically, flinging his hands in the air, but his voice was dubbed over by one of the comedians.

'. . . and ah promise you good folks out there that ah'm gonna have me a big ol' talk with God about a' bunch a' things.

Oh yeah. We gonna talk about puttin' things straight here in the US of A. First up, ah'm putting God in charge of the Federal Ree-serve. Maybe he can go rustle us up some real dollars, 'stead of the paper shee-it we call money now. Then, ah'm gonna get him to do some ass-whuppin' over in the Middle East . . .'

The barman leaned across and switched channels. 'Ass-holes,' he mumbled.

'You a fan?' asked Rose.

'Of the show or Shepherd?'

'The show.'

'Usually those two guys're pretty funny.'

'But not tonight?'

'No.' He switched over to a sports channel. 'That guy Shepherd's the only fella runnin' for the job who's worth a red cent. The others? Bunch of parasites or bleedin' heart liberals. Don't trust either party any more.'

She sipped her beer. 'Do you think he stands a chance?'

'I hope so. He's sure as hell got my vote,' the barman said. Rose heard the muted trill of a phone coming from the other end of the bar. The man excused himself and went to answer it.

A moment later Lance joined her and reached for the beer she'd got him.

'Wow,' she said, 'that was bloody quick.'

He grinned. 'Hell, I'm in a bar with, like, a real sexy English lady,' he said. 'I can work real quick when I have to.'

Rose smiled. His clumsy frat-boy smooth-talk had a certain charm. 'So, what's your verdict, Lance?'

He shook his head, laying the sheet of paper out on the bar and sitting down again on the stool beside her. She could see words circled and underlined and a tally of something in the margin. 'You know, this is pretty gross reading,' he said, shaking his head. 'This something that happened a while back? 'Cos, the language is a bit, you know, like . . . *old style.*'

Rose nodded. 'It was written about a century and a half ago.'

His eyes widened. 'Hey, that's cool.'

'So?'

'So . . . you wanna know if the person who wrote this was writing the truth?'

'Yes.'

Lance bit his lip for a moment. 'Well, it ain't conclusive, but, looking at some of the words the writer has chosen, I'd say some of this *could* be made up. There's words here that sort of distance the author, and what we call *displacement details*, where the writer is focusing too much on small, irrelevant stuff instead of the main thing which' – he looked up at her – 'would be, like, describing this body, I guess.'

'So, you're saying this might be an untruthful account of what happened?'

'Hey . . . *some* of it *might* be, is what I'm saying. That's all.'

Rose surprised herself by feeling a stab of disappointment. She'd read enough of Lambert's journal so far to feel she somehow knew him as a person, perhaps knew him better than she knew a lot of her friends back home.

Trusted him.

Lance placed his hand back on her thigh once more. 'But look, it's just a quick assessment in a bar. And shit, I've had a couple of beers.' He shrugged casually and flashed her a mischievous smile. 'My mind's on other things here. Ain't going to be a hundred per cent accurate, you know?'

'Yes.' She smiled. 'I suppose you're right.'

His hand wandered a little too far along her thigh in the wrong direction and she gently grabbed a hold of it and squeezed.

'Look, uh . . . Lance,' she said awkwardly, 'you're a gorgeous guy and I'm sure you break hearts right across the state, and I've really been enjoying talking to you . . .'

His friendly grin slackened a little. 'But?'

'But . . .' She nodded. 'I don't want to come back with you tonight.' She forced a rueful smile onto her lips. 'If that's all right.'

He sighed. 'Shit, that's a kicker.'

She guessed by the look on his perfectly chiselled face that being knocked back wasn't an experience he was too familiar with. She felt the slightest pang of guilt for exploiting the boy's hormones and despite Lance's chivalrous protest, she settled the bar tab.

She thanked him for a lovely evening, wandered out of the bar to where her car was parked, and decided she was more than sober enough to drive back to Blue Valley. All the while, she was wondering about the seed of doubt the young man had inadvertently placed in her head.

CHAPTER 63

I November, 1856

They'll be coming for us some time today. That's what Keats has been saying to the others. I can't help but think he is right. There are some – Mr Weyland and Mr Bowen – who have been arguing that we should all do as Preston demanded and leave immediately. But Keats said to do so would mean freezing to death. Instead of leaving, we are preparing to defend ourselves. Keats assures us that with a small enough space to defend, we could hold them off indefinitely.

The morning has been spent by every available hand ripping apart our sorry cluster of shelters and using the materials to build a small enclave, a barricade of branches and wood ripped from what remains of our wagons.

Which begs the question . . . what shall we sleep in tonight?

The air had been thick with heavy, tumbling snowflakes, jostling each other on the way down throughout the morning and reducing visibility to no more than a few dozen yards. It was letting up now, the downfall little more than sporadic dust motes, and the sky above them showed teasing glimpses of cerulean blue.

Once more they could see to the far side of the clearing.

Ben studied the crowd of people gathered around the other campfire and listened to the murmured chant of prayer.

If he could see them, then surely they could see the frantic activity going on here. Ben was surprised they had been left alone to build a stronghold in plain sight. He wondered if Preston was simply being very shrewd – watching them pull apart their shelters so all he had to do was wait. By tomorrow morning they'd be nothing more than two dozen frozen statues inside their hastily erected barricade, exposed, as they now were, to the elements. Once the sun went down, they would suffer the bitter, freezing night unprotected.

As he watched, the prayer meeting finally began to dissolve as people got to their feet and groups, families, meandered back to their shelters for warmth. Many of their faces – from this distance, no more than pale ovals framed by tightly wrapped shawls, dark beards or bundled scarves – peered furtively their way. He could feel their suspicion and anger wafting over the icy no-man's-land towards them like a toxic cloud.

He wondered what Preston's words throughout the morning had turned them into. A vengeful crowd? A lynch mob?

Behind him, leaning against their frail, waist-high barricade of stacked branches and lumber, he heard Keats frantically barking orders to the others as they – men, women and even the youngest children – worked industriously to finish shoring up their defences.

'What do you see, Lambert?'

Keats had entrusted the watching of Preston's people to Ben, whom he considered to be the keenest pair of eyes in their group.

'The meeting's broken up and they're dispersing . . . for now.'

Preston's people filtered away into their various shelters, leaving a few clusters of men brandishing guns and staring back at them. He scanned the men for sight of Preston. Even now, he wondered whether a last-minute dash across the empty ground between them and a plea at his feet for common sense and mercy to prevail would sway the man and allow them all to weather this ordeal together.

Of course not.

His eyes finally picked out the tall, slender figure of Preston. As the others clambered back inside for warmth and shelter, he pushed his way through knee-deep drifts towards the edge of the clearing, walking beneath the big cedar tree from which Vander had been dangling this morning and stepped up the incline. His head was lowered, abstracted in thought and prayer or perhaps internal debate; Ben could visualise the bloodshot and dilated eyes, the numerous little tics in his face, and skin slick with sweat . . . very much his last close-up recollection of the man. He climbed the gentle slope and without a moment's hesitation or any apparent fear for what might be out there in the woods, he disappeared amidst the thick tree line of snow-laden spruces.

'Where are you going?' Ben whispered to himself.

Ben looked down at his journal and for the first time realised how much the cold seeping into his aching hand affected his writing; or perhaps it was fear of what was to come. The jagged lines struggled illegibly across the page in a slant descending towards the bottom, the diluted ink spreading and blotting, making his words look uncontrolled like the scrawl of a child. Undeterred, he continued, his pen scratching dryly across the page, guided by fingers numb and struggling to hold the pen.

I believe I'm right in thinking now that it was Preston who killed the Dreytons. I had harboured a suspicion for a while that it might have been Vander. But clearly the butcher's blade was not held by him. Preston, I suspect, is the kind of man who can kill with brutal efficiency, and bury awful deeds behind the most compelling façade. He is a powerful man, powerful in his hold over those who follow him. That kind of man is dangerous. But what makes him a magnitude more terrifying is that he is also afraid. A man like that will do anything.

Did Emily see this man carve her brother and mother to pieces, like a shop butcher?

*

Ben looked down at his journal, at the childish marks his stiff hand was making. He suspected the scribbled lines would make sense to no one else. At the end of the last line, the pen's nib running dry had scratched a groove into the paper, the last few words etched rather than written. He shakily dipped his nib one last time in the diluted dregs of the inkpot — now no more than a ring of dirty blue water that settled in the rim at the bottom of the pot.

Keats is right. Tonight they will come for us. But I believe he's wrong to think we stand a chance.

The pen scratched dry on the paper again. He shook the pen to dislodge the last droplet held in the nib.

There's ink for no more. That's it. If none of us survive this night, let it be known it was no demon in a spiritual sense that did for us . . . just the madman William Preston. I am sure of it.

He closed the leather-bound book and placed it in the small travel trunk on the ground beside him. He had dragged that out, along with his other meagre possessions, just before his shelter had been pulled apart for its materials. From within the trunk he took out the photographic portrait of himself and his mother, taken the day before he set sail for the Americas. For a moment he caressed the plate with his fingers.

'Sorry, Mother.'

He suspected he wouldn't be bringing this book home for her to read and *The Times* to publish, after all. He put the photograph back in, snapped the lid shut and locked it.

Keats called across to him. 'You keepin' a watch, Lambert?'

Ben stirred, aware that he had momentarily abandoned his duty. He turned to look across the clearing. 'Their meeting's over. They've mostly headed back to their shelters.'

He looked again at them, bemused that their efforts at building a defence were not being prevented. Half a dozen faces watched them from afar, guns at hand. The snow falling this morning had disguised what they were up to; the noises might have been construed as the sound of them packing up. But now, with an unburdened sky, and clear air between them, Preston's men looked on. They—

His train of thought stopped dead in its tracks.

Disguise.

'Where's Preston?' Keats called out, but Ben ignored him.

Oh my God – a disguise.

He recalled Mrs Rutherford's faltering description – a description Preston had clearly *wanted* his people to hear. A description that sounded terrifying coming from the woman's trembling lips.

Made of bones.

'Lambert? If you ain't watchin' you can give us a goddamn hand!' Keats called impatiently, as he, Bowen, Hussein and Weyland pulled the remnants of a wagon chassis out of a bank of hardened snow.

A disguise. There would be proof of it, surely?

In that moment, Ben was convinced that evidence of Preston's bloody guilt would be up in the hills, in that place, evidence everywhere: blood-spattered tools, clothes, drips and smears over the snow, screaming out his guilt as loudly as it stained darkly. It was Preston who had decided unequivocally that the trapper's shelter be left well alone.

My God . . . yes!

Ben stood up and reached for his gun.

Keats looked on, confused. 'Lambert?'

He didn't want to stop and explain what he was up to. There wasn't time. He had seen Preston head into the trees and could only imagine the insane bastard was on his way up to the trapper's place to ready his appearance. Darkness was coming soon and he could imagine Preston appearing with the twilight, as the avenging angel of an enraged God, exhorting those frightened people of his to attack them. Eric Vander's body would be fresh in their minds; the likeness of themselves, their

335

loved ones, their children, superimposed on the man's contorted face.

I can stop this.

He strode quickly across the small, enclosed space of their stronghold and clambered over the rear wall of their pitiful barricade, keeping low as he scuttled away across the clearing, to avoid being spotted by any of Preston's men watching from the far side.

'Lambert!' Keats called after him. 'Where the fuck are you goin'?'

Ben reached the tree line and glanced back. It appeared that his scuttling departure had gone unnoticed by the distant men. Keats, however, was shouting all manner of colourful profanities at Ben for running away like a coward.

He looked up at the thick mesh of fir branches and the rising incline of the ground, dark and forbidding in the deep shadows of such a pale and lifeless afternoon, and reassured himself again: *There're no demons or angels out there — just a madman.*

That wasn't the comforting thought he'd hoped it might be.

He crawled up into the tree line. A few moments later, the clearing behind was lost from sight and he was alone in the snow-dampened silence of the wood.

CHAPTER 64

I November, 1856

'Speak to me,' Preston whispered hoarsely.

He pushed through a waist-high thicket of thorny briar that scratched at his hands as he stepped through into the small glade. Almost a week's worth of snow had transformed it from a grisly butcher's shop to a virgin-white, sylvan idyll. There remained no exposed sign of the frozen slick on the log or the violence that had been perpetrated here.

He walked forward across the snow, resting his hand on the log and brushing aside the fresh powder until he saw the jet-black slick of Dorothy's blood. He felt a solitary tear roll warmly down his cold, sallow cheek and instinctively checked that he was alone before allowing his grief to emerge with an audible sob.

'Why Dorothy?' His voice broke with grief. 'Why Dorothy? Why Sam?' he cried. 'Why do you punish me like this? Haven't I done everything you asked of me?'

His words faded into the stillness and remained unanswered.

'Eric and Saul . . . were not pure of heart, I know that now.' More tears rolled down his cheeks and settled into the dark bristles of his beard. 'But Dorothy was a good woman. She gave herself to you, gave herself to me.' He wiped his face with one grubby sleeve. 'Gave me a son and a daughter, both of them such good children.'

He looked up at the grey, tumbling sky. 'I had to sacrifice them. You know that. I had to. Dorothy had doubts . . . doubts that would have spread amongst my people and destroyed them.'

Preston sobbed. Overhead, the startled flutter of wings from the topmost branch of a tree punctuated the silence. The bird flapped noisily across the clearing and away over the trees.

'I loved her! And my children! And I gave them up for you!'

Preston dropped to his knees, for the first time in his entire life feeling utterly alone.

God has turned His back on me.

He closed his eyes, accepting a truth that drained away the very last of his will to live any longer.

I am not the one He wants to spread his new gospel.

'I've angered you, somehow,' he whispered. Unspoken, he sensed he knew what it was – the plates, those sacred plates of Joseph Smith's – were not his to have.

Have? Perhaps 'steal' would be a better word.

'No!' he cried, 'I didn't steal them! I . . . I thought it was Your will that they came to me! I thought it was Your wish that I take them!'

Preston's vague memory of a dark night and a deed done with the help of two other men came from another life, another time. The true memory had almost completely gone and had been replaced with a far more palatable one in which divine inspiration had brought to him two wayward men, Eric and Saul, carrying with them a gift from God of which they had no understanding. Only *he* had understood the true value of the book of metal plates, and the small canvas sack of bones they carried.

And yet, here it was . . . the truth he had almost managed to hide from, to forget, coming back to taunt him. They – the three of them – had stolen from God . . . and now His angel was here,

Nephi . . . risen from the canvas sack and fully formed, ready to implement God's wrath.

Preston felt tears of shame and fear roll down his cheeks. 'I . . . I'm sorry! I . . . I'm so sorry I took those things!' His broken voice echoed off the silent trees around him.

The bones, the remains of Nephi, had never whispered to him as he'd confidently announced they would. They had never risen as the angel sat with him and read to him from the plates in a language he could understand. And yet, impatiently, Preston had made a start . . . his Book of New Instruction.

'Oh God, forgive my arrogance!' he whimpered. 'But I had to begin the work. I had to. My children needed guidance. I thought you were steering my hand! I thought . . .'

He pulled a knife out of the pocket of his long coat and unsheathed it. His eyes still closed, he felt the cold, sharp edge of the blade in his hands. 'I've done wrong. I'll take my life right now . . . if you will spare them.'

He waited, eyes closed, sensing a freshening breeze on his skin, the whisper of the branches stirring, and knew it was the draught of something approaching.

I hear it.

He remembered a voice of wisdom from one of his many turbulent visions.

Never look on the face of His anger . . . or your soul is doomed for eternity.

His eyes remained firmly clamped shut as the breeze intensified and the trees swayed. He thought he sensed the ground beneath him vibrate with the footfall of something large approaching the glade.

It's near.

He heard the crack of branches splitting, being pushed aside by something large and powerful. All of a sudden, he was certain it was there in the glade with him, standing before him. His eyes remained tightly shut.

Do not look.

Preston had no need to open his eyes, though. In his mind he

339

already knew what it must look like: a presence as tall and as wide as a building, crackling and shimmering with the raw energy of God's rage. In his mind, he saw a giant skull-like head, the horns, the spines of bone towering over him.

'T-take me,' he whispered, his thin lips trembling, awaiting a powerful swipe that would empty his stomach onto the ground in front of him.

'Spare the others . . . p-please.'

There was stillness in response. He could hear only the deep, panting breath of the giant apparition in front of him, sensed its giant form swaying, looking down on this pitiful human who thought he was pure enough in heart to channel the word of God to mankind.

Preston could see that now. It was his heart, stained by arrogance, that had condemned him and perhaps condemned his people too. He wondered if the angel had hesitated like this before emptying Saul, before gutting Eric; whether it had listened dispassionately to their tremulous pleas for forgiveness before finally, cruelly, ripping them apart.

Preston realised poor Emily's eyes must have been open in this glade; she'd seen this apparition, and in that moment was eternally doomed. Her mind emptied by the horror of it, leaving behind the breathing carcass they had been tending this last week.

My God, poor girl.

A violent and messy death right now would be preferable to that. An eternity of torment to a moment of agony — seeing his insides steaming on the snow beside him as his consciousness ebbed away. This death, certainly no more than seconds away, was going to be a hard death, but infinitely preferable to the fate his daughter had suffered.

Poor, poor Emily.

'End my life,' he whispered. 'It's worth nothing.'

He sensed it moving around him, from the front, to his right, then behind . . . circling, studying him silently. He felt the vibration of its steps through the ground, the monstrous weight shifting from one foot to the other, and the energy radiating from it.

Heat trickled down his thighs and Preston realised that his shame was complete. 'Lord, I'm ready to die.'

A gust of wind swept through the branches above with a hiss, the leaves and fir-needles rustling in tacit agreement. He heard the angel shift heavily in front of him, felt the warm blast of breath on his face and smelled the sulphurous, fetid odour of death.

'S-spare them, p-please!' his own breath hissed past trembling lips.

It was silent, except for the deep, rumbling, panting breath. Then he heard the angel, deep inside his head, in a dark corner, a quiet, whispered voice.

Prove yourself. Kill the outsiders. Kill them all.

CHAPTER 65

\	cave iram Dei					
M	T	W	T	F	S	S
				1	2	3
4	5	6	7	8	9	10
11	12	13	14	15	16	17
18	19	20	21	22	23	24
25	26	27	28	29	30	

Friday
Heathrow Airport

'I'm boarding now, I think.'

Julian cocked his head and listened to the repeated announcement for a moment. Amidst the garbled words he thought he detected his flight number and the phrase 'now boarding'. There was movement from around the departure lounge and, almost instantly, the beginnings of a queue formed in front of the boarding gate.

'Yeah, this is my flight. You'll meet me at Reno?'

Rose sounded tired. 'Yup,' she mumbled.

'Okay then, I'll see you later on today,' he replied. Then as an afterthought, 'We've got a lot to talk about.' It was a probing, throwaway comment. Of course there was much to talk about, and not all of it would be about work.

'Sure,' she replied in a non-committal way, 'be good to have you back,' she said.

They said goodbye in the same professionally familiar way that they always had before . . .

. . . *before the other night.*

Of course, friendly and *laissez-faire* as always. He got up, grabbed his bag and ambled towards the growing, ill-defined,

342

meandering queue in front of the gate, pondering that last comment of hers.

Good to have you back.

He found himself replaying that in his head and trying to analyse the tone and timbre of her voice for the slightest clue on how exactly she meant that; how she felt about him. He shook his head at the ridiculousness of it all. Saturday night in that diner, they'd been mildly juiced on the beer, well and truly on a high over the discovery of Lambert's journal, and yes, they'd flirted a little – that's all. End of story.

This is getting stupid.

They knew each other well, better perhaps than most married couples. They'd worked out of each other's back pockets these last few years, on too many occasions wearily propping each other up with black coffee and trench-banter as they pushed a thirty-six-hour shift to rush together a last-minute edit. There had been the unavoidable intimacy of shooting footage from a variety of uncomfortable places, arms, legs and cables tangled round each other for lack of wriggle room. They had shared the exhilaration of seeing their work aired on BBC2, and the disappointment of sliding into the obscurity of various digital channels. They had got pissed together God knows how many times, swapped CDs and regularly derided each other's taste in music, slept together in the back of a touring Transit van with a sweaty teenage grunge band, and cowered together at the back of an equally sweaty BNP rally.

Not once had they ever flirted with the idea of *something more* . . . until the other night, that is. Since then he'd been troubled with the notion that he felt a lot more for her than he'd realised. The idea scared him. He enjoyed the security of the tight, solitary bubble in which he had lived most of his life, no one ever getting too close, no one ever hurting him.

Now here was Rose. The thought of folding her in his arms, stooping down to kiss her, feeling the tickle of her hair on his face, the trembling warmth of her body pressed against his . . . terrified him.

This is ridiculous.

'We need to talk,' he muttered to himself. A bull-necked man with a shaved head and a Rooney football shirt, standing to his left, shot him a bemused expression.

'Uh, sorry,' Julian smiled awkwardly, 'just talking to myself. I . . . uh . . . do that sometimes.'

The man shook his head and pressed forward into the shuffling queue with his boarding pass ready.

Julian decided enough was enough. The first thing he and Rose were going to discuss in the car on the way back to Blue Valley was whether there was something more between them, and whether they wanted that, or not.

'Hey!'

Julian felt a tap on his arm and turned round to see a man holding something out to him.

'What?'

'You left this on the seat.'

Julian looked down to see the man was holding his Black-Berry.

'Oh bugger! That was stupid,' he admitted and smiled dumbly as he grabbed it. 'Hey, thanks for—'

The man had already turned away, in a hurry to get where he was going. Julian wanted to thank him for not running off with it. He watched the man push his way out of the scrum; just another executive drone in a dark suit, nothing visible but the back of his head, and his raised hand holding a boarding pass. His eyes picked out an incongruous detail – a faint and blurred tattoo across the back of his hand. It looked very much like a fox's head.

Odd tattoo, he thought, and then his mind was back again on Rose.

He had an ideal seat, across the aisle and two rows back from Cooke. It allowed him to keep an eye on him, but remain outside Cooke's field of vision for the duration of the flight. Important fact: on an eight-hour flight, one can get very familiar with the few faces visible between the headrests; familiar enough to recognise that face for quite some time afterwards, even in an entirely different context – a crowded street, a shopping mall, on a bus, or a train.

He studied the man.

Cooke. He preferred never to use the Christian name of a target, just the surname; it preserved a formal distance. It made a great deal of sense to maintain that distance for a target he would be required, at some point, to finish off.

He allowed himself to relax. Cooke was tagged now. The discreet little pin he'd inserted beneath the BlackBerry's fascia had a minute lithium battery that kept the thing quietly chirping a signal for months. It was good only for a short range of a few miles, depending on line-of-sight intrusions, but good enough for the job, and perhaps not even necessary in the circumstances. Cooke was behaving as planned and heading where he was wanted – a discreet meeting with Mr Shepherd in some middle-of-nowhere, blink-and-you'll-miss-it place called Blue Valley.

He wondered whether Mr Shepherd was taking an exceptional risk agreeing to meet Cooke like this. Even under the pseudonym and a little disguise, Shepherd's face was becoming too recognisable.

He closed his eyes.

Mr Shepherd knows best.

The man had a keen tactical mind, one of the many things Carl respected about him; that and the courage to say the things most of the other parasites running for office this time around were too frightened to say. Even if this wasn't a paid job, he'd happily consider doing this one for free to ensure a smooth ride for his man into the White House.

Shepherd was exactly what this ailing, fucked-up country needed. Someone driven solely by the crackling energy of *belief*, instead of flip-flopping over the latest, fickle, issue-of-the-day poll results. In many ways, thought Carl, Shepherd reminded him of Kennedy: a conviction politician, a man ready to jump up, grab the steering wheel and pull this lumbering juggernaut back on track before it was too late.

As far as Carl was concerned, the Clintons and the Bushes had, between them, fucked over his country good and proper. Someone fresh, someone new, was needed to break the back-and-forth grasp the two main parties had over the reins of power.

Two different flavours of go-fuck-you.

He smiled. That was one of the favourite trash-talk sayings of his squad. Now, who the hell had first come up with it? He racked his mind, side-stepping fleeting memories – images he'd rather not call to mind – and finally it came to him.

Steve. Technical Sergeant S.T. Petray. It was his cracked-arse version of *between a rock and a hard place*. Another time, another life. He'd left too many of those strong, patriotic young men of his squad dead or dying in the shit-smelling back streets of a fucking Iraqi town, the name of which nobody on FOX, CNN or MSNBC had ever needed to learn how to pronounce.

Carl absent-mindedly caressed the fading tattoo on the back of his hand. The personal motif of their team – a desert fox.

He watched Cooke tucking into his in-flight meal, and saw in the willowy, bespectacled, dark-haired man across the aisle the personification of everything that was fucking well strangling his country; goddamned liberal media more concerned with the rights of terrorists than the families of fallen servicemen, more concerned with Nielsen viewer ratings than a moral message.

Cooke and his ilk, and the kids they were brainwashing with their flashy TV programmes that peddled explicit sexual content, me-first greed and selfishness, and a fast-food mulch of politically correct propaganda . . . those fuckers were eating away at America's Christian heritage. They were destroying the ethos of hard work, loyalty, good old-fashioned love for God and one's country.

The American Way.

Fuckers like Cooke wouldn't understand that. He suspected Cooke would sneer and deride that kind of quaint notion. He suspected Cooke didn't care a flying shit for what was right.

Because people like him cared about only one thing: themselves – making money, selling advertising space, hitting the ratings, selling sneakers, nailing a prospect, ID-ing a demographic.

People like Cooke were filthy fucking whores.

Fuck him.

When Shepherd gave him the nod that it was time, he was going to make the bastard understand what it feels like to see everything you value chipped away. He was going to make that bastard squirm before he died.

CHAPTER 66

1 November, 1856

Ben scrambled through the snow, tripping and tumbling into virgin drifts that had fallen since he'd last headed this way, over a week ago. It felt like a lifetime had passed since he and Sam had stumbled upon the place, along with Preston and Vander. He was sure he was heading in the right direction, though — uphill and drifting to the right. He passed the twisted and dying trunk of a leafless cedar, a tree he had unconsciously registered on that day as they'd been foraging for firewood. The greying afternoon pall beyond its splayed black branches and twigs urged him to hurry on: time was running out. The short day had already been showing signs of waning as he'd stumbled out of the camp; there was perhaps just another hour of light to make use of.

Keep your wits about you. Preston's out here somewhere.

Perhaps he was already at the hunter's shelter.

Doing what?

He could only guess, but he was certain that was where Preston was headed. His mind played snapshot images of the man preparing to kill once more; donning some crudely made demonic disguise to drive his people into a heightened frenzy of fear and panic.

Ben stopped to check once more that the long barrel of his

Kentucky rifle wasn't plugged with snow, that it was ready to fire immediately should he stumble upon Preston.

'I need to be ready for him,' he muttered.

He struggled another fifteen minutes in the direction he hoped the shelter lay and then a recognisable slope in the ground rose out of the gathering gloom. He scaled it as quietly as he could, dropping down to his haunches as he reached the brow and looked down into the dip, towards the shelter. He breathed as quietly as he could, his rifle raised, squinting down the barrel, and fully prepared now to fire at Preston on sight.

But there appeared to be no movement down there. It was silent and still.

He took several cautious steps down the shallow slope towards the shelter, listening intently for movement coming from within it.

Nothing.

He moved across the clearing, his gun trained on the ragged flap over the entrance. Every now and then the slightest innocent stir of movement in the woods – a breeze, the sloughing hiss of snow off a branch – triggered a panic-ridden three-hundred-and-sixty-degree whirl from him.

Stay calm.

There was no sign of Preston here, not outside. And not the slightest sound from within. He was about to concede that his suspicions had been ill conceived, that the Mormon leader might merely have left the camp to seek solitude, perhaps to pray – when his eyes flagged an incongruous detail. It took another second for his mind to understand what they had picked out. He strode towards the shelter.

Along the wall, hanging from lumber nails, was that curious assortment of skulls, cleaned and bleached white by the hunter's hand long ago. They hung in no particular order, in no particular pattern, the hunter's trophies, a proud proclamation of his skills as a trapper and a hunter. Close to the wall, he could see what it was that had caught his attention, not so obvious across the clearing but much more so now.

349

He spotted a faint outline against the weathered wood of the wall, and a single nail protruding. One of the larger skulls had been removed.

When?

He tried to recall whether there had been this gap in the row the last time they had come up here to this desolate spot. But his mind, like everyone else's that day, had been on the bodies.

He took a step back and felt something brittle crack beneath his feet. In the muted silence the noise startled him. Under several inches of new snow that had drifted against the bottom of the wall, the toe of his boot had found something hard and sharp. Ben knelt down and quickly brushed the powder aside.

His hand found a small pile of flecks of bone and jagged shards. For a moment he wondered whether the missing skull had dropped and shattered on the ground. It seemed unlikely. The ground was a soft cushion of decaying needles, cones and snow. There was nothing more of the skull to be found.

He realised that someone must have had to work it loose from the nail, dislodging crumbling fragments of bone.

'Where's the rest of it?' he muttered quietly amidst a fluttering plume of evaporating breath.

You need to go inside.

Ben looked warily up at the sky through the bare web of branches. Darkness was coming. He had no oil lamp to illuminate his way inside. If he dared go in and investigate further, he decided he had better do it now before too much more of the light was gone.

He moved cautiously towards the entrance. Girding himself with a deep breath, he swept the canvas flap aside. The meagre daylight seeped into the exposed interior, and he waited for a moment, allowing his eyes to adjust before stepping down. He was familiar with the layout from last time: a crude workbench to his right, a stack of traps, rotten pelt bales and paraphernalia against the rear wall, to his left the flimsy wattle and daub partition leading to the cot and the bones of the hunter.

His first step across the soft, peaty ground found the same

brittle flecks of bone that he'd encountered outside. He looked down and saw more jagged pieces of bone around the workbench. He looked at the bench itself, and saw it was dusted with more fragments, whittled pieces.

Ben fleetingly recalled visiting the cell of an asylum inmate who carved the most exquisite chess pieces from the bones of a sow, donated by the kitchens every Friday — ham-shank broth day.

'My God,' he whispered. He felt his scalp prickle and the hair on his neck rise as his nebulous suspicions found firmer footing. Here was evidence that something had been crafted in this place recently. Ben tried to recall how the young Paiute had described what he'd seen in the woods.

A giant head, a skull, with horns . . . a body of bone and spines.

He looked at the workbench and the floor and could now clearly visualise Preston feverishly at work by the light of a solitary oil lamp, fashioning a mask from the giant skull of a bison, or a stag. And all the while reassuring himself over and over in the muttered voice of a man utterly insane that he was engineering God's will for the good of his people.

And yes, he thought, *a mask of bone would be enough, wouldn't it?*

The mere fleeting glimpse of such a crudely fashioned mask amidst the bedevilling half-light of this forbidding place, and the low visibility of a gusting snowstorm, would certainly be enough to convince someone already terrified, someone already believing in such things as angels and demons, that something awful was in these woods.

There was no sign of such a thing here. Which he supposed could only mean that Preston had already been and gone.

What do I do now?

Presumably, he was already on his way back to the camp. He could try to pursue him and intercept him before they got back. Just the two of them, alone in the woods — one shot, and this could all be over.

If Preston's followers didn't lynch him first, Ben could show them the trapper's hut, the skull mask. He could explain to them that the medicine Preston had been taking had sent him mad. He could tell them of the confession the elder had made, which Dorothy had heard and planned to tell the others . . . he could tell them all those things, and perhaps it would be enough.

If I hurry . . .

He emerged from the shelter with relief, filling his lungs with the clear, cool breeze outside. He exhaled a large cloud of fetid air, purging the dank, coppery odour of rotting vegetation and dried blood.

Ben cast a hurried glance towards the subtle mound across the clearing; the grave of Sam and Dorothy lying side by side, now only a faint hummock beneath the thick blanket of snow. Beside their graves was Mr Hearst's; he'd been laid to rest not by his own people, but by Keats.

He wished Emily was standing with him right now. He wished he could show her the grave – that she could see both her brother and mother at rest side by side, properly buried, marked and prayed over. Instead, he imagined her last vision of them was an endless loop of sudden, barbaric butchery that dutifully played a performance for her time after time, night after night.

'I have to go,' he whispered. 'I'll save her from this madness, Sam. And come the spring, I'll take her out of this place with me. I promise you that.'

CHAPTER 67

1 November, 1856

As the last of the sun's rays shone daggers over the tree tops, and purple shadows like the claws of a giant hand grasped their way across the clearing, Preston emerged from the temple with his dark eyes seeming lost and far away. The whispered prayers of his people quickly hushed to silence as they all looked up at him from their clasped hands.

The campfire crackled and spat, and around them there was quiet save for the gentle hiss of shifting trees.

His remote, disengaged manner unsettled them. Right now they needed to know their First Elder was still empowered with certainty, righteousness . . . touched by the Almighty.

Mr Stolz was the first to speak up and break the silence. 'William? What are we to do?'

Another spoke. 'Night is almost upon us and they're still there.'

The flickering light from their campfire reflected in the deep sockets of his eyes.

'I entered the woods and prayed for guidance,' he said. 'I was ready to die for you, for God to come to me, to take my life and spare yours.' A tear glistened on his sallow cheek. 'I would do that for you, because I love you all like my children.'

His voice faltered. 'I thought we had been forsaken,

abandoned by Him, abandoned by His angel, Nephi, and left alone in this empty place with those *outsiders*. I thought we'd failed him. I feared He had judged us through Eric and Saul and found us wanting. But then it came out of the trees. It came to me, large and powerful.'

He took a deep breath, and smiled at them all. 'I was with the angel!'

Across the assembled crowd, he could hear the sharp intake of breath, whispered 'amens' and the keening tears of relief and joy from both men and women.

'God is with us. God has a mission for us still.'

One of the women dropped to her knees and cried with relief.

'There will be no vengeance wrought upon us tonight. We'll not face Eric's fate, nor Saul's, nor Dorothy's.'

'Thank you, Lord,' Mr Hollander bellowed.

'He asks of us one thing. To flush away those others across from us. They must be gone. And when what needs to be done here is done, we can finally begin work on God's beautiful message. Remember this well, because tonight will be the night the first true faith of our Lord is born, and the apostasy of all the false faiths will be at an end.'

Several voices cried out, and a feverish sound of lips and tongues at prayer spread across his people, like the roll and hiss of a wave across a shingle beach. He allowed them time to pray and give thanks before continuing. There was need for that now, to show God their humble gratitude. When he could hear the concluding mutterings of 'amen' uttered from the gathering gloom, he spoke once more.

'The angel confirmed what I feared. We have allowed devils to gather around us like jackals. They may look like people, they may walk and talk like people, they may bleed just like people, but they are nothing more than an evil deception.'

He shook his head. 'The Devil nearly fooled us with them, didn't he? With their fair skins, little ones resembling sweet, innocent children – looking so much like we do. But all along the Devil was mocking us with his clues. The dark-skinned

354

family, the Negro woman, the savages from the woods. The Devil was laughing at our stupidity, showing his presence amongst them and mocking God!'

'I heard say . . . that the white men over there have been sharing their wives with the savages!' called out Mr Larkin.

Several women gasped.

Preston nodded. 'I fear it might be true, Jed. I too have glimpsed things at night over there; gatherings around the fire, the noise of cloven feet, the chattering voices of evil.'

An uneasy murmur spread amongst them.

'I have seen . . .' Preston lowered his voice to a hoarse whisper that carried loudly across the gathering. 'I have seen the curved horns of the Devil emerge from amidst their fire, his head that of a goat, turning towards us, staring across the way at us . . . challenging us!'

'Oh Lord, please . . . please be with us!' someone cried.

Preston clamped his eyes shut and clasped his hands together. 'Pray now with me!' his voice commanded deafeningly. 'Pray with me now!'

They chorused his words.

'Oh, Lord, forgive us our weaknesses. We see now how we have let you down. We see now that those of us who died – that was your warning. That you are prepared to spare the rest of us, we are eternally grateful. That you are prepared to let us prove ourselves to you this night, we are eternally grateful. That we will be your first true followers of the true word of God, we shall be eternally grateful. Tonight, we make amends. Tonight, as you ask of us, so we shall obey! Now, we will purge this place. Amen.'

'Amen,' a hundred voices rumbled.

Preston unclasped and lowered his hands, breathing deeply, sending tendrils of vapour out through his nose. 'Gentlemen, gather your guns. Mothers, wives, sons and daughters, gather what tools you can find. Tonight we have to cleanse this place of poison. Make it a sacred place, so that Nephi can come in from those trees out there, and finally be with us.'

'Amen,' several of them chorused together.

'Amen,' he replied. He shook his head and lowered his voice, tempering it with regret. 'It is grim work He asks of us, but necessary work. None of them can remain here alive.'

He looked up at them. 'You understand what God is instructing us to do?'

'To kill them,' a woman called out.

'Yes, that's correct. To kill all those agents of Satan. Go now, get your guns and return here!'

Preston's people rose swiftly and disbanded in different directions; a hustle of activity, of boots crunching on compacted snow.

CHAPTER 68

cave iram Dei

M	T	W	T	F	S	S
				1	2	3
4	5	6	7	8	9	10
11	12	13	14	15	16	17
18	19	20	21	22	23	24
25	26	27	28	29	30	

Friday
Reno, Nevada

Rose glanced across at him as she overtook a sluggish container truck on the interstate.

'I still can't believe Sean's dead.'

'Yeah. Apparently he was stabbed by some care-in-the-community type while he was walking his dog.'

'That's awful!' she said, shaking her head. 'My God, poor Sean.' She hadn't seen him in the last year and a half since he'd worked with them on preparing to air *Uncommon People*. He'd almost been another member of the team, providing them with guidance on what they could get away with airing and what they couldn't.

'Nowhere's safe in London these days, is it?'

'Sometimes feels that way. If it isn't someone who should be on meds, it's a pissed-off hoodie carrying a shank. It depresses the hell out of me.'

She looked across at him. 'But that's so creepy, isn't it?'

'What?'

'You met him, then, a couple of days later, he's dead.'

He puffed air. 'Creepy. And bloody awful. I still can't quite believe it, either.' His fingers drummed on the dashboard.

357

They sat in silence for a while, both uncertain what to say next.

'This'll sound shitty, Rose, but it needs to be said.'

'What?'

'I was relying on Sean to fast-track a deal. That's not going to happen now.'

'You're right, it does sound shitty.'

'Well, sorry. That's the way it is. As I'm sure you've worked out, we're going to have to pull out of this story for now and head back home.'

'I suspected as much,' she replied. 'How much is left in the bank account?'

'It's not good. Just under four thousand.'

'Great.'

'I'll get my agent to pull in some work. We'll do some crappy corporate stuff, and then head back out here again in a few months' time. How does that sound?'

'I don't suppose we've got much choice, have we? Bills to pay.'

'Bills to pay,' he echoed quietly.

Rose overtook a slow-moving lumber-laden truck uphill.

'After I've met this guy, we'll see if Grace can take us out one more time, then we'll need to check out of the motel and head back.'

'What guy?'

'What?' Julian looked at her. 'You got the mail?'

She shook her head.

'Oh, it's no big deal. Some guy who has an interest in Preston. I hit upon his website. We've exchanged a couple of emails. Since I was already coming back, I thought I'd try and hook up with him.'

'Where?'

'Actually, he's coming to Blue Valley.'

'What?'

Julian shrugged. 'He's keen, I guess.'

'What's his name?'

'Arnold Zuckerman. Anyway, I'm sure I emailed you that.'

She shook her head. 'I don't think so. Communication isn't exactly your strong suit.'

'Damn. I could've sworn.'

'Maybe I missed it. Anyway, this Arnold . . . who is he?'

Julian laughed. 'I'm imagining a real hardcore historical anorak. But it looks like he's got some bread and butter on Preston's background. It'll be useful. Best we grab all the material we can in the time we've got left.'

'Are you sure he's not another journo?'

Julian shrugged. 'Who's to know? He doesn't come across as such, just a passionate amateur.'

'He's coming to Blue Valley to meet with you?'

'He offered. Said it wasn't a problem.'

'Well, don't stay up too late. I already arranged with Grace that she'll take us in again tomorrow morning. She's meeting us at the park's camp, early.'

'Oh, well done. How early?'

'Seven.'

'Bugger,' Julian grumbled. 'I could've done with a lie-in. Can't we start off a little later?'

'Let's not forget she's doing *us* the favour, Jules.'

'Fair point.'

They drove on in silence for a while, long enough that Rose suspected from Julian's awkward shuffling that he was on the cusp of raising a particular, awkward subject.

'How's the good Dr Griffith?' she asked.

Julian smiled. 'Looking well, doing well. He sends his best; he thinks highly of you.'

'As he should.'

'Actually,' Julian uttered, pulling out his cell phone, 'I tried him earlier, but he's not answering.' He checked his log. 'Not called back.'

'Was he interested in the Preston story?'

'Very. Perhaps there's something we can do with him. That's a follow-up meeting we can have when we get back.'

359

'He's putting some money in?'

Julian made a face. 'Not sure . . . maybe. More likely he'd want in on a book of some sort.'

'Great,' Rose wilted. 'Well, that's me cut out of the loop, then.'

He turned to her. 'Not at all, Rose, not at all. We discovered this as a team. Anything that comes from it, we share. I promise you that.'

He paused, and she knew he was putting together some thoughts.

'There's too much we've shared, too much between us, that I'd cut you out like that.'

Too much between us? She wondered what Julian meant by that. They both spoke at the same time.

'Julian, I—'

'Did we nearly—?'

She felt her cheeks flush in the deafening silence that followed.

Julian shuffled uncomfortably. 'Something almost happened between us, or am I mis-remembering and making a fool of myself?'

'No,' she snapped quickly, 'nothing almost happened. We had a few beers, and we were buzzed on the story, just having a laugh . . . as we always do.'

'Yeah.' He nodded, looking out of the window at the passing peaks, carpeted with a veil of dark green firs and dotted here and there with cedars and oaks turning a rich, burning, autumn gold against the October sky.

Was there a hint of disappointment in his voice? Or was she reaching?

That wasn't disappointment . . . that was relief.

She knew Julian was the kind of guy who didn't like anyone getting too close to him. That awkward little moment, back in the diner last week, had most probably frightened him back inside his reinforced shell. Nearly four years working together, building a trust, a tight friendship, a robust partnership . . . and she'd nearly blown it all because, for a moment, she'd let her guard down and shown him how she felt.

She sighed. It had been a stupid moment, a stupid impulse, and she ground her teeth, angry with herself.

CHAPTER 69

1 November, 1856

Ben tumbled over a root and fell to his knees in the snow. 'Shit!' he cursed, quickly picking himself up and pressing on.

'Dammit!' he cursed again.

He stumbled downhill towards the camp, through the tightly packed fir trees, coarse pine needles whipping and scratching his face as he pushed his way along by the last fading grey twilight.

He'd found no freshly disturbed snow, no sign of Preston. His hope of coming across the man alone had not happened. If he had, he wondered if he'd have been able to shoot him in cold blood.

Perhaps.

But now it looked as though he was going to arrive back at the camp with nothing to show, with only an unsubstantiated accusation to make. Ben had no idea as yet what he would do when he emerged into the clearing, no plan at all. Perhaps if he threw his gun down and crossed the clearing with his hands raised high, they might let him approach them without shooting him down.

And what if Preston is there, amongst them? You think he's going to let you talk for long?

'I have to try,' he gasped under his breath.

If he was right, if this was Preston's work, if Preston did have

362

some crudely fashioned devilish disguise and it was not being kept in the trapper's shelter, then perhaps it was stowed in the temple. Perhaps even stowed in that metal chest the man kept behind his cot.

All of a sudden, that seemed a certainty to him; in that chest he was sure to find something that would expose Preston; a blood-stained knife, a gore-spattered mask of bone . . . something. He wondered if there might be a way to creep around the edge of the clearing, to await a moment of distraction and steal inside the temple, hoping to remain undiscovered long enough to wrench the chest open and pull something out that would bring everyone immediately to their senses.

It was a pitiful plan, but short of running away into the woods alone and freezing to death, or joining Keats in some futile last stand, he could think of nothing else to do.

He caught a glimpse of light through the trees, the flickering orange of a flame. Keats had built a large pyre in the middle of their blockade to provide enough illumination that they'd clearly be able to see anyone coming for them. The pyre, it seemed, had now been lit and was already burning well.

It was then that he heard the first echoing crack of gunfire.

'Oh, God, no!' he gasped.

It's started already.

He watched Lambert struggling past, wheezing and panting, staggering through the branches and drifts of snow, making enough noise to awaken even the hibernating creatures of the woods.

Squatting in the branches, he watched the man pass beneath him towards the camp, whimpering and muttering to himself.

You're too late, Benjamin Lambert.

This man will try to stop them, the voice whispered to him from a dark corner of his mind. He didn't mind the voice being there in his head with him; it was comforting in a way. It knew just what to do.

This man might stop it. Kill him.

It's too late now. They're all going to kill each other.

He watched Lambert stagger blindly forward through the undergrowth and low branches, towards the peeling echo of an opening salvo of gunfire and the distant undulating twinkle of firelight.

The angel was right, of course. Lambert might yet put an end to this before it got going. The angel always offered the best advice, the best guidance – a voice to listen to and learn from. Alone, his own anger would have been the end of him. The angel had helped him channel the energy of his rage very cleverly.

Ingeniously.

It had become fun, watching the fear and paranoia eat into those people, watching the Elders become like frightened children, and Preston descend into madness.

He smiled beneath the mask. Listening to Vander beg, whimper and squeal like a pig had been the most fun of all.

Kill him.

He dropped down from the tree into the snow. He was hesitant to follow the angel's whispered instruction. Lambert was further away now, making better speed through the thinning trees, drawing closer to the clearing.

He is getting away from us.

He found an inner reserve to dare to confront the angel.

I wish for him to get away.

The bones stirred uneasily, and for a moment he thought he felt the warm smoulder of disapproval burning through the canvas sack to touch and scorch his skin. The warmth intensified for a moment, then the sensation quickly faded.

Perhaps. He is a good man.

They watched him stagger out of view, wading through knee-deep snow, calling out desperately to those in the clearing to cease. But the crackle of gunfire had intensified and there was a growing cacophony of voices coming from the clearing; some taunting, some pleading, some screaming – men, women and children all joining in a chorus of chaos.

I want to get closer, so that we can see.

The voice was silent in agreement. He stood up, spines of bone clinking softly against each other, then he stepped forward and followed with quiet, lithe grace in Lambert's tracks.

Tonight, the one we both want will die.

Yes. I want his death to be worse than that of the others. I hate him.

Then we should be closer.

CHAPTER 70

```
cave iram Dei
M   T   W   T   F   S   S
                1   2   3
4   5   6   7   8   9   10
11  12  13  14  15  16  17
18  19  20  21  22  23  24
25  26  27  28  29  30
```

Friday
Blue Valley, California

Julian checked the email on his BlackBerry to remind himself of the agreed time as he stepped inside.

It was, as he thought, four p.m.

He looked around Angel's Muffin House, a small and cosy teahouse with lace doilies, chequered tablecloths and a faux brass oil lamp adorning each table. Several small windows with net curtains allowed in some of the dull pallor of late afternoon, but it was dim enough inside that he needed a moment for his outdoor eyes to adjust.

It appeared to be deserted, not a single customer. Not that that surprised him. Like the rest of this quaint little holiday-season town, he imagined Angel's Muffin House bustled with trade in the summer but tumbleweed rolled through it the rest of the year.

It was a well-chosen spot for a discreet meeting. This had been Arnold Zuckerman's emailed suggestion. Julian hadn't noticed this cake shop, tucked away off Blue Valley's one, quiet, high street.

The guy's visited this town before, then.

Julian was busy wondering why the proprietor of Angel's would bother to keep it open like this, when he spotted

366

movement in a dimly lit corner. He noticed a middle-aged man sitting alone at a table. Self-consciously he wove his way past several tidily laid tables towards him.

'Arnold?' he asked, holding out a hand.

'Yes,' the man replied with a warm smile and a rich, deep, vaguely familiar voice. 'Mr Cooke?'

Julian nodded and they shook hands formally.

'Please,' the man said, 'pull up a seat. I ordered us a pot of Earl Grey and some delicious-looking cinnamon muffins.' He spoke with the warm, old-world charm of a storekeeper; very appealing and welcoming in a *come-and-join-me-by-the-fire-m'boy* kind of way.

Julian sat down and the man poured tea into his cup from the pot.

'You flew in from Britain today?' he asked.

Julian nodded. 'Into Denver, earlier this morning.'

'You must be tired.'

Julian added milk and spooned in some sugar. 'Yes, I am a bit.'

An awkward silence passed between them as Julian decided how to open up the discussion.

'Look,' said the man, 'this is a bit awkward. I'm not particularly good at playing games with people, Mr Cooke. I lie very badly, which . . . believe me, is a real handicap in the line of work I've chosen. I'm afraid I'm not who I said I was.'

Julian looked up at him. The man smiled a little guiltily. 'You might recognise me, or you might not. Depends how well you've been following the news lately.'

Julian realised he knew the face from somewhere – distinguished in the way a mature character actor might be.

In the news?

'Yes,' he replied, 'now you say it, I think I have seen you on TV.'

The man sighed and his smile widened. 'I suspect you probably have. It's getting harder and harder these days to find a quiet corner where I can be myself.'

'I'm sorry.'

He shook his head. 'Don't be. I should apologise for not being on the level with you, Mr Cooke.'

'Okay, *Arnold Zuckerman* is an alias.' Julian smiled. 'I thought it sounded like a badly made-up name.'

'Yes,' the man acknowledged with a soft laugh. 'If I place a cap on my head and a pair of glasses on my nose and try a change of clothes I can still – just about – walk up a street without being accosted by someone. But' – he sipped his tea – 'not for much longer, I imagine.'

Julian looked at him intently, trying to place this man's face in the right context. He remembered seeing that face recently as a still image, a picture on the front of a magaz—

Then it came to him.

'Oh shit!' he whispered. 'You're . . . you're the independent candidate, uh . . . Shepperton?'

He nodded. 'William Shepherd.'

Julian's jaw dropped open. 'Oh my God!'

Shepherd laughed. 'Not quite. I'm just a part-time lay preacher.'

Julian grinned. There was a warm, disarming familiarity to the man, which he found quite charming.

I'm sitting across the table from a man who may well be the next President of the United States.

Shepherd noticed Julian's sudden stiffness. 'Relax,' he laughed warmly, 'and please call me William. You know, despite being demonised, or lionised, depending on which news network you want to watch, I'm just a tired old guy trying to muddle through one day after the next and do what's right for my country.'

'You seem to be doing well, though.'

'It's still early days. There's another whole year of campaigning to go. There's a lot of work to do yet, to convince the American people it ain't the end of the world if they go and vote a Mormon into office.'

'A costly business.'

Shepherd sighed. 'Tell me about it. I believe the predicted spend on political campaigning by the others is likely to top two billion dollars by the time election day rolls around. I'm hoping to rely on the message, instead of slick campaigning.' Shepherd leaned forward and offered a sly wink. 'You know what? I think people are beginning to see through all that glossy crap these days.'

'Do you think you stand a chance?'

'I'm making a lot of new friends,' he replied. 'There're a lot of backers out there beginning to smell a good bet.' Shepherd shrugged. 'In any case, the Democrats and Republicans are both looking dirty, the amount of mud they've been slinging at each other. All I need do is convince middle America that voting for me won't let in the party they despise the most.'

He waved his hand dismissively. 'But look, if you'll forgive me, I'm bored witless of discussing campaign tactics. I have a man called Duncan who drives me up the wall with that kind of tedium. No . . . I'm here because we share a fascination with a certain obscure historical character.'

'Yes.' Julian reached for a muffin. He pulled it apart in his hands and picked at the hard-baked crust, not hungry but needing something to fiddle with. 'So then, I suppose the obvious question from me is: why your interest in this William Preston character?'

Shepherd took a moment to consider the question.

'I'll level with you. It's not so much Preston *himself* that I'm specifically interested in. As you saw on my web page, I managed to put together some background on the man, but it's what happened to the group of people that were travelling west with him that I'd like to learn more about.'

'So, what *do* you know?'

'They vanished in the mountains . . .' He looked out of the window, through the net curtains at the panorama of peaks towering over the small town. 'Somewhere out there.' Shepherd turned to look at Julian. 'One of them was my great-great-grandfather.'

Julian's eyes widened. 'No! Seriously?'

Shepherd nodded. 'My great-great-grandfather.'

'Preston?'

Shepherd hesitated. 'Lord, no. It was a young man.'

'Would his name have been Lambert?'

'Yes,' replied Shepherd – his turn to look astonished. 'Yes, it was. How on earth would you know that?' he asked, his deep voice dropping to a whisper.

Julian wondered how much of the truth he wanted to pay out to this man. He decided there was no harm in giving him a little bit more for free. 'We discovered what happened to those people. We found where they ended up.'

'Oh my . . .' Shepherd's deep eyes widened.

Julian smiled. 'Better still, we found the journal of one Benjamin Lambert. A very detailed account of what happened out there.'

Shepherd gasped. 'That's an incredible discovery!'

Julian nodded. 'Yes, yes it is.'

Shepherd spread his hands. 'And? Would you tell me what happened to them?'

Julian sipped his tea silently.

How much do I give this guy for free?

'Well, this is a little awkward, Mr Shepherd—'

'William.'

'William . . . I'm sitting on a historical tale I believe to be worth a lot of money.' Julian sighed. 'Look, I'm crap at talking money, but—'

Shepherd smiled. 'But, you're a journalist, you've worked hard to unearth the details and you're not that keen on giving it all away for nothing. I can understand that.'

'Yeah, that's about it.' Julian shrugged.

'Except now there's something of a topical link into this story, eh?' Shepherd added, with a wry smile.

'You could say that.'

Julian remained poker-faced, but his mind was racing to catch up with the situation. More information on this man was

370

coming to him, bits and pieces he'd unintentionally picked up from the background noise of daily news. William Shepherd, the independent Mormon candidate from Utah. The preacher, the businessman, the voice of common sense broadcast twice a week to tens of millions of the faithful, and a voice that broadly appealed to Christians from many other churches, the one and only candidate untainted by corruption and sleaze. And the guy who all of a sudden in recent weeks had started looking like a real contender.

'I imagine your concern is how your great-great-grandfather conducted himself?'

Shepherd nodded. 'I'd be lying if I said it wasn't a concern. In this ridiculous business we call politics, public perception is everything.' He sighed. 'If my great-great-grandfather went and ate someone in order to survive . . . well, I think my campaign manager, Duncan, would have a hissy fit.'

Julian appreciated his candour – and his sense of humour.

'I can imagine.'

'So I'm sure you can see,' Shepherd continued, 'I have a very cynical, vested interest in how my ancestor behaved.' He reached for the teapot and topped them both up. 'You could imagine, for instance, how much mileage the Republicans and the Democrats would get out of something that resembled another Donner Party incident, eh?'

'Yes. I can see how that would bugger things up for you.'

Shepherd looked at him, anxiously raising an eyebrow. 'And? Did he?'

Julian shook his head. 'No. There was no cannibalism . . . at all.'

Shepherd closed his eyes and sighed with relief.

'I'm sure you understand how important that is? It's such a taboo word and any kind of association with it . . . ?'

Julian understood.

'Politics is an awful game, one I genuinely detest. In some ways I'm not looking forward to the prospect that I might just win this election and have to play the political game in office for four years. But I'm doing it because someone has to. Someone has to show our people that there's another way, that they don't *have* to vote for one of two groups of corrupt sons-of-bitches. To be honest, it might be a relief not to make it to the White House.' Shepherd sighed and laughed gently. 'But don't tell my backers that, eh? They're bankrolling my campaign to win and nothing less will do for them.'

'I can put your mind to rest,' said Julian. 'Your ancestor comes across in the journal as a very good man. But,' he said, choosing his next words carefully, 'some very . . . *twisted* . . . things happened up there. Really very dark, unsettling stuff. All of it revolved around Preston. I'll be honest with you: whilst you personally may benefit from how Benjamin Lambert conducted himself, the Mormon faith may take a hit from Preston's be-haviour.'

Shepherd pursed his lips, deep in thought. 'Yes . . . but I believe from the little I've been able to research on the man that he abandoned the Church of the Latter Day Saints to follow his own path. He took his followers into a wilderness, literally and spiritually.'

Julian took his glasses off and wiped them. 'Yes, very much so,' he said. 'Lambert's description depicts a man tormented by something, by horrendous visions, capable of anything – even murder and mutilation. I've had a criminal psychologist exam-ine the journal and without getting into a long-winded profile' – Julian smiled edgily – 'there's something of the Charles Manson about him.'

'Lord. Really?'

'The psychologist's phrase was a *messianic narcissistic sociopath*. Bit of a mouthful.' He smiled. 'Perhaps it's just easier to say that he lost it. Went quite mad out there.'

'Yes,' Shepherd replied quietly, his eyes focused out of the window and on the mountains. 'So, Mr Cooke, what do you plan to do with this story?'

'I don't know. I really don't. I had plans for a documentary, but at the moment that's not looking so good. Perhaps a book.'

'Well,' said Shepherd, his gaze returning to the room, to Julian, 'you've certainly got my attention, and,' he added with a candid smile, 'I'm a man known to have quite a bit of money. Perhaps we can help each other out here?'

CHAPTER 71

cave iram Dei

M	T	W	T	F	S	S
				1	2	3
4	5	6	7	8	9	10
11	12	13	14	15	16	17
18	19	20	21	22	23	24
25	26	27	28	29	30	

Saturday
Blue Valley, California

'I still can't believe you did that,' Rose said, shaking her head angrily, 'after all the care we've taken to keep this to ourselves, to keep this story under our hats, and you go and invite along some guy who might be the next President of the United States!'

She swung the hire car left, onto the road leading out of town and up into the woods. 'Not only that, this guy's a media owner. He's the God-squad version of Rupert Murdoch. And here he is in Blue Valley, skulking around anonymously like some sort of Howard Hughes. Doesn't his keen interest in this strike you as odd at all?'

Julian shrugged. 'It's understandable, given his position. Think of it: in a country where a blob of semen in the wrong place can get you impeached, don't you think Shepherd is going to be somewhat cautious about a potential ancestral skeleton in the closet?'

'He wants to stage-manage our story, that's what he wants, Jules. He wants to be sure it's got a spin on it that makes him look good.'

Julian shrugged. 'Then there's not a lot he needs to do, is there? Benjamin Lambert seems to have behaved like a gent.'

'What if he wants to back-pedal the Mormon angle? What if he wants us to gloss over Preston being a psychotic nut?'

'We won't.'

Rose pursed her lips. 'Yeah?'

She dropped a gear as the car wound its way slowly around a hairpin turn, taking them up a steep single-lane road that hugged the contours of a rock-strewn gulch.

'I've got a question for you, Jules.'

'What?'

'What if we find something up there that turns things around?'

'Eh?'

'What if we find something that points to Lambert being responsible for those killings?'

The morning sun shone down through the tops of the Douglas firs lining the side of the road, dappling the windscreen with splashes of light and shade.

'Oh, come on, Rose. You're not still chewing over the Rag Man angle, are you?'

'I'm considering it. Lambert survived, we know that. But he came out of those mountains a . . . a haunted man.'

'Of course he did. But I mean, wouldn't *you* be changed by that sort of an experience? Traumatised, even?'

'I suppose. It's just . . .'

'What?'

Rose pursed her lips. 'Well, what if the story was very different?'

'What do you mean?'

'What if, I don't know . . . what if Lambert killed those people, but simply decided to leave a fictional account behind?'

'What? On the off chance it might be discovered a hundred and fifty years later?'

'Very funny, smart-arse. No, on the off chance he might be rescued by some other settlers or trappers and need something to corroborate his tale.'

Julian made a face. 'Possibly.'

'Come on, don't you think it's odd that Lambert chose to write it all up in so much detail? Surely he would have invested more of his effort in surviving, rather than writing? Unless, of course, he had something to hide.'

'He was a writer, Rose, remember; that's what he wanted to do.' He squinted out of the passenger-side window at the flickering sunlight. 'In some ways, just like an embedded journalist in Afghanistan. You don't *stop* documenting what you're seeing, hearing, feeling when the bullets start flying . . . that's when you really *start*.'

She shrugged. 'Maybe.'

They drove on in silence for a while, both of them drinking in the splendour of the mountainside and the wooded valley below – scenery that demanded their attention with every twist and turn of the road. Ten minutes later the car rounded a corner and the tarmac gave way to a potholed, gravel track that the bouncy Japanese suspension began to struggle with. A roadside sign announced the National Parks campsite was not much further.

'But what if . . . ?' She abandoned the thought unfinished and unformed.

'What if, what?'

The track curved to the right and a moment later a wooden board above them welcomed them to Blue Valley Camp. Beyond they saw the parking lot, two cars parked apart from each other. One of them Rose recognised as Grace's, and sitting in the front, she spotted her reading a paper, smoking a cigarette and enjoying the warmth of her car heater. The sound of tyres on gravel caught her attention and she perked up, offering Rose a smile as she parked their car snugly beside hers.

'The unsinkable Molly Brown,' Julian muttered under his breath, waving at her as he unplugged his seat belt.

'What?'

'Never mind. It's just a line from a movie.'

Rose snorted. 'Geek,' she replied, looking over her shoulder at the other car. 'Is that . . . ?'

Julian followed her gaze. It was a cream-coloured Lincoln

376

Navigator with shaded windows. 'It looks like the kind of car a President-in-waiting might drive. Hmm?'

They let themselves out and joined Grace on the gravel as she opened the boot of her battered Jeep.

'Morning, Grace,' said Rose, savouring the crisp, cool mountain air and exhaling a plume of steam.

Grace squinted up at the deep blue sky. It was patched with a smattering of combed-out clouds painted a dazzling vanilla by the rising sun. 'Lovely mornin' it is too.' She sucked in the air and blew it out. 'Snow should'a come before the end of the month. I reckon it's more than due. That's definitely a sky readying for the winter.'

'Hey, Grace.' Julian waved at her.

'Hey, Mr Cooke,' the old woman replied with a cordial nod and a wave, then shot a quick, questioning glance at Rose. She shook her head almost imperceptibly.

Grace shrugged.

'So, we set off now, we'll be there mid-afternoon,' she announced, pulling her backpack out of the boot of her Jeep. 'You two tourists good to go?'

Julian pointed towards the Lincoln. 'We've got someone coming along with us.'

Grace turned to look as the driver and passenger doors opened and a couple of men climbed out, both hauling backpacks of camping equipment out after them.

'I thought it was going to be just Shepherd,' Rose muttered.

Julian pulled a face. 'As a matter of fact, so did I.'

Their feet crunched across the gravel towards them.

'Mr Cooke,' Shepherd called out, 'I should have mentioned that I'd have company with me.' He closed the gap between them. 'This is Agent Barns. I recently qualified for a free Fed of my own. Apparently, when you hit a certain poll rating, you automatically trigger FBI protection.' He grimaced at the man. 'Barns has been my shadow for the last week.'

Agent Barns nodded politely to Julian, Rose and Grace and automatically produced his ID for them. 'You can call me Agent

Barns or Carl. I'm easy with either. I'll try and keep out of your way — just keeping an eye out for Mr Shepherd, is all,' he explained matter-of-factly.

Grace studied Shepherd with suspicion. 'Anyone tell you, you look a lot like that guy from Utah running for . . .' Her words trailed away quickly as her eyes widened with growing recognition.

'Yup.' Julian nodded. 'He's exactly who you think he is.'

Shepherd extended his hand. 'Pleased to make your acquaintance, ma'am.'

Her jaw fell open.

'Mr Shepherd, Mr Barns,' said Julian, 'this is Grace Simms, the National Parks ranger who's going to take us out, and this is Rose Whitely, my business partner and cameraman.'

A brief exchange of clumsy handshakes filled the silence, and then Julian turned to Grace, still thrown by their guest.

'Shall we make a move then, Grace?'

She stirred. 'Okay, yes . . . you folks all ready to go?'

They nodded.

'Mr Shepherd?'

He smiled warmly. 'Ready when you are, Grace.'

'Right then,' she said, her voice finding its back-to-business gruffness, 'it's about a six- to eight-hour hike up into the peaks from here. We'll stop halfway for a brief rest, and then press on. That should get us to where we want to go by about three in the afternoon. That gives us a couple of hours of daylight to set up camp.' She turned around and pointed to a worn footpath that led through the deserted camp site and up into the lowest apron of trees running down to the edge of the camping area.

'We're heading this-a-way,' she barked, turning round and setting off along the path at a brisk pace.

Julian looked up. It was a solid carpet of woodland as far as the eye could see, topped by the purple and jagged, slate-grey crowns of the nearest peaks. They looked deceptively close, towering over them like a gathering of curious giants.

Shepherd broke into a brisk walk, swiftly catching up with

Grace. A few moments later he had her laughing loudly, the bray of her coarse voice bouncing merrily off the hillside. The Fed followed behind them, dutifully keeping close to Shepherd, but not crowding him.

'Rose, what was that little thing between you and Grace?'

'Uh? What?'

'When we were getting out of the car. She gave you a look.'

'I don't know what you're talking about,' she replied.

'Oh, there was definitely a *look*.'

'You're getting paranoid in your old age, Jules.'

Julian shook his head. 'Pffft.'

CHAPTER 72

1 November, 1856

Ben emerged from the trees and stumbled into the clearing illuminated by the flickering amber glow of flames. In several places around the barricade erected that afternoon, flames licked up from inside the tangle of branches and cannibalised lumber. He saw small faggots of kindling and flaming torches being hurled onto Keats's defences by Preston's people.

'Stop! Stop it!' he shouted. But his voice was lost amidst the sporadic crack of gunfire, the chanting coming from one side and the screams of fear from the other. Above all of that he heard the loud roar of Preston's raging voice.

'Burn them out! Burn out the servants of Satan, the evil imps, the evil ones in our midst!'

A musket fired through the flames from inside the barricade and he saw one of Preston's men double over, grabbing his stomach. He looked back at the barricade again to see one of the Paiute frantically reloading a rifle. Several retaliatory shots rang out from amongst the Mormons. He saw half a dozen billowing clouds of blue-tinged smoke from the muzzle flash within, and showers of sparking gunpowder erupt from amongst them. The shots whistled through the smoke and flames and he heard the *thwack* and splinter of a shot finding wood somewhere inside the besieged enclave.

'You'll burn here and then in hell!' He heard a woman's shrill voice in a momentary lull.

This has gone too far to stop.

'Surround them; don't let them escape!'

It was Preston's voice.

His followers began to move, thinning out in both directions, beginning to spread out around Keats's small redoubt, dotted with small fires that were beginning to take hold of the dry wood and converge on each other.

'Don't let them escape!' Preston called again.

This morning, he had made it clear they weren't welcome in this place any longer. Now, Ben realised, Preston's resolve had gone one step further.

Preston wants us all dead.

Standing where he was on the edge of the clearing, he realised that they were moving swiftly towards him and would soon be close enough that one of them might stumble into him and be sure to recognise his face by the increasing brightness of the dancing firelight.

Another couple of loud cracks signalled gunfire coming from the flaming middle. Both shots were aimed frantically and whistled high over their heads, lancing white-hot into the night sky like shooting stars. Above the increasingly ferocious flames amidst the barricade, the sky was filling with a host of bright embers climbing, fluttering and dancing like fireflies.

Ben slowly stepped back up the slope into the tree line, aware that any sudden movement would catch someone's eye. Once there, he hunkered down behind the tall, straight trunk of a spruce, hidden enough for now, and watched with a growing sense of horror the fate that was awaiting all the others of his party out in the clearing.

They'll burn to death in there, or die if they try to come out.

'God help them,' he whispered. 'This is madness.'

The barricade was almost entirely alight now, a bright ring of flame whose heat he could feel on his face where he crouched. In the middle, the heat surely had to be unbearable, scorching.

He could see a couple of the women — Mrs Bowen and Mrs McIntyre — shielding their young ones as best they could from the searing heat, scraping hard-packed snow from the ground with their hands onto the exposed, blistering skin of their children.

Then, inevitably, it happened: a section of the barricade collapsed amidst a shower of sparks. A few seconds passed, during which he heard the distinct bark of Keats's voice shouting a string of commands from somewhere amongst the flames.

Then, through the burning gap, they emerged; a vanguard of the Paiute led by Broken Wing, their hand-me-down muskets from another era abandoned in favour of their *tamahakan*, now raised with savage readiness as they hurtled out towards the nearest, startled members of Preston's party.

Keats, and several of the other men — he recognised Weyland, McIntyre, Hussein — fired a volley of shots past the Indians, a couple of which found a target, one knocking a woman to the ground, the other clipping the side of a young man.

The Paiute were almost amongst Preston's people before the first crack of returning gunfire threw one of them off his feet and onto his back. Scrambling through the gap in the flames, the rest of the party tumbled out, some of the youngsters wrapped in smouldering blankets.

Keats and the menfolk emerged last, reloading rifles as they ran in the wake of their families, towards the ferocious melee being spearheaded by the Paiute.

Preston was quick to respond. 'Over there! Stop them breaking out!' he heard the man bellow. The Mormons, spread thin around the flaming redoubt, began to abandon the idea of surrounding it and instead converged on where the fight was happening.

Ben suddenly realised he was sobbing with grief, his cheeks stinging from the salt of his tears rolling down his winter-raw skin.

The screams of agony and the snarling of anger intensified.

He saw one of the Mormon women on her knees rocking back and forth, holding the still body of a teenage boy in her arms. He watched as one of the McIntyre children, Anne-Marie, the girl who had given Emily her doll, ran tearfully amidst the heaving bodies, calling out for her parents. She was suddenly caught by the vicious back-swing of one of the Indians. His *tamahakan* caught her neck as it swung, ripping a bloody chunk free before continuing its savage sweep and lodging itself in the face of a man he recognised as Mr Holbein, one of Preston's quorum. Anne-Marie dropped to her knees clutching at her throat. Holbein spasmed, firing his musket at point-blank range, ripping a jagged hole out of the back of the young Paiute.

Ben saw Keats push through to join the other Paiute, forcing their way forward. Their ferocious struggle had opened a gap in the loose tangle of people, standing warily back from their flickering blades. He called out for the others to follow him, but his voice was lost amidst the cacophony.

Bowen, McIntyre and their families had coalesced into one tight pack, fighting tooth and nail, back to back, doing their best to fend off the lashing blows of a taunting, goading circle of men and women and some of the older children.

Ben spotted Hussein and his extended family in an identical predicament, a few dozen yards away. He watched as Stolheim, one of the elders, aimed a pistol and knocked Hussein's eldest son, Omar, down with a point-blank shot in the chest. Hussein screamed with grief and swung the butt of his musket, catching the old man squarely on the chin. As he dropped to his knees, dazed, Hussein's meek and shy wife stepped forward and stove his head in with a mallet.

More of Preston's folk joined the churning mass of people. The swirling limbs, the dancing flames, the sporadic flicker of muzzle flash made the scene look like some bizarre occult square dance.

And Preston amidst it all, screaming encouragement, goading his people on. But no disguise. Not that it mattered. Perhaps Preston realised it was no longer necessary to play the avenging angel; his people were ready to do whatever he asked of them now.

They're all going to die.

Then a thought occurred to Ben — a promise that he felt like he'd made a lifetime ago; a promise to Sam. He looked away from the fighting, towards the far end of the clearing, and there he picked out the mound of the Dreytons' shelter.

Emily.

This is God's will?

He felt the angel stir in a quiet corner of his mind as he watched from the edge of the clearing. Bloodied women wrenched out the hair of other bloodied women; children punctured each other over and over with sharpened sticks, the snow darkening with sodden patches of freshly spilled blood.

No. It is Preston's will.

The fight was beginning to wane now. There were as many people squirming in pain on the ground as left standing and locked in the ugly struggle. Cries of anger, grief, pain and fear filled the night.

They kill in God's name, like trained dogs.

He ignored the angel for the moment, scanning the bodies, the squirming wounded, those still standing, recognising the faces, but no longer knowing them.

Curious . . . what people will do in His name.

He nodded, holding on firmly to the tree branch and looking down at the scene.

Yes.

A child squatted on the chest of a dead man, screaming and slashing repeatedly at the face with a hunting knife, leaving just a bloody chaotic pattern of fleshy ribbons.

There is hate in them all.

Yes.

Not like you. I see only good in you.

I hope so.

These could *never* have been the chosen people.

Why?

They are sick with a sin. It is a poison in them. It is in everything they do.

He was unsure what the angel meant.

You know the name of the sin. You have had to live amongst it, breathe it all of your life.

He nodded silently, beginning to understand.

It is this sin that defines these people.

Is it pride?

He sensed the angel approving his answer.

For believing themselves chosen . . . they are guilty of pride.

He nodded. Nephi was right.

You were always different from them.

I was?

That's why I let you take me away from *him*.

Preston.

His mind jumped to a certain matter, pending.

Preston! You promised me him.

Yes. This you deserve.

His eyes picked the man out, loading a rifle as he urged his people onwards. Three of the savages remained alive along with the guide, Keats. They now decided the fight was up, turned, and fled for the trees. They passed right below the branch he was crouched upon; any one of them would have seen him if they'd chanced to look up.

Preston called out to several of his people nearby. 'Don't let them escape! They must all be purged from here!' he screamed, leading the pursuit into the trees, followed by half a dozen men.

He is yours to do with as you wish.

Thank you.

CHAPTER 73

1 November, 1856

Ben stepped lightly between the shelters, afraid that Preston might have thought to station one or two of his people as guards. But it seemed no one had been left behind, and he wondered whether he would find Emily left unsupervised, lost in her trance, unaware of the slaughter going on outside.

He made his way to the snow-buried hump of the Dreytons' shelter, and squatted beside the low entrance, listening for the sound of anyone else inside. It was difficult to tell against the appalling sounds coming across the clearing. The hysterical cries of fighting had gone and now he could hear voices dotted around, voices that were starting to wail mournfully in the growing stillness.

He suspected the fervour Preston had whipped up prior to the fighting was at the point of being exhausted now. It occurred to him that Preston may well have induced such mania amongst them with the help of the medicine. Watered down and shared in a broth, Ben suspected its effect might have been enough to excite a certain tingling sense of euphoria amongst them. Preston's powerful exhortation would have done the rest.

He wondered if some of them might start drifting back towards the camp, perhaps to pray. He decided there was no more time to waste on caution and pushed his way through the canvas flap.

Inside he heard a gasp, and by the weak light of a candle saw the wide-eyed, tear-stained face of Mrs Zimmerman, beside Emily. Her lips trembled with grief as much as surprise at his sudden intrusion.

She looked at him, panting heavily, the red rims of her eyes sore with grief.

'Preston . . . he . . . he's turned us all into m-murderers,' she whispered between sobs.

Ben shook his head. He spoke softly 'No, not all of you, Mrs Zimmerman.'

She sniffed and wiped her nose. 'This place has . . . has become evil. I can feel the Devil out there.'

'It has.' Ben looked down at Emily. 'I've come to take her away.'

She nodded. 'Yes . . . yes, she must go with you. She can't stay here.'

He squeezed up inside the shelter and gathered the girl in his arms. Emily murmured something drowsily and her eyes darted anxiously around for a moment before lapsing back into a vacant, torpid stare. Mrs Zimmerman reached out and stroked the girl once more.

'Please, promise me you'll keep her safe,' she cried, fresh tears streaming down her cheeks. 'She's all I live for now. I have no one . . . family . . .'

'Then come with me,' said Ben. 'Help me with her.'

She stared at him uncertainly. 'Where will you take her?'

'I have no idea. All I know is we have to get away from here. You should come. Emily needs you.'

They could hear wailing outside, tormented grief and rage . . . tinged with madness. Her eyes met his uncertainly.

'I've seen depictions of hell,' said Ben, 'painted by asylum inmates and great painters alike, and they are what I've seen outside.'

A distant piercing scream echoed from the woods.

'If you stay here, Mrs Zimmerman, Preston's madness will kill you and all the others. One way or another you will all die. He's lost his mind.' He placed a hand on her arm. 'And I'll need your help with her.' Ben's eyes met hers. 'There's nothing for you here, not any more.'

She looked around, still uncertain, biting her lip, agonising for the briefest moment. Then she nodded. 'I'll come.'

'We must go now.'

Ben shuffled clumsily on his knees with the girl in his arms towards the entrance. He pushed the flap aside with his head and peered out. The fire in the middle was now beginning to dwindle and the circular barricade had collapsed in on itself, leaving a ring of glowing, sparking embers and languid flames. He could see silhouettes of people moving amongst the bodies. He hoped it was comfort being offered to those wounded or dying, but he suspected raw grief and rage was driving some to exact a cruel revenge on those not yet dead.

No one had drifted back towards the camp, just yet.

He scrambled to his feet with difficulty, encumbered by the dead weight of Emily, and loped across the space between shelters directly towards the nearest trees. Mrs Zimmerman followed, anxiously looking behind her at people she no longer recognised. She caught up with Ben kneeling down on the edge of the clearing, waiting for her.

'We will freeze outside tonight,' she whispered hoarsely.

'We'll keep moving tonight. That will save us from freezing. By daylight tomorrow we should be far enough away to consider our other needs and make a shelter.'

He wondered which way to head, having no idea where they were in the mountains or how far away, and in which direction, the nearest humble outpost of civilisation lay.

There might be other trappers out in these woods.

But he realised that coming across one was unlikely. They were going to have to find their own means of survival.

Mrs Zimmerman placed a hand on his arm. 'Head west, Mr Lambert . . . we should head west.'

She was right. He looked up at the clear night sky and made a rough calculation on where he recalled noticing the pale, milky sun rise and set these last few weeks.

'West is that way, I think,' he said, pointing across the clearing. 'We'll need to move quietly round the edge of the camp. Are you ready?'

She nodded.

'Come on then,' he whispered, scooping up Emily in his arms.

Keats struggled against the gradient of the gentle upward slope, winded and exhausted by the exertion of the last ten minutes, the desperate hand-to-hand fight and the ensuing escape. His tortured breath came in ragged gasps and wisps of steam rose from his hot body into the cold night air.

He stopped for a moment to catch his breath and turned round to look back the way he had come. The sky was mostly clear tonight, and in between the floating islands of dark cloud the full moon shone brightly, bathing the night with a quicksilver that made the snow's glow almost luminescent.

A hunter's light. A hunter's moon.

He cursed. The tracks of dislodged powder snow in his wake were unmissable even without the aid of lamplight. The dark spatters of blood he was leaving beside them — black by the light of the moon — only served to further betray the way he had come. The gash down his forearm, caused by the vicious swinging impact of a hoe, was still bleeding, but the flow of blood had slowed from a gush to a viscous trickle. He needed to bandage the wound so that it wouldn't get caught on something, tugged open, and the bleeding renewed.

But he also needed to keep moving.

Behind him, some way further down the hillside, he could hear someone's laboured breathing, the cracking of branches and twigs being pushed desperately aside; someone rapidly approaching him. Further down the hill beyond, he could see the muted flicker of lamps and flaming torches moving swiftly between the trees.

The sound of panting breath and the cracking of hasty strides taken carelessly was almost upon him. Keats hadn't time to mess with pouring powder and wadding a lead ball ready to fire. He dropped his rifle and pulled out his hunting knife. The panting quickly drew upon him, and by the pale glare of moonlight he saw a silhouette stagger out of the darkness and cross the clear, luminescent, snow-covered ground between them.

Keats sighed with relief when he recognised the outline and managed a dry and wheezy laugh.

'*Broken Wing*,' he said in Ute.

'Ke-e-et, you live,' the Indian replied in English.

They stared in silence for a few moments, both gasping hungrily for air.

Keats pointed downhill. 'Others with you?'

Broken Wing nodded. 'One Paiute brother, and the white-face with buffalo-skin squaw.'

'No one else?'

'They all dead.'

He heard Weyland and the others approaching now, making enough noise between them that Keats found himself grimacing and wincing with each deafening snap and rustle. They emerged into the moonlight, Weyland and a Paiute carrying between them the Negro girl, who flopped lifelessly in their arms.

Keats focused his attention again on the distant glimmer of torchlight. He counted at least a couple of dozen flickering orange auras moving amongst the trees. He watched as they halted, then a few moments later began to converge.

A meeting.

'My little girl's hurt badly.' Weyland's soft voice broke the silence as he lay down with the girl in his arms. 'My little darling, Violet. They hurt you, but you're going to be fine,' he whispered, rocking her gently in his arms. 'You're going to be fine, my little angel. We'll get you out of here, out of these

mountains and down . . . down into the land we came here for,'
he muttered, his voice thick with grief.

The young Paiute looked up at Broken Wing and shook his
head slowly.

'*Buffalo skin is dead.*'

Broken Wing nodded.

Keats ripped a strip off the faded polka-dot shirt beneath his
deerskin jacket and tied a bandage around his arm as he studied
the distant gathering of light, undulating in the darkness.

'They will come, Ke-e-e-t,' announced Broken Wing in
English for the benefit of Weyland. Following Keats's gaze, he
continued in Ute.

'*Even blind fool can follow.*'

There was some movement from down below. The gathering
appeared to be splitting in two. One of the groups changed direction and began to diverge into a dozen pin-pricks of light,
spreading out and covering the woods around the camp. Keats
realised they were looking for any escapees who had decided to
hide and not flee. The other group delayed a while longer before
starting up the slope towards them.

Keats balled his fist. *They've found our tracks.*

Weyland continued making whispered assurances to his girl,
promising a future that wasn't going to happen for her.

'We have to go,' hissed Keats.

The Virginian ignored him, whispering promises into her ear.

'Weyland!'

He looked up at Keats.

'She's gone, Weyland. She's dead. We have to go now.'

Weyland shook his head. 'Violet's tired. I need to let her rest
here for a while, and then—'

'The girl's dead!' he snapped. 'Ain't no time to argue 'bout
it. Look,' he said, pointing downhill. The glow of lights was
already growing brighter and more distinct. They were making
better speed up the hill, with the benefit of the light from their
flaming torches and oil lamps showing the way.

'*Why do white-faces still come?*' asked the Paiute in Ute.

Broken Wing glanced at the distant lights. '*White-face spirit has taken them.*'

Keats placed a hand on Weyland's arm. 'Say goodbye to her, Weyland, we're movin' along.'

Weyland nodded, kissed her still mouth and held her tightly, burying his face into her shoulder and rocking backwards and forwards.

'We gotta go,' Keats barked. 'Now!'

Broken Wing uttered a clipped command to the young Paiute. He then punched Weyland roughly in the small of his back. 'Come, or you die.'

He nodded, let her head down on the snow and got to his feet.

'This way,' said Keats, pointing uphill. He turned once more to look back down behind them as they filed silently past. Their pursuers were getting closer. Beyond them, he saw the muted glow of a smouldering circle, the fading embers of their hastily constructed defences. His assumption that the wood would be too damp to easily catch fire had been an error. They should have used the day to pack what they could and leave, as Preston had demanded of them, instead of digging in.

It was my mistake.

Lambert had seen sense, had seen they were doomed, and left before it was too late. The rest of them could have – should have – done the same. He realised now that there was plenty worse to be frightened of in these hills than the weather.

'Mebbe them preacher types are right,' he muttered to himself.

Maybe there are demons and angels . . . a God and a Devil.

CHAPTER 74

1 November, 1856

'Oh, no . . . no, that won't do. We can't have them skulking around in these woods,' Preston called out to the nearest of his people. 'You hear me?'

The men nearby nodded.

'Find them for me. We can't let them slip away and then come back. Spread out and find them!'

The swinging lights of dozens of oil lamps and flickering, sputtering torches filled the space around them with dancing shadows as they beat multiple paths through the coarse undergrowth and pushed through thick boughs of fir needles.

'And be careful!' he cautioned, raising his voice above the murmur of other voices, the snap of branches, and the rustle and tumble of dislodged snow around him. 'They're evil spirits. They will jump at you and cut you if they can. Be aware,' he said with a chilling certainty, 'if you corner them, they will try to confuse you. Whatever you do, do not listen to them! Do not look into their eyes; do not let them into your head! They may look like people . . . but they're not.'

Preston pushed forward with renewed determination, frantically scouring the ground in front of him, looking for signs of a recent footfall.

We cannot let any escape. This place must be purged.

The noises of movement from either side diminished as the men around him began to fan out, making their own way through the thickening woods. He turned to look over his shoulder and saw the familiar faces of two men following too closely in his wake.

'Pieter, Jacob . . . you must spread out some more. We must—' Turning forward again, the light from his lamp suddenly picked out a trail of kicked-up snow crossing directly in front of him. 'Look! There! More tracks.'

Several people by the looks of it, running together.

A drift of snow was disturbed and flattened to one side of the tracks.

Someone weakened and fell, perhaps stumbled.

'We have them!' He smiled.

The three of them veered to their right, following the recently made tracks, taking them up the gradually increasing gradient. Their breathing grew more laboured as they pushed onwards, and after a while the noises of the other men out combing through the trees were all but lost, except for the occasional distant voice calling out a find, calling to each other.

The tracks suddenly separated.

Preston stopped and studied them. 'Four of them, I would say. Three went this way, and one has gone to the right.'

Pieter Brumbaugh squatted down and pushed a lock of long, dark hair from his square face. 'Look! Can you see, one of the three is hurt – do you see it?' he said, pointing to a train of ink-black stains in the snow. He dipped a gloved finger in one and held it close to the lamp. He looked up at them, invigorated by the chase, his eyes wide.

'It's blood all right.'

'Then you and Jacob hunt them down,' Preston said. 'And mark my words, there's trickery in them. Don't let them talk. Be quick when you find them. Kill them immediately. They'll try to trick you, get inside your head and turn you on each other. Do you understand?'

Both men nodded, breathing hard with exhaustion, fear and excitement.

'God will be with you both. Now go!'

Both men set off, following the larger set of tracks. Preston turned right, to follow the one heading off on its own.

He watched Preston, hunched forward, his oil lamp held aloft in one hand, lighting the way ahead. The man moved with the clumsiness of one unused to tracking through woods, unable to find firm footing on the bumps and troughs beneath the deep snow.

He lacked agility; he lacked grace.

There is no beauty in him. He is as ugly on the outside as he is within.

My promise to you. He is yours.

Thank you.

He moved with effortless speed up behind the man, following delicately in his wake, stepping only on the compressed footsteps in the snow, no crunch . . . no noise at all . . . and now only a dozen yards from him.

If you turned around, you would see me, Preston. You might even have one chance to fire your gun at me if you were quick enough.

He smiled. This was fun. He had been following the outsiders like this, only a few minutes ago; the Indian, the tall southern man and his dying Negro girl, listening to their ragged breathing, the terror in their muted whispers. To be so close as to smell the odour of fear that trailed behind them and yet remain unseen was such good sport – he had to struggle not to laugh out loud with the excitement of the chase.

He'd been close enough to kill them.

But the angel was wise. The angel told him to use them as bait.

The tracks suddenly ceased.

Preston stopped dead. Confused, he knelt down, moving the

lamp closer to the ruffled folds of snow. The hurried, carelessly placed footsteps of one fleeing alone simply ended.

'What?' he muttered.

To his right he noticed the thick, gnarled trunk of a cedar tree. He looked up at the bare branches above him, each coated with undisturbed snow, like icing on a layer cake. Except one bough directly above him. The snow had been brushed off this branch, where two hands must have grasped it.

Tricky devil.

The angel, Nephi, had often warned him of that . . . the trickery of evil, the games of deception that Satan and his advocates played for their amusement. He stood up, craned his neck to look up into the dark branches above him, raising his lamp as high as he could to project the dim amber light further.

'I know you're up there!' he called out.

Only one of the smaller imps, one of the ones daring to masquerade as a child, would have had the agility to pull itself effortlessly up into the tree like that, like a monkey.

'Child!' He used the word, though the taste of it curdled in his mouth. 'Come down this instant!'

The tree's limbs swayed with the clicking of twigs on each other in the gentle breeze.

'Child,' he called out again, softening the cadence of his voice this time. 'Come down and I will help you eject the wickedness that has crawled inside you.'

Preston knew the Lord would forgive him that small lie; there was no cure for these creatures. But he was a man of compassion and love – he would make its death a mercifully swift one.

How can a man be so blind, so unaware of the space around him?

He stood behind Preston, now no more than an arm's reach away, swaying silently and struggling to keep from laughing aloud. He couldn't wait for the stupid, arrogant idiot to turn round and see him.

You are so blind, Preston.

The tall man in front of him, calling up a tree like a fool, was going to die in just a few moments. But before he died he wanted Preston to know who it was that was going to kill him . . . as he'd managed to do with Eric Vander. Saul Hearst's killing had been unprepared; it had happened in the blink of an eye, amidst a red rage that had clouded the moment. He would have liked to have taken his time with Saul, to let the dirty old man understand what fear truly was, for him to comprehend what a despicable creature he was . . . but most of all, to have him know for certain before he died that he would burn in the pits of hell for eternity.

He'd had that exquisite pleasure with Eric.

And now it was Preston's turn.

A gentle breeze tickled his bare skin as he rose up from his hunched posture, now standing straight, the soft clink of bones unheard. He whispered.

William . . .

Preston spun round at the sound of the gentle hiss of his name.

'Oh my!' His voice froze in his throat instantly. The head-rush of fear and awe, terror and elation left him momentarily rigid and silent, his pursuit of the child-imp in the tree completely dismissed from his mind.

Preston . . . the apparition before him hissed again quietly.

He dropped to his knees, and looked up in stunned, silent awe at the tall skeletal form standing over him. Love, joy and elation forced a choked sob from his throat.

'Nephi, is it you? You . . . you've come to me at last!' His voice quivered with gratitude. Tears rolled from the corner of his deep eyes, down hollow cheeks into the dark thatch of bristles beneath his jaw.

'Oh thank the Lord! I thought I had disappointed Him, disappointed you somehow . . . that you'd sought someone else for this work.'

The angel remained still. Preston's eyes wandered up the

pale form, over the spines and bones that protruded from it, up to the long, horned skull and two dark eye sockets through which he thought he saw the reflected glint of his flickering oil lamp.

'It's done! We . . . we have cleansed this place as you asked . . . cleansed it of devilish parasites; they've all gone.' His voice trembled with excitement. 'Pure enough that y-you've come back to us.'

The angel raised a long bony finger up to a jagged row of teeth. **Shhhhh.**

Preston felt the dark eye sockets studying him intently and was certain he sensed the angel was pleased with him – proud of him for having the strength of purpose to see through what needed to be done.

'Do you wish to b-begin our work?' Preston asked, ending the still and silent tableau. 'The golden plates are w-waiting in our temple, ready for us t-to begin—'

Shhhhh.

Preston stopped.

You have waited long for this, William – to revive me.

He nodded, feeling tears of joy welling in his eyes. 'I've wanted to see you, to talk with you, to hear the voice of an angel . . .'

But, William . . . why would an angel come to you?

'What?'

Why would God trust you to deliver His word from those sacred plates? Hmm?

Preston shook his head, confused. 'Because . . . He . . . He brought them to me, asked of me that I—'

No! You are a fake! A liar. A thief!

'No!'

Eric, Saul and you . . . the false prophet. You know what happens to false prophets?

Preston shook his head.

The angel suddenly took a step forward, one hand swiping across Preston's belly.

Preston was startled and confused by the sudden movement.

398

It was only when a twisting tendril of warm steam flickered past his eyes a couple of seconds later that he understood the angel had just cut him open. He looked down to see a growing pool of dark, viscous blood soaking into the snow at his feet, and a coil of glistening intestine protruding from the ripped gash in his clothes, hanging pendulously towards the ground.

He looked up at Nephi. 'Why did . . . ?'

There are so many interesting things inside you. You're going to see them all before you die. The angel giggled like a naughty child.

Preston felt an emerging sting of pain from his opened belly. But his confused, struggling mind was trying to comprehend a more important thing.

'Why? Why . . . do . . . this?'

The angel swung a hand of long, razor-sharp fingers across the open wound, catching the bulge of intestine and pulling a long loop of it out onto the snow. Preston felt the tender tug pulling him forward. He collapsed onto his knees.

Because you are not a good man. Not good enough for God.

Another swipe and Preston felt more of himself being eviscerated, landing with a wet splash on the ground between his legs. His mind dully registered that in one hand he held a gun, loaded and ready to fire. But that was irrelevant now; it was too late. He knew he was dying.

What mattered more to him right now, more than anything else, was trying to comprehend *why* this was happening to him, and what fate awaited him in the hereafter.

'Have I not been good? Have I not—'

'YOU'RE A BASTARD!' The angel's whispered voice had suddenly transformed into an all-too-human scream filled with anguish and hate.

Preston flinched. He rocked back drunkenly on his knees. The little world around them both, this small space of snow and bare branches, lit an amber hue by the flickering glow of his solitary oil lamp, was beginning to sway and spin. He felt light-headed.

That screaming voice certainly didn't sound like an angel.

'I HATE YOU!' the skeletal creature screamed. 'Your dark fucking evil soul is going to burn in hell! I want you to know that before I rip your heart out! You're gonna burn and burn and burn for ever!' it screamed with a shrill voice. For the first time in Preston's fogged mind, confusion gave way to fear, and the first inkling of suspicion.

'No!' he whispered.

The world suddenly keeled over to one side. Preston felt cool snow pressed against one side of his hot face as he lay supine. He turned to see this creature of bones and spines step over him and then kneel down, one knee planted either side of his pelvis.

'DO YOU UNDERSTAND NOW, WILLIAM?!' it screamed again.

A spiny hand disappeared into his gaping belly, and Preston felt the pull and rupture of tender things tearing inside of him. He gasped, convulsed and vomited blood. His eyes were losing focus, beginning to cross and roll uncontrollably . . . and then close.

'LOOK AT ME!' the thing screamed angrily, leaning down towards him, its face so close that the ragged teeth at the bottom of the long skull rested on Preston's bearded chin, hot gasps of fetid air billowing out into the space between them.

'See what I am!'

Preston's eyelids obediently fluttered open. He tried to focus on the bone-yellow face and the dark empty sockets inches away from him.

One hand of long spines came into view, covered in dark blood and shreds of tissue dangling from serrated edges, and Preston's dying mind vaguely noticed the leather straps tied tautly around a gloved hand, securing the sharpened blades of bone to it. In an abstract moment he wondered why an angel would want to construct such a strange device.

'I want you to see who I am,' it snarled with a keening whine, 'before those eyes of yours come out. I want you to *see me*!'

The hand grasped hold of the jagged teeth and pushed the long bone-face upwards. The skull – Preston's dulled mind managed to comprehend – was just a façade, a mask. And beneath that mask, dimly lit by the flickering amber hues of his oil lamp, he saw a face contorted with rage, every bit as terrifying as he'd imagined an angel might look.

It was *his* face he saw . . . only younger.

Sam smiled. 'You thought I was dead? Buried?'

Preston could only nod and gurgle in response.

Sam laughed at the pitiful, confused look on Preston's face. 'No, it wasn't me. That was the angel's idea.'

He's so very clever.

The angel had so deftly taken charge when he most needed it; his mind fogged with anger and grief, he had been incapable of thinking clearly. His memory of it was vague now. Mr Hearst's attack had been brutal and without warning. Momma had been slashed open once, twice and again; a deliberately barbaric attack to look like an Indian's handiwork. And as Momma collapsed, Saul had turned towards Sam and Emily.

Sam's memory was jumbled. He had killed Hearst in a rage, hacking and hacking at his open bowels as Emily stared in horror at him. He remembered a lone Indian arriving, and turning on the savage with Hearst's blade . . . the Indian snatching Emily from him and running.

These things had been a confused web of half-memories, until Nephi came to him and helped him make sense of it all – advising him with a quiet whisper, like a much wiser older sibling, a father, a mentor.

The angel told him there was work to do, and that work was not the translation of sacred metal plates – not immediately, anyway. The task at hand was to punish those arrogant people who presumed they spoke for God, and the charlatan who was leading them.

The grave for Momma; the same grave for the dead Indian

shot by Saul a week earlier and buried wearing Sam's clothes; making an example of Hearst's body . . . an example that let Preston know his secret was out. All of this, Sam knew, he'd not have been smart enough to conceive of by himself. The angel was so, so clever.

I'm glad you came to me.

You have a good soul.

His mind returned to the here and now, looking down at Preston's flickering, confused face. The man's lips were wet with blood and twitched, struggling to form what would prove to be his last word.

'Why?' he gasped.

'I'm doing this for Emily,' Sam replied. 'For me, for Johanna . . . and all your other bastard children.'

Preston squirmed and gurgled.

'I'm doing this for Momma. She was going to tell them all about you, but you had Saul kill her. I hate you!'

Take his eyes.

Sam raised his clawed hand and smiled. 'So, now you've seen.'

With a sudden thrust, the sharpened point of the bone claw strapped to his index finger penetrated Preston's left eye. It burst with a soft, wet pop. He pushed the claw in all the way to the knuckle, feeling cartilage and bone crack and surrender.

Preston thrashed convulsively for a moment, and then was still.

CHAPTER 75

cave iram Dei

M	T	W	T	F	S	S
				1	2	3
4	5	6	7	8	9	10
11	12	13	14	15	16	17
18	19	20	21	22	23	24
25	26	27	28	29	30	

Saturday
Sierra Nevada Mountains, California

'And this, ladies and gents, is it,' said Grace, stepping down over the moss-covered hump of a fallen tree into the clearing.

Shepherd followed her over and then stopped, surveying the open expanse of grooves and bumps covered with an undulating blanket of smooth, green moss.

'Oh, I assumed there would be more to see,' he said with a look of disappointment.

'Don't worry, it's all there . . . buried,' said Julian quickly, 'and surprisingly well preserved because of that.'

'And this place is where you found that journal?'

Julian nodded and pointed across the clearing. 'Over on the other side; you'll see where the moss has been disturbed.'

Grace looked up at the sinking sun. 'We're not goin' to have time for playing around in the muck today, people. We should get the tents out whilst we've got some light to work with.' She looked across at Shepherd. 'If that's okay with you, Mr Shepherd?'

'Sure.' He smiled genially. 'You're the boss out here, Grace.'

Grace smiled. She liked that he said that.

As they stepped cautiously across the uneven clearing, Rose

403

sidled up to Julian. 'Shepherd's doing a good job of winning over Grace, isn't he?'

Julian shrugged. 'Of course he is. He might end up being her next President.' He turned to her. 'Do I detect a whiff of jealousy?'

Rose wrinkled her nose. 'No . . . it's, it's just that, I dunno . . .'

'She didn't bow and scrape quite so much for us?'

She smiled. 'Yeah, I suppose.'

Julian looked up at the man ahead of them, and his bodyguard walking along warily to one side. 'Power does that. The smell of it stimulates our inner serf.'

Grace led them to the same relatively flat area they'd camped on last time. It was surrounded by a subtle, roughly circular hump. The blackened soot from their last campfire a week ago remained undisturbed.

'We've got about an hour of light to pitch our tents. Let's do that, then I'll get a campfire going for some coffee.' She turned to Shepherd. 'You okay putting up your tent, Mr Shepherd?'

'I'm okay, my dear,' he laughed. 'I've done my fair share of hiking in my time.'

'Mr Barns? You okay with that?'

The Fed nodded. 'I'm good, ma'am.'

Grace put together a surprisingly tasty stew from the contents of several tins and a perforated bag of spices that she threw into the bubbling pot a few minutes before serving.

'My word, this is delicious,' said Shepherd, blowing onto a steaming spoon.

'Nothing like a stew when you've been walkin' out in the fresh,' Grace replied.

The fire crackled warmly between them. Julian felt it was noticeably cooler this time around than a week ago. But then, it was into November and, according to the local weather man this morning, snow several weeks overdue would be covering these hills soon. Julian shuffled slightly closer to the fire and blew a cloud of steam out of his bowl. 'You said you've done a bit of hiking before?'

'Yes. My father and I . . . a long time ago now, I'm afraid. We took quite a few trips to the Rockies and the Sierra Nevadas. I don't seem to have much time these days to spend it like this, away from the end of a phone network. It's hard to truly get away from that.'

Julian smiled. 'I can imagine. Not that long ago it wasn't so hard to find somewhere off the grid, but—' He pulled out his BlackBerry and checked for a signal. 'Nope, nothing. Well, there you go. I guess you can *still* find places off the grid.'

'So, you were sayin', you've come along because you're interested in this story of Rose and Julian's?' said Grace.

'Yes. I've an interest in history from this time, particularly early Mormon history. Fascinating thing, the birth of a brand new faith, so recently – historically speaking.'

Rose blew on her spoon. 'Isn't it awkward timing for you to duck out from campaigning, just to join our field trip?'

Shepherd chuckled. 'I guess there's no such thing as a good time. But I felt like I needed time to recharge my batteries, have some quiet.' He looked across at Julian. 'And your colleague's email arrived at just the right moment. It gave me an excuse to get away from things for a short while.'

They ate in silence for a few moments, listening to the hiss of a breeze through the swaying branches around them.

'So,' said Julian, 'you're a Mormon yourself. That's right isn't it, Mr Shepherd?'

He nodded. 'I was born and raised one.'

'How does that factor into your voter appeal?'

Shepherd sighed. 'I was hoping to get away from work,' he replied with a weary smile.

'Jules, let the poor man eat in peace,' Rose chided him gently.

Shepherd raised a hand. 'No, I don't really mind.' He looked at Julian. 'As long as you're not interviewing me?'

He smiled and shook his head. 'No Dictaphone. Off the record. I'm just curious.'

Shepherd shuffled to get comfortable. 'It's definitely a factor. There're about thirteen million Mormons out there. And to be honest, not *all* of them would put a vote my way. But I hope the people I'm getting through to are not necessarily Mormons, not necessarily Baptists, but a large, quiet groundswell of middle-ground voters who are tired of the other two parties, the sleaze, the corruption, all that self-serving manoeuvring they do on every issue.'

'But your core voters, the ones you're aiming at are . . . are what? Protestant Christians?'

'Not at all. I hope I'm talking to people of every faith. I hope I'm getting through to Catholics, Muslims, Hindus . . . people of *all* faiths, Julian. People who see beyond the immediate *I am, therefore I will have.*'

Rose frowned. 'What do you mean?'

'This selfish, *me-first* society we've gone and built. There's no social bond left in this country of ours, no sense of community, of a greater good. We all go our own separate ways, grabbing what we can for ourselves . . . and screw everyone else.'

'Yup,' Grace muttered. 'That's about it.'

Shepherd nodded. 'We've spawned a generation of selfish, self-obsessed product consumers. A younger generation who know nothing more than their local mall, the internet, Mc-Donald's and their iPods. Kids who don't care a damn for their community, for their family even. Moms and dads both working double shifts to pay for the shiny gadgets the TV tells their kids they *need* to have.'

Shepherd shook his head. 'The great big capitalist experiment,' he sighed, 'went and broke our society big time. There's no *Thanks* in Thanksgiving, no *God* left in Christmas. Those days are nothing more than carefully branded herding to drive the cattle into the mall twice a year. And hell, we do it all over again for Easter.'

'The world *has* become too commercial,' agreed Rose.

'With no faith left in our lives, no meaning to our lives,' Shepherd replied, 'all that is left is' — he shrugged — 'buying things.'

Julian finished his stew and placed the bowl on the ground. 'You know, what you're saying sounds refreshingly left wing, for America at least. Don't you worry you might sound too . . . I dunno . . . socialist for voters to accept?'

Shepherd shrugged. 'People know what's right. In their hearts they do. Our broken country needs some kind of glue to put it back together. To reconnect kids with their parents and rebuild all those fragmented, dysfunctional families; to rebuild those isolated families into communities and those communities into a country that once more understands the notion of a common good.'

'And that glue is faith?'

Shepherd nodded. 'It's all we have left. Let me ask you a question, Mr Cooke. Who would you prefer as your neighbour: Homer Simpson or Ned Flanders?'

Julian laughed and pushed his glasses up. 'Seriously?'

Shepherd nodded.

'Well, it's got to be Homer, annoying though he is.'

'Because?'

'It's the God thing, I'm afraid. Sorry. I struggle with the ridiculous beliefs most religions insist on slavishly subscribing to. You know, the world being created in seven days and being only six thousand years old, that kind of thing.'

'If we're talking about the other faiths too,' Rose cut in, 'how about the idea of women being the property of men? Or heaven being a place where a man can get satisfaction from seventy-two virgins? Or to take another faith, that any sin, no matter how awful, can be instantly written off by muttering a Hail Mary.'

To their surprise, Shepherd nodded. 'You're right, both of you.'

Julian looked up from the fire. 'What?'

'It's all a load of crap.'

407

The crackle of burning firewood filled a long silence.

'The world's faiths are contaminated with age-old super-stitions, most irrelevant and many very dangerous. After all, every one of them was formulated and prescribed at least a thousand years ago. How, in God's name could any of them be relevant to our lives now? What we need—' Shepherd stopped short and looked around at them. 'I'm sorry. You got me whipped up into preacher mode.'

Julian sat back. 'Uhh, I'm pretty sure you've never preached *that* kind of message on your TV station.'

Shepherd shifted uncomfortably. 'No, you're right, I haven't. No one's ready to hear that kind of thing. It would sink my campaign in a heartbeat if they knew how I felt.'

Julian shook his head. 'What you say out here is off the record. I'm not interested in who becomes President eighteen months from now. It's Preston's story that I'm interested in.'

The kettle on the fire began whistling and bubbling. Grace leaned forward and carefully unhooked it from a small 'A' frame suspended over the fire.

'Mr Shepherd?' She topped up the stewing coffee with steaming hot water. 'I believe you were going to tell us what we need. You know, before you stopped short there.' She stared at him. 'You were just beginning to make some sense to me.'

Rose nodded. 'I'm intrigued too. I believe you just rubbished all the world's major religions. And yet you are a man of faith, right?'

'I am.'

She shrugged. 'Well, uh . . . isn't that a problem for you?'

He reached for the coffee pot and refilled the chipped enamel mug on the ground beside him in silence. He sipped the black brew hesitantly, his mind elsewhere for a moment.

He spoke quietly. 'I'd like to see those old faiths swept aside. And all the malice, the hatred, the bigotry, the ignorance that goes with them. More than anything,' he said, the slightest hint of passion stealing into the timbre of his measured voice, 'more

408

than anything . . . this broken world needs to have a new conversation with God.'

'What do you mean by that?' asked Julian.

Grace emptied the dregs from her mug. 'You're talkin' about a new faith?'

Shepherd nodded.

'And Mormonism is that faith?'

He shook his head. 'I was brought up to believe that . . . and perhaps I once did. But not any longer. The Lord's word was corrupted by ambitious men – not good men, not *pure* men. We've been living in a state of apostasy for too long.' He took a deep breath. 'I believe this tired, troubled world of ours needs to hear from God again in a language that makes sense of the twenty-first century.'

Rose stared at Shepherd, quiet now, lost in his thoughts, a detached, faraway look in his eyes. The silence continued long enough that Grace finally decided to cut in.

'I'm beat. I'll be turnin' in. The fire needs to be completely dowsed before we sleep, and the pan properly covered. And if any of you need a pee before bed, be sure to do it well way from the tents.'

She stood up and gathered their empty bowls. 'Mr Barns? Give me a hand?'

Agent Barns nodded. 'Sure.'

They headed across the moonlit clearing, a flashlight lancing out into the darkness before them, with bowls and cutlery in hand, and Grace carrying a two-litre plastic jug of water. Rose watched them stop at the edge of the clearing. Grace began to rinse the bowls and spoons.

'So, Mr Shepherd, do you mind if I ask something?' Rose spoke quietly.

He looked up at her and smiled. 'Of course.'

'Would you consider yourself . . . *pure* enough?'

'Pure enough to interpret the message of God? To listen to his quiet voice in the darkest hours of night and not twist it to suit my own ends?'

She nodded. 'Yeah, I suppose that's what I'm asking.'

'I'd like to think so,' he laughed. 'After all, I'm a very good listener.' He looked at his watch. 'Look, it's late, I've had a long day . . . a hectic week in fact, and I'm bushed. I think I'll turn in.'

'We'll see you in the morning,' said Julian.

They watched him head over to his tent, unzip it and climb inside.

'For a politician he does seem refreshingly honest,' said Rose quietly. 'Makes for a change, huh?'

Julian nodded. 'He's got it . . . whatever it is: charm, charisma . . . he's got it.'

'He sure has,' she replied, gazing back at the fire.

CHAPTER 76

cave iram Dei

M	T	W	T	F	S	S
				1	2	3
4	5	6	7	8	9	10
11	12	13	14	15	16	17
18	19	20	21	22	23	24
25	26	27	28	29	30	

21 October, 1973
Haven Ridge, Utah

'William, I'm glad we have this chance to talk alone.' The old man spoke with a frail voice. 'You know . . . I can see the burning light in you.'

'Grandfather?'

The old man smiled. 'You remind me of my own grandfather,' he added.

'What do you mean, *the burning light*?'

'The passion, William . . . the passion, the faith, that zeal. The knowledge that you're special, that God has marked you out for great things.'

William looked out of the window of his grandfather's study. 'I do feel a calling,' he admitted.

'Yes, I see that in you. You have a talent for communicating the word of God. I'm sorry to say I never had that kind of strength of purpose or faith, and nor does your father. We've both been good businessmen, hard workers, and we've made plenty of money in Portland and here . . . but there's something in you that I know will take you so much further.'

William felt it too, in a way.

'I have something I wish to share with you,' his grandfather uttered quietly, 'something I never shared with your father.'

'What is it?'

The old man turned to look at his grandson — a handsome young man, whose recent devotion to the faith, speaking publicly with such passion that he was becoming a regular attraction at the local temple, made him proud. And . . . it made him feel guilty for merely paying lip service to the church throughout his life.

'I have a secret.'

William stirred uneasily.

'It's to do with our past, our family.'

William knew a little of the family history from his father.

'You know that my grandfather,' said the old man, 'travelled west during the migrations? That his group, under an elder called William Preston, ran into trouble in the mountains?'

William nodded. 'They got snowed in, didn't they?'

'That's right, they did. And many people died.'

The old man sat back in his winged chair. It creaked. 'The only one of them who did manage to make it out of the mountains was my grandfather. He was young and fit . . . otherwise he would have died, I'm sure.'

'Dad told me the story. He emerged starving and in rags, didn't he?'

Grandfather nodded, stroking his chin thoughtfully. 'Yes, that's right. I do believe it was his faith alone that saw him through that nightmare.'

'Faith in God can get you through anything,' William replied earnestly.

'Well, see lad, there's a little more to that tale than you know.'

William sat forward, his curiosity piqued.

'Preston led his followers out into the wilderness for a reason. He had with him some very special things.'

'What things?'

His grandfather's eyes narrowed. 'Sacred things.'

CHAPTER 77

Sunday
Sierra Nevada Mountains, California

The words came back to him as his fingers traced the outline of the chest in the peaty soil.

'Sacred things,' Shepherd whispered quietly. Scrabbling in the pitch-black dirt by the light of his torch, he imagined himself looking very much like some small forest animal scratching in the earth for its first catch of the day – a pig snuffling for truffles.

A wry smile sloped momentarily across his lips as he tried to imagine what sort of pithy headline Leonard Roth, the *Washington Post*'s political editor, would come up with if he could see him now. Instinctively, he looked around.

It's always a possibility.

Some industrious paparazzi might just have managed to successfully track him down out here and be – even now – lining up the crosshairs of a telephoto lens upon him. He quickly dismissed the thought for what it was; unnecessary paranoia. No one knew where he was right now, not even Duncan.

As it needed to be.

'Sacred things,' he said again quietly, his breath a plume in the cold morning air. He turned to look at the Day-Glo tents across the clearing; none of the others had risen yet. It was still before seven, and the grey light of pre-dawn was just enough now that he no longer needed his torch. He switched it off, not wanting to attract any unnecessary attention, just yet. He wanted this to be a private moment, to share it with no one else, to perhaps feel that sense of epiphany and revelation that Joseph Smith must have once felt, unearthing these precious things from the Hill Cumorah.

His fingers felt the hard metal surface, pitted, rusted and caked with soil: it was beautiful.

Preston's chest.

This was the thing he *really* sought. Getting into the White House, getting his hands on political power to ready everyone for the future – that was all very important. But this . . . *this* . . . putting his hands on the plates, the actual spoken words of God, and interpreting them into modern, American English . . . *this* . . . he thought, looking down at the dark lid of the metal chest, *this is destiny.*

You seem like a good man.

A voice.

Shepherd froze. It had come from somewhere inside his mind, a gentle whisper at once familiar but also strange; like his own thinking voice, but quieter. He remained still, listening intently for a while, hearing nothing but the gentle ballad of shifting branches.

You seem like a good man.

So quiet, anything but a still mind would miss it. It seemed to come both from within his head and from the chest in the ground.

Open it.

'Do I hear you?' he whispered.

There was no reply. He was no stranger to voices. There'd always been voices as long as he could remember. Nasty, spiteful ones, ones that urged him to test his faith and steer into an oncoming truck, ones that teased and mocked him, ones that soothed and encouraged. But this one had a curious cadence to it.

He remained still, emptying his mind, and listened for a while.

But it was gone.

Shepherd craned his neck to look out of the excavated dip. There was still no sign that the others were about to rise. They were all zipped up snugly in their tents, glistening wet with morning dew amidst the lazy tendrils of a cool mist lying in pools across the clearing. Shepherd had risen an hour earlier, with the sky still dark, eager to make a start and unearth those precious things.

He'd had a fair idea where to search; his grandfather's hand-me-down tale had contained enough detail that he knew the largest shelter was Preston's temple, and that his people had the larger camp. His eyes had easily picked out the most prominent ridge of humps beneath the moss. It sat almost beneath the twisted form of an old cedar tree, one branch strangled by a creeping vine stretching out over the clearing.

A solitary crow pierced the quiet woods with an impatient *caw*, as if urging him to get on with his work. He dug his fingers deep into the soil, pulling it away from the sides of the chest. The metal was scarred with corrosion but still robust, still intact.

It's inside. I can feel it.

His fingers stumbled upon the latch at the front, triggering a tremor of adrenaline-charged exhilaration.

This is it.

Open it.

He took a deep breath, aware that both his hands were shaking. Forgivable, given how long he had been searching for this place, given how many times he had tried to find it over the years, always praying for guidance that God would lead him here. He'd always known the probability of his finding it by chance was one in a million – the proverbial needle in a haystack. But he also knew that one day a group of beered-up hunters, a family on a hiking holiday, some teenagers goofing around, *somebody*, would eventually stumble upon it, find the decaying remnants of the camp, dig up some long-lost personal keepsake with a name still legible on it. And eventually somebody would end up typing Preston's name into a search engine.

Shepherd smiled. 'And here we are.'

His heart thudded at the thought of what lay within the metal trunk before him, and his mind momentarily dwelled on a folly he'd watched on FOX news before coming to meet with Cooke. He had listened to a Catholic priest and an amateur archaeologist discuss with light-headed exhilaration the spreading ripple of anticipation amongst theologians and archaeologists around the world at the promise of a technology that would finally allow the last few Dead Sea Scrolls to be read spectroscopically.

Shepherd smiled at the ridiculous interest those worthless rolls of papyrus attracted. They were nothing but the words of mere scribes, templemen, inconsequential Judaean politicians of the time authoring their manifestos, supposedly with the endorsement of a higher authority. *Not* the words of God.

Here, before me, however — his heart pounded in his chest — *I have the real thing.*

The holy spirit, the angel Nephi was here too, ready to read to him from the plates. He was almost certain now that the quiet whisper he'd heard in his mind was that of the angel.

Yes.

I can hear you.

Yes.

Shepherd felt a tear roll down his cheek.

You're with me now?

Yes.

He realised he was soon going to bear witness to the original, undoctored, unchanged words of the Lord as the angel read to him; it would be almost like peering into the actual mind of God.

It's going to be wonderful.

Open it.

He slid his fingers under the ridge of the lid and lifted it up. Rust flakes crackled and fell from all four sides as it creaked open, and a dry, stale, not unpleasant, musky odour welcomed him inside.

CHAPTER 78

2 November, 1856

Ben shivered beneath his thick woollen poncho, wrapped tightly around the three of them. There was a growing fug of body warmth in the small spaces between them, enough to keep at bay the worst of the early-morning chill.

He raised his face from the faint warmth inside to look up at the sky. A steely grey light was straining through the clouds.

'The night's nearly gone,' he whispered.

The last faint glowing signs of pursuit had disappeared hours ago.

We're safe from them now.

Mrs Zimmerman stirred and shuddered with the cold. 'Thank goodness,' she muttered, her trembling lips almost blue.

Ben turned to look down inside the poncho at Emily, nestled between them, her head resting on Mrs Zimmerman's ample chest. Her small frame shivered in an inadequate cotton dress, her breath rattled and chattered, the occasional unintelligible murmur stealing past her lips. Her eyes were closed. She was sleeping.

'The Devil came to our c-camp last night,' said Mrs Zimmerman. 'He came into our camp and turned people – people I've known for years – into demons.'

Ben shook his head. 'It was fear that did that.' He turned to look at her – a stocky, ruddy-faced woman of middle years, her skin chapped and sore with the cold. 'That's all. Fear of the unknown.'

Ben looked out from the nook they'd found between two spurs of rock. The snow covered rocky, uneven ground that sloped downhill towards a tree-filled gulch. Beyond that, an uninterrupted carpet of woodland shrouded the way they had come during the night. From one small valley, they had stumbled into the next.

They were sheltered here from the sporadic gusts of ice-cold wind. That was good for now.

'It was Preston,' he whispered.

'Preston?'

He nodded. 'I saw his handiwork. He crafted some disguise out of animal bones and skulls. He wore this disguise and I'm almost certain it was he who killed Vander, Hearst, Sam and his mother.'

'No.'

The voice came from inside the poncho.

Emily spoke.

'Dear Lord . . . Emily?' gasped Mrs Zimmerman. She pushed aside the woollen cover and looked down at the girl's pale face, stroking her hair aside. 'Emily?' She turned to Ben. 'God be praised, I thought she would never speak again.'

He hunched over to look closely at her. 'Emily,' he said. 'It's Benjamin here.'

The girl's eyes remained closed and her breathing even. She seemed to be still asleep.

'Emily? Can you hear me?'

Beneath her parchment-thin skin, her eyes moved back and forth, following the progress of some horrendous scene being played out again. Her dry lips twitched and parted. 'Angel . . . an angel,' she muttered sleepily.

'Emily? It's Ben. Can you hear me?'

'. . . killing Momma . . . Sam . . . he's killing Momma!'

419

Her voice faded into a sleepy nonsensical drone, and then she was silent.

'She's coming back to us,' Mrs Zimmerman said, a tear trickling down a crimson-blotched cheek. 'Thank the Lord,' she cried quietly. 'She's finding her way home.'

'I'll thank the Lord, Mrs Zimmerman, when we make it down from these mountains and find *our* way home.'

'We will, won't we?' she asked.

He managed a confident nod. 'Of course we will.'

Later on, the sky broke up into a mixed chequerboard of heavy clouds and fleeting strips of blue sky that mercifully permitted the respite of the sun's warming rays through every now and then. They made some faltering progress westward and through a treacherous rocky pass that led down into a much broader valley. Ben wondered if this was the pass Keats had been taking them towards, the pass he'd assured them was his self-discovered shortcut through the peaks – the shortcut he hoped would one day bear his name.

Keats Pass.

The snow-covered hillside sloped gently down through a continuing canopy of firs towards the distant glinting ribbon of a river that snaked gracefully along the valley floor.

Ben felt his heart lift at the sight of it. The river pointed their way out of the mountains, flowing downhill and westward, hopefully leading them towards somebody else; a trapper's cabin, the winter stop-over of an Indian tribe, the moored resting place of a river-raft, piled high with beaver pelts . . . perhaps even the crudely constructed homestead of a hardy family of settlers. The river was going to lead them eventually to someone.

By midday they had shambled their way down to a flat shingle bank overlooking the surging flow of fresh water, and Ben, confident they had travelled further than they were likely to be pursued, dug away a space in the snow and set about building a fire around which the three of them now gratefully huddled.

Emily stared wide-eyed at the flickering flames dancing around the crackling wood, the thick smoke of pine needles and moist bark slowly catching. She was humming a tune to herself, a hymn.

'Little by little, she's coming back to us.' Mrs Zimmerman smiled.

Ben nodded. For now, though, his mind was on the gnawing tightness in his belly. There was food to be had amongst the trees, he was sure, if only he knew how to find it, catch it and kill it.

'I have to eat,' he said, rocking gently to take his mind off the discomfort. 'Preston denied our people any of the oxen after we took in those Indians. We've been living off packing oats and whatever they could forage for us.'

Mrs Zimmerman shook her head, ashamed. 'I'm so sorry.'

'He was trying to make us leave.' He looked at her. 'We should have.'

The kindness of a fleeting blue sky had deserted them once more as a seamless grey blanket of cloud rolled over. They had the fire though, and enough firewood.

'At least we won't freeze tonight, eh?' he said cheerfully. 'It'll be better than last night was for us.'

Mrs Zimmerman was about to reply when they heard the rustle of movement amongst the trees. Their eyes met.

'You hear that?'

She nodded and Ben jumped to his feet. They heard it again. It was not the gentle rustle and dart of a startled animal they'd heard, but the steadily approaching noise of careless feet.

'Oh please, no,' he muttered under his breath.

There was no hiding out here on this snow-dusted frozen bank of shingle and silt. They were trapped. He looked down at the fire, and up at the twisting column of smoke, curling languidly up into the sky.

Stupid. We led Preston right to us.

Mrs Zimmerman came to the same conclusion. 'Please!' she

421

called out, 'William Preston, it's Ellie Zimmerman here! Please don't hurt us!'

The noise was increasing, picking up pace.

'Mr Lambert's been very kind, caring for us!' she called out again. 'He's been very kind. Please, don't hurt him!'

They heard the crack of a branch snapping, and briar roughly trampled beneath hasty feet – almost certainly the sound of more than one person moving through the trees towards them.

Ben pulled a branch from the fire, one end smouldering and smoking, and held it before him. Then he caught sight of some movement; a man . . . two men . . . weaving their way through coarse undergrowth in the darkness beneath the trees, stooping beneath the low, heavy branches of a squat fir tree, emerging, blinking, into the daylight.

'Oh God . . .' Ben whispered.

CHAPTER 79

cave iram Dei

M	T	W	T	F	S	S
				1	2	3
4	5	6	7	8	9	10
11	12	13	14	15	16	17
18	19	20	21	22	23	24
25	26	27	28	29	30	

Sunday
Sierra Nevada Mountains, California

Shepherd reached into the metal chest and placed his hand gently on the faded cotton sack, feeling the hard metal plates through the perished material. The dents and grooves on their surface reminded him of braille. His fingers tingled as he felt the subtle contours of ornate curls.

This is the language of angels.

He puffed out a cloud of air and felt momentarily dizzy from the exhilaration of it all.

'You okay, Mr Shepherd?'

Shepherd looked up to see the sturdy outline of Carl squatting beside the shallow ditch.

'I'm fine, Carl.'

'This is what you came for?'

Shepherd nodded.

Carl looked over his shoulder at the tents in the distance. 'I should warn you, the others are stirring now. It's gone seven.'

Shepherd's mind was elsewhere. 'Thank you,' he answered absent-mindedly, as his fingers gently grasped hold of the threadbare cotton. He delicately lifted the bag out of the chest, warily holding one hand beneath it in case the frail bag ripped and dropped its precious contents.

'Could you open that for me?' he said, nodding towards a reinforced aluminium travel case on the ground beside him. Carl flipped the latches on the side and opened it, revealing a layer of black cushioning foam. Shepherd gently rested the tattered cotton sack inside.

'Can I see?' asked Carl, studying the bag with a puzzled expression on his face.

Shepherd nodded as he carefully opened the bag to reveal a glimpse of the tablets. They were each roughly the size of a sheet of foolscap — copper sheets, green with corrosion and richly textured with rows of indented glyphs.

'That's really the word of God?' he asked.

'You sound disappointed.'

'I guess I expected the word of God to look more . . .'

'Important?'

Carl nodded. 'Yes.'

'That's why I *know* this is genuine, Carl. The Lord speaks with the quietest whisper, not a shrill cry. If this were a shimmering golden tablet, I would be sceptical.'

The man considered that. 'I guess you're right.'

Shepherd turned back to the dark metal chest in the ground. Carefully he reached in and pulled out another tattered canvas sack. From within came the soft clink of fragile bones.

'What's that?'

'The remains of an angel, Carl.'

The man looked at him. 'An . . . an angel?'

Shepherd smiled. 'That's right, a real angel, one of God's own. These tablets are written in a language that you or I would never understand — the language of angels.' Shepherd gently placed the sack alongside the other in the case. 'This angel is called Nephi, and when I'm ready to transcribe these tablets, he'll appear to me in the flesh and read to me so that I can write it down.'

Carl's eyes widened. 'My God, Mr Shepherd,' he whispered, 'this . . . this is for real, isn't it?'

Shepherd placed a reassuring hand on his arm. 'Oh yes, Carl, this is the real deal.'

He closed the lid of the travel case.

Carl glanced back at the tents, leaned forward slightly and whispered. 'Mr Shepherd, they're up now.'

Shepherd stretched up to look out of the shallow ditch he'd excavated. He could see Cooke ambling casually towards them across the clearing, yawning out a cloud of breath as he made his way over, and the park ranger, Grace, heading into the trees to forage for some firewood.

You have it now.

Yes.

They are no longer needed.

The voice in his head was just a little louder than earlier, a little more insistent, as if it had emerged from a dark corner at the back of his mind and moved a step or two towards the front. Shepherd hesitated. There was something implied in what it had whispered.

Would that be necessary?

The voice was quiet for a moment.

I have what we both want now. There's no need for anyone else to die.

Do not be weak.

It's not weakness. It's common sense. We don't need any more bodies, not with what lies ahead for us. You understand the importance of my campaign? The potential to be President . . . how that can help us spread the new word of God?

There was no reply. Shepherd sensed it stirring, distracted with thought. Perhaps he could argue it round. *Is this what God wants? For us to start work on his message with blood freshly on our hands?*

Shepherd sensed the simmering heat of anger, disapproval somewhere amongst the dark recesses of his mind.

I wonder, have I chosen wisely?

Yes, you have.

Then do as I say.

425

Carl was watching him. 'Mr Shepherd? You okay?'

Shepherd looked up at him, his eyes barely registering the man. He stood up slowly, feeling an ache in his back from having crouched for too long, and watched as Cooke covered the last few yards towards them with a look of growing curiosity on his face.

'Morning,' Julian called out, approaching the edge of the ditch. 'You've started already? We've not even had breakfast.'

Shepherd offered him a tired smile. 'Yes . . . yes, I wanted to . . . uh, make a start.'

Julian looked down into the dark trench and spotted the open metal chest. His eyes instantly widened. He looked around at the faint outline of a much larger shelter than the others and instantly realised that this was the 'temple' Lambert had frequently mentioned in his journal.

'Shit!' He looked at Shepherd. 'Is that Preston's . . . ?'

'Yes,' he replied evenly, 'I believe it is. Preston's belongings.'

Julian shook his head. 'How the hell did you find it so easily?'

'I prayed,' Shepherd shrugged and offered a hazy smile, 'and the Lord showed me the way.'

Julian grinned. 'Well, however you managed it, this is fantastic. You know, having read through Lambert's journal last week, and reading about this' – he pointed to the ditch, the nubs of dark rotten wood poking through the soil and moss – '. . . and here it is!'

'Yes.' Shepherd replied dully.

You know what needs to be done.

'Perhaps, Mr Cooke,' Shepherd continued, 'you should gather up the other two and we shall celebrate this find properly.'

'Yeah.' Julian grinned. 'Yes, of course.'

Shepherd's slack face came to life with a generous smile. 'Then, I think you and I should discuss how much money you're going to need for your documentary. How does that sound?'

426

Cooke's grin widened. 'That would be good.'

'Excellent,' Shepherd replied, pulling himself up out of the muddy trench. Carl reached out a hand to help him. 'Off you go and get the others, then.'

Julian turned away and headed back towards the tents. Shepherd watched him silently for a moment, the false smile draining away swiftly.

'Carl,' he said, 'you know what needs to be done?'

'Now?'

He nodded sadly. 'Yes, I'm afraid so.'

Julian picked his way slowly across the clearing, confused. By all rights he figured he should've been tap-dancing across to tell Rose the news. But he wasn't. Instead his mind was on something else, something that was troubling him . . . something he'd just caught a glimpse of — the faint flash of a dull blue tattoo across the back of Agent Barns's hand.

I've seen that tattoo before.

It was distinctive: a fox.

Damnit, where've I seen that? On whose bloody hand did I . . .

A cold loop of realisation suddenly curled through his stomach.

That man was at Heathrow.

He glanced back over his shoulder and saw Barns watching him. If Barns was in London . . . ?

He's been following me.

Other things that he had almost managed to forget about, to dismiss as the product of an over-active imagination, came back to mind: a noise on his phone line, the suspicion that somebody had entered his flat. The unsettling curl of anxiety in his stomach turned into something more acidic and uncomfortable.

And Sean, dead twenty-four hours after doing lunch with me.

He remembered Tom's caution about looking for skeletons in the closets of the powerful.

'Oh, Christ,' he muttered to himself as he stepped across a

427

gentle hump in the ground. He knelt down outside Rose's tent and fumbled for the zip.

Or am I being paranoid? Shit. I dunno . . .

'Rose?' he called out softly.

There was no answer, no noise at all coming from inside.

'Rose, it's me . . . coming in,' he said, pulling the zipper up.

CHAPTER 80

Sunday
Sierra Nevada Mountains, California

Rose looked up at him as he stooped inside her tent. Still snuggled up in her sleeping bag, she had her laptop on and was staring intently at the screen.

'Jules, there's something that isn't right.'

He squatted down beside her. 'Rose, I need to—'

A slither of bright morning sunlight streamed across the floor and into her eyes. 'Close the zip – I can't see anything.'

He reached round and pulled it down.

'Jules, you have to see this,' she said, turning the laptop round so he could see the screen.

She moved the mouse across to the tab of another image. 'I got an email back yesterday morning before we set off to meet Grace at the camp. I just didn't have the time to read it and open the attachment before we set off.' She waved her hand at the unnecessary digression. 'Anyway, there's a small museum, well . . . it's nothing more than a photographic archive in Fort Kearny.'

Julian shook his head impatiently. 'Rose, look can this wait a—'

'Jules, just listen! It's an archive of portraits taken of groups of settlers on the eve of departure. It seems nearly everyone at the point of stepping out into the wilderness had one of these portraits done.'

'So?'

She clicked the mouse button on the image tab and a muddy brown portrait of a group of people, standing proudly in front of a wagon, filled the screen.

'They had one image in their database of a certain *Preston party*, stepping out in 1856, which they kindly sent me.'

Julian studied the group portrait; several dozen men and a few women, all of the men bearded, the women wearing bonnets that modestly covered their hair. Each had a face betraying grim determination, and a readiness for everything nature could throw at them. Clearly not the entire group, just those elders senior enough to warrant being in the photograph. To one side stood another man, tall and gaunt.

'My God!' he whispered. 'That's Preston?'

Rose nodded. 'And who do you think he looks a helluva lot like?'

'Oh, shit, yes, he does,' he whispered.

Shepherd.

It was the eyes – unmistakably deep and intense, the distinct brow above and the long, clearly defined jaw. She flipped the screen of the laptop down. 'I'm really not comfortable with this, Jules, getting so into bed with this guy—'

Julian raised a finger to his lips to shush her, and then spoke quietly. 'I think we're *way* past not feeling comfortable.'

'What do you mean?'

Julian pulled off his glasses and wiped the lenses, a stress habit he was vaguely aware of, but he felt too distracted to correct himself right now. Rose studied him with a growing expression of concern. 'Julian?'

'Shepherd is Preston's descendant.'

Rose nodded. 'Yes. That means he'll want to bury this story.'

He looked at her. 'I think we might need to leave.'

'Leave?'

'As in drop everything, no explanations, just leave.'

'Julian? Why . . . what . . . ?'

'It's something our friend, Dr Griffith, said,' he whispered. 'Something he said that's really, really spooked me . . . and I want to get out of here, like, right now.'

'Julian? You're spooking me now.'

'Get dressed. I'll explain this all later on.'

Julian pulled the zip down slowly and peered outside. There was now no sign of Shepherd in the ditch, nor Agent Barns, although he wondered whether the ID badge was genuine, and whether Barns was really his name.

'Shit, where are they?'

He turned round. Rose was dressed now, ready and crouching anxiously behind him.

'Where's Grace?' she whispered. And then as an afterthought, 'Grace has a gun.'

'I can't see her . . . or them.'

'Jules? I said Shepherd might want to bury this, that's all. Why the hell are you so jumpy all of a sudden?'

He turned round. 'I was being followed in London, Rose. I just recognised that guy Barns. I think he was tailing me. I think he might even have broken into my apartment and bugged the phone.'

She froze. 'Seriously?'

'And now Sean's dead,' he added, 'killed the day after I had lunch with him.'

Rose's jaw slowly dropped open. 'Oh fuck.'

He nodded.

'So, what are we going to do? We can't just run out into the woods without our stuff — we'll get lost, and this isn't the time of year to go doing that.'

'Rose, consider where we are right now. We're alone in the deepest, darkest wilderness with a man who stands to lose everything if we emerge from these woods alive with this story. I can't be a hundred per cent sure that Sean's stabbing is linked,

431

but you know what? I'm not prepared to hang around here a moment longer and, you know . . . ask.'

'Jules, I'm scared.'

'Me too.'

She placed a hand on his back. 'Okay, I'll go with the *leave* idea.'

'Right.' He peered out again. 'We're going to climb out very calmly and casually make like we're going to the trees for a toilet visit, okay?'

'What about Grace?'

'She's out there collecting firewood. We'll try to find her and explain we need to make a sharp exit.'

'All right.'

'Ready?'

'Not really.'

Julian lowered the zip the rest of the way, pushed himself out through the flap of the tent and stepped into the morning sunlight, dazzled and blinking. He stood up slowly, stretching and yawning, half-aware the whole routine looked pathetically theatrical.

Rose stood up beside him, shielding her eyes from the morning glare. 'Where are they?' she muttered quietly.

'We're right here,' replied Shepherd flatly, standing to the side of the tent.

CHAPTER 81

cave iram Dei

M	T	W	T	F	S	S
				1	2	3
4	5	6	7	8	9	10
11	12	13	14	15	16	17
18	19	20	21	22	23	24
25	26	27	28	29	30	

Sunday
Sierra Nevada Mountains, California

Julian spun round at the sound of his voice. 'Oh,' he gasped, and then managed a faltering smile. 'I believe we were all going to celebrate finding Preston's things, weren't we? Shall I brew us a nice pot of coffee?'

Shepherd cocked his head in an odd, unsettling way, a distracted, far-off expression on his face. Barns looked at him, one hand sliding discreetly into his jacket pocket for something.

'Mr Shepherd, sir?'

Shepherd shook his head silently, his lips fluttering in silent debate.

'Rose and I will get some firewood,' Julian added, reaching for Rose's hand. 'Get a nice fire going for the coffee? Have some breakfast too . . . okay?' Julian wondered if Shepherd had heard any of that, but then the man's troubled eyes returned from far away and locked onto his.

His thin lips spread slightly with a hard-fought and weary smile.

'Yes,' he said, his face flinching and flickering. 'Do that. Go get some firewood.'

Barns's hand hesitated in his jacket pocket. He looked confused. 'Sir?'

433

Julian turned to Rose and mouthed, '*Let's go.*'

They backed away from the two men, turned and walked, struggling with an instinctive urge to break into a desperate run.

Julian heard Barns's voice again. 'Sir? Are you sure about letting them go?'

Rose whispered from the side of her mouth. 'Shit, Jules, I'm sure they know. *They know we know.*'

'Keep walking,' he hissed back.

Behind them, Barns's voice came again, insistent. 'Mr Shepherd, are you all right?'

They stepped a little more quickly over the undulating mounds of moss, both desperately trying not to give in to the growing rush of panic. For some reason Shepherd seemed to have slipped into a listless state. Right now he was letting them walk. Julian figured if they started to sprint, that might snap him out of it.

Twenty yards ahead of them were the first saplings that marked the edge of the clearing and the start of woodland rising from it. To their left, in amongst them, making her way down the slope, weaving through the trunks, he caught the briefest glimpse of Grace's red anorak.

'Look, there's Grace up ahead—'

His words were interrupted by a high-pitched shriek of rage from behind them. It was Shepherd's voice . . . but somehow not Shepherd.

'KILL THEM!'

Julian turned to see Barns react instantly, whipping out a gun and adopting the well-practised firing stance of a trained killer.

'Oh shit. RUN!'

He heard several cracks of gunfire and felt the throb of a bullet passing his ear an instant later. Rose yelped beside him as they raced for the trees. The sound of two more cracks came in quick succession.

He felt the sleeve of his jacket tugged viciously and saw the white puff of inner lining exploding from a ragged hole.

'Shit!'

They reached the first narrow tree trunks as a third double-tapped volley was fired, sending splinters of young wood into the air. Julian and Rose ducked down and scrambled under the low branches into the undergrowth.

He lost his footing on a root and tumbled over.

'Jules! Get up! Get up!'

Rose held out a hand; he grabbed it and pulled himself up just in time to see Grace emerge from the trees, clearly confused by the ruckus. She started jogging towards the two men, unslinging her rifle. Julian realised that, in all innocence, she must have been thinking the shots were being fired at a bear.

'GRACE! RUN!' Rose screamed.

Grace turned their way, confused by Rose's call. She turned to Shepherd, her gravelly voice raised urgently as she asked them what the hell was going on.

Julian watched in horror as Shepherd's hired killer swiftly raised his pistol and shot the old woman point-blank.

'NO!' screamed Rose.

They watched in shocked stillness as Grace flopped lifelessly to the ground. Shepherd casually reached down and scooped up her gun.

'Oh shit-shit-shit . . .' Julian muttered. He grabbed Rose's hand and pulled her after him. 'Come on!'

They scrambled up the hillside, alternately weaving their way through dense clusters of undergrowth and brambles that scratched and grabbed at them, then bursting into small isolated clearings encircled by a thick, tall wall of dark green fir trees.

Julian stopped in one of them and turned to look downhill, through a gap in the trees towards the clearing. He could see the Day-Glo colours of their tents clustered together in the middle, and amongst them the darker, navy-blue anoraks of Shepherd and Barns. They seemed in no immediate hurry to pursue; instead Barns was picking through his backpack, and Shepherd was slowly scanning the hillside, a hand cupped over his eyes to keep out the low-angle glare of the morning sun. Suddenly his other hand shot up and pointed directly towards them. He heard the distant bark of the man's voice a second later.

'Shit!' snapped Julian. 'He's spotted us.'

'Jules,' Rose whispered, 'look at us.' She pointed at her anorak and his. One was lemon yellow, the other orange. 'We've got to lose these.'

'You're right.'

They pushed their way out of the clearing back into dense foliage, and there, hidden from view for the moment, they shed their anoraks. He tucked his into a small bundle and pushed it under his jumper, creating a pregnant bulge.

'We need to hang onto them,' he said. 'It gets cold at night.'

She nodded and did likewise.

'Okay, then,' he said, gasping for air after the last few minutes of exertion. 'You're better with directions — which way?'

Rose nodded up hill. 'That way is west, I think . . . and perhaps we'll get a signal on your BlackBerry at the top.'

'Right.'

They pushed on again, stopping to rest momentarily in a small rock-strewn glade a few minutes later. Julian looked back down at the camp clearing and saw the dark outlines of both men walking calmly across it, towards them and the tree line.

'They've stopped fucking around down there, now. They're coming for us.'

She turned to look. 'Can they find us?'

Julian shrugged. 'I don't know. It's possible we've left tracks behind us that could be followed . . . shit, what do I know? I doubt it, though.'

'Yeah,' she whispered. 'It's not like he's some Indian master-tracker, right?'

He watched them as they disappeared from view beneath the forest canopy below to begin their ascent up the hillside, towards them. He didn't like the calm, unhurried way they had made their way out of the clearing. If Shepherd's body language

436

said anything, it was: *I know exactly where you two are, and I'm coming for you.*

'Let's just hope not.' He grabbed her heaving shoulder. 'Come on! Let's move.'

Rose nodded wordlessly. They turned and continued scrambling uphill.

An hour later, the trees thinned out before them and they found themselves standing in the open, three-quarters of the way up one of the bare peaks that looked down on the valley in which they'd camped. Above them, dry brown tufts of grass gradually gave way to a sharp and steepening slope of bare rock that rose to culminate in a jagged horizon.

Rose sighed with relief to see a break in the peaks to their right, a quarter of a mile along the side of the slope – a narrow pass.

'There,' she said, pointing to it. 'I guess that'll take us into the next valley.'

Julian nodded as he pulled out his BlackBerry and tried for a signal.

'Anything?' Rose asked hopefully.

He shook his head.

'Let's go,' she rasped between breaths. 'Maybe we'll pick up a signal on the other side.'

The pass was little more than a modest gulch, hacked like the very first cut of an axe into a tree trunk. It was just about wide enough that a 4x4 might have made it through, if it weren't for the many fractured boulders and slides of rubble that clattered noisily and shifted unnervingly beneath their feet.

The sun was high in the sky as they emerged and looked down on a much broader valley.

'Anything now?' asked Rose.

Julian snapped his phone shut and shook his head. 'No.'

She scanned the world below looking for some sign of civilisation – even an empty road would have been worth heading for. Then she spotted it.

'Look!'

Julian followed her finger. 'What is that?'

A wide, shallow, slow-moving river wound its way westward down the valley, and on a major horseshoe bend in the river, they could see a row of squat wooden buildings.

'Looks like some kind of logging camp,' said Rose. 'Abandoned, though, do you think?'

'Yeah.'

'We should still make for that. There might be something there. There might be *someone* there.'

Julian nodded.

CHAPTER 82

2 November, 1856

'My God! Keats, you're alive!' cried Ben. The old guide clung to the shoulder of Broken Wing as they hobbled out of the woods into the open. Ben rushed towards them, the gut-wrenching, plummeting sensation of fear he'd been experiencing a moment earlier replaced by an energetic surge of relief.

'Oh bloody Christ!' he yelled with a grin smeared across his face, as his feet carried him across the snow towards them. 'I thought only the three of us had managed to esc—'

Then his eyes took in the pertinent detail. A broad strip of Keats's long-faded, polka-dot shirt was crudely wrapped around his waist, soaked with his blood and almost as dark as ink. Keats looked up at Ben; his face, normally the rich golden tan of worn saddle leather, was now ashen.

Broken Wing helped him across to the fire, then gently laid him down. Keats groaned with the pain, holding his hands protectively against the front of his body. Several new dark blotches of crimson bloomed across the material, as beneath the wrap a large wound flexed and opened.

Ben looked up at the Shoshone, his face a question mark. Broken Wing understood and uttered a rapid burst of Ute, gesturing back at the dark apron of trees from which they'd emerged, his hands telling a story Ben couldn't quite decipher.

Something back in there did this to Keats.

Ben needed to know more. 'Keats, what happened?'

The old man breathed deeply, gathering his wits and what was left of his failing strength. 'I seen it, Lambert. *I seen the fuckin' thing,*' he gasped desperately. His eyes, normally narrow flinty slits, were wide and dilated with fear. They flickered from Ben to the trees then back again.

'Seen what?'

Keats puffed clouds and clenched his eyes shut, grimacing at the pain from his torso. Ben noticed there was even more blood coming down his left leg, soaking through the deerskin. A torn gash in the worn hide above his knee revealed a protruding tatter of bloodied skin.

Ben knelt down beside him, knowing instinctively there was not a lot his medical knowledge could do for the old man.

'Let me have a look at this for you. The bandage needs re-wrapping.'

Keats shook his head vigorously. 'Leave it be!' He held a hand out. 'Only thing holdin' me in one piece is this here bandage.' He looked down at it and grimaced. 'You loosen that an' everythin' inside'll come tumblin' out.'

Ben suspected it was the same kind of wound he'd seen on the Paiute boy who had carried Emily into the camp. The same deep, horizontal gash that would have lacerated the organs, opened up the stomach lining and intestines, spilling digestive acids and faecal matter inside him. Even if he could completely staunch the flow of blood now, Keats was going to die painfully from the internal damage.

Looking at him now, however, it was obvious most of the dying was done.

'What happened to you?'

Keats licked his lips, dry and chapped. 'We heard them Mormons durin' the early mornin',' he wheezed. 'The ones followin' after us. There was screamin' an' shootin' behind . . . every now an' then. Kept happenin' through the dark hours. And

440

we got to seein' less an' less of their torches. Until eventually there was none.'

Keats opened his eyes again, scanning the tree line. He panted like a winded beast, struggling with the effort of talking. 'Me, Broken Wing and Weyland . . . kept movin' uphill. Thought maybe it was others of our group . . . who had escaped, was fightin' back or somethin'.'

Broken Wing squatted down and muttered something in his language, nodding towards Emily. Keats replied in the same language, falteringly, slowly.

'What? What did he say?'

Keats shook his head, ignoring the question. 'We was near the pass . . . when it happened . . . when it came right out the darkness at us.'

He closed his eyes again, panting rhythmically, replaying something in his head. Ben noticed he was shaking; his leathery, tobacco-stained lips trembled. The sight of that rattled Ben. He considered Keats unflappable, his gruff, unpolished demeanour impervious to anything. And yet here he was looking frail and frightened and, all of a sudden, a very old man.

He leaned closer to him. 'Come on, what? Tell me, what was it?'

Keats's eyes flickered open, focused on something a thousand miles away, then his gaze drifted across to Ben's face, the here and now. 'I saw it with my own eyes, Lambert. Ain't no *man* . . . ain't that son-of-a-whore Preston did those killin's — like you was sayin'.' He licked his dry lips again. 'Saw somethin' I can't explain.'

Broken Wing spoke a word Ben had heard the Paiute men utter sombrely amongst themselves over the last few days.

Keats nodded weakly. 'That's right . . . Goddamn right. It ain't nothin' natural — nothin' that by rights should be walkin' this world.'

Ben heard Mrs Zimmerman gasp. '*The angel*,' she whispered, 'come down to punish us.'

'White-face ssspirit,' said Broken Wing.

'That's what I saw, Lambert,' gasped Keats. 'Goddamned fuckin' demon – no angel. Came out of the trees and took Weyland's head clean off.'

'What did it look like?'

'Bones, an' a skull . . . Goddamned graveyard come to life,' he snorted with a dry scaffold smile.

Bones.

'Fuckin' thing moved so *fast*. I got me a little powder, but no shot left . . . might've put a ball in it if I had. If I got me another few—'

Ben placed a hand on his shoulder. 'Keats, listen to me. I think it might be Preston. It has to be.' He looked around at the others. 'Preston in some sort of . . . of a disguise.'

Keats grabbed his side and cackled. 'Ain't . . . that . . . fuckin' zealot fool,' he grunted. 'Maybe them Paiutes was right . . . after all.'

'What do you mean?'

Keats smiled. 'Mebbe . . . we took a little madness into the woods with us.' Keats grunted painfully, looking down at his seeping bandage. 'Gonna have me a one helluva fuckin' scar to show off.'

Broken Wing spoke, and gestured with some urgency towards Emily.

'What? What's that you're saying?' he said, looking up at the Indian.

He gestured to the trees. 'It comess. Iss come for Am-ee-lee.'

'What?' Ben looked to Mrs Zimmerman. 'Why? Why would Preston want her?'

She shook her head, confused. 'Emily is his daughter . . . most of the children were his.'

Broken Wing shook his head. 'Not Presss-ton.'

'Then it's the angel!' whimpered Mrs Zimmerman. 'The angel wants us all . . . all of th-those that followed Preston!'

'It's nothing of the sort!' snapped Ben. 'It's a man, that's all! And if it *isn't* Preston, then it's someone else amongst your group, someone who's gone mad!'

442

'It come,' uttered Broken Wing, 'it come this way.'

'You've been followed?'

Broken Wing pointed to the fire, the column of smoke. 'It seee sssmoke.'

'Oh God have mercy on us,' cried Mrs Zimmerman, burying her face in her hands and sobbing.

Ben turned back to Keats, perhaps the only other person here he felt he could engage with rationally. 'Keats, what the hell do we do?'

There was no reply. The old man was lying perfectly still.

'Keats?'

Broken Wing knelt down and held a hand above the guide's nose and mouth, feeling tentatively for the warmth of his breath. Ben could see by the pallor of his skin that it was too late.

The Shoshone's expressionless eyes met Ben's.

'Kee-eet . . . isss . . .' He splayed the fingers of one hand. Instinctively, Ben comprehended the unfamiliar gesture.

Dead.

Broken Wing anxiously looked over his shoulder, back into the woods. Speaking rapidly in Ute he pointed at the fire, the rising smoke, and then gestured towards the trees. And Ben realised what he was pointing out.

The smoke will attract . . . him . . . it, to this place.

'We go . . . now!' said Broken Wing, pointing towards the riverbank as he stepped around the fire towards Mrs Zimmerman, reaching out to grab an arm to lift her off the ground.

He's right; we must stick to the riverbank. Stay in the open.

The apron of ground between where the trees petered out and the river flowed afforded them a chance to react if it attempted to rush them.

'Come on,' Ben said to Mrs Zimmerman, 'we have to go now. He's telling us this thing's nearby and coming for us . . . for Emily. We have to move. Now.'

He bent down to pick up Emily, but she seemed no longer so listless and was able to pull herself up, as if inch by inch she was returning to this world.

'Foll-ow ri-verrr,' said Broken Wing, pulling Mrs Zimmerman to her feet.

All of a sudden, the stillness of the woods was shattered by something moving deep within, beyond sight – something moving too quickly to concern itself with stealth.

'Oh shit!' he whispered.

Emily looked towards the trees, no more than fifty yards away from where they stood on the riverbank. Her pale blue eyes came alive. She seemed to be almost back in this world with them. A small hand reached out for Ben's poncho, and tugged on it.

'Mr Lambert,' she said in a quiet voice, 'there really are angels.'

Broken Wing snapped out something in Ute and pulled a knife from his hide belt. He pointed along the bank, and Ben understood it was the *only* way for them to run.

Ben bent down and pulled Keats's hunting knife out of its sheath. The heavy blade felt reassuring in his grasp. He placed a hand on Keats's still-warm face. He would have liked to have a moment to assure the old man that he had brought his journal with him, that he'd make it out of the woods, eventually back to London, and Keats's name would end up in print, immortalised. That would have given the guide something to smile about.

'Goodbye, Keats,' whispered Ben.

Broken Wing, meanwhile, pulling Mrs Zimmerman along with him, began to make his way close to the water's edge, keeping his eyes on the tree line running parallel to the river.

'Come on, Emily,' Ben said, grabbing her hand. 'We have to go.'

CHAPTER 83

cave iram Dei

M	T	W	T	F	S	S
				1	2	3
4	5	6	7	8	9	10
11	12	13	14	15	16	17
18	19	20	21	22	23	24
25	26	27	28	29	30	

Sunday
Sierra Nevada Mountains, California

Julian stared at the row of bunkhouses. They were utilitarian but robust; almost a century of abandonment, but they looked to be firmly intact and ready to face another. Nature had made good use of the last hundred years in reclaiming the land the drab wooden huts sat on. Small Christmas-tree-sized saplings sprang out of the ground in and around the buildings, whilst patches of briar, hip-high, tangled in and out of the support struts beneath each bunkhouse, pushing fronds of green up through loose and warped floorboards.

He'd naively hoped there might have been *someone* here, a lone caretaker in a Portakabin, some other hardy all-year-round trekkers, a party of Japanese tourists even.

And still no fucking cell phone signal.

'At least it's shelter,' said Rose, shivering. She looked at him. 'Do you think they're still on our tail?'

'God knows. I'd say they're probably still picking their way through the trees in the other valley,' he replied, giving Rose's shoulder a reassuring squeeze. 'I'm pretty sure we lost 'em,' he added, hoping he sounded more confident than he felt.

The sun was fast approaching the jagged line of peaks on the far side of the valley, casting long, cool shadows that were sliding across the gentle valley floor towards the river and them. It was going to be cold tonight.

'Come on, Rose, let's get inside. See if we can't find a cosy nook somewhere.'

They stepped up onto a wooden porch and pushed aside a thick wooden door that creaked dryly. Skylights in the sloping roof – one broken, the other fogged with a green filter of algae and moss – provided enough light for them to find their way around the dim interior.

The bunkhouse was one long communal space. A row of coarse wooden bunkbed frames lined each lengthways wall. An iron wood-burning stove sat against the far wall. Above them several thick gable beams ran across from one side to the other, protruding metal pegs from which dangled coils of heavy rope, a loop of twine tied from one beam to another – most probably, once upon a time, a clothes line – and several rusting tools including a band saw, a rotary saw.

'Your basic two-star accommodation,' he muttered and managed a humourless laugh that trailed off quickly.

Rose wandered over to a bunk in the corner and hunkered down on the floor beside it, pulling her knees up to her chin and wrapping her arms around them.

'I'm shit scared, Jules.'

He reached up to one of the cross-beams and lifted a large, rusty canting hook off a peg. He held it by its wooden handle and examined the long, curved hook. He hefted it in his hand. It looked vicious but unwieldy. It felt good to hold.

He wandered across the floor towards her, examining the hook. 'Yeah, got to admit I'm a little scared too.'

'How scared? Am-I-going-to-die scared? Or just sort of a bit anxious?'

He laughed skittishly. 'Remember the time we followed that candidate to the BNP rally?'

She nodded.

'Or the time we got death threats from that Jihadi cleric?'

She nodded again.

446

'Well, more scared than that,' he replied, sliding down the wall to hunch up next to her.

They sat in silence a while, watching the coppery hue of the evening sun stream in through the fogged skylight windows, the shadows slowly climbing up the opposite wall.

'Jules, when you came into my tent this morning, you definitely had something to say to me, didn't you? But I was too busy yapping on about the photo. What were you going to say?'

He shook his head and laughed. 'That I was beginning to have a bad feeling about things.'

Rose smiled. 'Little earlier next time, hmm?'

'Dr Griffith warned me about this. That insanity like Preston's can carry down the line.'

Rose nodded. 'I must have got it wrong, then,' she sighed. 'The Rag Man story, the survivor who emerged from the woods – I thought that was Lambert.'

'Well, maybe it was.' Julian leaned his head back against the rough wooden wall. 'Perhaps Preston left behind some descendants in Iowa, before he set off with his followers, and Shepherd's family link is to one of them.'

'Yeah, I suppose.'

'Either way, Shepherd's unstable, right? Did you notice right before we ran how weird he was?'

'No I didn't really . . . it's a bit of a blur.'

'He seemed out of it, vacant, like he was slightly stoned.'

'I don't remember that.'

'I wouldn't be entirely surprised if he's got a few skeletons of his own to hide somewhere.'

'What . . . some bodies buried in his basement?'

Julian hugged his knees for warmth. 'Who knows? Maybe he's got himself a typical serial-killer basement complete with a Gothic well, where he's been busy stitching together a woman-suit.'

Rose snorted.

447

'He seemed prepared to kill us just to bury a story about his . . . what? . . . his great-great-grandfather?'

'It would have damaged his campaign. I can believe someone like that would do what he could to stop it.'

'Maybe. But would you *kill* someone for that?'

Rose shrugged. 'I wouldn't.'

'Would any normal politician murder someone just to bury a negative story?'

Shepherd looked up at the deep blue sky, robbed of the sun and left only with a stain of its memory on the horizon. It was going to be a freezing cold night; the thinly combed clouds stretched in front of a growing early audience of stars made that solemn promise.

Several paces ahead, a small piece of glowing technology was leading Carl forward. He held something no bigger than a slim cell phone, with a pale backlit screen displaying a direction and a distance. He'd assured Shepherd that although the tracker was a few years out of date – CIA surplus – it was more than adequate for the job out here.

Tracker's good for five to ten miles depending on line-of-sight obstructions. That had been Carl's crisp and businesslike explanation of the gadget's efficacy as they set out from the clearing after them.

'Not so good for urban detection,' he'd added. 'Lot of walls and electrical interference, but more than good enough for the job out here. This'll lead us right to them, Mr Shepherd.'

You disapprove?

Shepherd winced at the sudden intrusion of the voice in his head. It seemed a little louder than last time, more insistent, shrill even, certainly so much louder than any others he'd played host to.

We don't need to kill any more people, he replied. *It's an unnecessary risk. We didn't need to kill that old woman.*

There was no response. He managed an edgy smile in the failing light. If Duncan knew . . . if any of his campaign sponsors knew, if those millions of voters out there knew that his mind played out such terrible dialogues, that suggestions – malicious ones, spiteful ones, murderous ones . . . genocidal ones – were quietly whispered to him every day and then cautiously argued down, well . . . he could imagine spilling it all to Dr Phil or Oprah on live TV.

What a release that would be, to share his burdens with someone.

They will talk.

I can persuade them not to.

Are you a good man?

Yes . . . yes, I think I am.

You are also a weak man.

The hectoring, disapproving tone in its voice sent a sharp pain through his head.

I'm not weak.

The voice was quiet again.

Several yards ahead of Shepherd, Carl suddenly cursed under his breath and stopped.

'The damned signal keeps dropping. Hang on a second . . . we need to let it pick up again.'

While he waited for his tracker to sweep for the signal, he looked out at the wide, graceful valley below them, silently scanning it with sniper's eyes for any signs of life. Evening was settling across it fast, and amidst the muted tones of dusk he was reassured to see no pin-pricks of light anywhere; just more endless wilderness and no one else around. No one for miles . . . and miles.

His eyes, however, picked out the artificially straight lines of a man-made construction down by the river.

'Some buildings down there, Mr Shepherd,' he called out, pointing towards a horseshoe bend in the river.

Shepherd shook away his thoughts and looked at where Carl was pointing. He could see a dark huddle of huts nestled close to the river's edge in an area swept clean of trees. He was familiar

449

with the history of this area; he knew what it was. The trees down there had gone a long time ago.

'It's a logging camp, closed down like all the others round here, back when they started moving logs on rails instead of along the river.'

Carl nodded, then looked back down at the tracker display. 'Fucking mountains here are playing havoc with the line-of-sight signal.'

'I should imagine they'll be hiding in that camp,' said Shepherd. 'It's where I would head if I was running.'

Carl looked up from the display and nodded. 'Yeah, I guess that's where I'd head too. Ahhh . . . there it is,' he said, 'signal's picked up.' He studied it silently for a moment and then nodded. 'Yes, you're right. They're in there somewhere, Mr Shepherd.'

'Good, then let's not waste any time. If we can run them to ground there, that'll do just fine.'

'This is a straightforward locate and terminate, right?'

Shepherd turned to him. 'I'd like to talk with them first. But if an instant kill is required, then so be it.'

Carl nodded. 'Understood.'

CHAPTER 84

2 November, 1856

Broken Wing stopped and pointed ahead. Ben understood what he was drawing their attention to.

'What?' Mrs Zimmerman asked breathlessly.

The river they were running alongside curled to the left and, where it did, the trees they were so desperate to keep a distance from ran all the way down to the river's edge.

'If we want to go any further, we'll have to go through those trees.'

Mrs Zimmerman stared unhappily at them.

There was no indication whether it would be a short interlude through a thin spur of wood, or whether, from this point on, the safe margin of ground between them and the woods was gone.

Broken Wing still carried his ancient flintlock musket, a horn of powder and some shot. If there was just the one . . . *thing* pursuing them, he trusted the Indian's marksmanship to take a single, quickly aimed shot across open ground, should it emerge suddenly and charge towards them. In amongst the trees, however, should they be ambushed, he suspected the gun would never get to be fired.

Ben cast a glance at the tree line to the left of them, running parallel with the riverbank, and knew it was in there somewhere, looking out at them and urging them to go forward, into the trees ahead. To their right the river flowed swiftly, swollen with freezing water that would numb them the moment they stepped into it. It would swallow them up and certainly kill them all.

Broken Wing spotted his gaze and shook his head. 'Not cross here.' He gestured west. 'Down river . . . cross. Five day north, to Shoshone.'

'What does he mean?' asked Mrs Zimmerman.

Ben understood. 'He can take us to the Shoshone Indians. But we'd need to cross this river and head north.'

Broken Wing nodded.

'But' – he turned to Mrs Zimmerman – 'we need to carry on through those trees.'

She shook her head vigorously. 'I can't . . . I don't want to go in th—'

'Neither do I. But we can't stay here.'

Broken Wing stabbed his finger impatiently forwards.

'Yes, we're wasting time,' said Ben. He smiled reassuringly at Mrs Zimmerman and Emily. 'It'll only be a thin strip of woodland, and then we'll be out in the open again. We'll be fine.'

Emily stirred. 'Don't worry, Mrs Zimmerman,' she said with a small voice, 'Benjamin will keep us safe.' She smiled up at Ben and tightened her grasp on his hand. 'We should go,' she added.

Mrs Zimmerman nodded at her. 'All right.'

They approached the trees cautiously, huddled closely together. Broken Wing was ahead, his musket held ready, loaded with shot, and powder ready in the flashpan.

His *tamahakan* was tucked into a leather belt. Ben had seen how quickly the Indian could pull it out and use it, during the struggle back at the camp. He wondered, though, if he'd be quick enough this time.

Mrs Zimmerman and Emily followed the Indian, the woman's arms wrapped protectively around the young girl, both of them staring at the trees with eyes as round as saucers. Ben walked a few paces behind them, Keats's large knife in one hand and a thick and heavy stick, for what it was worth, held in the other. Together they stepped beneath the darkening canopy of branches, from a bed of crunching snow onto a spongy carpet of dry cones and needles.

Through the gaps in the branches he watched them move with slow deliberation, only a few dozen yards away . . . so close to him now.

His hot breath blasted back off the bone mask onto his face, warming his cheeks.

Emily.

He missed her, missed her so much. Before everything had changed there had been him and her – just the two of them. Momma only had time for Preston, never for them. Momma didn't care about them, not as much as she cared for God. Momma didn't want to know about the games Hearst and Vander played with the children.

It's always been just you and me, Emily.

But there was Ben. He had shown some kindness. Sam had even let himself believe that come the spring, the three of them might leave the wilderness together: an odd family, like three siblings – big brother, little brother and little sister. Emily liked Ben. She would have adored the idea of doing that, leaving Preston's temple and exploring the world alongside Benjamin Lambert.

You have *me* now.

Yes . . . I do.

Sam owed so much to the angel. He knew he wouldn't have survived alone. He would have gone mad; he would have been stupid the day Mr Hearst came to kill them. He would have returned to the camp and tried to attack Preston. And he would have failed. Mr Hollander always stood guard, ready to protect him. He would have failed and been killed.

You need me.

Yes.

Do you trust me?

Yes.

Sam watched them moving steadily and quietly through the wood, Emily dropping back to clutch Benjamin's hand, the Indian ahead of them, Mrs Zimmerman beside.

Do you see how she clings to him?

He did. He saw her holding tightly and peering out at the darkness in fear . . .

Of me?

You are different now.

I'm Sam.

You were 'Sam'. You are much more now.

The thick canopy above them had kept all but the slightest dusting of snow from reaching the ground beneath. Through occasional gaps, lances of light speared down ahead of them, dappling the brown forest floor. They stepped forward in silence, the muffled crackle of dry twigs beneath their feet and the soft, muted gurgle of the river to their right the only sounds the wood allowed. Looking hopefully ahead for any sign that the wood was thinning out once more, Ben could see only an endless forest of tall lodgepole pine trunks with a high canopy of branches, punctuated by clusters of squat spruce trees hugging the ground where the sun came through.

'I'm scared,' Mrs Zimmerman whispered.

Broken Wing looked back at them and frowned at her.

'Just keep going,' Ben replied softly, 'quiet as you can.'

They walked in silence for another five minutes before the Indian suddenly stopped and cocked his head, listening to something. Then he turned to face them, with the slightest smile on his stern face.

Ben shrugged.

Broken Wing pointed to their right, and cupped an ear.

Listen.

Ben did so, noticing nothing at first.

Mrs Zimmerman frowned. 'I hear something.'

Then he did too — the faint sound of rumbling. He felt it more

454

through his feet than he heard it with his ears. 'That's the river, isn't it?' he whispered.

She nodded. 'Yes . . . yes, I think it is.'

Broken Wing pointed ahead.

'It's coming from that way,' said Ben.

'Crosss riv-uhh ahead.' Broken Wing pointed insistently. The rumble of water could only mean the river had narrowed, perhaps offering them the opportunity to cross. The sound was heartening.

Ben placed a hand on Mrs Zimmerman's shoulder. 'Come on, then . . . it can't be that much further through the trees.' She nodded and set off after the Indian, eager that the Shoshone not leave them too far behind.

Ben turned to Emily. 'Come on, we'll be out of—'

The girl was rooted to the spot, her eyes wide, her jaw slackened and hanging open.

'Emily?'

Her eyes remained fixed on something above them.

'He's here,' she whispered.

Ben turned round and looked up at the branches. For no more than half a second, he saw the outline of something crouching on a branch. Pale like a ghost, but with spines or spikes emerging from its silhouette, and a long skeletal face. It uncurled from the branch, dropping soundlessly down to the floor of the wood and out of sight beyond a tangled veil of undergrowth.

'Oh God!' he shouted. 'It's here!'

Broken Wing stopped and whipped round. Ben pointed towards where he'd seen it drop. 'THERE!'

The Indian swiftly levelled his musket and dropped to one knee with practised and elegant swiftness. Mrs Zimmerman stumbled towards the Indian, sobbing with fear as she dropped to her knees at his feet and started muttering in prayer.

Ben reached out a hand for Emily. 'Come on,' he whispered quietly. Her small hand grasped his obediently, and they moved slowly towards the others.

'Anyone see it?' Ben called out, his eyes darting left and right. 'Where is it?'

His voice echoed around the wood, then diminished. In the stillness there was only the continuous muted rumble of the river and the sound of the four of them breathing.

'*I'm right here*,' a whispered voice hissed from somewhere nearby. The sibilant hiss echoed in the silence, bouncing from tree trunk to tree trunk. Broken Wing's aim darted swiftly from a bramble, to a cluster of ferns, to another. He muttered something under his breath – a curse.

'*This is fun,*' the voice hissed again.

Ben and Emily quickly joined the other two, and he let her hand go. Mrs Zimmerman reached out a comforting arm to the little girl and held her tight.

Ben stood beside Broken Wing, scanning the forest around them, the hunting knife and his stick held ready.

'What do you want?' Ben called out, hating the warbling sound of fear in his voice.

'*Emily.*' The whisper seemed to come at them from all sides, quiet yet deafening in the thick silence of the wood.

There was a long pause. He would have been happier with complete silence, but instead he could just about detect the quiet muttering of a voice coming from somewhere. A small, plaintive voice arguing under its breath, pleading with some kind of silent partner. It sounded like the insane one-sided conversations he'd heard echoing from the cells of Banner House Asylum; pathetic, quiet voices that asked nonsensical questions and moments later riposted the silent replies. He knew this was no angel, no demon – it was the pitiful sound of someone who had lost their mind.

He swallowed nervously. 'Who are you?'

There was no answer. The question peeled around the wood, and as the echo died away, he could hear the whispered debate had ceased. Ben had been sure he knew who this was last night, but now he was not so sure. There was a timidity to that small voice that just didn't square with the man.

456

'You're not Preston,' said Ben. 'I know that much.'

'No,' came a hissed reply. 'The dirty man is dead now.' The voice of the thing was changing, from a chilling hiss to something that sounded more human. 'He had it coming!' the voice continued to drift, gradually becoming the emotionally strangled cry of a person struggling to hold back tears of rage. 'He was a bad man, bad all the way through. Even the angel couldn't stand to be with him any longer!'

Ben looked from side to side, trying to work out where the voice was coming from, but the bewitching acoustics of the wood played tricks with it.

'He let Eric Vander play his games with all the children.' The voice laughed without joy, bitter and hollow. 'Well, I cut it off, didn't I? I cut his thing off and shoved it into his mouth before he died.'

There was something in the voice that Ben recognised, some signature beneath the visceral snarl of hate that he remembered from what felt like a lifetime ago.

It was a voice he had once taken pleasure in listening to; a young man he enjoyed being in the company of. 'Sam? Is that you?'

Silence.

'Sam? Is it you out there?'

There was no reply. A long moment passed in silence. Ben strained to listen to the noises of the wood and then he heard it: so quiet, the whispered one-sided conversation of madness once more, coming from somewhere ahead of them, somewhere behind a dense cluster of twisted and dead vines and brambles, long starved of sunlight and sustenance.

'Sam,' he called out. 'Sam, we're going to take her away from this place, take her away from Preston's madness. The man was insane. Whatever it was he was planning to do, it was the product of a very sick mind.'

There was something Sam had once asked of him, an awkward request that, back then, he'd had to turn down.

'Listen, I'll take you both out of these woods with me. You

and me and Emily. You and I, we'll both look after her . . . and we'll leave all this behind us, in the woods where it belongs.'

The sibilant, whispered conversation was at once quietened.

'Sam, just come out where we can see you. Put down whatever weapon you've made and join us. It's all over now. Preston can't get to Emily. She's safe.'

The silence continued. A minute, two . . . long enough that Ben was beginning to suspect the boy had left them and returned into the darkness of the wood, when a familiar voice called out.

'Emily, please come back with us. Back to the camp.' It was Sam, as Ben remembered him from weeks ago – a voice utterly without malice, broken with emotion, pleading.

'Please . . . Emily . . . please.'

Emily began to cry at the sound of his voice.

'Sam? You said *us*. Who else is there with you?' asked Ben.

The answer came after a few seconds. 'She belongs with us. There is God's work still to do back there,' the voice replied. 'You belong with us.'

Emily screamed at those words. 'Don't want to go back!' She grasped Ben's hand. 'Please don't make me go back!'

'Let go of him!' the voice hissed angrily.

'No!' Ben shouted back. 'She's coming with us.'

There was a rustle of movement to their right, followed by the deafening boom from Broken Wing's musket and the startled flutter of departing birds from the branches above them. Ben spun round to look towards where the end of the Indian's musket still pointed. As the thick haze of powder smoke around both men cleared, Ben anxiously peered into the darkness ahead, expecting to see a slumped form.

But there was nothing to be seen.

'Sam?' he called out. 'Sam?'

'Sam is gone,' the voice hissed back.

In an instant Ben realised they were in trouble. The musket had been discharged and nothing hit.

He turned to Broken Wing. 'Take them and go!'

The Shoshone hesitated.

458

'RUN!' Ben barked to the others. 'Run for the river!'

Broken Wing hurled the empty musket to the ground and pulled his *tamahakan* out, ready to bloody its small, jagged blade. He pulled Mrs Zimmerman roughly to her feet and pushed the woman ahead of him. Turning to Ben and Emily, he beckoned to them urgently.

'Lam-bert . . . come!'

'Emily,' said Ben, 'go with him!'

She shook her head. 'No, I want to stay with you,' she cried, anxiously reaching for his hand.

'Go!' he shouted angrily, shaking her off. 'Now!'

She was about to turn and run when the low bough of a squat spruce lurched to one side, sending a shower of snow to the ground.

It stepped out into the open.

Emily gasped at the sight.

A tall, thin figure, he stood before them, coiled ready to leap forward and disembowel them at any moment. Strapped to one hand were several long serrated blades, whittled and sharpened from bone. On his body, the ribs of a host of unidentifiable creatures had been stitched to a hide shirt with careless and unskilled haste. The head was half the skull of some larger creature, perhaps an ox or a stag. It appeared that Broken Wing's shot had found the target, shattering one side of the skull. Behind the jagged half-mask of fractured bone, he could see the blood-flecked face of Samuel Dreyton staring out.

'Sam!' Emily shrieked – recognition, relief and fear mixed into her shrill cry.

He took one small, uncertain step forward. 'Emily.' His young voice cracked with emotion; not the evil hiss of some demon, but the voice of a troubled young man. The side of his face that Ben could see was pulled into the tight grimace of someone fighting to hold back a flow of emotion.

Emily suddenly shook uncontrollably. 'Oh no! I . . . I remember!'

'I killed him, Em,' he admitted, his voice choked with a sob.

'I killed Saul. I had to . . . he would have killed you . . . he would have killed me. I . . . I had to, Em.'

'You . . . cut,' she whispered, her eyes wide, replaying that day once more, 'y-you . . . cut . . . and cut . . . and cut . . . and cut . . .'

A tear rolled down Sam's cheek. 'H-he deserved it. Saul and Eric—'

'You d-did those . . . th-things . . . those . . . things to Mr Vander?' she gasped.

He nodded. Ben thought he saw the slightest hint of revulsion and regret in his face. 'Yes, I did,' he uttered. 'And Preston too.'

'Oh, Sam,' Emily whispered quietly.

'I did it for you, Em. For me, too.' He took a step forward and she whimpered in fear, recoiling from him.

'It's me,' he pleaded tearfully, stretching out his hand to her.

Her eyes were drawn to the serrated blades strapped to his hand, clogged with dry blood and shreds of tissue.

She screamed.

It was a brittle, high-pitched scream that tore to pieces the cushioned silence of the wood. Emily wrapped her arms around Ben, terrified of her brother. Sam's face changed in that instant — the last sign of the boy replaced with the listless, bland face of a killer.

'Emily!' Ben looked down at her. 'Run!'

She let go of his hand and took a dozen uncertain steps towards Broken Wing and Mrs Zimmerman.

'RUN!'

She turned and fled towards them.

Ben faced Sam. 'Sam?'

The face he could see behind the fractured bone was still and lifeless.

'Not Sam, not any more,' it whispered and advanced several steps towards Ben.

From behind him, Ben heard Broken Wing call out. 'Lammbit! Come!'

Ben waved. 'Go! Dammit! GO!'

460

The creature in front of him eyed the long-bladed knife Ben held in his hand, and smiled.

'Sam,' he said quietly, 'let her go. Broken Wing will take her to the Shoshone; they'll care for her there. She'll be safe.'

It shook its head. 'Not Sam. I am the angel,' it added, one hand gently patting a canvas sack that hung from a belt. Ben heard the soft clink of bones as it swung gently.

'In that bag, Sam? Is that something Preston had? Is it what was in his chest?'

The creature managed a smile. 'I chose to leave him. I chose Sam.'

Ben could hear the crack of a branch echoing from the trees behind him. The others were getting away. The longer he could delay Sam here, the more chance they'd have.

'You *are* Sam,' he replied. 'Take off the skull . . . take off the bones.' He pointed to the canvas sack. 'Undo that . . . let it go, Sam. These things are affecting your mind, making you something you're not.'

It stood there in silence. The one eye Ben could see was no longer glancing distractedly over his shoulder at the others. They were out of view now.

'I know you, Sam. Before the bad things happened, you and I . . . we were friends. And we can still be, if you take all these bones off and leave them behind you.'

The creature cocked its head curiously. 'Sam is telling me he once liked you,' the voice hissed. 'Wanted to be like you.'

Ben glanced at the long, viciously jagged blades attached to the hand as the fingers flexed and the sharp serrated bones clinked together.

That's going to cut me to bloody pieces.

'Sam, listen to me,' he uttered, his mouth dry. 'Something very wrong has found its way inside you — inside your head. Something bad. But we can make it go away.'

'Sam is not listening any more,' it hissed. 'He needs to rest.'

Ben looked at the eyes; one he could see clearly, the other twinkled through the skull's dark orbital socket.

'I can cut you up like I cut all the others.' It took another step towards him.

'Stay where you are!'

Its twinkling eye appraised him silently for a moment. 'You seem like a good man.'

Ben left that unanswered, Keats's blade held out in front of him, watching the creature ease forward another step. Only three yards separated them now.

'Stay where you are.'

'You seem like a good man, with love in your heart.'

'And so are you, Sam.'

'I told you, Sam is not here now.'

'Let me talk to him again.'

'No.'

'Sam? Sam, talk to me.'

'He is not here now.' The creature took another step closer.

Ben backed up. 'Sam! For God's sake, wake up!'

The creature stopped, its head cocked slightly, listening for a moment.

'Sam? Is that Sam talking to you?'

The angel ignored him, still listening.

'Sam, are you there?'

The angel shook its head. 'No, I am still here, but . . . Sam asked me to tell you something.'

'What?'

It was fast. It crossed the ground between them with liquid grace – a blur of movement that left Ben's sluggish reaction in its wake. The lunge was aimed high, across his chest and throat. Before he had a chance to understand what had happened, Ben was on his knees, looking down and watching ribbons of dark red sputter out onto the snow in front of him.

Keats's knife fell to the ground, and a moment later he dropped down onto his hands, his mind now caught up with events.

My God . . . I'm dying.

The angel squatted down so that the shattered jaw of the long

462

skull was inches from his face. It pushed the skull-mask off and threw it on the ground.

Ben stared into Sam's young face, smudged with dirt and flecks of drying blood from the small shards of bone that had exploded into his face a few minutes ago. It was Sam's face that, not much more than a week ago, had been full of the silly dreams that young people have. Now it was listless, expressionless, even more terrifying than the skull on the ground beside him.

Ben felt light-headed. The blood, gushing out from his throat, was bringing his life to a rapid conclusion.

'Sam asked me to say he liked you. You were his favourite.'

Ben fell to the side and instantly felt the press of the cold ground against the side of his face. The angel stepped over him and then was gone, sprinting lightly in pursuit of the others. Then it was quiet, save for the rumble of the river, and a shifting breeze in the canopy of boughs high above. He watched the swaying movement of bare twigs and branches and the featureless white winter sky beyond, calmly savouring his last few moments.

Then finally, in a distracted way, he chastised himself that he'd not been able to bring his journal full of adventures, as promised, back home to Mother.

CHAPTER 85

cave iram Dei

M	T	W	T	F	S	S
				1	2	3
4	5	6	7	8	9	10
11	12	13	14	15	16	17
18	19	20	21	22	23	24
25	26	27	28	29	30	

Sunday
Sierra Nevada Mountains, California

Rose shivered, sitting on the rough wooden floor beside him. 'I'm freezing.' She pulled her anorak further down her legs, huddled up inside it like a mini-tent.

'We've just got to sit tight for tonight.'

'And tomorrow?'

'Tomorrow? If we stick to the river and follow it down, we'll come across somebody sooner or later, I guess.'

Rose's lips twitched with the cold. 'They won't find us here?'

Julian couldn't work out whether it was a question or a statement. 'No . . . no way they'll find us.'

'I just . . . I just . . . I can't believe they shot Grace like that.'

'I know.'

'Jules, I've never been so flipping terrified.'

'I know, I know, but I think it's going to be okay now,' he said, squeezing her shoulder. 'We've lost them. As soon as I get a bloody signal on my phone, we'll call someone – the police, a newspaper – and let them know what happened. Shepherd won't touch us then. It'll be all over for him.'

They endured the creeping cold in silence, listening to the gentle breeze play with the loose things it could find around the camp, and the chattering of each other's teeth.

464

'What the hell have we found out here, Jules?'

'What do you mean?'

'This story . . . I get the feeling there's more to it than we've worked out. I don't understand why Shepherd's doing this. He's risking everything just because of some ancestral skeleton?'

'Maybe he's got some skeleton of his own to hide,' he replied.

'You think?'

Julian shrugged. 'Who knows? I think it's safe to say the guy's unhinged.'

'Just like his great-great-grandfather.'

'If he's happy to see us dead, maybe he's killed with his own hands before? Who knows what goes on in that guy's base-ment . . . if you know what I mean.'

'But what about the Rag Man? Lambert?'

'I don't know, Rose. That may have nothing to do with Shepherd. So that guy survived? So what? Right now we've got a bloody psychopathic preacher who's running for President, chasing after us with his hitman. I'll be honest with you: right now that's my main concern.'

She shivered. 'You want to huddle up? I'm freezing.'

'Okay.' Julian shuffled up against her and placed one arm round her shoulders.

Rose sighed, her tremulous breath blowing out a cloud in front of her. 'To think someone like that could end up being President.'

'A very scary thought.'

'Yeah,' Rose replied thoughtfully. 'Another very good rea-son for us to make sure we get out of these mountains ali—'

Julian grabbed her arm.

'Ouch!'

'Shh!'

'What?' she whispered.

'Thought I heard something.'

'Wind-blowing-stuff-around *something* or . . .'

He squeezed her arm tighter. She got the point and hushed.

465

Then, listening intently for any other noises over the clatter of debris being teased by the occasional gust, they heard it. Faintly at first but quickly growing more distinct: two voices talking quietly and the sound of footsteps approaching.

'Oh shit-shit-shit,' whispered Rose. 'How the hell did they find us?'

Julian shook his head. 'I don't know. I don't know.'

It was impossible unless . . .

Unless there's some kind of tracking device stuck on either of us.

But there was nothing on them other than the clothes they were wearing, and . . .

And my fucking BlackBerry.

Carl studied the small screen. 'Right in this bunkhouse, I'd say,' he muttered quietly. 'Yeah, they're definitely in here.'

He pulled something out of his backpack and, with a click, attached it to the top of his gun. A green glowing light spilled from it.

'It's quite a long building. I'll take point,' Carl said quietly, 'and we'll sweep it from one end to the other. You best stay a few yards behind me, Mr Shepherd.'

'I understand.'

'Are you proficient with that firearm?' he said, pointing towards the rifle Shepherd was holding.

'I've fired a few hunting rifles in my time.'

'Good. Keep it muzzle down, sir. Unless I shout for back-up fire.'

Shepherd sighed. 'We're dealing with a television researcher and a camera girl.'

Carl turned to him. 'With respect, we're dealing with two people who saw their friend shot dead. They'll fight or flee. Either way, we've got to be ready to bag 'em.'

Shepherd conceded the point. 'Yes, you're right, Carl. Shall we?'

Carl took a step towards the hut's entrance, his pistol with mounted nightscope raised before him, in his other hand the tracking device, still counting down the distance, but now only tens of yards away. He took a step up into the hut, his boots clunking on the dry wooden floor. Shepherd watched him whip sharply from side to side, checking the corners, checking every angle.

'Clear,' he reported quietly. 'Room full of bunkbed frames. A long bench each side, wood stove at this end, some lockers. The signal's coming from the far end.'

He stepped further inside, making his way slowly to the middle of the floor between the two facing rows of bunk frames. Shepherd stepped up to the doorway of the hut. It was the only way in and the only way out; as good a place as any to hold position. He knelt down in the doorway, holding the rifle muzzle down as Carl had told him, imagining for a fleeting moment that he was a *real* soldier doing a house-to-house through some Baghdad back street.

He grinned in the dark.

This is fun.

'Checking this end first,' whispered Carl, sweeping his night-scope across the stove and around the nearest bunks. He crouched down low and looked quickly beneath the bottom bunks. 'Signal's here . . . can't see anyone, though.'

Shepherd decided to flush them out. 'Julian! Rose! We know you're in here! Your phone was tagged. I'm sorry, but there's no getting away. You best come out.'

There was no response. A gust of wind played with the skylight shutter in another bunkhouse further along.

'Why don't you come out? I don't really want to add to the body count if I can help it.'

Nothing.

'Grace was a mistake. Carl reacted too quickly. He didn't need to shoot her. I'm truly sorry about that.'

Shepherd held his breath and listened more closely to the faint sounds coming from inside the hut: the rustling, skittering sound of a rat, the soft moan of a gentle wind eddying inside

467

amongst the rafters . . . and yes, he could hear it now, the stuttering breath of someone trying to be ever, ever, so quiet.

'Come on out. We've got some matters to discuss. We'll come to some arrangement.'

Carl took another few steps forward, panning his scope left and right between the bunks that he passed by. 'The signal's ten yards from my position, right ahead.'

Shepherd swallowed back a nervous giggle. This was getting to be too much fun.

'Oh, you know what? Screw this . . . I'm lying. You're both going to die. I might kill you quickly, or I might decide to have some fun first. It really depends how much you piss me off right now.'

Shepherd listened intently again as the last vibration of his voice faded. He could hear that staccato breathing, faster now, fluttering with fear.

Carl took another few steps forward, whip-panning left-right. 'I'm nearly on the signal. Can't see 'em yet, though.'

'One of them, at least, is in here. Can't you hear the breathing? It's the young woman.'

Carl listened. 'No, not yet.' He looked at the display in his hand. 'The signal's just ahead, to the left, between two bunks.'

Carl took another few steps forward, crouching low to sweep beneath the bunks on both sides, then finally he drew up to where the signal was coming from. His display read just over two yards. Through the nightscope, he saw something lying on the floor.

'Shit!' he snapped out angrily.

It was the BlackBerry. He knelt down to pick it up. 'The fuckers ditched it and ran.'

'No!' Shepherd called out from the doorway. 'I can hear . . . I can hear her breathing. The girl's right in here with us.'

Carl held his breath and listened. He could hear nothing. He picked up the phone and then heard something else – the soft puff of exhaled air and the rustle of sudden movement from right beside him. He swung the nightscope to his left, just in time to catch a blurred streak of movement from the top bunk of the frame beside him.

With a sickening penetrative crunch, his eyes saw stars and his ears whistled and rang with a deafening white noise – the sound of his mind going into traumatic shock. His finger convulsed on the trigger and fired off half a dozen rapid rounds.

Julian's right thigh was punched hard. He heard the crack of his femur.

'Rose! Get out of here! RUN!' he screamed, letting go of the wooden handle, and watching Barns slump to the floor with the large, rusty canting hook through the back of his skull, little rapid breaths puffing out of his mouth like a steam train.

He heard the clump and scrape of feet on the wooden floor, someone scrambling. Then he heard Rose whimper and cry out in the dark on the other side of the hut – the sound of a struggle, and her desperate, muffled cries.

Then a heavy thud.

Oh Christ, no.

Julian struggled with the pain in his leg, trying to pull himself out of the bunk.

'Rose?' he called out.

It was quiet.

'Rose!'

Grimacing, he managed to swing his leg over the wooden bunk frame and lower himself to the floor. By the faint, ghostly blue glow of light from a device in Barns's twitching hand, Julian could see the metallic glint of something smooth on the floor; the man's gun.

As he reached down for it, everything went black.

cave iram Dei

M	T	W	T	F	S	S
				1	2	3
4	5	6	7	8	9	10
11	12	13	14	15	16	17
18	19	20	21	22	23	24
25	26	27	28	29	30	

Sunday
Sierra Nevada Mountains, California

The young woman was crying, her eyes fixed on the gun. Cooke, lying beside her in a small pool of blood from a cut on his scalp, was unconscious. He was breathing noisily, blowing bubbles in his own blood.

He looked at Carl. He was quite clearly dead. Pity. The man had been an extremely loyal and useful acolyte.

William Shepherd sat on the bunk in silent contemplation, Carl's pistol held in one hand resting in his lap, the more cumbersome rifle on the bunk beside him.

'Wh-what are y-you going . . . t-to do?' whimpered the woman.

Shepherd put a finger to his lips. 'Shh.'

He needed quiet to think. There were considerations to make, risk assessments. He had to think this through logically before he did something that couldn't be undone.

Why are you waiting?

The voice was very loud now in his head, almost uncomfortably so.

'I have to think,' Shepherd replied aloud.

Kill them.

470

'Is it necessary?' he uttered, and then realised he was speaking.

Is it necessary? I'm certain their silence can be bought.

What if it can't?

It's a risk, I know. He nodded. *But I'm not prepared to have blood on my hands.*

You already do.

No, I don't. Carl exceeded his authority. He killed unnecessarily.

The voice laughed unkindly.

It's true. I never asked him to kill. I asked him to . . .

Tidy things up?

Shepherd winced. Yes, he'd used those words and left Carl to interpret them, knowing full well what that would mean. The man had been fiercely loyal; loyal enough that he would happily have taken a bullet for him. Deep down, Shepherd had been aware that there would be a body or two before this was all satisfactorily resolved.

Your hands are already bloodied.

I have never killed anyone. I'm a man of faith.

You are a man with ambition. That's why I'm here.

I only wish to do God's will.

They need to die, then.

Shepherd's gaze drifted onto them. The voice was right, of course. Money most certainly wouldn't silence them. A threat might . . . but he couldn't take that chance.

No. If you want the things your heart desires, you must kill.

His hand tightened around the pistol, but he resisted the urge to raise it, aim it and pull the trigger.

I wonder . . . are you a good man?

I am.

I wonder.

I've just . . . I've never had to shoot someone before.

Certainly not like this, in cold blood, so close that he could hear her heart pounding. It took an iron will to kill so deliberately, so intimately. It would be easier if she were running, or struggling, but like this?

That is why you need me.

Shepherd's hand tightened on the gun.

I am what you need.

What do you mean?

Strength, William Lambert. Strength.

Lambert. That wasn't a name he'd used in a long time, not since he'd started preaching as a young man. He always preferred his mother's maiden name — *Shepherd* was so much more appropriate for his calling. What's more, the family name was one his father and grandfather preferred maintain a low profile; well away from the tittle-tattle of newspaper columns and latterly, glossy kiosk magazines.

I have all the strength I need.

Yes? Then finish the job.

'This isn't . . . this isn't what the Lord wants of me,' he uttered. 'Not if He wants me to make His word known. I can't do that with blood on me.'

Rose stifled a whimper as he said that.

You can.

Cooke stirred drowsily on the floor.

Hurry now. The man is waking up.

This can't be what God wants of me.

Yes it is. He wants them dead. He wants you to lead the world to Him. And I'm here to help you.

'No, I'm not sure . . .'

Yes! God sent me to you. Now do it!

If He wants them dead, then let Him do it.

The voice was silent.

Cooke opened his eyes blearily and moaned. He squinted drunkenly at Shepherd. 'Where's m' glasses?' he mumbled with a thick, clogged voice.

'Julian,' hissed Rose quietly, keeping her eyes warily on Shepherd. 'Shh, just be still, Jules.'

William Shepherd turned to look down at the tattered canvas

472

sack on the wooden bunk frame to his side. His hand reached for it, feeling the small, infant-sized bones inside through the threadbare cloth.

'It's an angel in there,' he said quietly to Rose and Julian. 'An angel.'

Rose nodded obediently.

'We need him,' he explained in a quiet, abstracted voice. 'We need him to read the words.'

Julian was still squinting, trying to make sense of what was going on.

'That's right,' whispered Rose encouragingly, 'we need him.'

Ignore the bitch! Do it!

Shepherd shook his head, a nervous shake that looked more like a tic. *No, I can't.* He couldn't murder two people in cold blood, and in the next moment turn to the holiest relic in the world and paw at it with his bloodied hands. That couldn't be what God would want, that couldn't be—

Do it!

He raised the gun from his lap, slowly, heavily.

'Shepherd!' cried out Julian. 'Stop! I got a signal earlier . . . I got a signal!'

Shepherd hesitated.

'I made a call!'

He held the gun on Cooke.

'I made a call, Shepherd! It's going to be enough to sink you,' said Julian. 'It's enough information to have the press sniffing around you.' He lowered his voice, making it sound as reasoned and calm as he could. 'That's enough to fuck your campaign up. It's over.'

Do it!

Shepherd's finger slid onto the trigger.

'Wait!' cried Julian, raising his hands. 'Listen!'

The gun remained on him, Shepherd's finger trembling on the trigger.

'Listen . . . the point is . . . you haven't killed anyone, have you? It was Barns who did it. Not you. We saw that.'

The voice fell silent in his head.

'What happened with Grace . . . yes, that's going to look bad, I know. But . . . but, you're not guilty of murder. Barns is,' said Julian. 'Do you understand? Lower the gun. Rose and I — we can still help you.'

Shepherd stared silently at him, the gun still aimed, but wavering.

'I know you're a good man,' Julian whispered. 'I know you just want to spread God's word,' he said shooting a curious glance at the linen and tattered canvas bags on the bunk and managing to force a smile through the jagged pain in his leg. 'That's a noble thing. This story . . . what happened out here in the past . . . is the past. It's just that. You're not Preston. You're not evil. I know that.'

Shepherd's hand was shaking. 'Who did you call?'

'I won't tell you,' said Julian, struggling to keep his voice even. 'You know that would be very stupid of me.'

'What did you say?'

'Enough.'

'WHAT DID YOU SAY?'

'Enough to make you look too . . . *unstable* to elect.'

Shepherd bit his lip angrily. The muzzle of the gun twitched and trembled erratically. 'Fuck you!' he snarled. 'FUCK YOU!'

'But . . . it's not murder! Shepherd, listen! I've damaged your reputation, okay? Forget about the White House — it's over. I had to make the call. But look, you're not guilty of murder. Not yet.'

Shepherd's eyes flicked from the gun down to the sack of bones beside him. 'You don't know what you've done,' he hissed angrily.

This man has ruined you?

Shepherd winced at the voice.

'If you lower the gun,' said Julian, 'please . . . we can still help each other. There's a story.' He pointed at the linen sack on the bunk. 'There's a message there . . . we can help each other.'

Rose nodded earnestly. 'We can help spread your word.'

474

This man has ruined you?

'Please.' Julian slowly held out a hand. 'Lower the gun . . . please . . .'

The gun *did* feel heavy in his hand now — heavier with each passing second. He lowered the weapon by a fraction. But the voice returned, angry and shrill.

God has no use for you, William.

What?

You're pathetic.

I've given my life to God.

But you are no use to Him now.

Please, let me prove myself to Him.

All right. Kill yourself.

He cocked his head and stared out into the dark, his troubled mind taken aback by the sudden request. A final test of faith, yes . . . he could understand that. With the most important task in the history of mankind yet to do, yes . . . it made sense. It made a lot of sense.

'Okay,' he whispered and slowly raised the gun.

'Shepherd?' cried Julian. 'What're you doing?'

He pointed the gun towards his face. 'You know I'd do this for Him,' he said quietly. 'I told you I'd do anything for Him.' He placed the short stub of the barrel in his mouth, his lips clasped around it dutifully.

You know I would do this, if He asked it of me.

Kill yourself.

Shepherd obediently placed a finger on the trigger and began to gently squeeze.

Do you see? I'd do it if He wanted. I'm prepared to do anything . . . to die for the Lord, if He wanted it. Do you see that now?

He knew God had once stopped Abraham from sacrificing his son at the very last possible moment; that the patriarch had to have every intention of killing his own child in order to make evident his fealty. Shepherd knew God would stop him too, but only if he could demonstrate his complete sincerity in this test of

475

faith. Shepherd pushed his promise a little further with another ounce of pressure on the trigger.

I'll do anything . . . do you see now? God was right to choose me. God was right to lead me here.

And another ounce of pressure.

Do you see?

And another.

God? Is this really what You want?

The small, delicately balanced trip lever inside Barns's pistol answered the question prematurely.

CHAPTER 87

27 April, 1857

I am alone now. I finally worked out how to stop the voice in my head. I put him back in the chest with the plates.

But I am alone.

He looked up from the journal on his lap. His measured handwriting contrasted with the deteriorating childlike scrawl of Ben's on the previous pages. The snow across the camp was melting in the warm light. It was warm enough, in fact, that he sat on a cushion of blankets in the open, with his shirt off, taking some small pleasure from the heat on his pale back.

The snow still remained in deep, slushy piles, but in the places where it had not been so thick, dark muddy patches showed.

There is a smell here in this place that I cannot take any longer, he wrote.

Across the mottled ground of mud and snow, the bodies lay rotting and bloated, both oxen and human. The meat from the beasts had turned too bad to eat.

He saw faces in the dirty slush that were once families he knew; faces that had once had names – Jeremiah Stolheim, Sophia Lester, Aaron Hollander – but were now swollen and purple and anonymous.

The angel killed so many of them. He came back here to this place and killed them all. I tried to stop him, but he wouldn't listen. He wanted to make an example of them.

Sam's hand stopped scratching words across the page. There were things sitting before him, in front of the temple, carefully stacked beside the campfire like logs. His eyes momentarily rested on them; grisly things that his hand refused to transcribe on the page.

The angel's rage had been complete.

The deeds that had been done on his return to the camp . . . Sam had managed to erase, or at least dull, most of those memories from his mind: the screams, the panic of slaughter. All that remained now, rotting in the melting snow, was the aftermath.

Now he is gone, I can see with my own eyes the bad things he did to the bodies. I see with my own eyes the heads carefully placed in a pile. I see with my own eyes the cuts, the gashes, the fear in those bloated, dead faces.

I see now what the angel is.

He looked towards the temple. The lumber frame, no longer supported around the base by dense, tightly packed drifts of snow, had sagged to one side, everything askew. Inside, the angel was sealed away in Preston's metal chest.

There had been a night, one particular night late in December, as he dined alone on frozen meat in the musky darkness of his shelter, when his wretched grief and the angel's tormenting voice had proved too much for him. He had pulled the canvas sack from his belt, staggered into the temple and as the shrill and suspicious voice screamed accusations at him in his mind, he had opened the chest and dropped the sack inside.

Sam hadn't dare venture within the slanting shelter since.

He knew if he did, he'd hear it whispering to him to be let out again.

I think I understand what the angel is now.

It is the darkness in our hearts, made a thousand times worse.

It made sense in a cruel, unforgiving way. It made sense to him that, guarding those precious plates on which God's true message was inscribed, were those bones. He realised now that they were a test of purity . . . and intent. As a magnifying glass could be to the sun's rays, so those angel's bones were to a man's soul.

Sam's grief at losing Emily, his rage, had been turned by the angel into a storm of wrath, visited back here in the camp on those poor people who had remained.

I see now that it was a good thing Emily left me. That she escaped with the Indian and Mrs Zimmerman. I fear if she hadn't, I might find her head stacked here amongst the others.

He looked up at the sky, clear and blue, promising an unbroken day of warmth. Today, he decided, was the day he was going to leave. Another night alone in this forsaken place and he imagined madness would finally take him completely. He looked at the space left on the last page of this journal, Benjamin Lambert's journal. This last page was dark with new ink, a bottle he'd discovered a few days ago whilst scavenging through one of the other shelters.

I have read all of Benjamin's words in here. Of all the bad things the angel did, killing him was the worst. He was my friend. He was a good man.

Sam wondered how different things might have been if the angel had chosen Ben to come to. His heart had seemed purest. It was a cruel joke, he considered, that the person most worthy of doing the Lord's work, most pure in heart and capable of making good of the angel's influence, was the one person who had no belief at all in God.

Sam had a wish.

I wish I were like Ben. I wish I could be him.

A solitary tear rolled down his hollowed cheek and dropped onto the bottom of the page, dotting his last scribbled line like a full stop.

He looked at his words, *The testimony of Samuel Dreyton*, and realised in that moment that perhaps he could have something of what he desired. Samuel Dreyton could die, as perhaps he should, and Ben could, in a way, live once more.

Sam realised his freshly written words should be the first thing to go.

He ripped the page out of the journal and tossed it into the muddy, slushy snow.

'My name . . . is Ben,' he uttered, with a voice weak and cracked and sounding like the frail rattle of an old man.

He stood up, painfully thin, and uncertain in his mind whether he'd make a mile from this place before collapsing, let alone finding civilisation once more. He returned the journal to Benjamin's chest and sealed it with the solemnity of someone burying someone dearly beloved.

'My name is Benjamin,' he whispered.

As he stepped out of the clearing and into the trees, he looked back one last time at the browning humps of dead fir-tree branches that had once sheltered people through an unseasonably early winter.

'My name is Benjamin Lambert,' he croaked one last time, and set off into the wilderness, heading west.

CHAPTER 88

```
cave iram Dei
M  T  W  T  F  S  S
            1  2  3
4  5  6  7  8  9  10
11 12 13 14 15 16 17
18 19 20 21 22 23 24
25 26 27 28 29 30
```

Monday
Sierra Nevada Mountains, California

The sky above them was stained grey and overcast as they stumbled awkwardly along the silted bank of the gently burbling river. The water seemed as black as ink and moved smoothly and calmly past them, showing the way out of the mountains, west, towards safety.

'Shit, I need another rest, please!' gasped Julian.

Rose eased him down onto the ground. 'Aghhh! Shit!' he cried. 'Leg's killing me!'

'It's broken in several places,' said Rose. 'I think I can hear it grating.'

He winced as he lay back in the coarse grass looking up at the sky. It was tumbling with thick winter clouds that threatened to open up at any moment.

'Yeah, thanks for telling me that, Rose. I can damn well *feel* it grating,' he grunted through gritted teeth.

She offered him a pitiful smile. 'Hang in there, Jules. I'll get you out of here. You thirsty?'

He nodded.

She opened the backpack. It had belonged to Agent Barns. Inside was a survival pack: foil wrap, a couple of high-protein bars and a flask of water. She pulled out the flask and gave it to Julian.

She caught sight of the linen sack inside and eased it carefully out, opening it to reveal half a dozen corroded plates of metal. Beneath her fingers, she felt the indentations and bumps of unintelligible letters and shapes stamped into the metal.

'What do you think?' she asked, passing him one of them.

Julian turned the plate over in his hands, inspecting it sceptically. 'Some kid's metalwork project, looks like,' he snorted wearily, passing it back. 'A sheet of scrap metal with a few interesting shapes banged into it. I'm going to be honest here . . .' he said. 'I'm pretty sure it's not the word of God written in the language of angels.'

'And this?' she asked, pulling out the threadbare canvas sack. The bones inside clinked softly.

'Ten quid says they were once somebody's bloody pet cat.'

'They're old,' she said. 'The canvas bag looks like it's seen a lot of years.'

Julian shrugged. 'I don't know. An old pet cat, then.'

Rose laughed. 'Yeah, maybe. What're we going to do with 'em?'

'Dunno. We'll get someone to take a look. If they're genuinely Joseph Smith's scrolls, then I suppose they have some historical value. I'm sure the Mormon church wouldn't mind having them back.'

Rose nodded. 'I guess. Ridiculous, though, isn't it?'

'What?'

'That there are people out there, people like Shepherd, who would kill for a bag of old cat bones and a few pieces of scrap metal.'

Julian laughed weakly. 'It's a world full of crazy people.'

She looked up at the sky. The first few snowflakes were coming down towards them, light and carried like pollen on the gentle breeze.

'Starting to snow,' she said. 'C'mon, we better get going. I don't want to be caught out here overnight.'

'No.' Julian winced.

She put the two cloth sacks back in the pack and slung it over her shoulder, then, grimacing at the pain she was about to inflict on Julian, began to help him to his feet.

'Shit!' he howled. 'Ow! Slowly, Rose . . . slowly!'

'Sorry, sorry,' she cooed apologetically.

He gasped, took a few deep breaths. 'Okay . . . all right, I'm good to go.'

'This river will lead us down to the camp site,' she assured him. 'We'll make it there by evening, I'm sure.'

He nodded. 'Yeah.'

They proceeded along the silted riverbank, puffing clouds of laboured breath and watching the winter sky above unleash the first tentative snowfall of the season.

Julian managed to conjure a faint, sanguine smile. If it wasn't for the jarring agony in his leg, this would be quite a pleasant hike. It was peaceful, almost silent except for the gentle, muted hiss of the river, the swish and thump of the backpack against Rose's shoulder with each staggered step, and something else . . . the soft, reassuring whisper of a breeze through the naked branches of elms and cedars along the riverbank; a whisper that sounded almost human . . . almost like words.

THE END

Author's Note

Inspiration for *October Skies*, came from an obscure little historical event known as the 'Donner Incident'. The 'Donner Party' were a group of settlers who set out across the American Midwest a little too late in the year and got caught out by early snows in the Sierra Nevadas — much like the characters in this book. That was the seed of inspiration for this book. Originally, I had planned to dramatise the story of these *real* people, but imagination and invention quickly got in the way and I soon realised that for me it would be a lot more fun to depart from writing an account of this bit of history and instead create my own cast of characters and tell a very different story.

Research as usual, required a lot of gophering for details, for which I must thank Google and Google Maps. But also, much of the feel for the characters of the time, and the tiny details of life I absorbed from several books; the one closest to my heart being *Centennial* by James A. Michener.

For those readers who might be intrigued by the origin of the Mormon faith, believe it or not, Joseph Smith's tale really *hasn't* been exaggerated for dramatic purposes; that really is the story he told to anyone who'd listen to him. Perhaps his story of Divine inspiration might have sounded somewhat more convincing if it had been separated from the present by 1500 or 2000 years and acquired some dubious credibility coming from *biblical times*. Instead, it's a faith that popped out of his mouth and into existence in the 1830s; a mixed bag of the current fads doing the rounds in New England at the time (Egyptology, archaeology, treasure hunting, codes and interesting mythologies).

The birth of Joseph Smith's new faith reminded me very much of that scene in Monty Python's *Life of Brian* where Brian, on the run from the Romans, disguises himself as a prophet on their version of Speaker's Corner. If you've seen the film, you'll know the scene I mean. It's that bit where the Romans have marched past searching for Brian and now he sees that he's probably safe, his impersonation of a prophet uttering bland and meaningless prophecies to the bored audience in the market square, slowly grinds to a mumbling halt. Only . . . he's left a sentence, hanging . . . unfinished, and the bored crowd, out of idle curiosity, nag him to finish his last inane prophecy. But Brian is more interested in making a smart getaway, and he scampers off, only to be pursued by a growing crowd of followers driven mad with curiosity . . . and thus a new prophet is born.

It sounds like I have an axe to grind with regard to faith. Maybe I do, maybe I don't. But more specifically, I do have something against *organised* faith. I could write another five thousand words as to why I believe them to be the curse mankind should have moved on from, to have *outgrown* by now. But I'll do that another day. If I have time for anyone though, perhaps it's for those people who have a quiet, *personal* belief in something beyond this world; something that doesn't have a prescribed way to behave, or a prescribed subset of people to victimise or label as *heretics*. Like Ben, I consider myself an atheist. But, you know what? I have to admit there have been several times in my life that I've been so scared, so completely terrified, that I've actually muttered a prayer. So . . . perhaps there *is* a tiny part of me that hopes there's more than we can see or measure or understand.